**WITHDRAWN**

# THE GIRLS WITH NO NAMES

# THE GIRLS WITH NO NAMES

## SERENA BURDICK

**THORNDIKE PRESS**

A part of Gale, a Cengage Company

**LIBRARY OF CONGRESS CIP DATA ON FILE.**
**CATALOGING IN PUBLICATION FOR THIS BOOK**
**IS AVAILABLE FROM THE LIBRARY OF CONGRESS**

ISBN-13: 978-1-4328-7815-3 (hardcover alk. paper)

Published in 2020 by arrangement with Harlequin Books S.A.

Printed in Mexico
Print Number: 03        Print Year: 2020

For the girls who lost their voices
to the House of Mercy;
for the women whose stories
will never be told.

# PROLOGUE

I lay with my cheek pressed to the floor, the cement cool against my spent rage. I'd screamed. I'd bitten and scratched. Now I was paying for it, but I didn't care. I'd do it again.

Rolling onto my back, I held my hand in front of my face, but only black stared back at me. They'd left me in complete darkness. My palm throbbed where a splinter of wood had pierced it, a glorious wound of rebellion. A wash of cold air drifted across my face and I shot upright, certain it was the ghost of one of the forgotten girls. Fear pricked the soles of my feet, turning into pins and needles nicking their way up my calves. How long would they leave me here? Would they starve me, forget about me until I began to rot and stink? I imagined Sister Gertrude dumping my wasted body into a grave next to other nameless girls. My family would never know what happened.

I crawled across the floor with the pressing need to urinate. My sister and I had spent our whole life thinking up stories, dreaming up our futures, but life was not a story. It was full of solid, irrefutable facts like the fact that I needed to pee; like this cold, hard cell and my inability to imagine any way out of it. I clenched my body trying to hold my bladder tight, but it was no use. Squatting, I hiked up my skirt and pulled down my knickers. Pee splashed down my leg and I sighed with hot relief. The acrid smell of urine mixed with the onions and garlic they kept in barrels on the other side of the door. I'd been planted underground, buried with the vegetables. I'd be found purple and bruised and unrecognizable.

I tried counting backward from five hundred, then from one thousand. I recited scripture, but became furious with God and switched to Shakespeare. I thought of the gypsy children performing *Romeo and Juliet* in the rain, of Tray and Marcella and the foretelling of my future. I thought of all the mistakes I'd made. I wanted to blame my father for them, for betraying our family and sparking a rebellion in our home, but down here, trapped in the bowels of the House of Mercy, I'd forgive him anything, if only he would come for me.

After a while, time became blurred and boundless, as it had when I was grieving for my sister. My mind grew hazy. In this windowless room, there was nothing to distinguish day from night. No way to tell a minute from an hour. When the door opened and a wan band of gray light slid in with a tray of food, I tried to guess between dawn and dusk, but I couldn't. The door shut and darkness slammed against my eyes. I sipped the water, bit into the stale bread crusted with old molasses. It didn't matter what time of day it was. Whether out of this room or in it, no one was coming for me.

When I grew tired, I lay on the unforgiving floor with my hands cushioned beneath my cheek. It was a relief to escape into a different darkness. It made my fear less palpable. I could be anywhere behind my lids. I could go back. I could make another choice on that night when the simple, beautiful sound of a fiddle, in another impenetrable darkness, called to us.

If only they hadn't played, or my sister and I hadn't listened.

■ ■ ■ ■

# BOOK ONE

■ ■ ■ ■

# CHAPTER ONE:
## EFFIE

Luella and I carved our place in the world together. More accurately, my sister carved and I followed, my notches secured inside the boundary of hers. She was older, courageous and unpredictable, which made it a natural mistake.

"Luella?" I called, afraid my sister would lose me.

"I'm right here," I heard, only I couldn't see her.

A moonless night had swallowed the woods of the upper Manhattan isle that we knew so well in daylight. Now we were stumbling, running blindly, bumping into one tree, turning and bumping into another, our hands held out in front of us, everything foreign and out of shape.

From the depths of my blindness, my sister grabbed my arm and yanked me to a halt. I gasped for breath, my heart rattling my whole body. There wasn't a star in the sky. My sister's hand on my arm was the only proof I had that she stood next to me.

"Are you all right? Can you breathe?" she asked.

"I'm fine, but I hear the creek."

"I know," Luella groaned.

It meant we'd gone in the wrong direction. We should have gone directly over the hill to Bolton Road. Now we were near Spuyten Duyvil Creek and farther from our house than when we'd started.

"We should find the road and follow it home," I said. At least on the road there would be lights from houses.

"That will take twice as long. Mama and Daddy will have the police out looking for us by then."

Our parents were worriers — Daddy for our physical well-being, Mama for our souls. I still wanted to take the road because, either way, they'd be searching soon. "It's better than not getting home at all," I pleaded.

Luella moved forward, pulling me with her until she stopped abruptly. "I feel something." She took another step. "It's a woodpile. There must be a house around here."

"We'd see a light," I whispered, the ground

14

squishy under my feet and pungent with the smell of manure.

"It's worth finding out." Luella let go of me. "I'm going on ahead. Follow the wood-pile."

I traced my gloved hands over the rough, rounded logs until they ended and I dropped a step into empty space, the darkness like a blindfold I wanted to rip off. I could hear the rush of the creek nearby. What if we walked straight into it? A few steps more and my shoulder grazed a tree. I stretched out my arm. The trunk was massive. I followed it, my gloves snagging over the dips and grooves in the calloused bark until I suddenly knew where we were.

"Lu!" I gasped. "We're at the Tulip Tree."

Her footsteps halted. Luella and I were staunch believers in ghost tales, and everyone knew the story of the oysterman who hung himself in the rickety house next to the Tulip Tree. We'd never dared come this close to the house; not even in the light of day had we found the courage to do more than peek from the hilltop.

There was a hiss of air through Luella's teeth, and her tone grew sturdy. "Even if it is haunted, someone lives here. At least it's too dark to see the oysterman's ghost dangling from a rope in the window."

This was not reassuring. My throat constricted, and my breath caught in my lungs. Luella had always been braver than me. Even in normal situations I panicked with shyness. Now I was frozen solid, and as always when afraid, my imagination took over.

When day breaks, the girls are nowhere to be found. The sun rises and warms the hill where they last stood. The river swells in the distance under the boat of an early rising fisherman who pulls up his net, the light catching the silver fish as they writhe in protest. He dumps them on his deck and catches sight of something floating in the water — a back, curved, buoyed to the surface by a skirt that bubbles up like a bloated fish. The girl's face is in the water, her dark hair trailing from her head like seaweed caught on a rock.

I shook the image from my head. The ground beneath my boots, the tree under my hands, the smell of rotting fish and manure were not my imagination. The twigs snapping under Luella's feet were real, the rapid knock on wood, silence, then the sound of a heavy bolt sliding back and the click of a latch. A light flared and the ghastly face of a man appeared, bearded, with red-rimmed eyes and gnarled teeth exposed in a mouth wide with surprise. I screamed. The man jumped and made as if to slam the door when he saw my sister.

"What the devil?" His voice boomed and the lantern in his hand swung, splintering light across the trees.

I was about to scream again when I heard my sister say, honeysweet, "I apologize for the disturbance, sir, but it appears we've gotten waylaid in the dark. If we could trouble you for your lantern, just to get us home, we'd be ever grateful. I'll have it returned first thing in the morning."

The man held up the light and stepped forward, peering into my sister's face, and then glanced down her dress. "We?" he said. It disgusted me the way he looked at her. I'd seen men look at my sister like that before, but we'd never been unchaperoned and alone in the dark.

"My sister is just behind me." Luella took a step back, closer to me, but still out of reach.

"The screamer?" The man barked a laugh.

"If you can't spare a light, we'll simply take the road." There was a quiver to Luella's voice as she retreated.

"Hang on, now." The man caught her by

the arm.

A ghost would have been better than this solid man of flesh and blood. I thought of crying out for help, but there was no one to hear us. Maybe I could lunge out of the darkness and take him by surprise, knock the light from his hand, then grab my sister and run.

I did none of these things, standing paralyzed with fear as my sister took a step closer to the man, the hem of her skirt brushing his leg.

"Oh, you dear, sweet thing." She placed her hand over his that gripped her arm, the affection startling him enough to ease his hold. "Aren't you kind to be concerned. Your chivalry will not be overlooked." In a flash she kissed his pocked cheek, at the same time slipping her arm free and plucking the lantern from his hand. Turning swiftly with two long strides, she caught me by the hand and rushed us up the hill as fast as she could.

Plunged into darkness, the man stood dumbfounded on his doorstep, knocked so far off balance by that kiss that I was sure for years to come he would think we were the ghosts who had come to haunt him.

We didn't slow down until we reached our front door where the fear of facing our parents replaced my fear of the dark and the ghost of hanging oystermen.

Out of breath, I pitched forward with my head between my knees.

"You're not going to have a blue fit, are you?" Luella sounded unsympathetic. If I had a fit, our parents would blame her, since she was older and therefore responsible for me. I was not allowed to run; it was a simple rule to follow.

I shook my head *no,* unable to speak as I took slow steady breaths, regaining my equilibrium.

"Good." She blew out the lantern, grinning at me as she stowed it behind the abelia bush, proud of her cunning to obtain it and not at all bothered at the idea of being in trouble for missing curfew. Daddy would get angry. Mama would scold. Luella would look appropriately regretful. She'd apologize, kiss Mama, throw her arms around Daddy and it would be as if she'd never done any wrong because, for all of my sister's rebelliousness, she was adored.

Tonight, however, we had no need to worry. Neala was dusting the glass panel on the grandfather clock as we stepped into the hall. It gave a resonant *tick tock* announcing our lateness. "I'm not even going to ask," she said in her Irish brogue. Neala, our household maid, was young and "spirited," as Mama called her. Maybe that's why she never tattled on us. "Your parents are out, and Velma's been kind enough to leave your dinner in the kitchen. No use setting the dining room for the likes of you two." She swatted the dust cloth at me as I passed, shaking her fiery-red head in mock disapproval.

The only person we had to look out for now was Mama's French maid, Margot, who had come with Mama from Paris. She was a solid, handsome woman, with dark hair that refused to gray and eyes the color of steel. Loyal only to her mistress, she reported our every misstep. Tonight, Margot's room off the kitchen was empty and Luella and I ate quickly, escaping to our rooms before she had a chance to return.

I was too tired to bother brushing my hair before crawling into bed with my notebook, where I would embellish our adventure into a story worthy of our tardiness. It was Daddy who encouraged my storytelling. As a child, my mind froze when people asked me questions. I'd stare at them, reaching for what they might want me to say, never finding the right words. When I was six years old Daddy gave me a notebook and a shiny black pen and said, "Your eyes are full of mystery. I love a good mystery. Why not write one for me?" After that, at least in my imagination, words flowed.

When my hand began to cramp, I slipped the book under my pillow and turned out the lamp to wait for Luella, who religiously brushed her hair one hundred times before bed. She'd read in *Vogue* it thickened limp strands.

Despite our separate rooms, we still slept together. When we were little our beds were so far apart in the nursery that one of us would creep across the room to climb in with the other. When Luella turned thirteen she got her own room and the nursery became mine. My twin bed was replaced with a double oak canopy, my child's wardrobe swapped out for a lovely, large one fit to accommodate all the womanly dresses I would grow into. I was only ten at the time and had high hopes for my future figure.

At thirteen it was becoming harder to pretend I'd ever grow into a dress meant to hang in that wardrobe. I had always been small for my age, but as the girls around me filled out and inched their way upward into the world of womanhood, I remained short and thin with no figure to speak of. Luella had long since left me behind. Her breasts filled out a chest that had once been as scrawny as mine, and her straight waist curved over enviable hips. Even her face had rounded out, her dimples sinking into full cheeks. But it was her fingernails I envied the most. Smooth and flat, her white cuticles like upside-down smiles, or tiny cresting moons. My cuticles were invisible under the murky lumps that grew like pebbles from my nail beds, bulbous and round as if I'd dipped my fingertips into melted wax.

Jumping into bed, Luella wriggled next to me whispering, "Wasn't it absolutely marvelous? I keep hearing the fiddles and that voice. I've never heard anything like it. It was wildly sinful, wasn't it?"

It was.

Our toes had been inches above the icy spring water at the base of the Indian caves when the music interrupted us. We had peeled off stockings for our pre-spring ritual of numbing our feet when fiddle notes pierced the air. Bewitched by a euphonious voice sailing through the trees we forgot about our mission to will the buds of flowers open, snatched our shoes and socks and scrambled up the grassy slope, halting at the tree line. The normally empty meadow was ringed with tents and brightly painted house wagons. Tethered horses munched on grass while dogs lay with heads in their paws, watching a group of people encircle a woman dancing with her hands above her head, her floral skirt swelling like the surf, voices and fiddles singing around her in circles.

Luella had wrapped her arm around my waist. I felt her body quivering. "Look at her. She's marvelous. It makes me want to move in ways I've never dared," she whispered, her desire beating off her like heat.

Since the age of five, my sister had trained as a ballerina under a Russian choreographer. *The French are good dancers,* our very French mother informed us, her voice lilting with her accent, *but the Russians are great dancers. The Americans,* she scoffed, *do not know the meaning of ballet.*

This gypsy dancer was something altogether different. I'd never seen anything like it. She was mesmerizing, her movements seamless and indefatigable. My sister and I stood for so long that we didn't notice the air cooling around us as the sun slipped behind the trees, leaving us in a darkness that twisted our sense of direction.

Safe now in our warm bed, with our parents none the wiser, we both agreed it had been worth it.

"What if we'd never made it home?" Luella wrapped her leg over mine.

23

"What if the oysterman got us?"

"And yanked me inside with his clammy ghost claw."

"And slit your throat."

"Effie!"

"What?" I could be as brave as anyone in my own fantasies.

"You don't have to be *so* gruesome. He could just smother me with a pillow."

"Okay, he smothers you and takes you as his spirit-wife. Meanwhile, I wander the empty house, hearing you, but unable to reach you."

"Mama and Daddy put out a search party."

"And I drown myself in the Hudson out of misery and fly up to Heaven, never to see you again because you're stuck on earth with the oysterman."

"You'd sink into hell for committing suicide." Luella was the least pious person I knew, and yet she still corrected me.

"Then the oysterman would be in hell too. Which means we'd be together, wandering in hell for all of eternity. A happy ending."

"I'm afraid you've got it all wrong." Luella twisted a piece of my hair around her finger and gave a gentle tug. "I'd never let you kill yourself for me, not even as a ghost, so the story is bunk. You'll have to start a new one."

Which, if I was going to be accurate —
even in fantasies, I tried to be as accurate as
possible — was true. Luella would never let
anything happen to me.

When something did happen, it was
Daddy who was to blame.

# CHAPTER TWO:
## EFFIE

I did not think my father capable of wrong-doing. When people spoke of him it was with admiration, if not slight reverence. Devilishly handsome, they said, quailing under his astounding blue eyes and full-lipped smile. It was a look you wanted to fall into and at the same time wriggle out from under. He was a man of few words. Not shy like I was, just stolid and taciturn, and when he spoke it was with the subtle hint that he knew much more about you than he was letting on.

My mother was straightforward and plain as paper, a disparity that I understood made my parents an odd couple. Once, I overheard a woman — homely herself with bony arms and a sharp chin — say to another woman as she sipped wine in our parlor, "I don't know what spell Jeanne wove over Emory when they were courting, but I wouldn't have risked it. Men that comely

26

always stray."

I was only seven years old at the time and all I could glean from this comment was that it had taken trickery on my mother's part to marry my father, and that somehow, she'd pay for it.

In public, Mama sang Daddy's praises, swooping to his side with the grace of a long-necked heron. But when she told us how she met Daddy, it was with a tone of warning as Luella and I sat rapt on her bed, watching her apply cold cream to her face.

"I was twenty-one," she said, this first bit already a travesty. "Living with my mother in a grand, old Parisian home. I thought I'd be stuck there for the rest of my life. No matter that I was a regular dancer on the Opéra stage, I had never had a single proposal." She wiped a glob of cream down the bridge of her nose. "These lengthy limbs of mine made me a lovely ballerina, but not a lovely catch. Never mind my height. Men don't like to be looked in the eye. The worst thing, of course, were my hands." Luella and I looked at them on cue. Mama's nightly cream application was the only time we got to see them gloveless. We knew well the story of when she was sixteen and her skirt caught fire over the limelights during a rehearsal of *La Bayadère.* She would have

27

died if she hadn't beaten the flames out with her hands. Hands now covered in scars. "A hideous embarrassment," she called them.

I loved those scars. They were badges of heroism, and proof of Mama's strength and survival. When I was little and I'd lose my breath, the only thing that calmed me was running my fingers over the folded, twisted skin on her hands. Pitched forward with my head to the floor, I'd pull off her gloves and trace her wounds like a map, memorizing the curve of each scar, until my heart slowed and I could breathe again. Then Mama, without a thread of panic, would say, "There now, that's done with," and pull me to my feet.

A blob of cream dropped to the rug. She laughed and said, "Why your father wanted to marry the likes of me, I can't imagine!" wagging a long finger at Luella. "Now you, my dear, will have none of my difficulties."

My sister stiffened. This part we'd heard many times before. Mama made a point of lauding Luella in the same way she lauded Daddy, often publicly, always demeaning herself in the process, saying things like, "It was Paris that turned Emory's head. It's a good thing he proposed before we left!" or, "Thank goodness Luella didn't get my looks. With her beauty, she'll go places in her career I never could."

Luella *was* beautiful. She was the spitting image of a photograph in the drawing room of our great-grandmother on our mother's side, Colette Savaray, a Parisian socialite who became a recurring character in the stories I made up. She'd died before Mama was born, and it was her husband, Mama's grandfather Auguste Savaray, who had taken Mama to the ballet every season. "He adored me," Mama reminded us. "It was for him I learned to dance."

"I'll never dance for anyone but myself," Luella retorted.

"You wait and see," Mama answered.

Where I was concerned, there was no talk of husbands or careers. My heart ensured that I'd never be a dancer, my clubbed fingernails that I'd never find a husband. Luella would fulfill our mother's dreams; my focus was only to stay alive.

I was born seven weeks early, on January 1, 1900. My father said only great things could come of a Tildon child born on the first day of the new century.

I surely disappointed.

According to Mama, my cry sounded like a cat mewing, which alarmed the midwife. Turns out, my heart wasn't right. "It's a malformation due to the imperfect development of the organ," the doctor informed my parents.

The way I saw it, God hadn't seen fit to finish me.

"You're lucky this one has no visible signs of cyanosis," the doctor went on to tell them, as if the fact that I wasn't born with gray coloring, like most babies with my condition, was something to be proud of. It was not much of a comfort, followed by what he said next: "Unfortunately, there's no way to close the abnormal opening in her heart. She's not likely to live through the year."

I imagined my mother accepting this information stoically, holding me in my pink newness like a breakable thing, her sinewy limbs draped on the bed, blue veins like fine thread running through her white thighs. According to her, it was Daddy who bellowed that no doctor was going to tell him his child wouldn't live to see her first birthday.

He was right, because despite my unfinished heart, I stayed alive, happily feeding on condensed milk from a glass bottle shaped like a banana. The doctor said I was too weak to nurse, but my mother believed I didn't have the will, that I wasn't trying hard enough. "I told the doctor that with a temperament like yours, you'd never survive," Mama told me, reproachfully, as if I was expected to prove myself even as an infant. Daddy, who loved modern inventions, said the feeding bottle was fascinating with its newly refined, rubber nipple. "I tried to convince your mother that it was an advantage, not a failure," he reassured me.

But I was sure she never saw it that way. She had already birthed Luella, and therefore knew what success looked like in a newborn. I imagine my sister came out kicking and screaming, attaching herself to our mother's breast with rightful ownership, growing into a plump, feisty three-year-old who already knew exactly what she wanted by the time I came along.

Mama told us that the first time Luella saw me she insisted, since I was the exact size of her glass-eyed baby doll, that I was *her* baby too. She'd swaddle me and place me in the stroller next to her doll, stroking my soft head, and the hard doll's, with equal care. I used to picture this doll as my strange twin, wondering if it haunted my mother to see this lifeless version of me, a reflection of what she feared I'd become.

Dr. Romero monitored my heart monthly during the first year of my life. After that it became a yearly examination, the fat, smelly, cold-fingered doctor declaring each time I walked in, "Ah, look who we have here," as if surprised to see me, when clearly I was expected.

During these visits I had Mama's sole attention, which made me not mind them so much. My heart didn't hinder me. I was agile and energetic, though small for my age, and if I didn't exert myself I could keep my blue fits to a minimum. Luella named them for the terrific shade of blue I'd turn.

Selfishly, I didn't think how these visits affected Mama until a chilly September afternoon when I was eight years old and she took me by train to the east side of Manhattan, to a quiet street lined with stately brownstones. When she opened a little black gate next to a sign that said, *Louis Faugeres Bishop, M.D.,* a prickle of fear went through me. I had the sense my mother was pushing me toward something dangerous I couldn't see. "Why aren't we going to Dr. Romero's?"

She clicked the gate shut behind us. "Dr. Bishop is a heart specialist."

"What was Dr. Romero?"

"Not a heart specialist."

The examining room was stale and bare, with a sharp vinegar smell like the pickles Velma canned in the kitchen. There were no pictures on the walls or even a vase of flowers to put us at ease, only a strange-looking contraption covered in rubber tubes with intricate dials and knobs. It made me think of Frankenstein's laboratory, from a book I'd snuck since Mama declared it *inappropriate.*

Steering clear of the machine, I hopped up onto a metallic bed covered in a starched white sheet that crinkled under my legs. Mama eyed the contraption, her gloved hands clasped tightly over the curved handle of her purse.

"What's that?" she asked the doctor when he stepped into the room.

Dr. Bishop was short and wiry with a glossy bald head that bobbed up and down excitedly, his round spectacles slipping down the bridge of his nose. "That is an electrocardiogram. Invented by a Dutch doctor. It's the only one in America." He pushed his glasses up, his bulbous eyes glistening behind his thick lenses. "Unfortunately, I won't be using it on the child. We're still in the early stages and have barely perfected it for grown men."

Mama gave a tight nod of relief as the doctor unceremoniously pulled my dress from my shoulders and stamped a cold stethoscope against my bare chest, cocking his head as he listened to the murmur caged in my ribs. The tips of his fingers felt cold and waxy against my back. He had white eyebrows with long hairs that curled toward his wrinkly forehead. *The face of an executioner,* I'd write in my journal later, *handing over a death sentence as solemnly as one slips a cloth over a prisoner's head at the gallows.*

Dr. Bishop unplugged the stethoscope from my chest and let it fall around his neck. I stuffed my arms into my dress sleeves and yanked it up over my shoulders. Mama quickly buttoned the back as I held my hair out of the way, my nudity a point of embarrassment for both of us. The doctor tugged the glove from my right hand and inspected my deformed fingernails — a side effect of my heart condition. One I've never understood, hearts and fingernails having little to do with one another. Like Mama, my gloves came off only at bath and bedtime. The air felt wonderful between my fingers as the doctor lifted my hand into the sunlight from the window. "How long has she had the clubbing?"

"It started when she was five."

"Has it gotten worse?"

"It's stayed pretty much the same. Will it get worse?" She glanced at her own hands concealed in expensive satin. Around my sister and me, my mother was a tower of strength; around doctors, or men in general including my father, she weakened, ready to be declared wrong at every turn. I thought now, as I'd thought many times, that if she took off her gloves she'd feel braver, like she didn't need to hide. She'd be as strong as she was sitting beside me when I lost my breath.

Ignoring her question, the doctor banded his fingers around my upper arm. "Has she always been this thin?"

"She eats plenty. She's just a thin child."

"She's not just a thin child, Mrs. Tildon. She's a child with a ventricular septal defect. Come with me." He strode into an adjacent room with the cold authority I had learned to associate with doctors. My mother, in her smart white blouse and gored skirt with pearl buttons, followed with her submissive shuffle. *Shut the door,* he said. Mama turned and gave me a warning look, closing the door behind her. As if anyone could get into trouble in this barren room, I thought.

I waited, lifting my legs up and down, my black boots making round shadows on the floor that appeared and disappeared like twin moons. Dr. Romero had never made a big deal of my clubbed fingernails or pointed out how thin I was. I'd never heard the words, *ventricular septal defect.* I didn't like the sound of *defect.* Bored, I peeked behind a curtain that hung to one side of the table and saw a tray of frightening tools. I quickly dropped the curtain and sat straight, eyeing the machine in the corner. If Dr. Bishop was a heart specialist, then he'd know especially how to heal me. Maybe he wasn't an executioner, but a mad scientist able to seal shut a heart like Frankenstein's ability to infuse life into an inanimate body.

A hand appears, thin and ashen. Wispy fingers float to the sheet that falls to the floor, revealing the body of a child. Her eyes are blank, colorless marbles, her skin transparent, her bones white lines of solid cartilage. In every aspect she is dead, and yet past the curve of her ribs, deep in her chest, there is a steady pulse of color, not vibrant red as one expects from a heart, but pale pink and blue. With each beat, the color brightens until the room is a wash of candied light. Slowly, she rises.

I tugged at the sheet bunched under my legs. I wasn't sure I wanted to be healed. I liked surviving. Others were expected to live year to year without incident, but my years were accomplishments. Each birthday meant I'd done a good job staying alive. What would matter now, I wondered, if I didn't need to work hard at living?

Mama emerged from the doctor's office frowning, the thin lines of her arched brows pulled together. *Come,* she beckoned, her fingers swooping through the air. I jumped off the table and my boots blasted to the floor. The doctor winced. "Sorry," I said, and he gave a weak wave, looking as if he'd just realized I was a child.

We took a cab home, driving slowly through the crowded Manhattan streets, the driver's duster jacket and goggles coated in a layer of dust that kicked up from the road. Mama wrapped her scarf over her mouth. I didn't mind the grit on my tongue. It felt satisfyingly real. I tried to focus on the sun on my face and the smells from the food venders, but Mama kept glancing at me with an anxious smile that made my stomach uneasy. Why didn't I get to know what was said in that doctor's office? After all it was my heart.

As soon as we stepped into the hall, Mama shooed me up to my room, but I snuck back down and sidled up to the parlor door. Daddy had come home early from work, which was unusual.

Through a crack in the partially opened door, I watched my mother pace over the Oriental rug, her skirt a vivid blue under the blaze of the chandelier, her face animated. Behind her, the fire crackled and spit inside the iron grate. My father sat on the sofa running his hand methodically over the seat like he was stroking an animal. His vest was undone and his tie askew. Normally Daddy was meticulously put together and I found something profoundly disturbing about his disarray.

Mama must have felt it also because she leaned over and compulsively straightened his tie, saying something in a low voice I couldn't hear. Daddy flicked her hand away, standing so abruptly he bumped the glass lamp on the end table. It tipped, threatening to fall before he reached out and steadied it. A sob escaped Mama. The sob was not for the lamp. I wanted him to reach out and steady her, but Daddy turned his back and gazed into the fire. "What did he say, *exactly*?"

Mama was very still, now. "He said, there is no treatment to close the abnormal opening in her heart."

"What kind of pathetic specialist is he?"

"He said there are new experiments happening all the time."

Daddy turned. "Then there's hope?"

"I don't know."

"Then why did he say three years?"

"He said, perhaps three years."

*"Perhaps."* Disgusted, Daddy turned back to the fire with his hands latched behind his back.

I moved away from the door with a heavy sadness. I didn't know how to comfort my parents. I was sorry to be the cause of all their worry, but what I couldn't explain, not even to Luella, was that I didn't mind having the hole in my heart. I viewed the world through that small, damaged portal. It was a weakness I sharpened my strength upon. From behind its protective edges, I could be brave. Just like Mama's disfigured hands were proof of her strength, my open heart was proof of mine. If only people could see it, they'd know how strong I was.

I decided right then and there that the bespectacled doctor was neither executioner, nor mad scientist, he was an overgrown fly trapped in an old man with a fancy machine who knew nothing whatsoever about children's hearts. I was not going to die on my parents. I would continue to gather years for them, pocket away birthdays. My survival would be long and exceptional.

That night, I didn't say a word to my sister about my doctor's visit, and she didn't ask. She'd never believed I was dying anyway. "Good night, Effie." She kissed my cheek and dropped onto her stomach. "Now, don't go yanking the covers off me," she added, falling asleep with her elbow jammed into my side.

I stared at the ceiling, envying how easily my sister went to sleep, her soft breath rustling the cool night air. The poke of her elbow was both irritating and a comfort, this point of solid, lasting bone.

# CHAPTER THREE:
## EFFIE

The morning after Luella and I discovered the gypsies I did not notice anything different about my parents. I should have. It was the beginning of the earth shifting beneath our feet, and yet all I hoped was that they didn't notice our late-night excursion.

Hungrily, I heaped my plate full of shirred eggs and stewed prunes, exchanging a look of complicity with Luella whose plate was as full as mine.

"Effie, really." Mama gave a disapproving look as I poured an unreasonable amount of cream into my coffee. She wore a blouse with a high, buttoned collar that made her look as if she had no neck at all.

"It's unbearably bitter." I took a sip, letting a small, undissolved lump of sugar slip into my mouth.

"If you are grown up enough to drink coffee, then you're old enough to get used to the bitterness," Daddy said, his eyes roaming down the page of his newspaper. His pinstripe vest was pressed straight as a board and his hair was parted on the side with a slight wave frozen over his forehead. I could smell the pomade from across the table.

My father, in spite of throwing lavish parties and hiring the best tailors, did not believe in indulging incidentals like tea when *he* preferred coffee. He was cheap in certain ways, we'd learned. My grandfather had been one of the founders of the soda water industry and Daddy had taken over the business when he died. It was thriving, according to Mama, and yet the only servants Daddy allowed were our housemaid Neala, our cook Velma — a middle-aged colored woman with towering hair who lived in Harlem and told me she took the underground at four thirty in the morning to get here in time to make our breakfast — and the formidable and ancient Parisian, Margot. There had been more servants when we were little, but Daddy believed in "economizing." There wasn't the need for servants like there used to be, he said. Consequently, Luella and I would not be getting our own ladies' maids, as did every other girl we knew. Luella had thrown a fit, but Daddy wouldn't budge. He said Margot could help us when needed. Otherwise, we'd have to learn to button our own dresses. I didn't mind. I admired Daddy's practicality, but didn't dare say this to Luella.

This morning, I wasn't dwelling on bitter coffee or buttons. I glanced at my sister rapidly eating her eggs, certain we were thinking the same thing. *The gypsies.* We had to go back in the light of day. Maybe they'd tell our fortunes. Maybe they'd play their music again. After all it was Saturday, a day without school or eleven o'clock mass. On the whole our parents did not approve of idle time, but somewhere Daddy had read about the importance of exercise in children, and believed that fresh air did our minds and souls good. He'd convinced Mama that developing an appreciation for the natural world would give us a greater appreciation for God. We would awaken Sunday morning with reverence and heaps of piety.

Incidentally, our delicious outdoor adventures only made Sunday mass more unbearable, but we weren't about to tell our parents that.

I sucked up my wiggly eggs, hoping we could slip away quickly, when Luella said, "Daddy, what do you know about the gypsy encampments?" This was so like her, to brazenly go to the edge of being caught just to prove she couldn't be.

Daddy folded his paper and set it aside. "Why? What do you know about them?"

"Only that they're camping near here. I read it in the paper."

"Then you know as much as I do."

"They are a vulgar people," Mama put in, *vulgarity* being a word she bestowed on most of New York City these days. "Immigrants," she added, knowing Daddy disliked the throngs of immigrants as much as she did. I had the urge to point out that she was an immigrant, but didn't dare. The French, apparently, had overcome that vulgarity by virtue of being French.

"They're well behaved and polite, from what I've heard." Daddy sipped his coffee.

"Well-behaved people do not let their children crawl in the dirt. They're savages, and thieves," Mama replied.

"They're honest horse traders."

Mama fussed with her napkin. "They tell fortunes and take people's money for it. That is thieving."

"What if the fortune comes true?" Daddy flashed her an indulgent smile.

Mama dismissed the remark with a click of her tongue, turning to Luella. "The gypsies are an ignorant people, which makes

44

them dishonest. If you want your fortune told you must understand that you are donating your money to thievery, not paying for an actual service. If they set up their booths on the street, I'll indulge you and we can call it charity. Otherwise, you're to stay away from their camps."

I glared at Luella, and we ate the rest of our breakfast in silence.

Once Neala cleared our dishes away, we excused ourselves and flew upstairs for sweaters. Mama was at her desk responding to invitation requests, and Papa was getting ready for his Saturday tennis match. We promised to be home by lunch, slipping out into the April morning with our sketch pads.

Our house was one of five brick homes on a wide cobblestone street that bordered a thickly wooded hill on the northwest end of Manhattan. No trolleys came up this far, and we had to walk five blocks for the elevated train into Manhattan for school. Mama used to walk with us to the schoolhouse when we lived on Fifth Avenue, but here it was too far and took too long for her to ride the train back and forth. Which left us on our own and gloriously independent.

As soon as we were out of sight of the house, we discarded our notepads behind a tree and ran to the stream where we pulled off our stockings, hiked up our skirts and tiptoed into the frigid water. Overhead the sky was a promising blue. Once our feet were properly numb, we waded out, pulled our dry stockings and boots over the bright red skin of our tortured feet and climbed the hill in silent, mutual defiance of our mother's prejudice against the gypsies. There was something fascinating about them that existed nowhere else in our lives.

Threading our way through the trees, we heard distant voices, the occasional braying of a horse and the shouts of children. This time we didn't stop at the tree line but walked boldly into the bright tumult of tents and caravans. Horses whinnied and dogs yapped. Cast iron pots straddled the morning fires, with smoke that coiled into the brisk air.

We passed a man squatting by a basin of water. He plunged his hands in, looking up with a crooked smile and two front teeth missing. Women in aprons and headscarves raised their heads to gaze at us, but kept to their tasks, arching over scrub boards, wringing clothes out to dry in the sun. A boy of around thirteen years of age followed us, swiveling his stick in the dirt like the trail of a snake. I had imagined all gypsies to be dark-eyed and dark-haired, but this boy was freckled and fair, with light eyes that bore into me every time I turned to look at him.

Without warning, Luella whirled to a stop. The boy pulled back, startled, but curious as Luella asked him whom we might speak with about hearing their music, enunciating her words as if he might not understand. When he didn't reply she asked if he spoke English, which made him laugh.

"Only my grandparents still speak Romani," he said in a pitched English accent. "Trayton Tuttle, at your service. You may call me Tray." He flourished his stick and rotated on his heels, turning from snake conjurer to gentry as he spoke. "I'll take you to my ma," he said, and marched in the opposite direction, his stick tapping the crude path as if it were Park Avenue. He disregarded the puddles, holding his head comically high and plowing right through them as mud splashed up his pant legs. I couldn't help smiling.

We were taken to a pillar of a woman who stood in the doorway of an open tent watching our procession. She wore a floral apron and matching headscarf. The door flaps were rolled to either side of her adding to the stage-like effect of the scene as Tray stopped, swept an illusory hat from his head and clasped it to his stomach. "I present my ma, the lovely Marcella Tuttle of Sussex."

He bowed with all the grace of a prince and Marcella swatted him on the back. "My little actor. Go steal someone else's show. Better yet, play the part of a servant boy and wash those pans. They're crusting over in the sun." An upward lilt at the end of Marcella's accented words made her sound as grand as the boy proclaimed her to be.

Ignoring her, Tray said, "These fair maidens of the hill have come to hear our accomplished music." He spread his palms as if we'd sprung from them, lowering an intense gaze at Luella. "If you're not careful, the music might change you in ways you're unprepared for." He turned his delicate face toward me, and I thought he'd make a fine actor one day, with a face like that. Cocking his head to one side, he said, "You, I believe, are not so easily influenced."

His sentence was cut short by a broad hand that reached into our scene and yanked him by the collar. "Enough of this dandy play. You get those pans washed or I'll wash your hide." There was a boot to Tray's behind. "Job and I already brushed down the horses and emptied the water buckets. You get on and do the one thing you're asked and stop messing about."

Tray stumbled, righted himself and straightened his imaginary jacket without missing a beat. "There are ladies present," he said, haughtily, lifting a stack of pans and carting them away with a wink at me over his shoulder.

The intruder was a gangly young man, youth persisting in his smooth face, the man-to-be surfacing in his baritone and swagger. He had a wide jaw and eyes that were dark, but not lightless. He stuck out his hand. "Sydney Tuttle," he said, shaking first my hand and then Luella's before addressing Marcella. "You can't let him go on like that, Ma. People will think him odd."

Marcella was a woman armed with size, her shoulders round and large as a man's, her back straight, her step deliberate. "You leave him be," she said, moving to the fire and setting her intention on prying a loaf of bread from an iron pan.

Sydney walked off, drawing Luella's attention without offering her a glance.

Marcella ripped the bread into sections, eyeing us over the snaking smoke. "Tray's friendlier than he should be," she said. "What is it you want?"

My tongue went heavy in my mouth, but Luella spoke up without hesitation. "We heard your singing yesterday. It was the

49

most beautiful sound. We hoped we might be lucky enough to hear it again."

Marcella remained taciturn. "We don't sing for strangers, not our own words, anyway. Not unless we're spied on."

I tugged on Luella's sleeve, but she plunged ahead. "We didn't mean any disrespect, we just happened by. It was magnificent. Any stranger would have stopped to listen."

Sparks shot up from the fire as Marcella poked it with a stick. "Like I said, we don't sing for strangers."

My throat was thick with nerves. I wanted to leave, but Luella stood rooted. "I'm Miss Luella Tildon and this is my sister Miss Effie Tildon." She gave a slight curtsy. "You are Marcella Tuttle of Sussex which makes us officially introduced and no longer strangers."

The corner of Marcella's lip curled as if suppressing a grin. She eyed Luella, giving a final jab to the fire. "Your parents know you're here?"

"Of course," Luella answered. "My father says you're fine horse traders."

"Ha!" The syllable rang out in disbelief. Marcella looked at me, jutting her chin at two chairs. "Sit." It was not a tone you disobeyed.

Luella pinched my hand as we sat which meant, *I told you so.* She always got her way.

Bone China plates, as lovely as the ones we had at home, were placed in our laps and we balanced them on our knees trying to keep hunks of bread from sliding off. The bread was crispy, dense and sweetened with raisins. I had never eaten anything baked out of doors and I imagined I could taste the crust of earth, the nectar of ash. Through the tent flap I saw a tidy room with a trunk and a double bed on a wooden frame with an ivory coverlet. These gypsies were as civilized as my father said, and yet I sensed what it was about them that made my mother fearful. There was a pulse around them, an enigmatic energy, as if the blood of their music, even in silence, vibrated up through the ground beneath their feet.

A little way off a girl watched us. She looked about Luella's age, or at least as mature in figure, with dark hair and skin. Her cheeks turned into a wide smile as she watched me rip the bread with my teeth. I felt on display, sized up by my ability to eat in an outdoor chair with a plate on my knees.

Walking over, the girl dropped to the ground with her legs curled back under a skirt embroidered in red, blue and yellow

51

flowers. "I'm Patience," she said, and we introduced ourselves in turn.

Marcella handed Patience a hunk of bread and she chewed it, watching us from the same dark, distinct eyes as her brother, Sydney. I wondered where Tray had sprung from with a paleness so unlike his siblings.

As news of our arrival spread through the camp, a crowd of children gathered around us, each with a pet of one species or another. One boy held a rope tethered to a goat that appeared perfectly content to be dragged around by its neck. Another boy, in dirty-kneed knickers, set a globed cage at my feet with a canary as bright as an egg yolk perched inside. The bird cocked his head and fluttered his resplendent feathers as the boy opened the little wire door and reached for him. "I've clipped his wings, so he won't fly away," he said, lifting the bird and letting him hop from the narrow branch of his finger to mine.

"How charming," cried Luella, watching the bird parade up and down my finger. "May I?" The bird hopped from my finger to hers, and Luella laughed and stroked its lemony head.

The other children crowded closer. A scrappy girl took the empty plate from my lap and dropped a bunny into the folds of my tan skirt. It was so ensconced in knotted, gray fur I could hardly tell its tail from its head. It gave a violent kick as I lifted it and tore a line of skin from the inside of my arm.

"Ouch!" I cried and the girl snatched the animal back.

"You can't hold him like that," she scolded, tucking the bunny into her chest and pinning his feet with her hands.

"Are you okay?" Luella said. "Let me see."

A string of blood beaded along my arm. It stung. "I'm fine."

The boy promptly took back his bird, as if Luella might also prove an unfit handler. Two children, matched in size, their hair wild and long, stared at us. The girl stuck out her hand and we realized they expected payment for their generosity. Despite our mother's warning, we'd both brought money in hopes of getting our fortunes told. We dug into our pockets and dropped a nickel into the children's palms. This, of course, brought more children with dogs, bunnies, birds, even insects, but we shook our heads, not about to waste what we needed to reveal our futures.

Marcella watched us, stationed by the fire with folded arms and an amused expression. She never reprimanded the children or called them off; she let us fend for ourselves until the gaggle turned away.

It impressed me how different Marcella was from my own mother, or any other mother I'd known. In my world, mothers stepped in to solve problems, arrange hair and clothes, and put everything in order. Marcella, with her eagle's eye, watched to see how things might arrange themselves.

It was Sydney who raised his fiddler's bow first, toasting his "brothers" and striking his fiddle with gumption. Clearly Tray had organized it, bouncing behind the musicians with glee, one man with a dulcimer, another the trombone. The three men formed a semicircle around Patience. She gave a dramatic pause, raised her hands over her head and then plunged into a dance as their notes struck the air and a man's deep, mournful voice rose above the instruments.

*It's evening already.*
*We took a long road.*
*Tie them up and Rest.*
*Oh my brothers, Oh my brothers.*

Patience's skirt lifted and her hands spun ribbons of color as she plucked the scarf tied around her braid, her loose hair creating its own commotion. The instruments quickened and just as I was certain she'd vanish in a heap of hair and fabric, her hand

54

emerged from the whirling mass and reached for my sister. Someone made a whooping sound. The fiddles double-timed. Luella needed no instruction. She danced with Patience as if it's what she'd always done, her arms and legs surging under the seams of her clothes, her limbs broken free. Caught up, I felt transported into a heavenly world of color and the voices of riotous angels, their haunting music opening up a longing in me that had no name.

Watching from my chair, I was aware of Marcella's presence only when I felt her hand on my shoulder, her fingers so close to my face I could see tiny cracks in her knuckles and smell the strangeness of her skin. It seemed an unconscious gesture, as if the music had softened her and she'd diminished, her body seeking earth instead of sky. Propped up by the narrow shelf of my shoulder, this large woman swayed and I began swaying with her from my seat. My shyness dissolved against the closeness of our bodies. My body racked with the pulse of the music, my chest with the thrum of my heart. I had never felt anything so powerful and disorienting, and there was a fluttering in my chest like the arrival of a swarm of tiny, caged canaries.

"Music feeds the heart." Marcella nodded

down at me, as if she could feel my quickening pulse through my shoulder. "And mind —" she tapped the side of her head "— and soul." She thrust her hands upward and the music seemed to come straight out of her fingertips as she lifted them into the vast bowl of blue above our heads.

Tray emerged from the chaos and took one of his mother's hands. She reached for mine with the other, and I was pulled from my chair. It didn't matter that I didn't know how to dance their dance. The fiddles drove the soles of my feet, the flutes my arms, the accordion my hips. Shaken from my inhibition, I soared until the wings in my chest weakened and faltered and I became breathless. I pitched forward, gulping for air, my lungs conspiring with my sneaky heart. No matter how many fits I had, I never got used to the terror of not being able to breathe.

"Are you okay?" Tray cried. He pulled me aside and tried to hold me up, but I pushed him away and squatted with my head bent forward bearing down with my whole body until my breathing slowed and my struggling capillaries opened their way back to my chest.

Tray squatted beside me, his hand tight against my shoulder blade. "I thought you were choking."

No one else had noticed and the musicians played on. "I'm fine. It's nothing." I stayed on my knees, disappointed that I'd ended such a glorious moment so pathetically. Tray eased to the ground next to me, cross-legged and yanking up tufts of grass, his head bobbing in time to the music. The top of his hair was dull with grease, the strands like dried wheat.

A final song trilled through the air. Fiddles and bows went limp. Patience and Luella bent over their knees, gasping and laughing, their limbs shaking. A large, bearded man with pitch-black hair put an arm around Marcella and kissed her. The dulcimer player slapped Sydney on the back. I watched my sister yank up the stockings that had bunched around her ankles. When she righted herself, her face was florid, drops of sweat sliding down the sides of her cheeks. Patience drew her away and I watched them splash their faces in a tin of water by the side of a wagon.

The bunny scratch on my arm began to throb. Tray tossed a clump of bluets in my lap, little bursts of yellow at their centers like a lapful of miniature skies holding their own suns. "The blue girl." He smiled, jumped up and careened away.

My tiny blue skies sprinkled to the ground

when I stood up, looking for Luella. I found her sitting on the steps at the back of a wagon with Patience trying to braid her hair.

"We should head home," I said.

"Did you love it?" Luella beamed. "How was my dancing?"

"Good." Her dancing was always good. She didn't need me to tell her that.

"I tore a stocking." She flipped up her skirt to flaunt the damage, her head yanked back by Patience.

"Hold still," Patience ordered, her forehead scrunched with concentration. She was doing a terrible job. Thin strands slipped out everywhere. Luella's hair never braided properly. Patience scowled, then pulled her scarf from her skirt pocket and wrapped it over Luella's hair, tying off the ends of the braid with a look of triumph. "Much better!"

Touching the silk, Luella craned to see the back of her hair. "I can't take your scarf."

Patience shimmied her liberated hair over her shoulders like a horse showing off its mane. "I'll just have to wear my hair like this until you bring me a replacement. Which means, I'll be in tremendous trouble until you return."

Luella hopped off the wagon and as she

slung her arm through mine, said, "I'll bring you a scarf so lovely, Patience, you'll never want to take it off."

"Then I'll never be in trouble again." Patience leaned back with one leg stuck out over the wagon step.

"And you'll owe me one," Luella said.

Their voices held a challenge, their look a friendly taunt. Later, I would realize that this teasing was a prelude to a friendship, but at the time it just drifted into the strangeness of the day. As we made our way out of camp, Sydney watched us over the crest of a horse, measuredly stroking the dip in her sleek brown spine. When he caught Luella's eye, he said, "You should come when the moon's out. We'll play again."

It was a ridiculous invitation, but my sister only smiled.

# CHAPTER FOUR:
## EFFIE

That night Luella crept into my room with a confiscated issue of Mama's *Good Housekeeping* magazine. We lay side by side, flipping through the spring fashion, Patience's hair arrangement displayed over Luella's shoulder.

"Gracious." She flicked a page. "I hope Mama doesn't see this YWCA summer camp. *'A hike to the lake with baskets and cameras . . . tennis, a little friendship fire.'* Well now, you can't beat that! *'Morning bible classes and afternoon vesper services . . . held out of doors it lays fresh emphasis on the beauty of God's world. Refreshment of the body and soul!'* Remember how there was talk of sending us off last summer. They're sure to do it this year." She pressed a theatrical hand to her heart. "Daddy fears for my soul."

"They wouldn't dare send me, and they won't separate us, so I'm sure you're safe."

"Promise to have a few fits to put them off?"

"Promise," I lied. I'd gotten good at hiding my fits and had no intention of telling anyone about my earlier mishap.

"Patience said they won't be moving on until fall, which means we can go to the gypsy camp every day."

"You mean to go back?" I wasn't sure how I felt about sneaking out again.

"I most certainly do. I'll dance with the gypsies all summer if we're not sent to some dastardly camp."

"But we leave for Newport in June."

"At least we'll have until then."

We never missed summers in Newport where we had family. I looked forward to it even though most of our time was spent perched in airy mansions, or parading with the other girls in white attire on clipped green lawns like flocks of egrets. I always held out hope that Mama would let us swim at the beach. She believed it unseemly to wear a bathing suit, and so far, all we'd been allowed was a fully shrouded walk on the sand with salt on our lips and spray sneaking under our dresses. It was agony.

Luella paused on a page where a model posed with a plume, plucked from some unfortunate bird, soaring from the back of

61

her head. Pearls cascaded from her hair and neck and waist like a strung instrument.

"What I wouldn't give for a dress like that," she breathed. "Daddy would never let me wear it."

"Not yet."

"Not ever." Luella clapped the magazine shut and slid it under the bed out of view. She turned off the light and pulled the coverlet to her neck.

"What did you do with Patience's scarf?" I whispered.

"Hid it under my mattress."

"Are you going to give it back?"

"Never. I want to remember today in every boring minute of my boring life."

I slid down and pressed my cold feet against Luella's. A full moon shone through the window and Luella's eyes sparked in the cool, bright light.

Church was unbearable the next day, the Reverend's voice droning on and on, everything stiff and colorless; seats, bibles, faces and pompadours. After, we were forced to sit all afternoon with our ancient grandmother in her town house on Gramercy Park, her powdered white face staring at us from under her black cap. She was a small, withered woman who made up for her size with dogmatic proclamations and a finely-honed sense of righteousness. I quailed in her presence and could never think of anything to say. I knew she thought me as dumb as a board.

Today, thankfully, she directed her sharp inquiries at Luella while I watched in silence, imagining if my grandmother dared to smile how her vitrified wrinkles would crack and shatter her porcelain skin.

School that week was as dull as church, and ballet was torture for Luella. I began to understand her ardor for the gypsy camp. There was fresh life in it. I wondered if Marcella had cast a spell making our day-to-day routine colorless without them.

On Friday, we conspired in the bathroom as Luella rubbed salve into her big toes. "Ivanov yelled at me three times because I didn't put enough padding in my shoes and I winced through all of my bourrées. *You look like a tortured fish! Smile, Luella, smile!*" Luella mimicked his accent and threw her arms in the air, nearly dropping the salve in the toilet bowl. "Whoever invented pointe shoes should be shot."

It was a rare moment when I didn't envy her ability to dance.

The next day, Saturday, we were halfway out the door when Mama stepped into the hall from the parlor, snapping shut the novel she'd been reading. "It's awfully cold to be gadding about out of doors. Which reminds me, where are your sketches from last week?"

Luella quickly lied that we'd turned our pictures in to the art teacher. Today, we were working on poems for the school poetry contest.

"Then where are your notebooks?" Mama raised a single, perfectly arched brow. Wordlessly, I produced the leather-bound notebook I carried for story ideas. "And yours, Luella?"

"We're working on a poem together," she smiled.

Mama narrowed her eyes at me. "How are you feeling?"

"Fine," I said. The previous day I'd had a blue fit I hadn't been able to hide.

Luella pulled me against her. "I'll keep an eye on her. If she shows the slightest sign of weakness, I'll bring her straight home."

Mama tapped a nervous finger on the spine of her book before giving a reluctant sigh. "Your sweaters won't do. It's drizzling. Go get your coats, and if it begins to really rain you're to come directly home."

We did as we were instructed, kissed Mama goodbye and strolled leisurely up the road as she watched from the doorway, tear-

64

ing off as soon as we rounded the corner. Bruised clouds grazed the horizon and a thin mist settled over our shoulders.

When we arrived the gypsy camp was lively with excitement. The children were getting ready to put on a play and everyone was being ushered to their grass seats in front of a set of sheets that had been strung up between two wagons for curtains.

Tray spotted us with a jump and a wave, popping out from one of the wagons to escort us to a rug spread over the grass. The play was *Romeo and Juliet* with Tray playing a gallant Romeo; and a girl as sprightly as an elf playing Juliet. Romeo kneeled in the grass. Juliet hung from a wagon window. Props were imagined, or mimed, as lines were thrown into a cooperative wind that tossed them our way.

The rain held off until our hero and heroine lay dead on the ground. Rugs and blankets were gathered up through a round of applause. Tray gave a quick bow and moved into the audience, taking my hand and pulling me toward a tent where Marcella stood inside slapping raindrops from her crocheted shawl.

I knew we should be getting home, but inside the tent the raindrops rang against the taut canvas like tiny cymbals. The gypsies, it appeared, could make music out of anything.

Taking an orange scarf from his pocket, Tray tied it around his head and said, "Shall I tell your fortune?" batting his lashes at me.

"Do you ever stop acting?" I laughed.

"I never act! I transform. Now, for your fortune?"

"I didn't bring any money."

"That's all right. If it's a bad fortune, people never want to pay anyway."

"Will it be bad?"

Tray shrugged. "You never know."

A red, medallion rug was laid out on the tent floor and he sat cross-legged on it, gesturing me to the ground. I kneeled in front of him.

"Don't go frightening the child," Marcella said, slipping out with a soft *thunk* of the tent flap.

I was annoyed she called me a *child.*

Tray slapped his hands together, rubbing them rapidly. "You'll need to remove your gloves."

"Why?"

"So, I can read your palms."

I pressed my hands firmly in my lap. Once, a teacher forced me to remove my gloves, took one look at my clubbed fingernails and told me, with disgust, to put them back on immediately. "Can't you read something else?"

Thoughtfully, Tray pressed his hand over mine, his palm warm as a mitten. "Sure." He smiled, crawling to the bed and producing a deck of cards from under the pillow. "It only works if you shuffle them."

The cards were bright and new with a Tudor Rose design on the back. On the front were moons and suns and kings and queens and beasts. I began to shuffle. They were large and awkward, nothing like the playing cards we had at home.

"I thought only women told fortunes?" I teased, trying to cover up how nervous I was. "Where's your crystal ball, your loop earrings? You look nothing the part."

He wiggled his eyebrows, grinned and latched a hand over each knee. A soft wind lifted the sides of the tent and cold, wet air slithered in. I shivered and placed the shuffled cards between us.

Tray swept them in a circle. "Choose five, but don't turn them over."

I chose carefully, hovering my hand over a card, almost touching it and then quickly choosing another, as if it was in the choosing that my future was decided.

When I finally finished, Tray arranged

them in a horseshoe pattern and unceremoniously flicked over the first card. I'd expected at least an incantation or a magical hand motion. The card was a picture of a woman surrounded by circled stars. Tray stared at it for a long time with a serious, contemplative expression.

I felt like he was teasing me. "What? What does it mean?"

He nodded, slowly. "This card is your present condition: material well-being, prudence and safety." He flipped over another showing seven gold goblets floating on a cloud with images emerging out of each. "This is your present desire: visions of the fantastic spirit, sentiment, things seen in the glass of contemplation." He turned over the third.

I bolted upright. "What does that mean?" I jabbed a finger at a skeleton riding a lovely white horse. It read, *Death.*

Tray remained calm. "It doesn't mean you're going to die."

"How can *Death* mean anything else?"

"It's not literal. This card means change. Extreme change like the end of something, loss, corruption, misdeeds, lies . . ." He flipped over the fourth card and the soles of my feet prickled. It was a heart pierced by three swords.

"And that?" My voice cracked. I'd picked the wrong cards.

"Is your immediate future."

"Is it literal?"

"Maybe." Tray looked straight into my eyes and I felt he was looking right down into the leaky hole in my heart. I didn't look away. As frightening as it was, I liked that someone could see the truth. And then I could see him too, the feeling between us shifting from something intimate and personal to an expanded awareness of each other, as if we were soaring through a larger future, a future that wasn't either one of ours, but one we were both, somehow, tangled up in.

A gust of wind lifted the tent flap and scattered the cards. Tray caught them with a slap of his hand. The heart with the swords still faced me.

"What does it mean?" I was ready for it.

Tray pulled the scarf from his head, like the joke was over. "It means removal, absence, rupture, total loss."

*Total loss.* I didn't like this. Not one bit. I wanted something good, something beautiful. I wanted the robed queen, or the angel floating in the heavens. "I should have chosen differently."

Tray shook his head, his face sad. "You

couldn't have. The cards choose you."

There was one left.

"You turn it over," Tray said. "It's the *Outcome.*"

Defiantly, I slapped the card over. There was a naked woman dancing with a wand in either hand. She was encircled by a garland with the four creatures of the Apocalypse staring out from each corner, a lion, ox, eagle and man. It read: *The World.*

Tray smiled, relieved, and seemingly unflustered by the woman's exposed nipples that were embarrassing me. "You see, all good things in the end. She is sensitive, vulnerable, enjoying the joys of the earth while guarded by the divine watchers. This card is the secret within, the universe that understands itself as God. It is the soul, divine vision, self-knowledge, truth."

This didn't make me feel better. As far as I was concerned this was the dead me dancing within the Divine.

Tray put a hand on my knee. "It's good."

I nodded, giving him a weak smile as Luella abruptly stuck her head in the tent. "Effie, we'd better go."

On my way out, I looked back at Tray who sat with his chin propped on his fist staring at the cards. I wondered if he was worried for his future, or mine.

"Tray?"

"Yes?" He looked at me.

Luella was already halfway down the path. "It's not your fault, my heart has always been damaged."

"I know." He smiled. "Bye-bye, blue girl."

Rain dusted my hair into curls as Luella and I pushed our way through the underbrush in silence. I was grateful she didn't want to talk about our morning. I didn't want to tell her about my skeleton and stabbed heart future, and I didn't want her to ask Tray to read her fortune. I was sure it would be better than mine, every card bright and promising. No doubt she would have turned over a queen and a soaring angel.

But more than that, I wanted Tray to myself. I hardly knew him, and yet I had this sense of familiarity, like he'd been a part of my life forever, accompanied by the panicked feeling that I was going to lose him.

# Chapter Five:
## Effie

As spring became flush with warmer weather, we managed on Saturday afternoons to sneak into the gypsy camp without rousing suspicion. This was thanks in large part to our headmistress, Miss Chapin, announcing at assembly, "I will not tolerate my girls getting up to no good now that the weather is warming." Low titters circled the auditorium. We all knew she meant *fraternizing with the opposite sex will not be tolerated.* "So . . . our traditional student outing to the athletic fields in Westchester on Saturdays will begin this week."

I wasn't allowed to participate in athletics, but I swayed Daddy to let me go by promising to play a single game of tennis and rest the remaining time.

Our train to Westchester left the station at 6:00 a.m., which left the morning for tennis — or in my case "resting," which meant scribbling in my writing notebook — eating a picnic lunch with our classmates and arriving back in the city by 1:00 p.m. Luella and I decided it was safe, if we both stuck to our stories, to tell our parents the train arrived back at 5:00 p.m. Then we could take the elevated train to Dyckman Street and walk the rest of the way to the gypsy camp.

I found comfort in Tray's quiet company, in Marcella's cooking, the children's loud games and the evening songs. I'd never noticed before how quiet and empty our home was. Even when our parents were there, it felt lonely in comparison.

Luella was happier than I'd ever seen her. She no longer grumbled about the possibility of summer camp, or leaving for Newport, or complained about ballet. At school, in the yellow-walled library, there was no more bemoaning the difficulty of the biology exam or Miss Spence's ethics class. She didn't even show the slightest interest when Suzie Trainer disappeared from school, with everyone whispering that her father had put her in the House of Mercy for receiving a telegram from a boy. The telegram had been delivered to the school and, according to Kathleen Sumpton, a gossip, Suzie was told she must become engaged to this boy immediately. Only she had refused and her father had her locked away for it.

"They would have driven right past your house." Kathleen twisted in her chair to look at me, the gaggle of girls huddled around her turning too. Our history teacher had stepped out of the room.

"I suppose." I shrugged.

The House of Mercy was just up the road from us, a Protestant Episcopal home for wayward girls. When I was young it held a mythological place in my stories, but it became a very real threat two years ago when a boy at a dance was caught with his hand on the small of Luella's back. Daddy went wild with fury. Not even Luella's charm could calm him. He said he wouldn't hesitate to send her away, if that's the sort of girl she'd become. Luella swore she thought the boy's hand was in the middle of her back where it should have been. "How can I feel anything through my stays?" she cried, and Mama said she had a point.

I hadn't thought of the incident until Suzie Trainer's disappearance.

After that, the worm of guilt wiggling through me on Saturday mornings when I'd kiss Mama and Papa goodbye grew larger. There were no boys involved in our sneaking around to the gypsy camp, not specifically, but I began to worry about our week-end escapades. What if we got caught and Daddy sent us away? It's not like we'd done one small thing, we'd been lying for a whole month, which was not something we'd be able to talk our way out of.

I was also worrying over exams, which were just around the corner. Most of the Chapin girls thought little about grades and instead competed over who would be the first graduate to have four babies. I shuddered at the thought. Luella said she might have *one* baby, someday, but never four. And she was certain to have a smattering of lovers beforehand. I was certain not to have any lovers, but I also wasn't interested in learning to cook and budget and keep accounts to run a household. I planned to go to Bryn Mawr and become a writer. Which meant I had to do well in all subjects. I focused on Latin and French, wrote short stories and essays, observed cells wiggling like living stained glass under the microscope, and dutifully memorized the periodic table and the classification system.

Since the gypsy camp, my studies had dropped off. I'd do well in English no matter what, but my math and science would suffer if I didn't focus. When I said this to Luella, she was unconcerned. She'd never been particularly interested in her studies, but this spring she hadn't bothered studying at all. When I pointed this out, she just shrugged, indifferent. She even started telling Ivanov her arches ached and skipped ballet class.

Then things changed for the worse.

Daddy started showing up at school in his red Empire runabout, with the top down, to escort us to luncheon at Delmonico's. This made us the envy of our peers. Girls clumped together watching from the steps of the Georgian schoolhouse as we settled into the car, our father plucking a gold-tipped cigarette from his lips with gloved fingers, his derby hat at a rakish tilt, pointy shoes so shiny you could see the steering wheel reflected in them.

In any other circumstance, I would have relished this kind of attention from Daddy. It was a mean trick, giving it to me now when I was consumed with guilt and couldn't enjoy it. These luncheons were out of the norm and every day that first week, I hurried through whatever exquisite dish was set in front of me and waited for him to tell us he knew about the gypsies. I thought maybe this was reverse punishment, showing us how good we had it before taking it all away.

It took me three long weeks of watching Daddy lean back in his chair, smoking and scanning the room, catching the attention of everyone, before I understood that these luncheons had nothing to do with Luella and me. It never crossed my mind that the stunning woman we passed every day taking lunch by herself, a woman who possessed the room in a manner more like a man's than a woman's, was the reason. She was remarkable, with a confidence I'd never seen in our sex. Daddy would tip his hat and smile and the woman would return the smile with a toss of her head, her face round and sensual, her lips a devastating red.

I intended to mention her to Luella, if for nothing more than her red lips, but somehow kept forgetting. Then came a day in May, as we sat eating our lunch and luxuriating in the sudden warmth of spring, when the woman rose from her seat and crossed the room to us. Luella and I stared. For all the dinners and parties we'd been to, we'd never seen a woman dressed like this. This was no mother clinging to the Victorian era, or schoolgirl pining after a magazine photo. This *was* the magazine photo. Here was the New Woman of 1913. A woman we'd only read about. Bold, confident, stripped of convention. Under strings of pearls and twists of sapphire tulle, she wore a flesh-colored dress of *peau de soie* so tight it looked like a second layer of skin. The effect was shocking.

There was something disturbingly familiar in the way my father looked at her.

"Emory Tildon," she said, her voice floating into the room, light and carefree. "I thought that was you. These lovely creatures must be your daughters?" She narrowed her eyes at us with exaggerated interest, the sound of the other diners fading to a quiet din in her presence.

Daddy stood up. He tugged at his cuffs and cleared his throat with a nervousness that embarrassed me. "Yes, these are my girls. Effie, Luella, this is Inez Milholland. Her father is an editor," he said, as if this was supposed to explain something.

*Inez Milholland?* Luella and I gaped. Here was the woman we'd gazed at on the cover of *Woman's Journal and Suffrage News.*

My speechlessness was nothing out of the ordinary, but Daddy gave Luella a sharp look indicating that she, at the very least, shouldn't be rude. My sister only stared, awed into silence for the first time in her life.

Miss Milholland remained poised and unflustered by our gawking. "It's a pleasure to meet you both." Her smile widened as she turned her dusty brown eyes on Daddy. "Won't you step outside for a cigarette? It's awfully warm in here and I could use a bit of air." Her hand fluttered out, delicate as the fabric shifting over her hips. Our father took her hand without pause and they slipped away from the table.

Luella's fork clattered to her plate. "How does Daddy know her?" she gasped, her mouth creeping into a smile. "He's more liberated than he lets on. Come on, I want to get another look at her."

She pulled me from the table and out the restaurant doors to the bright and crowded street. It took a moment before we spotted Daddy helping Inez into the back of an open cab. A couple passed and I smelled the woman's sickly-sweet, gardenia perfume. Luella started forward, halted and froze as Daddy leaned into the car and kissed that bright, red mouth of Inez Milholland. The kiss seemed to stretch for an endless amount of time as we stood frozen.

Luella spun around, her face leached of color, her eyes crinkled into little slits of rage. In spite of Luella's rebellious nature, she thought the world of our father. She pushed against him because she believed it was safe. She believed, as I did, that our father was principled and scrupulous, that he would rein her in when she dared go too far, as any good father would. She might not like it, but she respected the natural order of things.

When that order shattered, she became wild.

She shoved me back through the restaurant doors and into our chairs at the table, where we sat wordless. The clink of flatware and hubbub of voices prickled my skin. My potatoes looked pasty, the gravy mud. I pushed my food aside and bit the inside of my cheek until it bled. I wanted to make an excuse for Daddy. Explain the woman away. But, I couldn't.

Luella had her elbows on the table, her eyes fixed on the cut-glass saltshaker as if counting the grains. Her silence unnerved me. She always had something to say.

When Daddy returned he was chatty and casual, as if nothing out of the ordinary had taken place, draping his arm over the back of his chair with an air of privilege. I looked for a smear of red on his mouth, but saw only the blush of his own lips.

Luella and I never discussed it, but I knew it was that haughty moment, even more than the kiss, that Luella refused to forgive. If he'd been unnerved or jumpy we might have convinced ourselves that his morals were intact. Passion had blinded him. He'd regain his balance. But he wasn't thrown, not in the least; even with the sin of another woman on him, my father was jaunty. Genial. Proud.

It was the first time I saw him as a man who'd been given everything, as a man separate from the person who was my father. I thought of the night when I was eight years old and I'd watched him pace in the parlor after my doctor's visit. Maybe his anger back then had nothing to do with my possible death. Maybe he'd bellowed at the doctor when I was born, not because he believed I was a strong baby, but because he refused to believe something he wanted could be taken from him.

I felt crushed under the weight of our discovery. It sickened me watching Daddy's bright, blue, unapologetic eyes as he waved the waiter over. I thought of Mama in her well-fitting dresses and her nightly cold cream applications, of her pride in Daddy marrying her despite her scars and homely limbs. The words of those women in the parlor came back to me; *I don't know what spell Jeanne wove over Emory when they were courting, but I wouldn't have risked it.* Well, Mama had risked it, I thought angrily.

She had risked it because of those scars. It wasn't her fault the spell wore off.

When Luella and I returned home from school she shut herself in her room without a word to me. I tried to study, but I couldn't concentrate so I moved my desk chair to the open window and tried to think up a story. The gauze curtains fluttered. The sun melted, golden and powdery over my lap and I could smell spring, the newness of it. No story came. Writing was what I shared with my father. Mama treated it like a silly pastime, glancing at a story I'd hand her with a distracted smile like I was a child handing her a scribbled drawing. Daddy took me seriously. Every Sunday morning he'd fold his paper, set it by his plate, and look up at me as if he'd just remembered something incredibly important. "Where's my story, peanut. Did you forget about me?"

I never forgot. I'd slip the notebook from my lap and offer it gravely. Recently, Daddy had started wearing glasses, which only added to the professional air he'd put on as he read, nodding, smiling, grimacing, every now and then offering a hearty laugh. Luella and Mama went about their usual breakfast business, chatting, spreading jam, pouring coffee while I waited with my hands pressed into my lap for Daddy to raise his head and

say, "Fine work, peanut. Fine work indeed."
Then he'd launch into his honest critique,
telling me what did and didn't work, treating me like a writer worthy of this solid
advice.

In the window glass, I caught my reflection, pale, thin, lips like pencil lines. I'd
never be a woman who wore lipstick. Daddy
would be ashamed of me. I pulled off my
gloves and held my hand to the light. My
nails were a bulbous, milky yellow. They
disgusted me, but I forced myself to look at
them, imagining God an ugly giant pouring
tallow from a massive pitcher, a drop landing and hardening on each finger. Maybe
I'd write that grim story for Daddy. Who
cared what he thought. His advice meant
nothing now.

At six o'clock I went down to dinner, even
though I didn't want to face anyone, not
even Luella, who, to my surprise, was
already at the table. I sat across from her
relieved she wasn't protesting. This was
good. We would slip the moment under the
rug. Bury it. Forget it.

Roast pork, potatoes and green beans were
heaped onto my plate, but I couldn't eat.
Neither could Luella, who kept her hands
glued in her lap. I, at least, pushed my food
around with my fork.

"What is it?" Mama asked. "Don't you girls feel well?"

"We ate a large lunch," I offered, hating how innocent she looked, how plain. I wished she'd worn her green dress instead of this severe, black one.

"You took them to Delmonico's again?" She smiled at Daddy. "You're spoiling them. It's so unlike you to be that frivolous."

"It *is* unlike you to be frivolous, Daddy," Luella said, her tone daringly confrontational. "Although we did have the pleasure of meeting the most astounding woman today, a Miss Inez Milholland."

My chest squeezed. I worked the torn skin on the inside of my cheek with my tongue and prayed my sister would stop talking.

Daddy reached for the pepper with an easy smile at Mama. "Do you remember her father, John Elmer Milholland? He's an editor for the *New York Tribune.* He used to be on Mother's guest list before his views on women's rights became too vocal for her tastes." He ground the pepper a little too vigorously over his pork.

Not an inkling of concern crossed Mama's face. "The name's familiar, but I don't remember him."

Luella was not going to let this go. "Inez Milholland is the woman who led the Suffrage parade on Washington, the one on the white horse, remember? It was all over the papers. I remember thinking how beautiful she was. Daddy admires beautiful things. Don't you, Daddy."

Daddy's smile fell. "There were more people at that spectacle than at Woodrow Wilson's inauguration. There's no respect for our presidential election system anymore, not a whit!"

"Not when it excludes women," Mama replied. We all looked at her, startled. "What?" she said. She had finished eating and sat in her chair with a self-composed dignity, her gloved hands in her lap. "I'm not as old-fashioned as you all think. I believe in votes for women. Don't get me wrong. I don't approve of their protests, or the way they make showy statements, like the sixty-year-old woman who stood on a mountain in Peru with a banner. I believe there must be a quieter, more diplomatic way of going about it."

"No one would listen." Luella shot Daddy a look.

He held her gaze. "Not if you're insolent, they won't."

"How else are women supposed to be heard?"

"One's actions have consequences."

"Precisely what I was thinking."

Their words batted back and forth like a tennis ball, each waiting for the other to smash the net. "I'm terribly glad you introduced me," Luella forced a laugh. "I think I'll take up the good fight with the glamorous Miss Milholland. I'm sure she'll have me. Women in numbers."

Color rose in Daddy's face. "You will do no such thing."

"That's not what I meant, Luella." Mama looked confused that the conversation had gone so far off the rails.

I slunk down in my chair, hating what Luella was doing.

"You can't stop me fighting for the rights of women. I'll do what I want." She flicked her head toward Daddy. "*You* most certainly do."

Daddy's fists thumped the table and my plate jumped. "That's right. I do. I've earned that right by growing up."

"I'll be sixteen in a few months. That's old enough to marry, if I want."

Mama sucked in her breath and Daddy's jaw bulged under his smooth high cheeks. "Not without my permission, you're not."

"I don't need your permission. If the law permits it, I can do it." Luella looked triumphant.

Generally, Mama defended Luella to Daddy, but this was too much. She remained silent, her eyes like a paralyzed doe caught in the cross fire.

Daddy's clear eyes sparked with anger. "Goodness," he mocked, "do you have someone in mind?"

"Maybe."

I knew Luella was making this up, but the vein swelling across Daddy's forehead was a sure sign he did not. "There are homes where indecent girls like you are sent and I am absolutely not beyond it." Daddy's voice was a low threat.

"How dare you call *me* indecent. I'm not the one who's done anything wrong." A thread of panic trailed Luella's anger. "You're the —"

"Out!" Daddy roared, leaping to his feet, his arm raised as if he meant to grab her.

Luella fled the room before he had the chance. The door slammed. Footsteps banged up the stairs. There was an awful silence as Daddy sat down and picked his napkin up off the floor.

"Good gracious," Mama breathed. "What's gotten into that girl?" No one answered. I quickly looked into my lap as tears sprang into my eyes. Mama reached across the table. "It's all right, dear. It's a phase. Ring Neala for dessert, won't you?"

I nodded, reaching for the bell on the sideboard.

Lemon tarts went down in silence, my jaw clenching with each sour bite. I ate all of it, noticing how my parents were carefully not looking at each other.

After dinner, I found Luella's door flung open and knew she was waiting for me. She'd kicked her shoes off and was pacing the rug in her stockings. Her room was north-facing and always had a chill. I sat on her canopy bed, the carved cherry posts like stately trees holding a maroon cloud of fabric that dipped over me like a soft, wide belly. The room was darkly furnished in a crimson theme that was not my sister. A hot, lurid red might have suited her, not this restrained, masculine rust color.

Back and forth Luella went at the foot of the bed, her skirt sweeping the floor. "How can Daddy be such a hypocrite? Holding to his morals, pretending to be old-fashioned and provincial enough to send me away when he's the one going to hell for his sins."

"Luella! You shouldn't say such things." I was glad I'd shut her door behind me.

"I'll say whatever I want."

I paused, working an idea I'd been convincing myself of. "Maybe it wasn't what we thought. Maybe we misunderstood. Or didn't see properly what was going on."

My sister shot her hands on her hips and reeled toward me. "I know a kiss when I see one."

"You've never kissed anyone."

"How do you know?"

"You have?" This was a revelation almost as shocking as Daddy's indiscretion.

"So, what if I have."

"Who? When? Why didn't you tell me?"

"I don't tell you everything, Effie."

This fell like a stone in my chest. "Well, maybe Daddy was just whispering something to her."

"Stop protecting him." Her face was flushed, her eyes huge.

I wanted to ask who she'd kissed. "I'm not protecting him, I'm just saying we don't know. The woman came over to *us*. She's the one who asked Daddy to go outside. It would have been rude to refuse. Maybe *she* kissed him. We didn't stay to see if he pushed her away." It could be true. Maybe she'd lifted herself from the seat and forced herself against him.

Luella made a throaty sound of disgust. "You're so ignorant." She pivoted, hauling open the window and dropping her hands on the sill. Outside, dusk had turned the hillside purple.

I stared into the advancing darkness with a feeling of shame.

Luella turned suddenly. "I'm sorry." She came to the bed and flung an arm around me. "I'm a wicked sister. I haven't kissed anyone. I just said it to prove you wrong. Do you know what I hate more than anything? I hate that Daddy used us. That we were his excuse to run into her every day."

"You noticed her before too?"

"How could I miss her? Those lips? I thought she was beautiful. Now, I think her a wicked witch in disguise. You should put her in one of your stories. You know," she faced me, slapping her hands on my knees, "I feel like that sometimes, like a wicked person in disguise. I tell people what they want to hear. Everyone thinks I'm good at ballet, but I'm not. I just pretend and everyone believes me." She stood up, energized. "Do you know the place where I'm real, where I don't have to pretend at all? With the gypsies. They don't care who I am or what I say. Everyone dances and sings whether they're good at it or not." She gave a hysterical laugh and flung her arms out. "It's positively freeing."

I felt like a cloud was settling over me, isolating me in a grainy mist that put

90

everything out of place. Luella was someone who did and said exactly what she wanted. If that was a lie, everything was.

For a few days I repeated Mama's words in my head, telling myself that Luella was just acting out, going through a phase. I held on to the idea that Daddy's kiss was a mistake, that he'd leaned in to tell Inez something and I hadn't seen properly.

Then Saturday came.

The Friday before I'd forgotten two of the history dates Miss Chapin required, but Luella had forgotten *all* of them. Worried her transgressions would multiply beyond what our parents would tolerate, I tried to convince her to stay home and study. She refused.

"I'm going with or without you," she said. "And this time, I'm going for the *whole* day. Bother with athletics. I'll forge a note to Miss Chapin from Mama saying I'm sick."

Frustration boiled in me. "You're being careless and selfish and Daddy's bound to find out."

"Daddy won't find out, as long as you don't go and tell him just to spite me," she glowered.

Her words stung. I'd never done anything to spite her. "Fine. Go," I said.

In the early morning sunshine, I sat at my

desk with my botany textbook trying to concentrate on the photosynthetic function of fronds, but my mind kept wandering to my sister. What began as listening to music and getting our fortunes told — a single lie for a day or two — was turning into a string of lies stretching over the summer horizon. I wasn't sure it was even about the gypsies anymore. There was something prowling in the depths of my sister's being, something longing to be set free.

The girl slips out the front door and up the hill, glancing back, hoping her father is watching from a window and will witness her defiance firsthand. He isn't, this time. The girl keeps going, her eyes fixed ahead as the fires and wagons come into view. Her breath quickens, her skin tingles with excitement as she slips into the camp. This is where she becomes herself, inevitable and powerful. It is not something she will give up, not for anyone.

I was shaken from my imaginings with a shout out the window. Mama had left to visit a great-aunt in Kensington and Daddy was playing tennis. I pulled the lace curtain aside, leaning into a warm square of sunlight to see where the voice had come from. The smell of lilacs wafted from below where the sweeping form of a woman in a wide-brimmed hat stood on our stone walkway. She wore a tan coat, open, a string of dark beads dangling between the richly embroidered lapels.

And there stood my father next to her. He'd traded his winter felt for a straw hat, which suddenly flew from his head as a man in tennis flannels knocked him to the ground. I slapped a hand to my mouth as Daddy leapt up and threw a punch, sending his attacker reeling into our rosebushes. The woman screamed and backed away. The man scrambled to his feet, his face flaming, yanked a thorny branch from the sleeve of his coat, threw it at Daddy's feet and stalked off. The rosebush looked defiled. I felt stunned. I'd never seen anyone punched before. Daddy plucked his hat from the ground, gave a decorous bow and beckoned the woman through the front door as if he'd given her a grand show and it was time for tea. She entered, glancing over her shoulder. Her unmistakable bright red mouth winked at me from under her hat like a taunting third eye.

My pulse raced as if I was the one about to be caught at something. I held my breath as their laughter echoed up the stairs.

Margot and Mama were out, and I was supposed to be with Luella in Westchester. Saturday was Neala's day off and Velma kept strictly to the kitchen. Was this why Daddy kept so few servants? Their shoes clipped past my door, the lingering reverence I held for my father shattering with each step. This could not be mistaken for anything but what it was.

Bold, female laughter reached me through the walls. I slid to the floor with my legs stretched straight out over the beige rug. Eventually the laughter stopped and the house fell silent. I yanked off my gloves and bit the skin around my deformed nails. After a while my bottom grew numb and I began to worry Mama would come home early. A few minutes after the clock struck two, I heard my father's low voice in the hallway, then quick, light footsteps down the stairs and the front door open. I peeked over the windowsill to see Miss Milholland, hat in hand, rest her arm over my father's as he guided her into a car. He shut the door, rapped the frame and tipped his hat to the driver as if she was any old guest on any old afternoon. The car pulled away and I watched him saunter off down the street.

I crawled to my bed and lay staring at the pale blue wallpaper of my nursery days.

Mama had never seen fit to change it. I wondered about this, and how Mama was the only one in the family who never made plans for me to grow up. Luella talked to me about college and Daddy said I'd be a great writer one day. Mama stayed quiet. Maybe she was blind to Daddy's indiscretions, but knew things about me that hadn't even come to pass.

I pressed a finger to the inside of my wrist, something Daddy used to do when I was little, after I was in bed. "Still ticking," he'd say. Luella would already be asleep beside me. Sometimes, and I never told anyone this, I'd tell him I was scared I was going die in the night. "We can't let that happen," he'd say, pulling a chair up to the bed. "I'll sit here until death comes and tell him he's got the wrong gal. 'This is *my* peanut,' I'll tell him. And if that doesn't work I'll give him a licking he'll never forget. I'll beat death, literally." He'd wink, then take my hand and hold it in his until I fell asleep. When I woke, I believed he'd done exactly as he promised.

I was no longer scared I'd die in the night. Despite the flutter in my chest, no one believed my survival was exceptional anymore, least of all me. I wasn't expected to live this long, and yet I wasn't expected to die either. I was thirteen, in limbo between girlhood and womanhood, between life and death, between Mama and Daddy, between Daddy and Luella. I didn't fit anywhere.

Indirect sunlight brightened the room. Through the window white clouds swept the sky. The lace curtains rippled. And then the tiny pulse under my finger became erratic, speeding up, pausing, slowing down, until suddenly it stopped. There was no fit, no breathlessness, just a freeze in my chest as the windows fell out of their casing and the walls expanded and the room rippled outward with a luminous translucence. I was aware that I was still here, on my bed, but the margins had fallen away.

It was all back in an instant, the crisp edges of things, my solid universe. I sat up with a gasp. The windows were in place. The walls upright. I felt the inside of my wrist. The steady little beat was back. Maybe it hadn't stopped? No, it had. I hadn't imagined it. I went to my desk and forced myself to read from my tedious, wordy textbook, hoping the boringness of it would help ground me in my concrete reality. I didn't want my extremities melting. It was hard enough to hold onto my surroundings as they were.

That night, I dreamt Miss Milholland was

dancing in a grove of fir trees, naked, wands in her hands. A winged lion circled her, each graceful, prowling step taken in time with the woman's feet, his veined wings rising like a dragon's from the sides of his body. There was no music. Round and round they went in silence until an eagle joined them, emerging from the trees with a winged ox and a winged man. They were the creatures I'd seen on the tarot card, but as they circled the woman their wings multiplied and their bodies became covered with eyes like the apocalyptic creatures from the bible. The man moved in closer and I saw that he had my father's face, and that his lips were painted the red of the woman's. I felt a sense of panic that he was going to kiss her, but then the woman was gone and her white horse lay dead on the ground where she'd stood. The apocalyptic creatures danced around it, their mouths dripping red saliva as they chanted, *holy, holy, holy, The Lord God almighty.*

# CHAPTER SIX:
## JEANNE

I'd forgotten to bring a book to read on the train ride home from Kensington. Frustrated, I stared out the window and tried to enjoy the budding forest flying past, the trees a bright new green. Visits to Emory's aunt Sylvia were tedious, to say the least, and my one consolation was the quiet hour I had to read on the train. Sylvia was my mother-in-law, Etta Tildon's, sister, and they were identical in every abusive, provoking, miserable way. I visited Sylvia solely to please my mother-in-law, a woman who found fault with every aspect of me despite my efforts. At one point we'd been on amicable terms, but since her husband's death the old woman's bitterness hung about her like a noxious cloud. As far as I could tell she wasn't on good terms with a single soul.

Removing my hat, I placed it on the empty seat next to me and rummaged through my purse for something to eat. The truth was, a book kept my mind from cycling through tragic scenarios that might have befallen my family while I was away. I was never a worrier before Effie's birth, but the fear that bore its way into me when she was a baby, wondering each day if I'd lose her, had persisted for years. It had contorted into new fears, but persisted nonetheless. The girls believed they were wonderfully independent when I let them take the elevated to school alone, or wander into the hills behind our home, but I was never more than a walk or a quick car ride away. Except for these monthly excursions to Kensington, which, after being berated by Aunt Sylvia for "refusing to adopt an American accent," as she so ridiculously put it, and in my bookless, anxious state of mind, I was seriously considering giving up.

There was nothing to eat in my bag, not even a stale mint, and I snapped the clasp shut with vigor.

"What's your poor bag done wrong?"

Looking up, I saw an unnervingly handsome man standing over me. "Excuse me?"

"Your bag." He pointed. "You look awfully angry with it. May I?" He indicated the seat where my hat was placed and I quickly moved it to my lap.

The train lurched and he caught the back of the seat to steady himself as he slid in next to me. "Cigarette?" He took one from his breast pocket and held it out with a full-lipped smile.

The cigarette was tempting. "No, thank you very much, I don't smoke."

When I first met Emory, he had the old-fashioned idea that women shouldn't smoke, and I'd given it up. At the time, I thought it was an American thing. Turned out it was a Tildon thing. His mother, the influential Mrs. Tildon, did not think it decorous in a woman.

"That's a shame. Wonderful stuff, cigarettes." He lit his and leaned back, smoking in silent satisfaction, his hat tilted high on his forehead.

I clutched my hat and looked out the window, the man's good looks unsteadying me. I'd always been a fool for a good-looking man. I suppose most women are. My mother had warned me of that with Emory.

He'd been courting me for three weeks before my mother met him. Despite his charm, I knew what was coming when she called me into her studio the next morning. While all the other society mothers were trying to marry their daughters off, mine was desperately trying to keep me in her clutches.

Her studio, with its pure bright light and smells of turpentine and paint, was a place that usually filled me with comfort. But that morning it felt stuffy and oppressive. My mother stood at her canvas in her stained apron, her dark hair hanging down her back. She never bothered to tie it up anymore and it gave her an unfettered appearance. The brushstrokes on the canvas behind her had the same careless, slapdash look to them. Over the years, her paintings had become more and more undisciplined.

"Don't hover in the doorway, Jeanne." She set her coffee cup on the table and picked up her paintbrush, pointing it at me like a weapon. I was a good deal taller than my mother, but this didn't intimidate her. "That man is dangerous. You'd best put him out of your mind straightaway. His attention is flattering, no doubt, but it won't last. It's fine for an ugly man to take a beautiful woman. It won't do to have it the other way around. You'll age like a stinky cheese and he like a fine wine. Moldy cheese is an acquired taste, while everyone loves a good wine, and they'll drink their fill, you take my word. It's a tale as old as time." Satisfied with her elaborate metaphor, and assured the subject was now closed, she turned her back to me, the light from the window catching the silver threads running through her dark hair.

I did not heed her warning. I'd never had a single suitor, and when Emory started showing up at the theater every night with an armful of flowers telling me I was the loveliest creature he'd ever seen, the compliments went to my head like a rush of champagne. I couldn't think straight. I could barely compose myself onstage knowing he was waiting for me afterward. For the first time, I was the envy of the other ballerinas. A proposal was more than I dared dream. Men often became struck with a dancer, but rarely did they want anything more than a mistress, something I would undoubtedly have become if Emory hadn't wanted me for his wife, a title that still filled me with pride.

The proposal was spontaneous. The evening he asked me, we'd attended a dinner party separately, finding our way to each other on the dance floor and dancing until midnight. When Emory offered to take me home, I didn't hesitate. It was snowing lightly and the boulevard sparkled in a hushed, empty silence. It was just the two of us, not even a carriage rolled past. I remember thinking how perfect the moment was even before Emory stopped me under the glittering light of a lamppost, kissing me in a bold, unhesitating manner that made my legs quiver. I'd never been kissed before, and when he pulled away, I was filled with a craving I hadn't known existed. His eyes were an intense, otherworldly blue.

When he lifted my hand and began delicately pulling at the fingers of my glove, I panicked. "Don't," I whispered, but he silenced me with his finger to my lips, the leather of his glove as soft as his mouth had been.

When my hand was exposed, he held it up, and I saw in his face that I was not hideous to him. He seemed in awe of my scars, and for the first time I recognized what Effie would, years later, show me every time she pulled off my gloves: immeasurable strength and endurance. Then, Emory bowed his head and kissed my healed wounds, snow dusting the arms of his coat and melting on the back of my hand under the warmth of his lips.

Any young woman in my place would have said yes.

We were genuinely in love, for a time. I was still not comfortable exposing my hands in the light of day, but at night, in those early years of our marriage, Emory caressed them with as much delicacy as he would later caress our babies' heads.

It was obvious from the start that Emory was not a complicated man. He liked his job, took pride in his family and was content to do as he pleased. Before Effie was born, he'd had no hardships, no toil or struggle. He was an only child with wealthy parents who adored him. There are people who simply have a good life. Emory was one of them. I was lucky to be his wife, to be a part of that simple, good life. At least in the beginning that's what I told myself.

Leaving my mother was the hardest part, and my brother, Georges, who was only a lad of eleven. I had no good reason to leave them other than falling in love. Reason enough, some would say. My life, before Emory, was also blessed. I grew up wealthy, fatherless — which didn't bother me as I'd never known him — with a mother who painted most hours of the day and a grandfather who worshipped me. He'd steal me away from my lessons and walk the streets of Paris with me hoisted onto his shoulders, proudly pointing out all the modern architectural advancements as if he had a hand in them. On Saturdays, he'd take me to the ballet. He would wait for me at the bottom of the stairs in his shiny black coat with his white cuffs peeking out like strips of peppermint, whistling that I "looked a picture," as I skipped down to him. My world revolved around pleasing him. That's the problem with being worshipped. You do whatever you must to keep the attention.

Greedy for praise, I learned to dance for my grandfather. I was competitive and liked to win, which made me an excellent ballerina.

I was ten when my grandfather died a shocking, sudden death, a fever that took him in the night. I screamed and pounded my small fists, refusing to believe my vivacious, sturdy grandfather was dead until my mother took me into his bedroom and I saw his ashen, lifeless face. I wept for days. My mother abandoned her brushes and canvas and sat with me until I cried myself dry. It was the most time I'd ever spent with her.

After that, I danced harder, to keep my grandfather's memory alive, but also because I had become addicted to the attention in the spotlight.

Then it was just me and my mother, who marveled, half-heartedly, at everything I did: my mediocre sketches and lackluster piano playing, as well as my dancing. She knew talent when she saw it. She acknowledged an object when it had value. But when it came to me, she half listened, partly looked, smiled, praised faintly and walked away. She cherished me like one might an heirloom, or an antique, something of great value that you're not sure what to do with. I think it would have suited her to keep me behind glass doors, to be taken out and admired only when she felt the urge.

Then my brother, Georges, slid into our lives. His birth was as shocking to me as my grandfather's death. I knew nothing of how babies were born and believed that my mother had just grown fat and a stork had dropped the boy through her window, as my governess told me. Not until I was sixteen and brought into society did I understand he was a bastard, and I wondered if this was why my mother seemed to hate him.

The half-hearted admiration she gave me turned into a full-blown loathing for my poor baby brother. She needled him, scrutinized everything he did from the time he could walk. Only as a grown woman did I wonder about the circumstances of my mother's pregnancy. I had come to the conclusion that it either happened against her will, or else she'd loved the boy's father and he'd scorned her. Either way, she deeply resented Georges, and from the tone of her letters still did, even though he was the one who'd stayed behind to take care of her.

I had not seen my mother since I married and moved to New York. We wrote regularly, but I couldn't risk the trip with Effie's health, and my mother had become too frail to travel. I hoped, very much, that Georges would come see us one day. My brother and I had written every week for the past seventeen years. From his letters, I could tell that he had grown into a thoughtful, wise young man. I was certain he would be a good influence on the girls.

At the thought of my daughters, I pulled my watch from my pocket to check the time just as the train lurched to a stop and my purse went careening to the floor. The gentleman, his cigarette finished and disposed of, leaned over and picked my purse up, dangling it by its silver chain with an amiable wink.

"Thank you." I took it, blushing like a ninny and thinking how shamelessly bold and cruel young men were these days to flirt with a woman like myself.

"Is this your stop?" he asked, standing as if already certain it was.

I glanced out the window. "Why, yes, it is." Forgetting to check the time, I put my watch back into my pocket and took the hand he offered. Humiliating desire raced through me as I clutched my purse to my chest and angled past him.

"Your hat," he called as I hurried down the aisle.

"How silly of me."

I turned back and he caught my hand, grinning felicitously. "You really must take up smoking. It's divine. It will ease that worry creasing your forehead."

A creased forehead was not a compliment, but I smiled and thanked him, graciously taking the cigarette he held out along with my hat and slipping it into my purse.

It was an encounter I would think of often over the next few months as my manicured life was swept out from under me. A strange man's seductive manner and genial smile, his faint scent of sage and cigarette smoke trailing my senses. It was the first time in years that I'd felt anything close to desire, and I would wonder, afterward, if God was punishing me for my sinful thoughts.

In a moment, I forgot the stranger, hurrying home with my usual sense of urgency only to find everything as it should be. Luella came to dinner flushed and excited after her day of athletics in Westchester — I always knew the outdoors suited her. Effie was quiet, but that was nothing out of the ordinary. If it weren't for Emory, avoiding my gaze and speaking sideways at me as if I was slightly out of his line of vision, it would have been a pleasant enough dinner. Not that my husband's avoidance of me was anything unusual, but there was something aflame in his face, a heat similar to what the young man on the train had ignited in mine.

Stupidly, I tried to touch my husband that night, slipping up behind him as he undressed for bed. He jumped, shoving me away with a mumbled apology about not feeling well.

I must have looked pathetic because when he turned, he softened. "I'm sorry, Jeanne, darling. It's just a spring cold. You know how I get them with the change of weather."

It was obvious he had no cold, but I said nothing as he climbed into bed and turned off his light while I quietly undressed, my gloves the last thing I removed before stepping into my nightgown. When had Emory stopped taking them off for me? I hadn't thought about it in a long time, but after that first kiss under the lamppost, the removal of my gloves had often become a seductive act between us. My resistance, Emory's gentle determination followed by my quiet submission, something I imagine most couples played out removing a corset.

I sat heavily on the edge of the bed. I rarely exposed my bare hands to Emory anymore. He never said as much, but I knew they repelled him. What had once been seductive had grown stale, and like our relationship, was better kept hidden under something shiny.

"Oh —" Emory's arm fluttered from his side. "I almost forgot, I bought you a new perfume. It's on your vanity."

As I moved to the vanity, I saw a tiny glass bottle I hadn't noticed earlier, *Farnésiana* printed in black lettering on the side. I picked it up. There was no card. No box or wrapping. This was not a gift, it was an apology. *My husband could use a lesson in deception,* I thought with disappointment. As I pulled out the glass stopper, a sickly-sweet smell hit me, a powdered sugar vanilla, a confection. I wondered if he thought this maternal scent suited me, or if he'd stood at the perfume counter in Gimbel's and pointed to the first bottle he saw without bothering to smell it.

I was utterly fed up, with myself, with my husband. I'd been stupid to touch him. What had gotten into me? We hadn't laid together as husband and wife since Effie's birth. It wasn't her fault, of course. I'd never dream of blaming our daughter. Not even a little bit. She couldn't help being born damaged. Not wanting another impaired child, I'd kept my husband at arm's length after her birth. At the time it was easy enough. I was an exhausted mother with a tantrum-throwing three-year-old, and a baby who turned blue every time she cried. I refused to let a governess, or nurse, care for Effie. If my daughter was going to die, I was going to be there.

Emory couldn't stand being denied. I should have seen that coming, but it was too late by the time I realized my mistake. And once he'd tasted his freedom, he liked it.

Climbing into bed, I could smell my husband's cedarwood aftershave, and the lingering scent of pomade that left a slight grease stain on the pillowcase even after he'd washed it from his hair. I flipped onto my side, irritated at how the blanket rose up over his high shoulder and let a draft under the covers.

Looking into the dark, moonless room, the furniture indistinguishable from shadows, I told myself what I'd been telling myself for years. *You were warned, Jeanne. You're lucky to have him at all.*

Only tonight, I didn't feel lucky.

# CHAPTER SEVEN:
## EFFIE

June arrived with a burst of tulips in the front yard, their pink tips bleeding into cupped white petals like watercolor. School was out and there was no talk of going to Newport for the summer. I was sure it was because of Daddy, who was seldom around these days, but Mama seemed unconcerned. She said it would be nice to stay home.

"I can see my lilies bloom," she'd said, and smiled. "I always miss them."

I hated holding Daddy's lie. It was anchored in the pit of my stomach, deadweight, that woman entering our house, her laughter through the walls. I'd been careful not to write it down or work it into a story in my head. Daddy never asked to see my writing anymore. Sunday mornings he hardly looked up from his paper.

I never told Luella what I witnessed that day she went to the gypsies without me. I didn't trust what she'd do with the information. Ever since the day we met Miss Milholland, Luella had grown smug and emboldened in a way I'd never seen. Whenever Mama was out, she'd skip off to the gypsy camp with the fearlessness of someone who no longer cared about being caught. As much as I worried about losing Daddy to some strange woman, I was more terrified of losing my sister.

I went to the gypsy camp with her, even though my blue fits had become a weekly occurrence. Hiding them was easy now, compared to all the other lies, especially since no one was paying attention. The day on my bed when my heart stopped haunted me. It was a message, a warning. Time was catching up with me.

As much as I hated deceiving Mama, I found comfort with the gypsies, in their liveliness, in the intimacy of the crowded families who lived all very out in the open. In the walled-in, echoing, high-ceilinged rooms of my home, secrets could get stashed away forever. I felt cloistered in comparison.

In this way, I could also keep an eye on Luella, sitting in the grass with my notebook watching her shed the trappings of her privileged identity and step into what she imagined was freedom: dancing in Patience's clothes until her feet hurt, singing until her throat was raw.

Tray would sit with me, quietly pulling up tufts of grass. Keeping me company got him out of chores, he said. I liked spending time with him, the feeling of familiarity between us another comfort. Only once did he ask about my writing. "Just stories," I said. He told me his mother loved fairy tales from the old country, and I soon found myself sitting with Marcella as she wove her tales. "Things not of this earth must be kept in the hearts of young people," she said. "Goblins and fairies, elves and dwarfs, ghosts and curses." She told me of the evil eye cast on her husband's people, of the spell put on her sister when she was born, and how the women in her family are given the sign of death before it comes. "Life can be ugly," she said. "You must keep your imagination alive. That way you will have somewhere else to look if things turn unbearable."

I liked Marcella. She had an open strength and confidence my mother lacked and the freedom my sister craved. She was a grown woman with a grand imagination, and an unshakable calmness even in the midst of the chaos of the camp.

The gypsies, I learned, fought as much as they sang. Insults, Tray informed me, were often hidden in their songs and fights broke out easily. These were usually between Sydney and his older brother Job, an intimidating pair. I was used to men with a disciplined, polished masculinity like Daddy, not the uncontained energy of these brothers.

At first, I wasn't sure why the gypsies accepted us, or let my sister get so close. When I asked Tray about it, he said it was his father, Freddy, who allowed it. "My brother Sydney is his favorite," he winked. It was no secret that Sydney was mooning over Luella.

Even though she never spoke about Sydney, I'd catch her dropping him a glance or a quick smile while she walked in lockstep with Patience, who I found more intimidating than her brothers. There was something about Patience I didn't trust, and she knew it. She also made a point to avoid me, keeping Luella to herself, gifting her small trinkets that required something in return.

By July, Luella had grown wide-eyed and agitated. The more time we spent with the gypsies, the more restive she became. Her rebellion took on a dutiful quality. I'd wake at night to find her sitting at the window, saying how unbearably stifling the room was and how nice it would be to sleep under the stars.

"The gypsies don't sleep under the stars,"

I reminded her. "They sleep in tents and wagons." But I had the feeling she wasn't listening.

It was the day after Luella's sixteenth birthday, July 13th, when she threw a fit about having to go for an audition at the Metropolitan Opera House. The previous night we'd had a quiet birthday dinner and Daddy had given her a pair of tiny pearl earrings, which Luella had accepted graciously. It was the first meal she hadn't spent glaring at him since the incident at Delmonico's, and I was hopeful things were on the mend. But as I came down the stairs the next morning, I found Luella storming out of the parlor. She banged past me up the stairs with exaggerated disdain. Mama watched from below, her accusatory eyes flicking to me. "Come down here," she ordered. I obeyed. Suspicion creased her forehead. "Is there something going on with your sister I should know about?"

My first thought was relief she didn't know already, the second panic that she knew enough to be suspicious. I kicked my shoe into the bottom rung of the stair. "No."

"Speak up." Mama propped her finger under my chin and lifted my face.

I pulled my head away, hating how small I felt. I was sorry, but also angry Mama couldn't see what was going on with Daddy. The least she could do was show signs of distress, gaunt eyes or ashy skin, make Daddy feel guilty. Instead she looked clear-eyed and healthy as ever, smelling cheerfully of sweet vanilla.

She looked as if she knew I was keeping something from her. "I said, speak up."

"And I said, *no,*" I answered loudly.

Mama pulled back, and I was sorry I'd spoken so sharply. It wasn't her fault we were all deceiving her. I looked at her self-consciously gloved hands with the urge to pull off her gloves and feel her twisted, bumpy scars under my fingers. It had been so long since I touched them. Marcella would have worked hard with those hands. Miss Milholland would have flaunted them. They were Mama's strength and she hid them away. I didn't want her to be weak.

"Very well," she said, and dismissed me.

As mad as Luella was about having to go to that audition, she danced well enough to be given her first role as one of the seventeen angels in the *Hansel and Gretel Ballet Divertissement.* She never went so far as to thank Mama for making her do it, but the honor, at least for a short time, raised her spirits. A glint returned to her eyes, and the rehearsals exhausted her into a sound sleep again.

Mama and I went to every rehearsal with her, happy to escape the city heat in the cool theater on 49th Street, sitting in the plush velvet seats, watching the dancers glide and leap across the stage as if their bones were weightless, their arms rippling like wings. It was Marcella's fairy tales come alive.

One day, as I sat in my usual seat next to Mama, caught up in the swirl onstage and the rising crescendo of string instruments, the choreographer halted the music with a swoop of his arm and marched over to Luella. Clapping his hands inches from her nose he barked, "Fouetté!" Without missing a beat Luella raised an arm above her head, whipped her leg out and spun in a single rotation.

Mama tensed, her hands moving in small extensions from her lap as she whispered to herself, "Croisé, yes, yes, fifth position."

"Fouetté!" The choreographer clapped again. "Fouetté, fouetté, fouetté!" Again and again Luella whipped around. There was no music, just the sharp clap of his hands and the soft thud of Luella's toe shoes on the wooden stage. Finally, the choreographer dropped his arms and the theater went silent. Luella's chest rose and fell rapidly against her tight bodice, her cheeks red-hot.

The choreographer pointed a finger in her face. "I will not waste any more time on you. One more mistake and you'll be replaced." He waved his hand at the conductor, who raised his baton, and the ballerinas shuffled back into position.

On our way home, Mama sat between Luella and me in the back seat of the car. The top was down and it was scorching hot. Pearls of sweat dripped down the back of our driver's neck as we crawled along, the sun beating down on us, the noise of the trolleys and cars dizzying. Mama had just begun an animated critique of Luella's performance when we passed a popcorn wagon and I burst out, "Can we stop for popcorn?"

"No, and don't interrupt," she snapped, and I huffed and leaned out the window. The buildings shimmered in the heat and the humidity cast a hazy curtain over the river of suits and hats flowing alongside us.

"Your pirouettes are lovely, you'll get the timing," she said. "But your extensions need to be longer. Extend, extend!" She threw one arm forward. "And you must point your toes the *instant* they leave the floor."

I glanced at my sister as she angled away from Mama, staring into traffic. She used to love talking about ballet, going over every detail. Lately, she hardly said a word.

It was painful watching Mama struggle to be encouraging. She'd start to say something, sigh and give up. We drove in silence for a few minutes before Mama finally got out what she'd been trying to say all along. "Your father and I have decided to send you to Paris in the fall."

"What?" Luella's head turned sharply. "Why?"

"You're sixteen. It's high time you went abroad. You've never met my mother, or your uncle Georges, or seen my native homeland."

"What about Effie? Why doesn't she have to go?"

Have to go? I would have loved to go.

"You know perfectly well Effie can't make that trip."

Luella crossed her arms. "I don't want to."

"Don't be ungrateful. It won't interfere with your dancing. Your show's in September, so we'll plan it for October."

"What about school?" Luella challenged, even though I knew she didn't care one whit about school.

"We'll call it a holiday. You'll catch up. Traveling to Europe rivals any textbook."

"I'm not going."

"Don't be silly. What girl doesn't want to

go to Paris?"

"I don't. And I don't want to dance in *Hansel and Gretel* either."

This silenced Mama. Her gaze shot forward and she clasped her hands as if crushing something. There was an uncomfortable stillness before she said, "You made a commitment. You have no choice."

Luella crumbled, her shoulders sinking as she looked pleadingly at Mama. "You heard Mikhail. I'm terrible. He's going to replace me. Anyway, I'm too heavy. The other ballerinas are like string beans. They're half the size of me. I don't know why I was cast in the first place. My feet won't do anything I want and there are blisters on my toes. I can't get my *fouettés* right, and I don't *want* to do it anymore."

"That's childish. You have worked too hard to give up now."

"You gave up."

Mama yanked herself forward, turning to face Luella as she latched a hand on the seat in front of her. "I most certainly did not. A ballerina has a short life. Mine was over." In a flourish, she tugged off her glove and held her hand in the air, exposing the misshapen scars of her right hand, tender and pink like newborn skin.

"Do you think anyone wanted to see *these*

121

arching through the air?" Her voice was pinched and high. "You have had none of my hardships, and I did not raise you to be lazy. Lose some weight. Bind your feet. You will figure it out, but you will not quit."

The car lurched and Mama steadied herself against the seat as she yanked her glove back on. From my corner of the car, pressed up against the door, I watched them stare each other down. Luella was almost as tall as Mama, and there was a new maturity in her face that had appeared the moment she turned sixteen. In Mama's face was a sternness I hadn't seen in a long time. The tension between them was palpable, a battle of wills. Then my sister did a wicked thing. She lifted her ballet slippers by their pink laces and held them out with a taunting expression, letting them rotate in a slow circle before calmly and deliberately dropping those beautiful shoes out of the car. I had always envied her those slippers. Shocked, I careened my head over the side of the car as they landed on the street and were instantly crushed by the car behind us. There was a slight gasp from Mama, but she didn't say anything.

The car slowed to a stop in traffic. I slouched in my seat, just wanting to get home. A boy sped by on a bike. I stole a glance at Mama and Luella sitting shoulder to shoulder. Mama stared straight ahead, her lips a thin line, her hand fixed back into its glove. Luella looked off into the street. I hated how effortlessly she had let go of those shoes, as if tossing away everything Mama had given her was the easiest thing in the world.

Dinner that night was tense and silent, the air through the open window warm and stagnant and filled with noisy crickets. Daddy was as withdrawn and sullen as the rest of us. I wondered if Mama had told him what happened, or if his own conscience was brewing.

I nibbled the end of a green bean, glancing at Luella across the table. She hadn't eaten a thing. Her eyes were downcast, her expression unreadable. What would she do if she didn't dance anymore? I couldn't believe she'd thrown away a chance to be on a stage, gliding with all the other angels. Tray had told me the gypsies would head south once it turned cold, so she'd soon lose them too.

After dinner, Luella went straight to her room without a word to me, or our parents. More and more she slept in her own room. I climbed in bed and tried to write, but I was finding it difficult to think up creative stories. Giving up, I turned the light out and lay picturing my sister's self-satisfied expression and her shoes being ground to pink dust in the street. At some point I heard the front door open and crept to my window in time to see Daddy getting into a cab. I watched it pull away, a pall of exhaust dissolving under the streetlight behind it. The solid body of my family was being ripped apart, Daddy and Luella the first limbs to go. With a dreadful feeling in my stomach, I crawled back to bed and fell asleep listening for Daddy's return.

I woke to Luella shaking my shoulder. "What's wrong?" I sat up. It was still dark out, but the curtains were pulled back and the moon projected a square of light on the floorboards like a box waiting to spring open.

"Turn around so I can braid your hair."

"What?" Even groggy with sleep this sounded like a ridiculous request.

"Remember how I used to insist on doing your hair for you, even when you were old enough to do it yourself?" She kneeled on the bed and began brushing my tangles out with her fingers, pulling against my scalp. "You have the most beautiful hair. It's just like Mama's, and so much thicker than mine. I always envied you your hair." She stopped combing and began plaiting. "I envied your blue fits too."

"Why would you say that?" The night air was warm and humid and I felt sticky with sweat.

"Because nothing is expected of you."

I found this insulting. "Why did you throw away your slippers?"

Tiny hairs snagged as Luella threaded the strands together. "It was a test. I wanted to see if Mama would stop the car and make me walk into the street and get them back, crushed and all. Daddy would have."

"I don't see what that would have proved, and you would have hated Daddy for it."

"I would have hated her for it, but that's not the point."

Finishing my hair, Luella lay down onto her back and I lay next to her. The braid bunched against my neck. "What is the point?"

"That she didn't do it. That she lets all of us push her around."

It wasn't a surprise Mama failed Luella's test, just a disappointment. "Do you think she'll tell Daddy and you'll be punished?" I asked.

"I'm already being punished. I'm certain it was Daddy's idea to send me away."

"Going to Paris is not exactly punishment."

"Don't you see they have no intention of letting me come home? Daddy wants me gone so I won't give away his little secret. Why else would they do it *now*? They've never mentioned sending me to Paris before." She punched her pillow into a mound and sank into it. "They can't make me go. I won't."

The thing was, they could make her and we both knew it. "If you refuse they'll send you somewhere worse," I said, thinking of Daddy's threat to lock her up. "Especially if you're not dancing anymore. You have to apologize. You love to dance. It's your future. What will you do without it?"

"I don't know." She didn't sound troubled by this uncertainty, but I needed her to care. We'd always conspired about our possible futures. "You, on the other hand —" she smiled, as if remembering her role to play in our conversation "— will go to college and become a great writer, an enviable, independent woman like Inez Milholland."

I cringed. "I don't want to be enviable, or anything like her."

"I do. She does exactly what she pleases. Daddy sneaks around with a woman like that and expects us to live by different standards. Who says we have to? You know, the gypsies aren't really free either." She propped up on an elbow. "Patience turns sixteen next month and will be forced to marry a boy she despises. She's been promised to him since she was three years old. Their fathers shook on it and that was that. We're all trapped."

It occurred to me that Luella might be married before long, especially if she wasn't dancing. She might even find a husband in Paris. Then I'd never see her. "Are you wildly in love with Sydney?"

"No! I'm wildly in love with their music. When will we ever hear music like that again? If I have to listen to Enrico Caruso belt out one more operatic note on the Victrola, I'll smash the thing. I keep telling myself there's only one year of school left, but then what? A failed dance career . . . a wedding veil and slippers?"

I used to believe she'd be as famous as the dancer Anna Pavlova, which was foolish. She would not be a ballerina, and I would not go to college. Tracing moon patterns on the ceiling with my eyes, I saw our future plans for what they were: childish stories. We were no longer little girls able to pretend. I lost the ability the moment I saw Daddy kiss that woman. It made what I believed to be true, wrong. Maybe that's why Luella threw her shoes in the street, because she couldn't make herself believe her own story anymore either. I glanced at her, lying flat on her back with her hair spread out over her pillow, her wide-open eyes staring at the ceiling. I wondered if she saw the same moon patterns I saw, or if hers made entirely different shapes. I wanted to tell her about my heart stopping, how I'd seen the walls fall away. I wanted to tell her my chest felt tight all the time, and that I was worried I'd lose her to Paris and a husband and a future I'd never have. That I worried we'd already lost our father, and that our mother would be left all alone.

It was too much to say. I was sleepy, and didn't know that I'd never get the chance to tell her these things. Closing my eyes, I listened to the shifting of my sister's wakeful body beside me until I finally drifted off. It was the only time I remember falling asleep before her.

I woke at nine o'clock the next morning in the exact position I'd fallen asleep. An empty pillow faced me. I sat up, the weight of sleep heavy on me. Luella was gone and a bright day peeked through the curtains. No one ever let me sleep this late and I felt an eerie sense of foreboding as I scurried into my clothes and downstairs, my stomach doing an anxious flip as I saw the empty dining room, all signs of breakfast cleared away.

"Effie?" I jumped at Mama's voice. She stood in the doorway, her skin a seamless white from her collar to her forehead. "You've slept through breakfast, you naughty girl." She smiled a bud of color into her cheeks, but there was a false cheeriness to her voice.

"Why didn't Neala wake me?"

"I've given her the day off."

"Why?"

"It's good to indulge your servants once in a while. Let's go out for lunch?"

"Just the two of us?" Mama and I rarely did anything alone. "Where's Luella? Has Daddy left for work already?"

"Get your hat," was all she said as she secured hers to her head, a thing so weighted with feathers it looked as if an entire flock had lost their wings for it.

We stepped out into suffocating heat, slate clouds pressing overhead like the top to a cooking pot ready to boil us alive. If it rained, I imagined the drops would sizzle and evaporate on the steaming bricks.

Mama and I took the elevated into Manhattan and dined at Café Martin's, everyone sedated in the warmth, fans and hats waving languidly, red-faced waiters in white jackets suffering behind steaming plates of food. People looked down from their balcony tables as if from the rail of a ship and I thought of the sunken *Titanic* last spring, and how guilty the onlookers must have felt when they realized that they had waved those passengers off to their deaths.

I watched Mama consume a single bite of duck, put her fork down and draw a silver cigarette case I'd never seen before from her purse. My mother didn't smoke. And yet here she was, smoking while I ate, her eyes roaming around the room. My duck was tender and salty, but I hardly had an appetite for it.

For dessert, she ordered caramel custard for me, and two Brandy Alexanders for herself. Mama never took a drink anywhere except in the parlor room after dinner with Daddy. The alcohol fueled the color in her cheeks and gave her voice an urgent quality. It undid her in the most beautiful way. Her bouffant hairdo cresting like a wave under her hat, her waist cinched into a swan-bill corset, with that name fitting her figure, sleeves billowing, eyes alert. She seemed utterly attractive, and wholly not my mother.

Under normal circumstances I would have

relished an outing alone with Mama. These were not normal circumstances.

The cigarette case lay on the table and Mama began clicking it open and shut with one hand, her eyes flitting above my head as she said, "Let's shop for new dresses, shall we?"

She was too giddy, too bright. Worry curdled in my stomach next to the duck and custard, which I wished I hadn't eaten. I wanted Luella. I wondered if Mama had forced her to go to rehearsal in spite of the tossed slippers, but I knew better than to ask.

Instead of heading to Céleste's, where we usually bought dresses, we walked to 23rd Street. Mama kept a few paces ahead of me, reaching her hand back from time to time to make sure I was still with her, sashaying our way past windows that glinted with shades of violet and amethyst. She took a sudden right through the doors of Stern Brothers department store, and her pace slowed as she lingered at the perfume counter and fingered cloth at the haberdashery.

After purchasing a pair of white gloves for her and salmon-pink ones for me, we left the store without trying on a single dress, and made our way through Madison

Square. No rain came. The clouds broke up and blue swatches of sky appeared with ragged edges like torn fabric. Sweat dampened the underarms of my dress and Mama's face flushed under her hat. She kept slipping her watch from her purse and checking the time, clasping and unclasping the latch on her mesh bag, as if the clicks propelled her forward.

I was thankful when we finally crossed Madison Avenue and climbed aboard the train for home. By the time we arrived on Bolton Road, the sky had turned cerulean. Storm clouds rested on the far horizon and the late sun pierced through a crack like a slit eye, rays so defined they looked graspable.

Mama stopped abruptly when we reached the front door. Daddy stood in the hallway with his jacket unbuttoned, his tie removed. There was a mad look in his eye. Mama stepped up to him, the box of gloves trembling in her hands.

"Effie, go to your room." His voice was harsh and the box slipped from Mama's hands and hit the floor. Neither reached to pick it up.

I ran up the stairs. Dread washed over me as I flew into Luella's empty bedroom and saw the sharp corners of her tucked-in bed and her neatly organized vanity. I flung open her wardrobe; all of her clothes still rustled and shifted on their hangers. Rehearsal never went this late. Where was she? She wouldn't have been sent off to Paris already, and without her clothes. My heart pounded and a ripple of pain eddied out from my lungs into my ribs. I crouched down with my forehead in my hands, trying to breathe slowly. When I stood up the blood rushed to my head and the room went black for a split second before everything came back into focus. A skinny, wan girl mocked me in the wardrobe mirror. I banged a fist against the side of my head. She banged hers.

Trying to calm myself, I went to my room and sat at my desk tracing leaf patterns, focusing on each tiny vein while I listened for the sound of Luella opening the front door and running up the stairs to tell me about her day. It was Daddy who shouted at me from the bottom of the stairs. "Effie, come down into the parlor immediately."

The lights had not come on yet, and the early evening cast a bruised hue over the room. My mother sat crumpled on the couch, her shoulders at an odd angle, her dress withered from the heat. My father stood to the side with his arms crossed over his chest. He seemed shrunken, as if recent events had taken height off of him. Then I saw my grandmother sitting in an armchair, her tiny form wrapped in her black dress like a tightly bound package, her face heaped with disapproval. My thoughts raced. What was she doing here? She never left her home on Gramercy Park. The last time she'd come here was when our grandfather died.

"Where's Luella?" I cried.

My parents looked at each other, hesitating long enough for my grandmother to jump in with a crisp, "She's been sent away to summer camp."

Summer camp? I wanted to laugh at them, or scream. How ignorant did they think I was? They knew about the gypsies. "Where is she?" I repeated, choking up. "Has she already been sent off to Paris?"

"Hardly." My grandmother pursed her lips and jerked her head to one side.

"Effie." Daddy stepped toward me, looking like he used to when he worried I was going to have a fit. Those were the only times he ever looked uncertain of himself. "Your sister's gone away for a bit, but she's fine. She'll be back, and she's not as far away as Paris so you needn't worry about that."

"Why can't I know where she is?"

"You have to trust us. It's for your own good."

I shook my head, tears streaming down my face as Daddy's strong arms pinned me in a hug. His heart beat against my ear and I pulled away, gulping for air.

Mama stood abruptly. "Take a breath. Don't get worked up." She patted the air with her hands, her anxiety visible on her face as she came toward me.

I backed to the wall, everything pulling away, my feet and hands distant, floating objects. I couldn't bear Mama touching me and I ran from the room, hearing Daddy say, "Leave her be, Jeanne."

Upstairs, I kneeled on the floor with my head dropped forward on my bed, the tightness in my chest suffocating. I slammed a fist into my breastbone wanting to rip out my stupid heart. I didn't want to view the world through this damaged portal anymore. It didn't make me special or different. There was no strength in my survival. It was just time, slowly wearing away at me.

If it wasn't for my condition, Daddy would have sent me away too. I'd lied and snuck out and gone to the gypsies. Maybe this was why Luella envied my blue fits. Did she know what he was going to do?

When the girl comes down the stairs, her father is waiting for her, slapping his driving gloves against his thigh as he opens the front door. Early morning light halos his head like a saint, which makes the girl laugh. She is told to get her hat and does so, only because she believes her father is going to try and convince her to go to Paris and she will have her chance to tell him she has no intention of being sent away. The girl pauses at the door and looks up the stairs, wondering if her mother and sister are still asleep. When the door closes she has no idea she won't be home for dinner. Only when the car winds up the road and the gates to the House of Mercy close behind them does she begin to cry out.

No. I put my hands over my eyes. That's not how it went.

I jumped off my bed and returned to Luella's room. Twilight lingered, casting shadows around the room. As much as I didn't want to believe she'd abandon me, I hoped with every bit of my racked heart that Daddy hadn't locked her away and she'd escaped with the gypsies. I fell on my knees and reached under her mattress, driving my hands around the flattened space. If Luella

136

had left willingly, she would have taken her treasures with her. We had agreed to hide all things associated with the gypsies under our mattresses. Mine housed a book of Wordsworth that Marcella had lent me, a feather and a yellow ribbon that Tray and I found in the woods. I reached up to my elbows, scooting my hands around, willing them to find nothing, my breath catching as they bumped into a bulky object. Pulling it out, I tossed Patience's blue silk scarf on the bed. The knot slipped open and glass beads spilled over the coverlet like pearls of water. There was also a silver comb and two spools of embroidery thread. I rolled a single turquoise bead between my fingers, a drop of red in its center like the spell of an evil eye.

As certain as I was that she wouldn't leave these treasures behind, I still brokered hope that she might, after all, be at the gypsy camp.

Gathering Luella's things, I went back to my room and dumped them on the bed. A sound outside drew me to the window where I watched Daddy help my grandmother into the car, her back hunched and rounded. I saw the elegant Miss Milholland in her place and felt a twist of rage at Daddy. The car pulled away and he stood

with his hands shoved into his pockets looking down the street for a long time.

I didn't go down to dinner. At seven
o'clock my father knocked on my door. "Effie? Are you all right?" I didn't respond.
"Like I said, your sister's fine. She'll be
home before you know it. Effie, I need to
hear your voice so I know you're all right."

"I'm fine."

"Are you hungry?"

"No."

The tips of his fingers drummed against
the other side of the door. "Well then, at
least get some sleep, you hear?"

That night, I lay fully clothed on top of
my covers with the window flung open so I
would catch every sound. Carriage wheels
creaked on the road, a dog barked, a motor-
car revved past. When I heard the clock
chime eleven, I crept into the hallway. No
crack of light shone from under my parents'
bedroom door and I tiptoed down the stairs,
hugging the wall where the stairs creaked
the least.

Outside, the bright, hard light of a full
moon lit my way as I hurried through the
woods, past our stream and the Indian caves
and up the hill into the meadow. Fear
pricked my feet with what felt like a thousand needles. I was afraid the field would

be an empty bowl of moonlight. The gypsies would be gone, and my sister would be gone with them. I raced forward, my chest heaving with a gasp of relief when I reached the clearing and saw the gypsy fires puncturing the sky with their glow. I charged through the grass, half expecting Luella to rush up and tell me to quiet down. But it was a man who stopped me. "Christ almighty. I almost clobbered you over the head." I recognized Job's voice. "Hey, Pop, it's Effie."

Job's father, Freddy, emerged out of a pocked circle of light. He was large, like his wife, with black pits for eyes and a heavy beard. With a silent jerk of his chin, he directed Job back to the camp. Marcella appeared beside him, regarding me with suspicion, as if she'd forgotten who I was.

"What are you doing here?" Freddy's voice was cutting.

"I came . . ." I stammered, "to find Luella." My chest fluttered and my breath came out ragged. In the flickering firelight, I caught a glimpse of Tray with his hands stuffed in his pockets. He looked right at me, but didn't approach.

"Your sister is not here." Marcella moved from her husband's side, blocking my view of Tray and the fire. Lit from behind, the soft lines of her figure hardened against the night and her form looked herculean. "You shouldn't be here either."

"She's gone," I said, trying to look around her and catch Tray's eye.

"We know," Marcella said. "Your father has already come and threatened us." Her tone held the strength of one used to being threatened, and the conviction of one used to thwarting it.

"She is bad luck, your sister." Freddy put an arm around his wife. "We won't have you bringing more. I should never have allowed the two of you here in the first place."

A log fell into the fire. Sparks shot up, flickered and sputtered out like dying fireflies. Freddy stood, wide and still as a wall beside Marcella, blocking the way. I wanted to talk to Tray

Marcella put a hand on my shoulder. The touch was motherly, her voice resolved. "We can't help you. You must go."

I thought of the time she'd rested her hand on my shoulder when the music played, how close I'd been to her worn knuckles and raised veins. I turned back to the woods, a motionless army of trees and bracken waiting to trip me up. The moon seemed to dim in my fright and I fumbled over roots and fallen twigs, remembering the night-blind adventure Luella and I had only months earlier.

Back home, I paced in my ro‿ nocturnal creature tracking a 1 scent. For months Luella had lo‿ Daddy with caustic, accusing eyes, kr‿ ‿ng his secret, holding it over him. I slammed my window shut against the night and buried myself under the covers, shaking out Patience's silk handkerchief and pressing it to my face, the beads and comb and thread spilling onto the bed. A bead lodged under my shoulder, one under my neck. The handkerchief smelled of lilac water and fire smoke.

Sometime in the night the wind woke me, rattling the windows and hammering a tree branch against the glass. The handkerchief slipped and the scattered beads slid farther under me as I sat up. I'd fallen asleep not caring what indentation their round, hard shapes made against my skin. The room was stifling and I had no sense of what time it was. A figure rose from the chair in the corner and I threw the coverlet.

"Are you awake?" It was Daddy, and I crumbled with disappointment.

He sat on the edge of the bed and took my hand, pressing his fingers to the inside of my wrist, checking my pulse like he used to when I was little. "It's been a long time

I've asked about your writing. I'm sorry for that," he said, his voice sedated, like something thick lay over his tongue.

I wanted to tell him I was sorry too. Sorry that I wasn't the great Tildon child born on the first day of the new century that he'd hoped for. Sorry that Mama and Luella and I weren't the perfect family he'd wanted.

In the bright moonlight, I could see faint creases around his eyes and stubble on his chin. He looked tired. "You're the one I always worried about. Which is ironic now, isn't it?" He patted my shoulder. "Look at you with your solid heart thrumming away in that chest of yours. I knew you'd beat it. Doctors be damned, right?" He leaned into my ear, a sparkle of fun in his eye like when he used to sneak Luella and me candy from his pocket before dinner. "We'll keep the curse word between us, yes? Your mother wouldn't like that. It will be our little secret, damning doctors."

I hadn't beaten anything and I didn't want any more secrets. "Where's Luella?"

Daddy pulled away, our moment of colluding intimacy broken. "You have to trust your mother and me. Your sister is learning the consequences of her actions. She'll be home soon enough." He stood up to crack open the window. Air whistled in and

Daddy tucked the sheet around my shoulder. "Sleep, Effie," he murmured.

I didn't want him to leave. I didn't want to be alone. "I'll show you my writing tomorrow."

He smiled. "First thing in the morning?"

"First thing."

"You know, if it's good enough, we might consider submitting it for publication. I know an editor who'd take a look at it for us."

"Miss Milholland's father?"

Daddy gave a startled laugh. "Yes, that's the one."

"I don't want him to."

We could see each other clearly in the moonlight. His expression told me he understood that I knew.

"No, well, we'll find someone else then," he said, and left the room.

I kicked the covers off and curled my knees into my chest, squeezing my eyes against the hot tears rolling over my temples. Behind my lids, the House of Mercy loomed massive and impenetrable, fortressed by high white walls like the gates of a duplicitous heaven.

The girl kicks and bites and screams as they drag her through the door. Her father,

143

watching from the car, worries he's made a mistake. He sits for a long time pounding his palms against the steering wheel, wondering if he should go inside and get her back. The sky is heavy with clouds and he wishes it would rain and wash away the heat. He thinks of his wife and feels the first pangs of real guilt. He's done this for himself, and yet, as he chokes the engine to a start, he tells himself he has done it for his daughter. It's the best thing for her. She's learning the consequences of her actions. She'll be home soon enough.

The crying made my heart race and my chest tight. I had only heard rumors about the House of Mercy from the girls at school, who'd read stories in the newspaper about quelled riots and attempted escapes. Other than the gossip about Suzie Trainer, I didn't know anyone who'd been inside. Whatever it was like, I couldn't imagine Luella surviving in such a place. She'd be like a caged tiger, sure to start riots, attempt escapes. Didn't Daddy understand that Luella couldn't be tamed?

# CHAPTER EIGHT:
## EFFIE

All night I tossed and turned, waking up with tearstained cheeks and eyelids so crusted that opening them felt like peeling dry paper from my eyeballs. Every part of me hurt. The morning sunlight assaulted my eyes and the twittering birds pierced my ears.

Coming down to breakfast, I slid into my chair not wanting to eat anything. Mama sat with her arms on the table, her own eyes puffy and red. Daddy was nowhere in sight. I guess he wouldn't be asking about my writing after all.

"Coffee?" Mama reached for the pot, her hands shaky as she poured it into my cup. She wore a light summer dress, her face drawn and pale as the fabric. There were dark circles under her eyes, the signs of distress I'd hoped for a month ago. "Cream?"

I nodded, watching the cream swirl and

145

color the coffee. "Where's Daddy?"

"He left for work early."

The forced, animated lilt of her voice angered me. Daddy lying was one thing, I already knew he was good at it, but I hated that she was lying to me too. "I know Luella's not at summer camp."

In a flash, she reached across the table, her sleeve fluttering like a wing as she took hold of my arm. I was struck by the pressure of her grip. She might not be a fighter, but not because she lacked the strength. "We know about the gypsies, young lady, and I know you're not as innocent as you look. Your father, on the other hand, has chosen to believe your sister is the only reason you went." She let go, drawing her hands into her lap and surveying me from across the table with calculated control. "You are not to make any more trouble. Is that clear? I expect impeccable behavior from you. If your father says your sister is at summer camp, you *will not* question him. And you will not question me."

Mama's saucer clattered as she lifted the cup to her lips. She took a sip before picking up the silver tongs and dropping three lumps of sugar into my cup. "Just as you like it, yes?" Her voice was conciliatory. "Or I can have Velma make you tea since there's no Daddy here to tell us otherwise."

I spent the day curled on my bed with my collection of Arthur Lange's fairy books. Luella's absence left me gutted. I felt heavy with anxiety and I had a blue fit that made me feel as if I was sailing out of my body. When night fell, I arrived at the dinner table and ate in silence, choking down colorless fish and buttered carrots. Mama looked aged and distracted and as abandoned as I felt. Daddy did not come home for dinner and Velma brought the dishes to the table in grim silence.

The next morning I stayed in bed and no one came for me. The heat had broken and a cool breeze came through the window. Outside the sky was a baby blue. When I finally made my way downstairs, wearing the same gingham dress I'd slept in, the house was empty. Where was Daddy? Had Mama left too? I ran back upstairs to their room, imagining empty drawers and wardrobes, my family packed up and gone. I pushed open the bedroom door so fast it banged against the opposite wall.

"Gracious." Mama flipped over the piece of paper she was writing on. "What on earth is the matter?"

"I thought you were gone." I felt foolish, but relieved.

"Don't be silly." She capped her pen, the kimono sleeves of her robe billowing as she pivoted on her chair. The front slipped open, revealing her smooth chest above her nightgown. She was not wearing her gloves and the scars on her hands stood out like white veins. When she came over and cupped my chin in her palm, I found no comfort in the uneven bumps. Instead, I found her touch disturbing. I saw her in flames, fire leaping up her bathrobe, consuming her.

She pulled away. "Come. Sit. I have something to ask you."

I sat on the edge of her chaise longue, fiddling with the tufted yellow buttons as I watched her light a cigarette. Was this a habit now? I couldn't tell if it was an old one she'd kept well hidden, or something she'd picked up since Luella left. There was a wariness in her gaze and nerves in the quiver of her smile. "Tell me about the gypsies."

My stomach iced over. If I told her, everything Luella and I shared would turn into incriminating evidence and the sacredness of it all would be ruined. Our collective enchantment would crack and float away.

"I'm sorry about yesterday. I won't be

angry with you, I promise." Mama's tone softened as she sucked on her cigarette, holding her robe closed with one hand. "I'm sure your father's right and that Luella made you go. It doesn't seem the sort of thing you'd think up."

"Why not ask her?"

Mama sighed, pressing a single finger between her brows, "She's not talking to us at the moment." She dropped her arm and looked at me. "How long have the two of you been going up there? Since Luella first asked about them? The time I forbid you to go? I remember being gracious enough to tell you I'd take you when there was a charitable event." She walked over and wrenched open the window, taking a moment to exhale her smoke. "What did Luella do there?"

"Dance," I said, even though I knew this would wound her.

"Dance? What kind of dance?"

"I don't know . . . gypsy dances."

She made a disgusted sound. "What else?"

"Sang."

"She danced and sang?" Mama jerked around, stubbed out her cigarette and shed her bathrobe onto the back of a chair with quick, angry little movements. She shimmed out of her nightgown and let it fall in a heap

149

at her feet. Wavelets of white crepe lapped the floor like frosting slipped from a cake.

It was distressing to see the naked, pale dip of my mother's back, the gentle rise and fall of her buttocks as she flung open her wardrobe. I couldn't remember seeing her naked before. She opened the wardrobe and tossed a dress on the bed, pulled a chemise from a drawer and slipped it over her head, then gathered her hair over one shoulder and stood twisting it into a thick band, her eyes wide open. "What could she have possibly seen in that sort of thing? How could that vile, dirty life appeal to her?"

I shrugged, fighting rising tears. "I don't know." Luella would have faced Mama head-on. Maybe she had. Maybe she'd spat and screamed as they carried her off.

"What did *you* do there every afternoon?" She braced herself, ready to hear the worst of my improprieties.

"I watched, and wrote." I wasn't about to give her details so she could grind our precious moments out like the butt of her cigarette.

Mama lifted a wire corset from its hook. "Help me with this." A deep inhale passed over her teeth as she sucked in her breath, squeezing her hands on her hips so I could hook the tiny metal clasps at the back. She turned to me, looking resigned, as if the corset had squeezed the anger out of her. Her eyebrows lowered and her lips sank, her whole face surrendering. "When you were little, I worried Luella was too attached to you. She'd carry you everywhere, check on you when you cried and tell me when you were hungry. And then it was *you* who ended up too attached to her." She sighed deeply. "I wish you hadn't followed her to the gypsy camp, but I know you won't do a thing like that again. Just don't go and get sick on me now, okay? You stay strong while your sister's gone. Promise me?"

I nodded, grateful I'd managed to keep my blue fits from her all summer.

Over the next month my father made himself scarce, working late and going to the office early, or so he said. Not once did he ask about my writing, but I had nothing new to show him anyway.

The energy my mother mustered in his absence was impressive. Her movements became rapid, brittle; her skirts snapped and her bracelets jingled. Summer was almost over, but she and I still went on picnics, attended the theater and took day trips to the beach. Not all of society was in Newport and the remaining ladies filled our drawing room with their rustle and chatter.

Luella, Mama announced gaily, was at summer camp. What summer camp? The mothers were intrigued, pronouncing that their daughters — the girls wearing polite, bored smiles next to them — could use the discipline of summer camp. "Upstate," Mama answered vaguely. "The name's escaped me, but I'll let you know after I've paid the bill." She gave a trickle of laughter at her foolishness for forgetting details.

The girls drew me aside to ask where Luella *really* was, their breath coated in the herring Mama served on tiny crackers that crumbled as you bit into them.

"She's truly at summer camp." I gave the vague smile I'd practiced, wondering if Mama's false laugh had tipped them off, or if they knew Luella would never stand for any loathsome summer camp.

One quiet girl with a sneaky way about her asked, "Why didn't you go?"

"Mama wanted me home with her, for company," and for now this felt true.

When I managed a walk by myself, I went up Bolton Road to the curve where the driveway to the House of Mercy broke off and wove up the hill. I stood with my face pressed into the iron gate, watching for any sign of life, but no girls came down as far as the road and I never saw anyone come out of the whitewashed house at the gate's entrance. From the road, I could only see a portion of the dark building, gabled windows and arched doorways, the spire of a chapel twisting above the trees. I made up a hundred stories about what was happening to Luella in that place.

September arrived. School began, and still, no Luella. Bruised shadows deepened around Daddy's eyes and he hardly spoke to me. At night I heard him pacing the halls. If I happened to meet him in the morning, he'd look as if he had forgotten my very existence. A polite, stilted "good morning" was all that passed between us.

When fall arrived, Mama's energy collapsed and she no longer bothered making up believable lies. She told me that Luella had been sent to a distant cousin in Chicago.

"Not Paris?" I said, and Mama looked confused. "Remember," I said, "you were going to send her to Paris?"

"No, not Paris," she said sadly.

I wanted to scream that she was lying, but the tightness in my throat and the weight on my chest pinned me into silence.

In school, I couldn't pay attention. My mind was easily muddled. Teachers' voices confused me. The blackboard blurred and text seemed to slide off the page. With each passing day, the rope of life knotted under my feet; there was no balance, no equilibrium.

I never returned to the gypsy camp. I was afraid if I crossed that stream and climbed that hill, all I'd see would be a deserted meadow, empty holes where the fires had been, wheel tracks leading away, the ghost of my sister dancing in the moonlight. I fingered Tray's ribbon tied around my wrist — pale yellow like a fading wisp of sunlight — and tried to remember Marcella's tales of magic and evil.

Then one day in early October when Miss Paisley left the art class, three girls moved their sheets of paper to sit near one another, bending their heads over their drawings and whispering loud enough for me to hear.

"Did you hear Suzie Trainer's *never* coming back to school?"

"I heard she wouldn't be let out for three years."

"Three years!"

"There are girls who get put away for more, if they're not reformed."

"Or repentant."

"It's like prison. You get put away for however long fits the crime. There are girls who've been in there for ten years, twenty. Some never get out, but I heard three years was the minimum."

"That can't be true."

"I'm just telling you what I heard."

The door swung open and Miss Paisley's heels clipped back into the room. She glanced at the trio. "Girls, separate yourselves . . . now!" They scattered back to their seats.

Miss Paisley stood close enough that I could see the flabby skin under her arms, and smell her breath reeking of onions. "You've drawn nothing?" She rapped the empty sheet on the table.

I had dropped my pen, and my gloved hands were splayed on the paper like wounded wings. I stared at the satin tips of my fingers trying to find a point of focus.

Three years. Three years *if* you showed remorse. Luella would never show remorse. My vision clouded. My ears filled with a muffled sound like distant waves crashing. I didn't have three years. I wouldn't live that long without her.

I picked up my pencil and began drawing a thin, sharp outline of the vase in front of me. A spark of determination broke through the shadows in my head. For the first time since Luella left, I began to compose myself.

Each line on my paper darkened with each purposeful stroke as the fog of my confusion lifted and I narrowed in on a single plan.

# CHAPTER NINE:
## EFFIE

The lantern was still where Luella had stowed it. A bit rusted, and with dirt splattered on the glass panels, but intact. Once I'd pulled it from its resting place beneath the ovate, glossy leaves of the abelia, it seemed thoughtless that we'd never returned it to the oysterman.

That morning I avoided my parents, skipped breakfast and left for school early. In my first class I told the teacher I wasn't feeling well and he sent me to the infirmary, where I had no intention of going. Instead, I made straight for the front door of the school. Dark clouds scurried across the sky as I hurried down 57th Street. I'd taken the train home, and now here I was, holding a rusted lantern, not knowing if Mama had gone out or was sitting in the drawing room looking out at me standing in the shrubbery.

Tucking the lantern on one side of the

front steps, I gently pushed the door open. Mama's gloves were next to her silver-chain handbag on the hall table. I peeked into the drawing room. It was empty. I tiptoed up to my room, where I wrote a quick note and left it on my pillow. Back downstairs, I clicked open Mama's bag, the mesh rippling like the metallic scales of a fish. The inside leather held a belly of money.

I took all of it and slipped out, picking up the handle of the lantern. My breath quickened as I followed the road to a place where I could duck safely into the woods, leaves crunching underfoot like aged paper. At the stream, I peeled off my shoes and socks and waded in up to my ankles. It was ice-cold, but I didn't move. The wind picked up, shaking red and yellow, perfectly veined leaves from the trees. I left the few that had fallen onto my hair as I stepped out of the water, stamping my numb feet on the bank.

The oysterman's house teetered on the edge of Spuyten Duyvil Creek. Its frame tilted to the east, as if the wind had been blowing from the west for a hundred years. The white paint had long since worn away, and its drab clapboards seemed to cling on for dear life. I picked my way down the slope and up the dirt path, past an abandoned shovel and a bucket of dead fish. The creek stretched wide and shallow behind the house. It was said that if a man tried to wade across the devil would drag him by his trousers to the bottom.

I knocked on the front door, hoping not to lose my nerve, telling myself the oysterman ghost was a figment of my imagination.

It took a long time for the bolt to slide back, the door opening just enough to reveal a single, squinty eye. "Yeah?"

I'd left the lantern on the woodpile where he'd find it on his own, rather than admit my sister and I were the ones who had broken our promise to promptly return it. "I've come to ask for your help," I stammered.

"You in trouble?" He eased the door open enough so I could see the whole of his face. It wasn't an ogre's face after all. In the light of day, it was just worn, tired, and in need of a shave.

The stench of fish wafted up from the creek. A docked boat groaned as the water shifted beneath it. "I'm not in trouble, just in need of your assistance. I can pay you."

I stood on his dirt threshold and told him what I needed as simply and quickly as possible, the man looking suspicious to the end.

"Odd thing you're askin'." He let go of

the door and it swung back, allowing me to
see a fireplace, and a wooden table with a
nub of a candle in a silver holder. The man
ran a hand through his hair, white and
patchy with age. "How much you payin'?" I
pulled the wad of money from my pocket. I
hadn't counted it, but the man's eyebrows
rose at the bulk. "Looks like a lot? Where'd
you get that? You steal it?"

I shook my head, another lie.

He didn't look convinced, but reached for
the money anyway, his fist swallowing the
last tangible tie I had to my mother. "You
want to go right now?" he asked.

"Yes."

"Hang on a minute."

The door shut in my face. I slipped off
my tailored coat, hoping I'd look shabbier
without it. The wind blew cold off the water
and I shivered as I reached down and
yanked at the pocket of my blue serge skirt.
The seam ripped and the pocket wilted
open. I wished I could remove the lace cuffs
on my blouse, but that would require scissors. A ripped pocket would have to suffice.
Reluctantly, I pulled off my gloves and
shoved them into my coat pocket, curling
my deformed fingernails into my palms.

When the man returned, I handed him
my coat and asked if he could get rid of it

for me. He shook his head. "You don't make no sense," he said, taking it from me and hanging it on a hook inside the door. "Let's get on then."

We backtracked, following Bolton Road to the south, stately elms lining our way. It began to drizzle and a wet mist settled over my cheeks. The man yanked his coat around his neck and bent his head in silence. Slivers of wind snuck under my dress and I held my arms across my chest and tried not to shiver. If we kept going to where the road wound around the southern part of the hill, we could cross to Emerson Street and loop back to my house. For a minute I entertained the idea, but then the man cut to the right and I followed him up a steep, grassy hill. It would only be for a few days. As soon as Mama took my note to Daddy, Luella and I would be home.

The man and I came out onto another section of Bolton Road, and within a few paces we were standing at the iron gates of the House of Mercy, gazing up the winding drive where white stucco walls stretched to either side of us.

"I never asked your name," he said.

My name. I hadn't thought about that. "I suppose I have to take your name."

"Rothman, Herbert Rothman."

I looked at Herbert. The drizzle of rain had stopped and the wind had whipped his hair into a puff over his head like something gone to seed. His coat hung down to his knees and bagged over his thin shoulders. I stuck out my hand, "Effie Rothman. Nice to meet you, Herbert."

His hands were buried in his coat pockets and he made no attempt to remove them. With a puzzled expression, he said, "You don't look like a gal who's done anything wrong." I dropped my hand. "It ain't too late to turn back, you know." He gazed up the road as if it held the worst possible ending. "Can't you just repent at church or something? Don't seem right, doing this."

I wanted to tell him that this was the bravest thing I'd ever done. But all I said was, "You won't get into any trouble."

"It certainly ain't me that's gonna be in trouble."

Herbert yanked the brass ring hanging from a large bell on the gatepost and a loud *clang* rang out. A woman appeared from behind the whitewashed lodge brushing her hands together, fragments of dirt scattering. "Admittance?"

Herbert nodded. The woman barely glanced at us as she rummaged in her apron pocket and produced a substantial key ring.

Her face was aged and brown from the sun. She wiggled the key until the lock gave way and the gate swung open. "Go on up to the main door. Sister Gertrude will let you in."

We walked through and the metal gate clanged shut behind us. Herbert pulled his hat over his ears and trudged ahead. I followed, the click of the lock etching a pinch of fear at the base of my neck.

The house was a massive brick structure on a high plateau overlooking the Hudson River, a battlement defending its stronghold. Rooftop and gabled dormers seemed to stretch for miles. Looking out over a vertiginous groomed lawn, fortified at its base by a lofty white wall, I could see the thickly wooded valley and the river, a winding slice of gunmetal reflecting the dismal sky.

I followed Herbert up the wide stone steps and through the arched portico where leafless vines, thick with age, snaked up the mortar to the top of the parapet and disappeared through the holes in the balustrade. The gong at the front door reverberated loudly as Herbert rang it. Quick footsteps sounded and the door opened.

"Sister Gertrude?" Herbert asked.

"No." The sister regarded us from under her veil and cap with small, dim eyes. "Sister Mary. What can I help you with?" Her words were wisps in the air, barely audible.

"Just lookin' to, um," Herbert glanced at me. I kept my eyes on the sister's clasped hands, pale and curved like seashells against her pleated habit. "Just lookin' to admit my daughter here."

"You've not come with a magistrate?"

"No, ma'am. Do we need one?"

"No, certainly not. It's just the usual way, but girls are admitted without a court order. Come, I'll show you to Sister Gertrude."

Sister Mary stepped aside with a slight nod. She was so thin and pale she looked like a sickly child kept from the outdoors, the weight of her cap burdensome, a punishment that kept her head perpetually tilted to the side. The hallway was clean and white, the floor polished. It was cold, but not unpleasantly so. We stepped inside a small room with a sterile smell that reminded me of a doctor's office. Sister Mary told us to wait, returning within minutes to lead us into an even smaller room where another sister sat dwarfed behind an enormous desk, bare save for a single lamp shining over the dark pool of wood. To my left, a heavy oak table ran the length of the wall with a row of books, a clock and a marble sculpture of Jesus bowing his head. On the windowsill, a spindly plant sat in dim light.

The woman behind the desk excused Sister Mary, who gave an obedient nod and backed out of the room, her movements as cautious as her voice, afraid of taking up too much space or too much air. I wondered how any of the girls obeyed her. One glare from Luella would knock her over. *Luella.* Where was she? In the dining hall? The chapel? Some barren room? I looked at the woman behind the desk and did my best to hide my eagerness.

The sister regarded me with a neutral gaze; the only sound in the dim room was a soft tick of the clock. She looked at Herbert. "I'm Sister Gertrude," she said kindly, glancing away momentarily to pull pen and paper from her desk drawer. "The child's name?"

Herbert twisted the brim of his hat round and round in his hands. "Effie Rothman." The uncertainty in his voice was aggravating. I willed him to be believable. Sister Gertrude uncapped her pen and recorded the information. "Age?"

At a desperate glance from Herbert, I answered for him. "Thirteen."

The pen hovered over the paper. Sister Gertrude looked up. She seemed old, and yet had a round, unlined face and smooth, veinless hands. Her life under her habit —

out of the sun, with small meals and hours of kneeling worship — had preserved her nicely.

"Thirteen?" she said skeptically.

"I'm small for my age."

She gave a disbelieving grunt. "Birth date?"

"January 1, 1900."

Her eyes went to Herbert. They were a snapping blue. "You're her father?"

Herbert cleared his voice with a guttural sound, managing a "yes," through the phlegm.

A speck of disgust flickered across Sister Gertrude's face as she continued to take down his age, address and employment. She asked my mother's name and Herbert gave one easily. Who she was, I had no idea: a dead wife, a daughter. Sister Gertrude pushed the paper to the edge of the glossy desk, proffering her pen and directing him to sign on the bottom line. Herbert did.

"Now then." She wove her long fingers together and clasped them in front of her, leaning forward with a soft, empathetic look. "We all fall short of God's glorious standard, and yet I wholly understand that you would not be here if your daughter was not in peril of ruin. How, sir, has this girl fallen from the path of purity?"

The twirling hat was now being compressed between Herbert's hands. "She ought to tell you herself."

Shifting her attention to me, Sister Gertrude said, "Go ahead, dear. Nothing will shock me. I've heard every impropriety."

"I lied," I said, quickly.

"Is that all?"

I tried to think up a better sin. "I kissed a boy." I blushed and bowed my head.

"How often?"

"Many times."

A quiver traveled over her face. "What drove you to do this, child?"

I didn't hesitate. "My sinful nature."

Sister Gertrude rose from her chair and the heavy cross around her neck swung forward and threatened to knock into the lone lamp. She came around the desk. "Recognizing the sin, my dear, is one thing, driving it out another. Are you repentant?" I nodded. Sister Gertrude smiled and wrinkles creased the corners of her eyes. She took my hand, flinching at my clubbed fingernails. "What's wrong with the girl's hands?" She looked sharply at Herbert.

"A birth defect," I answered quickly and Herbert nodded in consent.

Sister Gertrude lifted my hand to the light, inspecting my nails. "As long as it

167

doesn't require medical attention."

Herbert looked at me. "No, ma'am," he said, cautiously.

"That must be a relief for you." She smiled again, dropped my hand and went to Herbert, leading him gently toward the door by his arm, his face red with discomfort. "We do our best to rescue our unfortunate sisters. Some find salvation. Some do not. That will be up to your daughter. All we can offer her is our protection and guidance." The door opened and they stepped into the hall. "We find that a quick goodbye is easiest on them." She cocked her head in my direction and Herbert gave a weak wave, looking genuinely concerned as he crushed his hat on his head and disappeared down the hall with Sister Gertrude. I felt the urge to rush after this strange man and cling to him, but Sister Mary was already in the doorway motioning me to follow.

# CHAPTER TEN:
## JEANNE

The night after my eldest daughter tossed her ballet slippers from the car, I couldn't sleep. It was hot, and I lay next to Emory with the sheet tossed off and my hands clasped over my stomach, sweat beading under my nightgown. I kept picturing the brazen look on Luella's face as she dropped her shoes into the street. Besides cutting me to the quick, my daughter's blatant disrespect was infuriating. Was this the natural consequence of raising children in America? I would never have dared such a thing with my own mother.

I rose and went to the window. Pulling the curtain aside, I looked into the yard at our lone oak tree, its huge branches cradling the pale moonlight. I hadn't told Emory what happened in the car with Luella. I didn't trust how he'd handle his daughter's effrontery. Her quick temper — so much like his own — always set him off. They were more alike than either would willingly admit.

There was no breeze to relieve the stifling heat and I slipped back into bed, tired, but restless. First thing tomorrow morning I'd write to my brother. He was sure to have advice on Luella. I wasn't about to let my mother know her granddaughter had refused to go abroad.

Something caught my attention and I rose up on one elbow, listening. The house was quiet and I dropped back down, clammy and uncomfortable. I spent the rest of the night tossing and turning until a gray dawn crept through the windows and the birds nesting in the oak set up a ruckus. Giving up on sleep, I climbed out of bed deciding the best thing to do was wake Luella before anyone else was up. We'd have an early cup of coffee and talk. If she went back to rehearsal and gave up this nonsense about quitting ballet, I'd agree to try and convince her father not to send her to Paris. Not that it would do much good. Emory was determined. Ever since Luella threatened to elope he'd been uneasy about her. It was nonsense, of course, but the fact that she made the threat was worrisome.

I pulled on my robe quietly so as not to wake my husband. There was so much tranquility in his sleeping face. It was like watching a child sleep and wishing you could hold onto the serenity of their slumber after they woke up to plague you.

Creeping to Luella's partially closed door, I pushed it open, not surprised to see her empty bed. I smiled to think the girls still slept together. I used to sit in their nursery and watch them all tangled up in the same bed, Luella sprawled with a limb off the edge or thrown over her sister; Effie curled in a ball.

I expected to find them that way now, but when I walked into Effie's room all I saw was Effie's thin face on the pillow, with the half-moons of dark circles below her closed lids — permanent reminders of her failing heart. On the pillow next to her was a folded piece of paper. Tiptoeing around the bed, I slipped the paper from the pillow and crept into the hall. The note was written in pencil, the words coming through in the dim morning light like a whisper.

My dearest sister,
Our time at the gypsy camp has changed me. No matter what I keep telling myself, I can't forgive Daddy, and I can't go on lying to Mama. I won't ask you to forgive me, because my actions are as

171

wretched and unforgivable as our father's, but I am leaving. Patience said if she's forced to marry the miserable boy she's been promised to she'll stab herself through the heart, and I don't blame her. She and Sydney asked me to go with them weeks ago, but I only made up my mind tonight. Sydney is mad about me. He's told me more than once, and Patience said he wouldn't help her if I didn't come along. The truth is, I want to go. Not because of Sydney, I don't feel an ounce of love for him. I want to go so I know what it's like to come to the end of a road and not have it matter whether I turn left or right. Can you imagine wanting to live by the ocean, or the mountains, and simply doing it? To not be bound to any place or person?

I love you, sweet sister, but I'm suffocating. I have to do this.

When I miss you, I will remember holding your hand at the edge of the field when we first heard that glorious gypsy music. That was the moment everything changed for me. I promise to make this up to you one day, and I'll write as soon as I can. You're stronger than you think and I know your heart will last forever. You're not to have a single blue fit while I'm away. Kiss Mama. Tell her I know she won't understand, but I love her too.

Your sister forever, Luella

Stunned, I looked into the empty hall, the swinging pendulum from the clock dizzying, the resonant tick in my chest like a faint, second heartbeat. Luella's door was cracked open. To think that she'd left in the middle of the night at lord knows what hour, that she was gone from the house at this very moment, sent my customary fear racing; and yet, this was not the tragedy I'd imagined. Never once rushing home from the train station, or eyeing the clock for the girls' return from school, or watching out the window for them to emerge over the hill, was this the scenario I played in my head. In those plots, my girls were victims. Crumpling the letter into a ball, I strode back to my room and shut the door with a bang. Emory sat up.

"What? What's wrong?" He looked dazed, still half asleep, his hair sticking out at odd angles.

I threw the ball of paper onto the bed, went to the window and heaved it open. A single, cool breeze, that's all I wanted. My fingernails bit into the wooden sill, but the air remained petulant and heavy below a miserable overcast sky.

Behind me, I heard the crinkling of paper and the sound of Emory's eyeglass case clicking open. When I turned around, he was already yanking trousers over his thin hips, his eyes puffy from sleep, the color in his face rising as he pulled on his shirt, buttoned and jabbed it into his pants. Standing his collar straight up, he slung a silk tie around his neck, making a mess of looping it. "Blast it!"

I crossed the room, steadying my fear with the task of righting Emory's tie while he rubbed a finger up and down the bridge of his nose, careful not to look me in the eye.

"How did this happen?" My voice cracked.

"She's insolent and ungrateful. She always has been. We trusted her and gave her too much freedom and now she's gone too far." The vein over Emory's temple pulsed.

"What are you going to do?"

"I am going to go get her."

"You think she's with those gypsies over the hill?"

"What other gypsies are there?"

"She says she's leaving with them. What if she's already gone?"

"She can't have gone far. I'll have her

174

home by supper. Whatever you do, don't show that letter to Effie." I nodded. The one thing we always agreed on was keeping Effie calm, whatever it took.

Emory's tie slipped through my fingers and fell against his chest. I stared at it, unable to look into his face. His confidence was reassuring, his unwavering certainty that things would go his way. It was a quality that attracted me to him, that put to rest my perpetual ripple of panic. A line in the note I'd breezed over in my shock came back to me, *I can't forgive Daddy, and I can't go on lying to Mama.*

"What won't Luella forgive you for?" It was a dangerous question. Making him admit it in that moment wouldn't do either of us any good, but I wanted to hear it anyway.

Without missing a beat, he said, "Cursed if I know," and snatched his waistcoat from its hook.

He stepped into the hall and I followed, reaching up to smooth his cowlick. "Your hair's a mess."

"Stop fussing." He pushed my hand away and dropped a kiss on my forehead before hurrying down the stairs, leaving me alone in the hall.

The air prickled around me. My husband

had not kissed my cheek or lips, but my forehead, like pandering to a child. The clock struck six and I reached up and wiped the kiss from my forehead. It would do no good to wallow, or panic over the horrors that might have befallen Luella in the hours she'd been gone. Despite Emory's faults, he took good care of this family. He'd set things right.

Sucking in my stomach, I walked briskly to my room. I'd get dressed, eat breakfast and take Effie out. By the time we came home, Luella would be here — brooding in her room, no doubt — and Emory and I would have to decide how to handle her.

But at the end of the day, when Effie and I rode the elevated back to Bolton Road with our new gloves in hand, the sky an arresting gold, Luella was not there. I knew it the moment I stepped inside the foyer and saw the stricken look on Emory's face. My husband was not the type of man who allowed himself to be defeated, and as he ushered me into the drawing room, I knew the situation was dire.

My mother-in-law sat on the edge of her chair looking like an ancient, porcelain figurine, her knuckles clasped, her dark eyes accusing. Etta Tildon hadn't left her house since her husband's death a year ago. Dread

176

rose up in me. Only the worst news could have brought her here.

I stood rigid while Emory paced, the parlor aglow from the setting sun. "Luella wasn't at the gypsy camp. I spoke to the parents of those children she wrote about in her note, and they're no more informed about their whereabouts than we are. They said their children left with Luella in the middle of the night, took a horse and a wagon. Apparently, both belonged to this Sydney fellow. His father said this meant the boy wasn't stealing, and even though he didn't approve, if his children chose to leave it was their right. I told him they were an ignorant lot and as far as I was concerned he stole my daughter. It got ugly. The boy's brother, this Job fellow, raised his fist at me and I threatened to get the police involved."

Relief washed over me, followed by a stab of anger. At least Luella wasn't murdered and left in the stream as I'd let myself imagine. She'd run away, just like she'd said, without any regard for how worried we'd be. I pictured her face in the car as she dropped her shoes out the window, her confident defiance. She was just like Emory, doing exactly as she pleased, certain the world would take care of her.

I sat coolly on the edge of the sofa.

"Where did they go? Their parents must know where they went?"

A grunt came from Etta, but she stayed quiet.

Emory's arms smacked his sides. "They don't know," he said.

The breeze I'd been waiting all day for finally came through our open windows. I turned my face toward it, watching Emory pour himself a scotch from the beveled decanter on the table beside me. The crystal clanked against the tray and the sound chimed through the room.

"Bottom line is," he went on, "if the gypsy parents plan to track down their children, they have no intention of telling us about it. They're a roaming people, and a tight-knit family, and don't take kindly to strangers barging in. I imagine they're just as keen to get rid of Luella as we are to have her back, but we'll have to track her down on our own."

"What are we going to do? Can the police go after them? How are we going to find her?" I pulled at the collar of my dress.

Emory drained his glass and poured himself another. "The police will do nothing. Luella left of her own accord. She's sixteen. If she wants to leave, there's no law that says she can't. Worse, if they choose, all she and this boy need is a magistrate to marry them."

This had not occurred to me. A marriage like that would be irreparable. "We should tell the police she was kidnapped. They can find her and make her come home."

Emory glanced at his mother. "Mother and I think we should keep this mum. No authorities. No reporters. We've decided the best course of action is to hire a private investigator to track her down. In the meantime, if people ask, we'll say that Luella is away at summer camp."

I felt as if the air had been sucked from the room. Etta's eyes bore into me and I tugged off my gloves and ran my fingers over my scars. I didn't care who saw them.

"And Effie," I finally asked, "what do we tell her?"

The reminder of our youngest softened Emory. It was ironic that her birth had unhinged our marriage as she was now the only thing that kept us close. Emory set down his drink and came to rest his hand on my shoulder, glancing at my bare hands. I think, for a moment, he considered taking ahold of one.

He sighed. "It wouldn't be right to ask her to lie for us."

"I agree."

"It would break her if she knew the truth."

"To know her sister left her willingly would be devastating."

"Best to let her think it's our fault."

"Yes, but what do we tell her?"

"I suppose the same as everyone else, that we've sent Luella to a summer camp."

I wanted to lean into Emory's hand, to feel his fingers against my neck. "She won't believe us. She knows her sister better than we do."

This intimacy was more than Etta could stand for and her voice cracked into action. "She'll believe what she's told. If she questions you, silence her. It's your tolerance that's produced this hedonist nature in Luella in the first place. Don't make the same mistake with Effie."

The insult caught me under the ribs like a bullet. This was my fault. I should have sent Luella away in the spring like Emory wanted. Taken her threat seriously. Watched her closer. I wriggled my fingers back into my gloves as Emory's hand slipped from my shoulder.

Revving up, Etta tapped the heel of her boot and barked, "Bring Effie down here before I atrophy sitting in this chair. It's getting dark. It's not safe to be out after dark anymore with foreigners crawling out of every crack in this city."

As I predicted, Effie didn't believe a word of Emory's story. Her small voice, asking where her sister was, sliced at my decorum until I couldn't hold the tears back. I reached out to her, but she pushed me away and fled the room. As much as I wanted to, I didn't follow her. Even as a baby she'd hold her arms out only for her sister, never me.

That night I couldn't sleep. At three o'clock I got up to check on Effie, her small features still so childlike as she slept. Her pallor was worrying, the dark circles under her eyes more prominent. Seeing her in bed without her sister sent a terrible fear through me. How slight and weak she was, how vulnerable without Luella. For over an hour I sat and watched her sleep, listening for the slightest catch in her breath. She was the one I'd always worried about losing, not Luella. And this backward order of events confused me. I had a longing to lay next to her, but resisted. I always resisted comforting Effie. I didn't want to coddle her. Treating her like a normal child was the only way to get her to survive. If she thought she was weak, she would be.

Over the next few months, I avoided Emory, slept fitfully, found food distasteful

181

and smoked too much. Despite this, I ran the household as if all was normal, keeping a firm grip on order and routine as I waited for news of Luella. She'd tire of that filthy life, I told myself, praying on my knees at the foot of my bed that she not come home married, or, worse, unmarried and in a compromised condition. I held out hope.

Effie surprised me. She held herself together admirably without her sister, did as she was told, repeated our lies even though she knew they were falsehoods. She was stronger than I'd ever given her credit for, which was why I stopped worrying about her and focused on willing Luella home.

It took until October for the detective to arrive with news. The temperature had dropped twenty degrees overnight and by ten o'clock in the morning frost still covered the ground. I'd crunched through it earlier to dig up my lily bulbs, the grass blades looking deceptively soft and fuzzy in their coats of ice. My trowel didn't make a dent in the frozen ground and I decided to wait until afternoon, as it was bound to warm up, which put me at my writing desk in the parlor when Neala announced the detective.

He was a tall, weedy man with deep brown eyes. When I saw him in the doorway, I leapt up so fast my calendar slipped to the floor with a bang. I left it, approaching the man with such urgency he retreated a step. "What news?"

He glanced behind me. "Is your husband at home?"

"He's at work. I'll relay any message."

The man removed his hat with a nervous flourish before fishing a letter from his breast pocket. "Your daughter's in a town outside of Portland, Maine. She doesn't want to come home. And she was right furious that you sent me to find her."

I snatched the envelope from his hand. "You were not supposed to go to her. You were to tell us when you found her so we could contact her."

"Don't get mad at me, ma'am. Take it up with your husband. I was just doing what he asked." He settled his hat back on his head. "I'll see myself out," he said, hastening from the room before I could ask another question.

When Emory came home, I was on the sofa with the letter in my lap. Neala had telephoned him at the office, the maid's lilting Irish sailing from the hallway. "I was nervous calling you at work, sir, but your wife's been sitting in the parlor for over an hour now without moving. She's white as a sheet. I think you'd best be coming home."

I heard the car pull up and turned my gaze to the window. The room smelled faintly of lemon oil from Neala's cleaning, and wood smoke from the fire that crackled in the hearth. A log fell, startling me, and a shower of sparks shot up the chimney. I noticed that the candelabra on the mantel was off center, and that the photograph of the girls and me taken at Christmas had been moved to the bookshelf. I'd have to tell Neala to take more care, I thought. It was imperative that things were kept in order.

The door opened and I heard the heavy thud of Emory's shoes in the hallway. I kept my eyes straight ahead as he entered the room. "Read it," I dared, waving the letter over the curved arm of the sofa.

He left me dangling the letter in midair as he walked to the decanter on the side table and poured himself a scotch. I'd never thought of him as a drinking man, but lately scotch was the first thing he went for.

I dropped my arm. My skirt, plum colored, rich as jam, shifted around my feet as I angled myself to look directly at my husband. "If you'd be so kind as to pour me one."

His drink was halfway to his lips. He paused, his clear blue eyes searching me curiously. I held his gaze, resisting their allure. Those eyes could drown a girl; I learned that a long time ago.

Emory extended his drink with an audacious look. Possibly this side of me would have excited him, under different circumstances. Careful not to touch his hand, I took the drink, feeling instantly more confident as the biting liquid coursed down my throat. I waved the letter like a red-dare before a bull. "Go ahead. It will only hurt a little."

I didn't usually speak to my husband this boldly, and I couldn't tell if it intrigued or worried him. He drew the paper from my hand and glanced into the fire, as if pondering whether to toss it in, before he pulled his reading glasses from his waistcoat pocket and unfolded the letter.

I'd already read it three times. And each time, I was struck that even the angle of Luella's handwriting seemed indignant. I could hear her voice upbraiding us as plainly as if she was standing in the room. She wasn't sorry, she wrote, especially not after we sent a *detective* to find her. Sydney had found a job with a local fisherman and they were doing just fine. If we were worried about her, we should have come ourselves. We were clearly more concerned over the family reputation, which she didn't give two whits about. She had no plans to come home, and if we didn't leave her alone, she'd marry Sydney just to spite us. Couldn't we see that this was why she'd left in the first place, because we were more interested in controlling her than understanding her? And had Daddy changed his ways? Because she wasn't doing anything he wasn't. *At least I'm brave enough to stand up to him,* she wrote. And we were to tell Effie she was sorry. This had nothing to do with her. She loved her, and they'd be together again. She promised.

There was no closing, just a hasty signature.

Emory looked at me over the wire rim of his spectacles, the blue of his eyes diminished. "When did our daughter become so mean?" he asked, carefully removing his glasses and folding them back into his pocket.

I myself had been enraged since reading the letter. It was not Luella's place to stand up to her father on my behalf, to shame me. What a man did in his spare time was his business. If I chose to turn a blind eye, that was mine.

"At least we know where she is and you can bring her home. I've already checked the train schedules. There's a train to Boston tonight that leaves for Portland at seven tomorrow morning." I didn't generally take charge, but I didn't generally drink scotch in the afternoon either.

He dropped the letter on the end table. He didn't look angry, just put out, inconvenienced. "I will do no such thing. Clearly, Luella refuses to come home, and I have no intention of pleading with my daughter. You think she'll last a winter in Maine in a wagon? I daresay she'll be home before the first snow falls." His self-possessed confidence needled me. He was so assured of my compliance. And why not. When had I ever questioned him?

Never. That was the answer. I could sway him in my direction, at times, when it came to the girls, but I never questioned him. In the beginning it was because I loved him, later, because I didn't want the truth.

Finishing my drink, I set the glass on the coffee table to leave a ring of sweat on the exquisite wood, an eighteenth-century Tildon heirloom. I was happy to leave my mark. I stood up to fetch my cigarette case from the hall table. When I returned, Emory tilted back on his heels, watching me as I lit my cigarette and tossed the case onto the sofa, the metal object sliding over the velvet and thumping the arm.

I drew a long breath and blew a satisfying puff of smoke in Emory's direction. "Maybe your daughter would see fit to come home if you apologized for whatever it is you've done."

This took him by surprise. "You'd like to give her that much satisfaction? She dictates the terms?" He yanked loose his tie and unbuttoned the top button of his shirt, facing me as I sucked hard on my cigarette. At least he did not say *I have nothing to apologize for.*

In a placating gesture, Emory reached for my hand, but I yanked it away. I was not going to be mollified. I had never let myself be angry with him. But I was angry now. "I want to know how you plan to get our daughter back."

His usual tactics failing, Emory took a step closer, trying now, I think, for intimidation. "What do you want me to do, lock her in the attic? Threaten to disinherit her? She's not going to come home unless she wants to."

"Or is it that *you* don't want her home?"

"Don't be ridiculous, Jeanne!" His composure slipped. Tiny, red blotches like champagne bubbles burst to the tops of his cheeks. He wasn't used to being hemmed in and I found his discomfort pleasurable. Steadying his voice, he said, "You're too upset to discuss this right now. We'll talk when you're feeling rational."

Dismissing me, he headed for the door. I'd finally cornered him and he was getting away. I followed him into the hallway. "I'm perfectly rational," I said, my voice gravid with years of resentment. He ignored me, pulled on his coat and snatched his hat from the hook. "Where are you going?"

"Out. I need some air."

"You can't ignore me!"

"I'm not ignoring you. I just need a minute to think straight."

"Think straight about what? Your indecencies?"

Emory moved in front of me and bent his head close to mine. "Stop this, Jeanne." Moisture collected over his upper lip, his mouth near enough to kiss. Maybe he'd kiss me now to shut me up. "Just stop it," he said again.

I didn't want to kiss him. I wanted to hurt him. "Stop what, exactly?" I jeered, sounding like a malicious schoolgirl.

"This is not the time." Somehow, he'd managed to make this look as if I was the one who'd veered away from what was important.

He wrenched the door open and I cried, "Just bring Luella home!" as Emory dropped his hat, stumbling into Effie who stood startled on the top step.

We stared at her, but in our tangled blindness with each other, failed to truly see her. Our second daughter slipped into the house and up the stairs.

Neither of us said a word to her, or turned to watch her go.

# CHAPTER ELEVEN:
## EFFIE

I followed Sister Mary up two flights of stairs to a dormitory lined with beds, each with a flat pillow and a gray wool blanket tucked around a thin mattress. Here there was no view of the river. The high, barred windows faced a mass of tangled trees, the tops swaying against a colorless sky.

I was made to bathe and scrub my hair in the bathroom down the hall. "To get the lice out," Sister Mary said, so confident of my infested head I didn't bother telling her otherwise. Ice-cold water sputtered out of the pipes and I bathed quickly, scrubbing my head with a bar of brown soap. The bathroom had no toilet, just a porcelain sink with exposed pipes and the tub that I scurried out of as soon as my hair was rinsed, grateful for the wool dress I'd been given despite how scratchy it was.

When I stepped into the hall, Sister Mary was waiting with patiently clasped hands.

191

She nodded for me to follow and we moved down the stairs, my wet braided hair cold against the back of my neck. As we walked, Sister Mary explained that the third floor was the dormitories, the second the classrooms and Ladies Associates dining rooms, which I was never to go into, and the first floor was the chapel, reception, laundry, dining and bathroom. I was not to use the toilet at night. There were chamber pots under our beds for that.

We entered a large room with narrow, high windows covered in rivulets of steam. The air was thick with moisture that settled over my face as I stepped inside, dusting my cheeks like the tip of a paintbrush. Laundry lines were strung from wooden beams, hung with all manner of clothing, and there was an unfamiliar smell to the air that I would later come to recognize as a mix of bleach and starch and wet wool. Girls hunched over washboards that rested in large barrels, their arms moving rapidly in and out of the mist that rose from the tops like a fog burning off of miniature lakes.

I scanned the room for Luella, trying to peer under the lowered faces that dripped with sweat as I was led to a long table. A row of girls stood pressing hissing black irons over wide swaths of linen. Sister Mary went to the tallest of them, a girl with high cheeks and fine hair pulled tight behind her head, white wisps scattered at her temples, her skin ivory, chiseled, her eyes slices of pale sky.

"Effie, this is Mable," Sister Mary said. "Mable, dear, would you please instruct Effie on the ironing?"

Mable propped a hand on her skinny hip. "Why doesn't she have to start with washing like the rest of us?"

"Do as you're told, Mable," Sister Mary said, singsong. She was used to this sort of talk back and she moved away, gliding as if on wheels, fluid as a ghost.

Mable snatched my hands and the feeling on my bare skin was a shock. "What's wrong with your nails?"

"Nothing. I was born that way," I mumbled, not used to the exposure. I wanted my gloves back.

She inspected my palms, her hands rough and dry. "Never ironed clothes, have you?" I shook my head and she dropped my hands. "Burn something and I'll slap you. Come on."

I followed her around the table, standing on my tiptoes to look out over the room. Maybe Luella would see me first.

"Pay attention," Mable snapped, handing

me an iron so heavy I almost dropped it. My hands felt tender, like freshly healed wounds. "We'll start simple." Mable spread out a pillowcase edged in lace, covered it with a square of linen, flicked water over it from a bowl beside her and told me to get to it. The iron hissed as I pressed down. "Smooth," Mable ordered. "All the way to the edge, and keep it moving or you'll burn it."

"I'm looking for my sister." I moved the heavy iron back and forth as I'd been instructed.

"She in here?" Mable took up her iron next to me.

"Yes."

"What's her name?"

"Luella."

"Luella!" Mable shouted and I looked up, my hand stilling, the iron spitting. "Get over here!"

A girl walked toward us, her plump face bobbing in front of Mable as disappointment washed over me.

"Blazes!" Mable cried and the iron was ripped from my hand as a blow struck my cheek so hard I gasped and grabbed my face. "You dunce," she hissed.

Stamped in the white cloth was the perfectly singed shape of the iron, the edges blackened like burnt toast. Mable slammed my iron on the massive black stove behind us and knocked me out of the way with her hip. Scrubbing, ironing and wringing halted as every girl turned to watch. Snatching up the pillowcase, Mable heaved open the door of the stove and shoved it in. Hot coals lit with flames. The door clanked shut and she turned to the room, brushing a clammy piece of hair from her forehead as she raised her finger, stringing an invisible line between the staring faces. "Not a word. Got it? Sister Gertrude finds out about this and I'll drag each and every one of you from your bed and beat you." The girl whom she'd ordered over stood startled in front of her. "You this halfwit's sister?"

"No," the girl muttered.

"Well, you got her anyway. Show her how to use the wringer. Maybe she'll lose a finger instead of costing me another pillowcase."

I kept my hand clasped to my throbbing face as I followed the imposter Luella to a tub where one girl stood feeding clothes through two large rollers while another worked the crank that squeaked with every turn. The girl at the crank was solid and strong. She took one look at me with her thickly lashed, brown eyes and said, "Those scrawny arms of yours won't last a minute at this. Helen, step aside and let her feed the clothes through."

"Gladly," said Helen, passing me a mound of wet fabric.

"Shake it out," ordered the girl at the crank. "And guide it through flat, but don't get your fingers near the rollers. They'll take 'em right off. I'm Edna." She offered her namely flatly, no smile, her round face dewy and bright with sweat.

"Effie." I touched the welt on my cheek. It felt red-hot. Where was Luella? A wave of panic ripped through me. "My sister's here somewhere," I said. "But I don't see her."

"We're not all on laundry. The younger ones are in the classroom. How old is she?" Edna relaxed her hold on the wringer and straightened her back, giving a little moan of discomfort as she stretched out her arm.

"Sixteen."

"Then she'd be in here. Millie!" she shouted at a girl dumping a boiling bucket of water into a tub. "Anyone in the pit?"

"Don't think so," the girl called back.

A bell tolled the hour, and there was a rustle of commotion as the girls put away their work and scurried to untie their aprons.

"Supper," said Edna. "We all dine to-gether, so as long as your sister's not in the pit she'll be there."

The dining room was large, with white walls and wide, gleaming floorboards. There were kitchen smells, bone broth and onion, but also polishing wax and tung oil, as if everything had been newly varnished. I'd never been in such neat, barren spaces. Nothing felt lived in. No paintings, no bookshelves. Were there books here? Maybe in the classrooms, surely the girls were allowed to read and write.

Our shoes echoed over the slick floor as we made our way to long oak tables with chairs pushed smartly in. From the high windows, past the thick metal bars, I could see the hillside. It had begun to rain. The bars struck dread in me, the reality of being locked in settling fresh in my gut. Where was Luella?

We didn't sit, but stood behind our chairs until Sister Gertrude entered and positioned herself at the head of our table. There was a lengthy pause as she scanned the room before giving an imperious nod for us to take our seats. I followed the girls as they scrambled into chairs and bowed their heads in prayer, keeping my eyes on the bits of onion floating in my bowl. When prayer finally ended, I glanced around the table at the girls spooning soup into their mouths and had to resist a consuming impulse to jump up and shout my sister's name. No one spoke, and when I tried to whisper something to Edna who sat next to me, she pinched my thigh under the table and I stayed quiet.

The room buzzed with clinking spoons and shifting chairs, coughing and breathing and the thrashing whir of my heart. My cheek still throbbed where I'd been struck, and I felt the approaching panic of a blue fit.

Nudging the girl next to her, Edna whispered under her breath, "Is there anyone in the pit?" The girl shook her head *no* without moving her eyes from her food. Edna put her head close to her bowl and whispered, "Your sister's not here. Now eat before Sister Gertrude thinks there's something wrong with you. The last thing you want is to get sent to the infirmary."

I reached for my spoon and gripped it as if that small piece of metal might hold me up. My sister was not here? My brain somersaulted through the events of the last few months, a frenzy rising in me. I took slow deep breaths and finished my soup. Luella had to be here. Pushing back my chair, I followed the girls to the back of the room where we scraped what was left in our bowls into a garbage pail and set them on a long counter. Silently, we tramped back to the laundry where I guided wet clothes through the wringer, my mind a tangle of irrational thoughts, my legs weak and my fingers slippery. The fabric kept going in unevenly and Edna glared at me as she made a show of heaving the crank up and repositioning the cloth.

I was exhausted by dinnertime. My wool dress was damp and heavy, as much from my own sweat as the wet clothes I pulled from the bucket. Dazed, I left my apron on a hook and followed the gaggle of girls back into the dining room. Edna didn't sit next to me this time and I found myself beside a pasty girl with sunken eyes who kept coughing and wiping her nose on the back of her hand. Dinner was a tough piece of meat and a baked potato that I found hard to choke down. I looked for Luella in every face around the room. She had to be here, otherwise nothing made sense.

After dinner, we assembled in St. Savior's Chapel for evening prayer. The chapel adjoined the main building in the center and extended out into a central courtyard. Shuffling our way past the hall windows, I could see the rain slicking over a lawn filled with golden leaves. Only hours earlier, a leaf had clung to my hair, water had eddied through my toes and the wind had chilled my neck.

In the ancient, musty chapel, we were forced to kneel in rows on hard, wooden benches. Gas sconces blurred in front of me and a pallid evening light eked through the stained-glass windows where St. Paul, with his sword and scroll, stared disapprovingly at me, and Jesus, shepherding a baby lamb, gazed at me with sympathetic eyes. I clasped my hands, following Sister Gertrude in prayer: *we have left undone those things which we ought to have done; And we have done those things which we ought not to have done.* Tears welled behind my lids. I squeezed my eyes shut and bit a trembling lip. It was cold and there was a draft at my feet. I wiggled my toes inside the soft leather of my shoes. Sister Mary had let me keep my shoes and I felt a sudden irrational attachment to them. Hours earlier these shoes had been sitting in the hallway of my home, a home that was just over the hill, and yet, somehow, existed in an entirely different universe. In what universe did my sister exist? Where was she? I looked around the dim chapel. Luella was truly not here. How had I made such a tremendous mistake?

Stripped of physical strength, I managed

to get through evening prayer and stumble up to the dorm room where a sour girl wordlessly tossed a nightgown at me and pointed to an empty bed.

I clutched the nightgown to my chest, my heart accelerating. I'd never spent a night away from home. I'd left my parents a note saying I was going to get Luella, but if she wasn't here, where would they think I'd gone? I imagined Mama pacing my empty room, tapping out the seconds on the back of her hand the way she used to when counting the length of my blue fit. What if she tapped all night and into the morning, her worry consuming her? I saw Daddy walking down the street with Miss Milholland on his arm, her hat tilted to one side, her cream-colored coat swishing from side to side. What if he didn't care that I was gone? What if he was glad to be rid of me so I wouldn't tattle like Luella?

Edna appeared beside me, linking her arm through mine as if we were old chums as she drew me to a bed where a girl was turning down the covers.

"Get on." Edna jerked her chin at the girl. "You're sleeping over there now. You snore."

"What about my sheets?" The girl darted her sharp eyes at me. She was small, but

201

looked vicious as a badger.

With a sweep, Edna yanked the sheets and blanket from the bed, and dumped them in the girl's arms. "Go." The girl sulked away and Edna nodded at the nightgown still clutched to my chest. "You waiting for someone to help you on with those?"

The room was frigid, but none of the girls seemed to mind as they stripped naked, flinging off dresses and chemises to pull nightgowns over their heads, some lingering in their underclothes, chatting and laughing while others crawled wearily into beds.

Embarrassed, I pulled my nightgown over my head and wiggled my wool dress out from underneath.

"That's a good girl. Now, go get your sheets and make up this bed before Sister Mary comes for the nightly check-in."

The sheets were in a large wardrobe at the end of the room. When I returned, Edna eyed me as if she knew I'd never made a bed in my life. Remembering how Neala did it, I found the gathered corners of the bottom sheet, tucked them over the mattress and shook the top sheet out over it.

Edna looked unconvinced. "There's something funny about you." She reached around and unbuttoned her dress, pulling it over her head, her bare arms pale and round, the outline of her heavy breasts visible beneath her chemise.

With a creak of springs, Mable leapt onto the bed opposite us, landing on her stomach with her hand propped under her chin.

Without thinking, I touched my tender cheek.

"You still sore about that?" Mable kicked her legs in the air, her nightgown falling down to expose her shapely calves. A smattering of freckles dotted her tight, pale skin. "I have to establish myself with the new girls right away, otherwise, no respect." She flipped onto her back and hung her head over the edge of the mattress, her hair like a white flame licking the floor. "It looks like Edna's given you a bed right between us. She must like you, but then she's a softie, especially for the newbies."

Edna dropped onto the mattress next to Mable. "There's something suspicious about this one." She twisted her hair over one shoulder as they exchanged conspiratorial glances.

Mable nodded, slowly. "I suspected as much." Swinging her feet to the ground, she drew something shiny from under the mattress and stood in front of me. "Put this on." She held out a small cosmetic pot with a gold label that read, *Rouge Coral, Bourjois.*

I didn't move to take it. I'd never been pushed around by anyone. At school, the girls knew to leave me alone. I was Luella's little sister, and besides, I was sick. No one pushed around the sick girl.

Mable smirked. "Haven't you ever painted your cheeks? You'll insult me if you don't take it. Do you know what it took to sneak this in here? Show her, Edna."

With a toss, the pot went sailing through the air and Edna caught it, pulling down the strap of her chemise to reveal her large white breast with its bright pink nipple. Lifting her breast, she promptly secured the pot beneath and raised her arms with a little curtsy, the pot held in place.

Mable clapped. "Stupendous what one can hide under those things. Now, give it here."

Retrieving the rouge, Edna tossed the pot at Mable who snatched it in the air like a ballplayer and unscrewed the lid. She smiled, rubbing her finger methodically into the red cream.

From behind. I felt my arms pinned to my sides. "Don't struggle," Edna hissed, her breath hot on my neck. "Otherwise it'll get all over and you'll look like a *whore* instead of a lady."

I thought of Luella's fierce glare and the

determined purse of her lips when she was angry. She'd never stand for this. She'd destroy these girls. I squirmed, trying to twist out of Edna's grasp, but all I could do was yank my head to the side as Mable came at me with her red-tipped finger. Frantic, I kicked her, hard, right in the shins. She winced, screeching, "You devil!" and together they threw me on the bed.

Edna sat on my stomach clapping her hands over my ears and holding my head still as Mable smeared cold, sticky rouge on my lips and cheeks. My breath caught and my heart sped up, the room muffled beneath Edna's hands. Mable's suffocating finger pressed to my mouth as I kicked and twisted, weakening. I'd never win. I'd never be like Luella. I was as flimsy and frail as the filaments I traced in my botany note-book. These girls would shred me like a leaf.

This time, the room didn't brighten and dissolve peacefully like the time on my bed. This was a violent death, a black noose closing around the edges of my eyes, around my neck. I choked and slipped and fell at a terrifying speed, images flashing like a deck of cards: Daddy's fingers on the inside of my wrist, Luella's braid on a pillow, a baby doll with glazed, taffy curls, piano keys, a ruler rapped over my knuckles, a pot of cold cream spilling to the floor, the white of Mama's scars.

Gasping, I clawed my way back through smothering darkness, dug at empty space until a ceiling beam came into focus, the edge of a window frame and the corner of a wall. The rush in my ears gave way to a ringing and I recognized Sister Gertrude's face floating out of reach.

Her mouth moved and I heard, "How long has she been like this?" I couldn't make out a reply.

The walls fell into place around me and I sat up, feeling like I'd been sucked through a tunnel and dropped out on the other side. The room was silent, save for the rain battering the windowpanes. Sister Gertrude stood cradling the pot of rouge in her palm, her coif and wimple shrouding all but the intimidating circle of her face. Mable and Edna lay in their beds gazing at the ceiling with innocent, bored expressions.

"You think you can lie here and pretend to sleep with a painted face? It seems the girls failed to inform you that I check each and every one of you before the lights go out. Or maybe —" she tilted back on her heels "— they didn't care if you were caught. Come with me."

My legs wobbled as I stood up. Finding

my footing, I followed Sister Gertrude out of the room and down the hall into an antechamber where Sister Mary stood on a braided rug in front of a bright fire, a small figure secured in black, a witness.

There was a clink as Sister Gertrude placed the pot of rouge on a round table positioned between two wing-backed chairs. This room was lived in, with its bookshelves and trinkets, a figurine of the Virgin Mary on the mantel, paper and pen on a desk. "Go, wash it off. All of it." She pointed to a washstand in the corner of the room.

I'd forgotten about the rouge smeared on my face.

As I closed my eyes to lather and rinse, I could have been at home, with the violet scent of soap and the crackle of the fire, Neala ordering me clean. When I looked up at the sisters' blanched, stern faces, I felt disoriented.

Propping a finger under my chin, Sister Gertrude ran her thumb roughly over my lips and I was reminded of my mother lifting my face the day she asked about Luella, how I'd pulled away from her. I should have told her everything.

Satisfied that no residue of sedition came away on her thumb pad, Sister Gertrude folded her arms over her bulky chest and said, "I did not peg you for a troublemaker when you arrived this morning, but it appears I misjudged." She savored each syllable, drew them out like flavors on her tongue. "I do not tolerate behavior of this sort. Which of the girls enticed you with this?"

I understood few of the social cues here, but I knew enough to realize it would be suicide to tattle. Whatever punishment Sister Gertrude handed over wouldn't be as bad as the girls' revenge.

"It was in my skirt pocket when I arrived this morning." This was a quick thought up lie as good as any Luella could tell.

"What possessed you to put it on before bed? Were you trying to make a show of it for the other girls?"

I bit my lip and said nothing.

There was a clucking from Sister Gertrude as she wagged her head in disapproval.

"Sister Mary," she snapped and Sister Mary's still form came to life as she shuffled to the desk under the window and drew something from the drawer. "Turn around," Sister Gertrude instructed.

I turned to the window. There were no bars, just little squares of glass with tears of rain weeping down them. My stomach seized. Was she going to whip me? I'd never been whipped in my life. Some of the girls at school got the switch, but my father would never do such a thing.

Before I knew what was happening, I felt my hair yanked backward and heard a sharp snipping. I whirled around to see my braid hanging like the pelt of a dead animal in Sister Gertrude's hand. I clapped the back of my head as if I'd lost a piece of my skull, watching the sister drop my hair in the wastebasket and slide the scissors back in the drawer.

She turned kind eyes on me, her disapproval sanctified by her righteous actions. *"I will inform thee and teach thee in the ways wherein thou shan't go, and I will guide thee with thine eyes."* She smiled. "It may appear a harsh punishment, my dear, but I assure you, rooting out one's vanity is the first step to salvation. Beg forgiveness for your sin, and God will look kindly on you. Your hair will grow back. I have faith that, by then, you will be strengthened in goodness and no longer fall into temptation." She looked at me as if the amelioration of the entire female race lay in our hands, as if we were in this righteous plan together.

Again, I thought of Luella. "I haven't done anything to beg forgiveness for. I'm not supposed to be here. My father's Emory Tildon. Get him on the line. I want to speak with him. If he knows where I am, he'll come straightaway for me." I drew on my sister's voice, held myself upright, chin lifted. I'd never stood up to anyone like this before.

Outrage buckled the sister's forehead and her lips pinched into hard lines, her soft face calcifying before me. She'd miscalculated. I was not as pliable as she thought. "I do not tolerate liars. Are you looking to spend your first night here on the basement floor?" Her hand clamped around my upper arm and she marched me from the room, the tips of her fingers digging into the tender muscles under my arm. Halting outside the dormitory, she dropped her voice and flicked a piece of my cropped hair. "Leaving you this was a kindness. One more misstep, one more lie, and I will shave this head of yours to the scalp and you will find yourself in the basement on bread and water for a week. Is that clear?"

She tossed me through the open door and I stumbled and caught myself on the foot of an iron bed frame, the metal frigid, my confidence dissolving as I crept along to my empty bed. I had dared to imagine Sister Gertrude would do as I said. How was I going to reach my parents if she didn't believe me, and how would I ever find my sister now?

Sister Gertrude's shrouded form receded into the hall and the door closed with a bang. The room went black and the ceiling snapped out of view. I touched my clubbed fingernails trying to resurrect the calming feel of Mama's scars, picturing Luella's face the night she woke me to braid my hair. Why didn't Luella send me any message at all? I needed a word, a sentence, a beginning or an ending, something to explain this.

There was nothing, just the pulse of a room filled with a hundred sleeping girls. Dear God, what had I done?

■ ■ ■ ■

# BOOK TWO

■ ■ ■ ■

# CHAPTER TWELVE:
## MABLE

I had no idea, watching Effie make her way across the laundry that first day, that the two of us would wind up tangled in each other's lives. To tell the truth, I didn't think much of her. Just one more girl added to the pile. What I could see, right off, was that she wasn't as weak as she played it. That's why I slapped her. It was nothing personal. She messed up and had to pay for it — that's how life is. I knew she could take it. I'll admit for a minute I thought I might have killed her with that rouge business, but she came back from that too.

How little I knew of that girl's true strength back then.

But I'm getting ahead of myself. I'm no good at this storytelling business. Stories are Effie's domain, not mine. Life, as far as I can tell, is a series of events best left untold, and yet here we are.

I suppose some things you just can't get

away from. Not when you've done wrong like I have. Committed the worst sin a person can commit in this world. I've searched my soul for why I did it and haven't come up with any answers. At least I'll go to hell for it, so there's that. I've tried to come clean, but I can't. So, I'm hiding out until the devil comes for me.

In general, I didn't care much for people. It was burying Mama's fifth baby that stopped me caring. After a while, you can't look at their tiny blue faces and balled fists and feel anything but sorry you have to dig that hole.

I buried the last baby on an early morning in July. It was raining. Water streamed down the dirty widows of the cabin and hammered against the roof. The rain made the sad day worse, the whole sky crying down on us as I stood in my parents' bedroom doorway watching the doctor's fat behind as he leaned over Mama's splayed legs.

"Now, Mrs. Hagen, you're going to have to push. You don't have a choice here." Dr. Febland was round as a barrel with whiskers thick as corn husks and cheeks that looked like he was holding peach pits in them. He sounded tired and fed up. He looked at Papa leaning against the wall with his arms crossed. "Einar —" the doctor was on first-name terms with Papa by now "— talk to her."

Papa's face remained fixed as stone, his ashen hair sticking to his sweaty forehead, his mouth shut firm, accepting the inevitable. When Mama gave up there was no encouraging her and we all knew it.

Sighing, the doctor took the flat of his hand and began pushing down on the hefty lump of my mother's stomach.

I didn't want to watch. I wasn't of any help anyway so I climbed the ladder to my loft bed over the kitchen and lay on my back tracing the rhythm of the rain in the air with my fingertips.

My parents wanted ten children. At least that's what Papa told me. Mama kept whatever she wanted to herself, but her stomach kept swelling and the small mounds under the birch tree kept adding up. I was the only baby that made it past a month.

"Born easy and grew into the beauty you are without any help from us," Papa liked to remind me.

I was their firstborn, and reckoned it was my fault they imagined the rest of their children would be as easy.

Between the slats of my bedrail, I could see the kitchen table below and hear the hiss of the fire dying in the hearth like someone was squatting between the stones spitting at me. I couldn't figure why my parents kept trying to have babies when there was nowhere to put them. We lived in a small cabin, deep in the woods outside the town of Katonah, New York. The walk from the main road — more a dirt path full of holes than a road — to our clearing was a good twenty minutes. Papa worked in town at the Hoyt Brothers furniture store for a man neither Mama, nor I, had ever met. Papa said Mr. Bilberry was a kind man when he saw fit, but that he didn't see fit very often.

A moan from the bedroom clawed its way into a wail. I was glad not to see my mother's anguish oozing out onto the bedsheet. I pulled the pillow over my head and waited until the moaning faded before tossing it off to listen. There was no sound of a baby's cry. Through the patter of rain, I made out the click of Dr. Febland's bag and the tired shuffle of his feet to the door. Before he left I heard him tell Papa it was a girl, and he was sorry there was nothing more he could do.

The house fell silent. I stayed where I was until hunger drove me down to the stove where I dug a chunk of spoon bread from the pan with my fingers. Mama was Italian, but a few months ago, when she and Papa were in their hopeful stage, Papa brought home a book that read *Knoxville Cookbook* in bold red letters next to a lady with a fancy hairdo I'd never seen the like of. I could read the word *Knoxville,* but couldn't make out what it meant. I'd never been to school and my education under Mama was spotty. Papa said he found it in a box of free books outside the village library, and since the only other book we owned was the bible, he figured he'd pick it up. He was Norwegian and had long since given up on Mama cooking anything he might recognize anyway.

Licking crumbs from my fingers, I noticed Papa sitting perfectly still in the rocker with his hands on his knees staring into the cradle at his feet. Blazes, I thought, they've gone and swaddled that baby and put it to bed again. The fire in the hearth had gone cold. I looked out the window at the rain washing our panes clean. Careful not to look into the cradle, I moved to the bedroom door where Mama lay, so fragile and wasted, all twisted up in the sheets, mounds of dark hair knotted around her head, a stain of watery blood at her feet. Her face was buried in the pillows and I couldn't tell if she was asleep or not.

Instead of crawling in next to her as I usually did, I went and stood by Papa. I was only twelve years old, but already came up to his shoulder when we stood side by side. Papa said I'd inherited his mother's Norwegian height. "If you keep growing, you'll break through the roof and we'll have to feed you through the chimney," he said.

"Then you'll have to take care of me forever," I replied, hopeful.

"Nah, you'd soon learn to snatch birds from the sky and not need us at all."

I put my hand on his shoulder and leaned against him, looking down on his full head of hair, pale and thick as milkweed. He didn't say anything, the quiet made worse by the fact that he insisted on stopping the clock when a baby died so there wasn't even the tick to distract us. I was the only one who ever started it up again. My parents kept trying to stop time, but being twelve years old, time was all I had.

Pulling my hand away, I leaned to kiss Papa's cheek before going outside into the warm rain. I took the shovel from the barn. Rain droplets trickled down my neck and soaked the shoulders of my dress while I dug the deepest hole I could manage. Maybe if this baby was buried far enough down, she couldn't haunt us like the others.

When the shovel no longer touched bottom, I threw it to the ground and went back inside. Papa was hunched over the cradle praying on his knees. I didn't know what time it was — that blasted, stopped clock — but guessed, by the light coming in, that it was getting on around four. Moving the leftover spoon bread to the warming oven, I struck a match and lit the paper in the firebox, grateful Papa had prepared it this morning as I was no good at getting the right amount of air between the sticks. When the flames were hot enough, I closed the damper and pressed my lips together, hard, steeling myself against the urge to climb back into the loft and pull the pillow over my head.

Going to the cradle, I lifted the baby. Papa didn't move. The poor thing was as light as air, and I couldn't help looking into the baby's tiny face as I moved toward the door. Her skin was pearly and translucent, her closed lids like drops of milky water. From the looks of her, she'd stayed a spirit all along.

When I reached the hole, I dropped to my knees and lifted that baby girl to Heaven, holding her up in the rain. There seemed a rightness to God washing her clean of this world. As I lowered her, I felt Papa's big hand on my shoulder. I hadn't heard him come up behind me, but I knew he would be there. He never made me put the dirt over them. Kneeling down, he took the baby from my hands and cupped her in his palm. She was so tiny it was like she'd been tucked into a mitten. Very slowly, whispering words of salvation, Papa leaned over and placed her gently into the earth, the rain already turning my hole to mud. This was the saddest part, separating that tiny creature from our bodies and leaving her alone in the ground. There was no other way, but it seemed cruel regardless. Closing my eyes, I lifted my face to the sky as I'd lifted the baby, the raindrops making it safe to cry without worrying Papa none. I stayed like that, listening to the hush in the trees and the soft thud of dirt as Papa filled the ground back in, the warm air heavy with the smell of wet soil.

A scream startled me. I leapt up to see Mama rushing from the house, her white nightgown billowing behind her like a reluctant cloud. Her bare feet slipped in the mud and she sank to the ground, clawing at tufts of weeds as she groped toward us. Papa didn't even turn around. He carefully patted the flat of the shovel over the filled-in hole, then moved out of Mama's way as she sank over it, bowed on her knees, crying and cursin' under her breath. My dress was soaked with rain and I felt chilled even in the warm air. I wanted to go back inside, but it wasn't right leaving my parents out here alone, Mama weeping and Papa kneeling beside her caressing her back. When they'd sobbed and prayed themselves clean, Papa lifted Mama up and I trailed them back to the house, Mama's frame so tiny in Papa's hulking arms she might as well have been his baby.

Inside, she shook herself down and stumbled to her feet. Mud plastered her nightgown against her swollen breasts and lumpy middle like a layer of dark skin. My mama was small and fierce, with deep brown eyes and a voice that ripped clear through anything. "No more!" she cried, shaking her clenched fist at him. "I will give you no more." With a swift kick she sent the cradle skidding across the floor. It hit the stone fireplace and split neatly in two, the ends falling away as softly as sliced butter.

Seemed that cradle had been waiting to let go.

I stared at the broken wood, stunned and uncomfortably relieved, water dripping from my dress and pooling at my feet. I'd be the last baby — alive, at least — to rock in that meaningful piece of furniture. It had come over with my great-grandmother from Sicily and cradled every one of her thirteen children. Mama didn't even glance at it as she stumbled into her bedroom, slammed and latched the door.

The finality of that latch clicking into place stayed with me as I set the pendulum swinging on the clock, and went into the kitchen to see if the spoon bread had warmed up. Papa was holding the broken cradle and was apologetically caressing the two split pieces. It wasn't even his grandma's, but I imagined his heart had split in two with it.

It made no difference how deep I'd dug that hole, I thought, moving around the kitchen. The delicate, papery face of that dead baby was going to haunt us anyway.

If my parents bothered to name her, no one ever told me.

# CHAPTER THIRTEEN: EFFIE

A resounding bell woke me. It was dark and the rain was still coming down as girls moaned and tumbled from their beds. Not until I stood up did I remember my chopped hair, light and swinging freely around my ears.

Mable knelt on her bed licking her hand and smoothing her hair into a knot at the nape of her neck. Neither she nor Edna looked at me as we dragged ourselves to chapel for morning prayer, and then to our porridge breakfast. I learned quickly that our meals had no variety: pasty porridge for breakfast, thin stew for lunch, stringy, dry meat and potato for dinner. There was rarely butter, and only once in a while an extra pinch of salt.

After breakfast, we trudged to the laundry room where irons stood like ready soldiers over the huge, black stoves. I was ordered to a washboard and given a pile of shirts to scrub. Within the hour, my fingers were wrinkled and blistered raw from the scalding water, and my rolled-up sleeves and apron soaked.

In a moment of dazed exhaustion, I lifted my head and spotted Suzie Trainer folding a sheet with another girl, their movements rapid and seamless. I'd forgotten all about her. I had hardly known her at school, and yet the familiarity of her robust face and curly brown hair gave my heart a leap. When I caught her eye, I gave a small wave, but she stared through me without a flicker of recognition.

The girl next to me nudged my arm and whispered, "Mable's eyeing you, you'd better get back to work."

From behind the ironing table, Mable watched with her cool, sharp eyes, one hand rhythmically moving the iron as she managed to find the exact edge of cloth without even looking at it. I arched over my vat and resumed scrubbing, the steam making my newly shorn hair spring into curls around my face. The blouse in my hands was of a fine silk, shrunk into a wad of blue from the hot water. Whose laundry was this, one of the Chapin girls'? A neighbor's? My mother's? She must be frantic with worry, I thought, twisting the blouse into a thin, wet rope.

In the light of day, I felt more rational than I had last night. I would not be in here long. Daddy would never abandon me. He hadn't locked Luella away, the worst he'd done was threaten to send her to Paris, only she'd refused.

I thought of the last day I saw my sister, her humiliation onstage, her defiance against Mama as she threw her slippers into the street, her frantically braiding my hair in the middle of the night. Our parents hadn't been acting wild and irrational, Luella had. It was Daddy who came to my room the next night and promised Luella would be back. I remembered how sad he'd looked, not angry. He didn't want to be rid of her, he was as sorry to lose her as I was. Why hadn't I seen that then?

Dropping the blouse into the clean pile to be squeezed through the wringer, I picked up another dirty shirt and shoved it into the hot water. The bump and hiss of the irons, the creak of the wringer and the splash of water were a constant rhythm of duty, an orchestra of work. I found it almost soothing, despite the exhaustion. I liked that no one talked, or expected me to. It gave me room to think.

I didn't know where Luella was, but Daddy and Mama did, which made her absence tolerable. I, on the other hand, had actually disappeared on them. They'd never stand for it. They would contact the police, hire a detective. Maybe I'd even be in the paper, and Sister Gertrude would be publicly humiliated for her mistake. I remembered a story I read in *The Times* about a wealthy heiress who went missing from Fifth Avenue. A story delicious enough to be fiction. She had charged half a pound of chocolates to her account at Park & Tilford's, purchased a book of essays at Brentano's and was on her way to meet her mother for lunch at the Waldorf Astoria when she disappeared. The police searched for weeks, the Pinkerton detectives were called in, but they never found her.

Under her heavy coat, the woman feels her thin blouse catch and tear on the pin of her brooch. The crudeness of this makes her smile as she slips in and out of the crowd, the brim of her wide hat grazing her shoulder as she tilts her head, her chocolates tucked into her muff, her book under her arm. A sound catches her attention and she stops to watch a street musician play his fiddle. The music drowns out the trolley bells and carriage wheels and the woman soars on the notes, lifted from all things detestable — brooches and fine blouses amongst them. There is a monkey on the man's arm, and this reminds her of the time her father took her to the circus and she wished to become a trapeze artist.

It is an easy decision to take the man's arm when it's offered and walk to the water's edge, the monkey on the man's shoulder between them. She likes the idea of secrecy, of disappearing, of leaving her story behind. When the boat pulls away she knows her family will miss her, but not enough.

I scrubbed the blouse hard over the rippled board, water splashing. My family would miss me. I'd be found. I had to be. I was just over the hill from my own home. Tears sprung to my eyes and I batted them away, reminding myself to breathe slowly and not scrub too fast. I couldn't afford a blue fit, not here, not now.

A hand landed on my shoulder and I looked up into Mable's eyes, struck by how much force there was in their washed-out blue. "Leave that." She took the blouse from my hand and tossed it into the bucket.

"Come on."

Nervous, I followed her to the back of the laundry where we were completely alone. She faced me, arms crossed. Behind her the shelves were stacked with bars of soap wrapped in white paper, *Sunlight Soap* stenciled in tiny red letters on them. There were boxes of starch, soap powder, borax and *Watson's Matchless Cleanser.* I tried not to look into Mable's eyes. Facing her was more nerve-racking than facing Sister Gertrude. Her intentions did not come from any sense of devout righteousness. There were no rules. She could do anything she wanted to me.

Standing on tiptoes, Mable reached inside a basket on a high shelf and retrieved a pair of scissors. I pulled back and she grinned in such a way that even her small, crooked teeth became attractive. "They're dull. I couldn't slit your throat with them if I wanted to. What I can do is even up that dastardly hair of yours."

Suspicious of her kindness, I kept a foot between us and stared her down. She was not coming at me with those scissors.

Mable laughed. "You see, *that* right there," she said and pointed the end of the scissors at me, "there's a fighting spirit in you most girls don't have when they come in here because it's already been beaten out of them. We pull that stunt with the rouge on every new girl. Not many have kicked me in the shins, and none ever pulled that trick you pulled. How'd you do it? You turned the deadliest color. Edna thought for sure we'd killed you. Scared the dickens out of us. I was so out of my wits, I dropped the rouge on the bed instead of hiding it. A shame, since there won't be no gettin' it back now. I bet Sister Gertrude paints her face when she's all alone. Wicked woman."

Mable twirled me around with a brusque shove of my shoulder. She was like a rougher version of Luella without the grooming. I heard the careful, slow snipping of scissors, and felt the brush of Mable's hand near my ear. "Then there's the thing about you not ratting us out. I'm gathering from this cropped head, and since no punishment's come down from the almighty sisters, you took the blame. Girls don't do that unless there's loyalty between them." Mable turned me around to scrutinize her work. "Well, you were no Lillian Gish to begin with, but it's the best I can do."

I reached up and felt the short curls at the back of my neck. Mable stood on tiptoe once more to return the scissors to the basket.

"We'd better get back before the hand of God strikes us down." She dropped on her heels and yanked her apron into place. "Tomorrow's Saturday, which means we're allowed an hour of leisure time between dinner and bed. You come find Edna and me."

I still didn't trust her, but her confidence in me was reassuring. It made me feel less alone.

The next night, after dinner and evening prayer, there was a hubbub of excitement amongst the girls as we were led into a room on the second floor. Here was a lived-in space, filled with fine furnishings and religious art framed in bronze, castoffs from the Ladies Aid Society, I was told. The room had a look of worn opulence, as if it once held grand parties long forgotten. Overhead, a gas chandelier flickered, giving everything a bright, gauzy glow. There were heavy velvet curtains at the windows, a dust-covered piano and peeling wallpaper in repeating clusters of roses. Lace, yellowed with age, covered round tables where girls sat embroidering or stitching, watched over by two sisters seated in tufted armchairs with squares of lace over the back, bibles open in their laps. Every now and then they'd lean over and speak in low voices to each other.

It was the first time I'd been in a room with the younger children. They sat on the rug facing each other in twos, playing hand games, their movements listless, as if tired puppeteers moved their arms. I could hear the slap, slap of their palms and the chanting rhymes. I wondered how little children came to be in a place like this. These girls weren't old enough to have done anything wrong.

Seated at a table embroidering obediently with two other girls was Suzie Trainer. The house was run on such a tight schedule I hadn't found a moment to approach her. About to go over, I saw Mable and Edna beckoning to me from across the room and hesitated, shifting direction. It might not do to make friends with them, but it wouldn't do to make enemies either.

With disquieting intimacy, Mable embraced me around the waist and drew me toward the window. "Can you keep a secret?" she whispered, glancing over my shoulder at the sisters.

I nodded, wishing she wouldn't stand so close.

"How do we know we can trust her?" Edna leaned against the wall with crossed arms, her dark hair piled in fashionable waves on top of her head. I couldn't imagine how she managed it after a hot day in the laundry, and without a mirror.

"Hasn't she proven it?" Mable flicked a piece of my shorn hair as evidence.

"I suppose."

"All right then." Mable faced us toward the window, our backs to the watchful sisters. Through the panes of glass, past the bars, there was a sliver of moon with a single bright star beneath it. I thought of the stream running at the bottom of the hill and felt a stab of longing for Luella.

"You see those bars?" Mable whispered. I nodded. "They've come loose on the bottom. If you lean out you can pull them right out of the siding."

"So?" I was instantly suspicious, imagining they had another prank in store for me. "And how do you know that anyway?"

"Edna discovered it last week when Sister Agnes told her to close the window. She was mad about something and slammed her hand into the bars. It's the one time Edna's anger's served her. Isn't that right, Edna?"

Edna grinned and bit the air with her teeth like a wild animal. "Won't be the last."

"We're only on the second floor. It's not a far drop. Once we're on the ground, we'll find a tree we can climb to reach the top of the wall. From the wall we jump to the other

234

side and find ourselves free as birds, so long as no one breaks an ankle."

Escape? This hadn't occurred to me. I could run straight home, I thought, my heart quickening.

"Girls?" A voice behind us made me jump. "What are we finding so engrossing out this window?"

I turned to face one of the sisters who was no longer reading in her chair.

Edna smiled. "The glorious moon, Sister Agnes."

Sister Agnes was short and plump, her jowls wobbling when she spoke. "I find that hard to believe, coming from you two."

"Are we not allowed to take in the miracle of God's work in nature?" Mable mocked.

"Don't." Sister Agnes pointed a finger at her. "Just don't. I'm in no mood. Go mingle and stop scheming. And you," she said, as her finger moved to me. "You've just arrived and from what I hear from Sister Gertrude, you're as bad as these two. Go on now and find something useful to do."

"Useful?" Edna mumbled as Sister Agnes went back to her chair. "Useful would be to kick her teeth in."

"Are you in?" Mable curled her hand around my wrist. I didn't stop to think why they were including me. Escaping out that window looked like the easiest thing in the world. Drop to the ground and run, just like Mable had said.

I nodded. "I'm in."

"You see, Edna, I told you she had spunk."

Spunk I had, along with gullibility. For some reason I believed what Mable said about loyalty.

# CHAPTER FOURTEEN: MABLE

All right, I still feel bad about fooling Effie. I never said I was any kind of saint. Far from it. And maybe our escape's partly why I'm telling you all this. Seems I have to make amends everywhere I turn.

I'm to blame for a lot, but in that cabin with Mama and Papa, I only tried to do right.

Normally, after a baby died, there was a period of time when Mama went cold and silent, taking a solid month or two before she allowed Papa to put his arm around her again. He'd nuzzle her neck while she stood over the stove and she'd soften and lean against him, and we all knew her mourning was over.

I used to think that no amount of sorrow could keep them from each other, but after that last baby Mama never softened. She kept her small, compact body tight and unrelenting, flicking away Papa's touch with a look of dark determination. Every night she'd latch the bedroom door, and Papa would shake his head and grin at me shame-faced, like I was the one who needed an explanation. "She'll come around," he'd say, continuing to make his bed on the floor.

Even though Papa had a job in a furniture store we only had one rocking chair and the four wicker chairs he'd built for the table. I hated that fourth, empty chair. By the end of September, when it was clear Mama intended to keep Papa locked out of the bedroom forever, I said, "Papa, it's time we get rid of that chair."

Papa was kneeling on the hearth raking the ashes into a tin bucket. Running a soot-covered hand through his hair, he looked up at me with a glint in his blue-green eyes. I'd never seen the sea, but I imagined the water looked just like Papa's eyes. "We might have a guest one day."

"No one ever comes out this far."

He nodded at the violin leaning against the wall. "A hunter might hear you playing and fall in love with you. Where would he sit, now, if we got rid of that chair?" He shook his head as if I was the biggest fool he'd ever seen, hooked the bucket of ash over his forearm and ducked out the door.

Despite this absurdity, I smiled. Our violin

was the one thing that kept us from total misery. Papa had taught me to play when I was five. Neither one of us could read music, but I memorized the songs he knew by heart. When Papa played that violin, it healed our wounds and melted the sorrow from our bones. Even Mama relaxed, a hum escaping her lips, her shoulders letting go.

But when the music stopped everything froze back up.

By the time the leaves fell, and Papa had a pile of wood stacked against the house for winter, nothing had changed between them. Those babies had shredded my parents' hearts to pieces and it didn't look like there'd be any recovery.

I spent the last winter I had with them trying to mend things with the foolish intention of a child who believes she can make a difference. I'd keep them sitting together at the table while I read scripture, hoping their hands might touch, or one might look up and realize how sorry they were. I'd call Papa to the barn to help Mama with something just to have him near her, or I'd ask Mama to stay up and sit by the fire to give Papa a little more time before the bedroom door shut on him.

At some point through all of this, I realized that my birth hadn't been enough to fulfill them, and my existence wasn't enough to keep them going.

I wonder if that's why, when I was forced to change my name, it wasn't too hard a thing to do. Since I'm outing all my lies anyway, I might as well admit Mable's not my real name. It's Signe Hagen, a name my father was proud of. A name I haven't used for a very long time.

It still makes me think of my papa on that early morning in April, standing on the ladder shaking my shoulder, the loft creaking under his weight. It was dark, but a lamp had been lit below and his eyes hovered like small moons over me.

"What's wrong?" I sat up. I could hear ice melting off the roof and dropping from the eaves. He was crying and it frightened me. I reached out and wiped the wetness along his scratchy cheek.

"Do you remember why I gave you your grandmother's name, Signe?" he asked.

"Because she lived to be one hundred years old?"

"No." He smiled. "Because it means victorious."

He'd told me this before and I'd always thought it silly. He should have given me a practical name. One I had a chance of living up to.

With a hand on my cheek and a sorry shake of his head, he said, "I need your help, Signe. Your mama seems strong, but she's not. You're a brave girl, stronger than the rest of us. I need you to take care of your mama for me now, okay?"

The truth of what he was saying came over me with the waiting breath of a storm. "No!" I clung to his arm.

"You must, Signe." His voice brimmed with agony and I squeezed his arm harder. "I can't stay. It's for your mama's own good. Every time she looks at me she sees those babies. All I've become is a reminder of what she's lost. You . . ." He put his hand under my chin. "You, my beautiful girl, remind her of the one thing she didn't. All you have to do is keep on reminding her."

"No. I won't. You can't go."

"I love her too much to stay, Signe. I love you too much. It's better this way, you'll see, in time." He pressed his fingers over my lips to stifle my sob. "I won't be gone forever."

"What does that mean? When will you be back?"

He shook his head. "I can't say, but I will see you again, my girl."

"Don't go!" I tried to hold on, but he slipped from my grasp, the ladder groaning with each descending step. I wanted to lunge for him, to scream for Mama, but the face of the nameless baby swam in front of me and I did nothing but picture the day we buried her, the rain and sadness and Mama screaming. If Papa left, maybe he could find happiness where Mama and I couldn't. He'd stow it in a bag, come back and pull it out to throw over us like sunshine.

From the slats in my loft, I watched him hoist his bag over one shoulder, lift the glass housing of the lamp and blow it out. The room went dark. The door opened and the shape of Papa, tall and broad-shouldered, was silhouetted against a moonlit sky. The curtains lifted and fell, rustling into place as the door shut and the house stilled, the silence immense.

I clamped my jaw and balled my fists, summoning up all of my indifference. If I squeezed everything tight enough, I could shut off tears and stop up my heart.

It wasn't long before dawn crept in through the windows. As reluctant as I was to start the day, I climbed from my loft, lit the fire in the stove, shoved my feet into my boots and stomped outside, my breath visible in the air as I made my way to the barn and pulled a stool up to Mandy, our one cow who gave a sorry amount of milk. She cast her mournful, brown eyes at me as if she too was sad to see this day begin.

When I returned with the milk bucket and a handful of eggs, Mama was seated at the table in her brown muslin, her hands clasped and her head bent in prayer. Mama had lustrous hair that reached past her hips and when she twisted it up on her small head, as she had this morning, it took on a life of its own, moving and spilling every which way since she never used enough hairpins.

I couldn't hear what her prayers said, but her mumbled words soothed me as I went about heating milk, cracking eggs and grinding coffee. By the time I set breakfast on the table, the fog had burnt off and a strip of sunlight warmed Mama's face through the window, her skin smooth and tight over her cheekbones, her lips moving silently around the hard lines of her mouth. Even in early spring there was a dark tint to her skin that she told me I was lucky to be born without.

She finished her prayers and opened her eyes, blinking and squinting as if startled to see the sun shining. "I hope your papa had the decency to say goodbye to you," she said, emotion threatening to crack her steady voice.

I hooked an egg on the end of my fork. "He did."

Mama was as tough as she was compact, and I knew she wouldn't cry in front of me. "Good." She poured warm milk into her coffee. In the deepest place in my heart, I hoped she was going to tell me her plan to get him back. Instead, she said, "The ground's thawing. We should get the peas planted."

It was hard to eat, but I forced my eggs down for Mama's sake, keeping my eyes on Papa's violin case resting against the wall. The only pure happiness he knew was in that violin, and he'd left it behind for us.

After breakfast, Mama shut herself in her room and I went out to dig up a row of dirt in the garden. I hadn't gotten a single pea in the ground before Mama came out and thrust a letter at me.

"You can finish the planting later. I need you to walk into town and post this letter for me." She held out two pennies. "For postage."

"Who you sendin' a letter to?" I asked, brushing dirt from my hands and slipping the pennies in my skirt pocket.

"My sister, Marie, in New York City." I'd never heard mention of a sister in New York

City. Mama and Papa said their families were too far away to bother with. "Go on now."

"Yes, ma'am." I slipped the thin envelope into my coat pocket, tightened my bootlaces and headed down the path.

The road to town was still frozen in the shady spots so I managed to keep my boots out of the mud. It took over an hour to reach the wide, main street of Katonah where the houses bumped up next to each other, like folks couldn't stand the idea of being alone. I couldn't stand the thought of being that close to anyone. I didn't have much interaction with strangers and it made me nervous being in the post office. The postman wore round spectacles and a funny hat. He smiled and said *what a fine day* it had turned out to be as I wordlessly slid the letter and coins across the counter. Maybe fine for you, I thought, hurrying out.

After Mama went to bed that night, I put out the fire and set Daddy's violin case by the door before going to the mantel and opening the little glass door to the front of the clock. I watched the pendulum swing for a minute before holding it still, stopping the hands at 8:32. When Papa came back I wanted him to see that the clock didn't just stop for dead babies, it stopped for real living people who left too.

Once a week Mama sent me to town to check for a return letter from her sister. She warned me there was no telling how her letter would be received. "You're old enough to know the truth of my family," she said. Turns out Mama grew up in New York City and fell in love with Papa when he came to sell apples from his papa's farm. I couldn't imagine Mama anywhere but this cabin. "I was quite the city girl, at one time." She smiled.

When the fall apples ended, Papa came down with Christmas trees piled in his wagon. Mama said he made any excuse he could to see her, and when she turned fifteen he offered to marry her, but her parents didn't want her leaving the city. Her mother wailed in protest and her father beat the daylights out of her. When Mama said she was going anyway, they threw her clothes in the street and turned their backs. After that, she told me she never dared write them. The only family member she'd heard from in the seventeen years she'd been gone was her sister, Marie, the eldest who'd cared for Mama when she was little. If anyone would help us, Mama said, she would.

Sure enough, we got a letter — it was mid-August by then — crinkled, Marie wrote, from her soaked tears. My grandparents were no longer alive and Marie said we were to come to her as soon as possible, that she'd been waiting her whole life for the return of her baby sister.

A week later, I stood in the shade of the crabapple tree, watching Mama lead Mandy down the road. The cow's thoughtful, sad eyes seemed to know she was going to be sold off and replaced with a shiny leather bag and a lumpy package wrapped in butcher paper. When Mama came home, she held the package out for me like she'd won a prize, her unruly hair scattered around her face. Since the letter from her sister came, she'd been happy in a way I only remembered when Papa would press his hands over her swelling stomach.

As I peeled the paper back, it crackled with newness, revealing a square of cream-colored fabric sprigged with yellow flowers. The heavy material tumbled to my feet as I held up a tailor-made dress. The waist was cinched, the sleeves and collar edged in yellow satin. I'd never owned anything so beautiful. Mama's eyes leapt with excitement and I hoped she would think the tears in mine were from happiness, when what I was wondering was if every good moment in my life would be filled with sorrow since

Papa wasn't there to share it with me.

"You need a proper dress for the city." Mama flicked the hem of the one I wore. "Can't let your ankles show. You're a woman now."

Our last morning at home, Mama and I washed the breakfast dishes, put out the fire and left the house as it was. Marie wrote that there was little room and we weren't to bring anything but a change of clothes, clothes Mama had packed carefully in the newly purchased bag that she now lifted over one shoulder as she shut the door behind us.

I thought of the clock I'd never rewound, and Papa's violin case resting against the wall. "How will Papa know where to find us?" I said.

From the look on her face, I knew she thought it was a silly notion he'd come for us. To appease me, she said, "He knows my family name. He'll find us if he wants to."

I didn't look back as we walked past the crabapple tree and the stump where Papa and I had sat in the moonlight waiting to shoot coyotes. I was glad to focus my attention on the wonders of an unknown city and an aunt who cried for you, but I was still afraid. Afraid we'd never come back and I'd never see Papa again. Afraid I wouldn't be able to take care of Mama like he asked.

I should have paid more attention to that fear. Fear, I've learned, can be a very useful thing. If I could have seen what was in store, I would have endured that quiet, lonely cabin for the rest of my days. But life's a blind business, none of us can see up ahead, and none of us would move forward if we could. So, there you have it: Mama and me walking straight into our damnation while I took care to lift my new dress out of the dirt.

"You look lovely," Mama said, and I smiled.

There was so much hope in that dress. Maybe a little hope is all it takes to blind us.

# CHAPTER FIFTEEN:
## JEANNE

Every year since Effie's birth, Emory and I had been told that it was only a matter of time before we lost her, and yet she kept growing. Doctors said we were lucky, blessed, but even though her survival was exceptional, her condition was incurable. It was unlikely she'd see her thirteenth birthday. And yet she had. The fact of Effie's inevitable death had become a way of life, moving from a fear at the front of my mind, to a nagging dread in the back. It was a feeling I was used to and as often happens with things we become used to, I stopped paying attention.

The day my daughter Effie went missing, October 16, 1913, was now seared into my memory, a physical pain in my temples that persisted long after the police stopped looking for her. Luella's loss was at least explainable, whereas Effie vanished into thin air.

Everything about that day was vivid and

clear, the pictures in my mind vibrating with urgency as I dug into the depths of my memory, convinced I could uncover that one, overlooked detail that would lead to the whereabouts of my little girl.

I was in the garden digging up my calla lilies for winter when I felt the first drops of rain. Tucking the last bulb into the tray of dirt, I hoisted myself from my knees and called for Velma. She emerged from the back door of the kitchen, looking austere even with a bloody chicken gizzard dangling from one hand. She moved like a tornado in the kitchen and could get anything done in a small amount of time.

"Yes, Mrs. Tildon?"

The gizzard swung in the air and I watched a drop of blood hit the stones at Velma's feet — afterward, this particular memory would shimmer, a single splat of red blood on the stones next to the clear, pinging drops of rain.

"What time is it?" I untied my gardening apron and pulled it from my shoulders.

"Going on about four, I believe." Velma jutted her chin toward the excavation in the garden bed. "It's awful cold to be doing that. You ought to get Neala. She knows a thing or two about gardening."

"Oh, no, that's quite all right. I prefer to

do it myself." I never let anyone touch my lilies. "If you'd be so good as to bring the tray into the basement for me. And Emory won't be joining us for dinner, so you need only set the table for two."

"Very well, ma'am. He working late again, is he?"

"Not tonight. He'll be gone for a few days. Until then," I forced a smile, "you'll have a lighter load with only Effie and me to feed."

Velma nodded, keeping quiet. I hadn't told her any details about Luella's vanishing, but I was sure she had her ideas.

"If you'd be so kind as to send Margot up to my room, I'd like to change for dinner. You can give these to Neala for washing." Steering clear of the chicken gizzard, I handed her my apron and gloves and went around to the front of the house, noticing that the abelia bush was crushed on one side, as if someone had fallen into it. *I have to remind the gardener to trim it up properly,* I thought, entering the front door and mounting the stairs to my room.

Faithful Margot was already waiting for me, her gray eyes set in her hard face like silver coins, her dark hair in a coil at the back of her head. Margot had been with me since I was fourteen and I'd always confided in her. Consequently, she knew all about Luella.

"I don't know how you bear it, madam," Margot said, helping me into my evening gown and fastening the hooks at the back.

"Not very well, I'm afraid." I smoothed the front of my dress. "Why am I even bothering to dress for dinner? I won't be able to eat a thing until I hear from Emory."

"Well, you should try. Keep up your strength." Margot took a comb from the vanity and fastened it in my hair.

"I'm sure I'll need all the strength I can get when Luella returns. I can't imagine how I'll handle her," I said, even though my argument with Emory yesterday had planted a new seed of confidence in me. Despite his resistance, he'd listened to me and had gone to Maine to persuade Luella to come home after all.

In the hallway, I stopped at Effie's door and gave a gentle knock. "Effie, dear? I'm headed down to dinner." There was no answer and I pushed the door open. "Effie?"

The room was empty. My daughter's satchel of schoolbooks had been dropped on the floor at the end of the bed, and her desk chair was yanked to one side with an uncapped pen on the edge of the desk threatening to roll off. How careless, I thought. It would leave an ink stain on the rug. Walking over, I capped the pen, slipped it into the drawer and turned to leave when I noticed a note on Effie's pillow. Anxiety rose at the memory of the last note I'd found on her pillow. I snatched it up, telling myself it was nothing more than a silly poem or piece of writing.

*I've gone to get Luella. If you want me home, you have to bring her home too.*

I pressed a hand over my mouth, stifling my panic. What in Heaven's name did Effie mean? How could she have gone to get Luella? This was absolute madness.

Hurrying down the stairs to the telephone in the front hall, I lifted the brass receiver, abruptly setting it back down when the operator came on, frantic with confusion. Who was I going to call? Emory was unreachable. There was no chance I was calling my mother-in-law. I pitched forward, the runner beneath my feet blurring. I needed to calm down, to think.

Rummaging in my purse for a cigarette, I realized with increasing shock that all of my money was gone. Not a single dollar remained, just Luella's letter in the side pocket where I'd jammed it after my fight with Emory. Oh, dear god, Effie must have found the letter. Had she taken my money and gotten on a train all by herself? If she had a fit no one would be there for her. No one would know what to do.

Dropping my purse, I snatched up the telephone. This time, when the operator came on I said, "Get me the police department straightaway."

Sergeant Price came right over — a thick-set, authoritative-looking man, just what one hoped for in a sergeant, with soft eyes that indicated an understanding of a mother's heart. I gave him Effie's note, told him that she'd gone into my purse, seen Luella's letter and taken money for the train, at which point I explained about Luella and asked directly that he keep the information out of the papers. Promising discretion, the sergeant asked if I had a photograph of Effie. I gave him the one on the bookshelf, taken last Christmas of both girls and me. I looked pinched and somber. Luella stood to one side bursting with youth. Effie was on the other side, a wisp of a figure, so pale and thin it hurt to look at her.

The sergeant slipped the photograph into his breast pocket, promising to keep it safe. "We'll get word to your husband just as fast as we can," he said. "Now, I know you can't help worrying, ma'am, but a young girl

255

traveling alone on the train isn't the worst thing that can happen. The porters are good at keeping an eye on them. I'm sure she'll be just fine until we can bring her home."

It would have been useless to sleep that night. To be suddenly without both my daughters was paralyzing. All I could do was sit at the window pleading with the starless, godless night.

How had I missed so much? The girls had been visiting the gypsy camp right under my nose. And now, Effie — my assumed innocent youngest — had snuck into my purse, stolen from me and gotten onto a train out of the city. Had she known where Luella was all along and been lying to us? Maybe she was lying about her blue fits too? Only a week ago, I saw her doubled over in the yard, but when I questioned her she told me she was searching for leaves to press into her botany notebook. I pictured the darkening circles under her eyes and how thin she'd grown. I thought it was because she missed her sister, but maybe her condition was worsening and I'd failed to notice?

Out the window, the darkness became a chasm. I felt pulled toward it, sucked downward into a blackness I would never be able to claw my way out of. The night I caught fire came back to me, the sense that

I was being devoured. I saw the flames rising up my skirt, felt the pulsing heat of their consumption. Only this time, there was nothing to beat out, no way to stop it. Sweat broke out on my forehead and I yanked off my gloves and gripped the windowsill. I was out of all reason. "Get ahold of yourself," I said out loud, my voice dropping like a stone in the empty room as I stood up, tapping the back of my hand like I used to when counting the seconds of Effie's blue fit.

I'd compose a letter, I thought, something practical and tangible. It had been months since I'd written my brother. I never told him about Luella. I couldn't bear to admit my failure. I'd planned to tell him when it was all over and mistakes had been rectified, but things were only getting worse. I scribbled a jumbled, incoherent letter, telling Georges everything, even Emory's indiscretions. It was too much. I crumpled the paper and tossed it in the wastebasket.

Pulling my chair back to the window, I wrapped a shawl over my shoulders and sat watching the rain gather speed and start battering the glass. Maybe I was being punished for leaving my brother in the hands of a mother who tormented him. Now I was being tormented.

For hours I sat running my fingers over the pits and grooves on my hands, listening to the wind wail around the house. Where was Effie in this torrent?

All that night I waited for the telephone to ring, fear traversing my body in small waves. The rain would ease up and then start in again, the wind howling like a rabid dog. Not until the wan light of dawn crept into the sky did the peal of the phone echo through the house.

I tripped down the stairs and grabbed the receiver. "Yes?"

The line crackled over a woman's voice. "Mrs. Tildon? I have a Sergeant Price on the line. Would you like me to put him through?"

"Yes, yes of course."

More crackling, and then the sergeant's husky voice. "Good morning, ma'am, Sergeant Price here. I hope you got a bit of sleep. Can't say I got any on this end."

"Not a wink, but it's no matter. What news? Did you reach Emory? Is Effie with you?"

There was an excruciating pause, and then, "A girl matching your daughter's description was seen boarding a train to Boston, but no one on the other end recalls seeing her get off. I have an officer in

Portland who's waiting to see if anyone matching her description shows up. It's a small station. She wouldn't be missed. That same officer is on the lookout for your husband to make his return trip."

I closed my eyes, pressing my thumb and forefinger to the lids. I had to keep my head. "Where would my daughter have spent the night?"

"She had money. I imagine she was smart enough to get herself a room."

"A room? She's a child! What hotelier in their right mind would give a child a room? Has no one in Boston reported a child wandering on her own?"

"To be fair, ma'am, the girl is thirteen. It's a shame, but many girls that age are on their own, circumstances not being so good at home, if you gather my meaning."

"Well, not my child!" I held on to the table, my nails clawing the wood.

"I'm just saying it wouldn't look that unusual, is all."

I could no longer hold the phone to my ear. "Have Emory call me the moment he arrives at the Portland station."

"Yes, ma'am." Static buzzed over the wire. "There's one more thing."

I wasn't sure I could handle one more thing. "What?"

"Your daughter Luella is not in Portland."

"What do you mean? Of course she is. The detective brought us a letter from her."

"She was there, but it seems they moved on a few days ago. Packed up and drove out, as gypsy folks tend to do."

A surge of fury at my eldest daughter overshadowed my fear for my youngest. *If anything happened to Effie . . .*

"We can track them down," the sergeant was saying. "But it might take time. So far we haven't found anyone who knows which direction they were headed."

"No," I said, firmly. "I don't care where they've gone. You put every bit of your resources into finding Effie."

"Yes, ma'am. We're doing the best we can. She's our top priority."

The following day, Sergeant Price escorted Emory home. When my husband walked through the door, I expected him to look willful and disbelieving, like all those times when we were told Effie wouldn't live. Instead, he looked stricken, grasping me in his arms as if he'd feared I'd be gone too. "It's going to be all right," he breathed into my hair, trying to convince himself as much as me. "She's going to be all right." He squeezed so hard the air pinched in my lungs. I let him hold me, struggling to remember how we had once loved each other. His chest was as wide and taut as the first time he held me, the smell of his orange-scented hair oil and his hand on the back of my head the same, and yet I felt nothing of the light-headed intoxication that came from his affection. I felt suffocated.

When he released me, I could see an apology forming on his lips.

"Don't." I pressed my finger to his mouth. "Not now."

In the parlor, Emory sat beside me on the couch holding my hand. The sergeant stood before us, rigid, militaristic. The rain had stopped and the sun shone through the sheer curtains, collecting dust motes in its wavy streaks. As the sergeant spoke, I focused on the tiny particles floating in slow motion, glinting and dancing, this beautiful, mysterious world existing only in a beam of light.

He told us that there was no news of Effie, other than a lone witness who reported seeing a girl matching her description boarding a train to Boston. "Many young girls fit Effie's general description and witnesses might be easily confused. There is no way of knowing for certain if the girl that was seen was your daughter, or not. At this point, we have no real evidence of her whereabouts."

I pulled my hand from Emory's and stood up, moving around the room, a sharp pain hammering at my temples.

"What do we do now?" Emory cried, at a loss for the first time in his life. "There must be something we can do."

"We'll keep searching, of course, but I advise you hold a press conference. Get as much publicity as possible. Offer a reward for any information leading to your daughter's return. It'll bring a lot of false sightings, but we'll weed those out. All it takes is one good lead. I'd say it's your best chance."

I steadied myself against the bookshelf, staring at the empty picture frame wondering what the sergeant had done with the photograph.

"Jeanne?" I heard Emory's voice, but didn't answer. "Jeanne, did you hear the sergeant?"

"Yes, yes of course I did."

"It will be all over the papers."

I felt a cool anger. "That's never been my concern. It's been your and your mother's." I moved to the window. It looked bright and cold outside. "And what of Luella? What do we say about her?"

Sergeant Price cleared his throat. "There's no need to bring her into it, at least not into the papers. I've no doubt we'll find her soon enough."

"I appreciate your confidence, Sergeant, but you don't know Luella." I tugged at the curtain, wishing it would come crashing down. "Effie's a sick child, did you know that? We don't have time for all of this. Her heart is failing." Flames were consuming me again, heat rising up my neck, setting my face on fire. I pressed the backs of my gloved hands to my burning cheeks. "There isn't time." I breathed heavily. "We don't have enough time."

"Jeanne," Emory spoke as if easing me away from the edge of a cliff. "Effie's going to be fine. We have to stay reasonable if we're going to get through this." He was right behind me, loosening my fingers from the curtain and I couldn't decide whether I wanted to sink into his touch or slap his hand away.

The sergeant set his hat on his head. "Begging your pardon, I'll be taking my leave. I'll schedule that press conference for tomorrow, if you've no objection. Best to move quickly on these things."

"Yes, of course, first thing in the morning," Emory said, wrapping his arms around me.

The next morning, I stood in the back of

Emory's office on 22nd Street watching reporters from the *Times,* the *Tribune,* the *Herald* and even the *Boston Sunday Herald* scribble down the one-thousand-dollar reward being offered for any information leading to the whereabouts of Effie Tildon, a thirteen-year-old girl weighing ninety-eight pounds with dark brown hair and hazel eyes. The reporters were eager and hopeful.

"It should only be a matter of days before she's found," one of them reassured me.

I did my best to believe him.

# CHAPTER SIXTEEN:
## EFFIE

*Escape,* I mouthed into the dark as I ran my hand over the notches I'd engraved under my wooden bed frame with the tip of my hairpin. Thirty-eight notches for thirty-eight days, and no one had come for me. When Mable and Edna first proposed escaping out the window, it seemed simple enough, but as the weeks went by I realized it was nearly impossible. We were watched at all hours of the day, save for bedtime, but at that hour the door to the room was locked and the keys secured on a massive ring attached to a belt under Sister Gertrude's habit. One would have to strip her naked to get at them, or leap out the window on a Saturday afternoon under the sisters' watch, neither of which would get us anywhere.

My only real hope was that my parents would come for me. For the past five weeks I'd anticipated one of the sisters appearing unexpectedly in the doorway of the laundry, or dorm, to tell me that they'd made a terrible mistake. "Your father is here," they'd say, humble with regret. "He's waiting in the front hall for you."

But, my father hadn't come.

In the bed next to me I could hear Edna's heavy breathing and I closed my eyes and tried to imagine I was at home in my soft bed with Luella. But it was too cold to pretend the warmth of a body next to me and I sat up, taking in the bare room and rows of beds, letting the longing for home and my sister twist and knot inside me.

It was a useful pain. My desire to get back to them motivated me out of bed each day. In the first few weeks it was solely because I yearned for them, but now a tinge of anger drove me forward. Not knowing the truth of what had happened to Luella, or why no one was coming for me, was infuriating. More and more, I felt convinced that my sister had left me for the gypsies, and that my parents kept it from me to hush up the scandal. Keeping secrets was Daddy's specialty after all. My parents lying to me was no surprise, but to think Luella hadn't trusted me enough to tell me where she was going, and not being able to confront her or ask her why, was agonizing.

The shadows of tree branches stretched over the ceiling, reflections of an outer world I could no longer reach. I thought of the simplicity of a tree branch, and of all the things I took for granted, pen and paper even more so. The House of Mercy was a world unto itself, a thing of cold entrapment, boredom, mindless physical labor, spiritual practice, redemption, cleansing of our souls and sins. And hard work, mostly just hard work.

I had done my best to keep up, to blend in. It was clear that there were things I should know, but didn't. Girls gave meaningful looks to each other that eluded me. They had phrases and a slang language all their own. Most of them came from the factories and tenements, places I'd only seen from the seat of my car — a matrix of laundry lines strung between skeletal buildings, underclothes flapping in the breeze, women leaning from windows to shout to one another, children in the street, everything dirty and raw and exposed. It struck me that I'd never once made up stories about those people. They were less real to me than my ghosts. Even the gypsies had been more familiar and approachable. The tenements were something you turned away from.

I'd tried to approach Suzie Trainer, thinking she was the one girl I could confide in, but she'd leaned into my face and whispered aggressively, "You've already made an enemy of Sister Gertrude, don't make one of me." No one at the Chapin School spoke like that. She'd clearly found a way to blend in. "Go on." She'd swatted her hand at me as if slapping away a bug, and I'd blurted out, "I need to get a message to my parents," thinking, for some stupid reason, she'd know how.

She laughed, as if I'd asked for something trivial, indulgent, like chocolate pudding. "How am I supposed to help you? I haven't spoken to my parents since they locked me in here. If you don't want trouble, you'll keep where you came from to yourself. Fit in. That's the only advice I'll give you," at which point she shoved me into the wall and walked away.

Later, I'd learn that Suzie Trainer was one of the "good girls." The pious, earnest girls — even the ones who faked it — got certain privileges, an extra blanket, heftier portions at dinner, some were even allowed into Sister Gertrude's private quarters. What went on in there, no one was certain, but we were sure it involved extravagances like cookies and tea.

I wasn't one of the good ones, my first night in here ruined any chances of that, but I wasn't a dissident either. As usual, I was suspended in between, sticking to neither identity. For the most part, I wasn't thought of at all. A weary look might be cast in my direction, but I was flimsy, meek and unthreatening, which made me easy to ignore. At least at the Chapin School I'd been Luella's little sister. In here, I was invisible. I envied these girls their camaraderie, their womanly bodies and filled-out identities, their selfdom.

The Irish girls stuck together, as did the Italians, Russians and Romanians. Everyone kept to their roots, as if the borders of countries still divided them. Only Mable and Edna were a world unto themselves. I didn't know their ethnicities, but it didn't matter. They were competent, resourceful. They didn't need anyone. The smattering of girls who thought of themselves as American, like Suzie Trainer, also stuck together. But Suzie squashed any hope I had of belonging with them. "You don't know me, got it?" she snarled. "Don't sit near me at dinner or chapel. And if you so much as look my way . . ." and her eyes became tight slits, "I'll make your life *miserable.*"

*Misery,* I thought, was relative. The longing for my family had become a permanent bruise in my chest. My arms trembled with exhaustion. My lower back ached and my legs were so sore it hurt to walk. The hot water in the vat stung my cracked, bleeding knuckles, and no matter how fast I scrubbed, there was always another pile in front of me. My heart raced with the exertion. After the first few weeks my blue fits became a daily occurrence, and I would squat down next to the vat with my head between my knees until I could breathe again.

It was quickly understood that I was too weak for scrubbing and Mable put me on sorting. "Not out of any kindness, mind you," she assured me, escorting me to a table piled with laundry bags. "A girl who can't keep up brings us all down, so don't mess this up."

Mable speaking to me at all was a rare occasion. There had been no further talk of escape. At first, I had the wild fantasy of stealing pen and paper from Sister Gertrude's chamber and sneaking a letter to one of the laundry boys, but the wagons didn't drive up far enough to the house for me to attempt it.

*Slaves* were how the girls referred to themselves, stating how much money the laundry brought in with presumption. Six thousand a year. "Peeves me washing rich folks' laundry by the ton." Edna flung herself down on her narrow bed, addressing Mable in the bed across from me as if I wasn't there. "The sisters collect the money while we clean bloodstains out of them posh bloomers!"

"Don't let the sisters catch you saying so," Mable said.

We all knew how the sisters looked for opportunities to whip and gag us. There was talk of straitjackets, and being sent to the pit, a windowless room in the basement where you were forgotten for weeks. A wide-mouthed Russian told me that a girl had died down there. "When the sisters found her, she'd coughed up blood all over the floor and now they say she haunts the place."

Tonight, past the moon shadows, I looked for that girl's ghost in the rafters. Maybe she'd keep me company. Thirty-eight notches for thirty-eight days, and no one had come for me.

Needing to pee, I tossed my covers off and slid the chamber pot out from under my bed, crouching over it and peeing as slowly as I could so as not to make much noise. There was nothing quite as humiliating as squatting in a room full of girls looking for opportunities to ridicule you.

When I was done, I crept into the hall and slid open the window, cold air chilling my arms as I tipped the pot out. The world seemed motionless. Maybe time had stopped, and my life would be right where I left it when I got out of here, I thought, sliding the window shut.

A muffled sob startled me and I turned to see a sniveling girl, no older than six or seven, standing in the doorway of the children's dormitory. She tried to say something, but choked on her words and I shook my head fiercely at her. If someone heard us, we'd both be in trouble. Stifling her sobs with a hand to her mouth, she hiccupped through her fingers, "I wet myself," her desperate eyes planting a seed of empathy into my belly.

I glanced down the hall at Sister Gertrude's closed door and with a finger to my lips, motioned the girl to follow. We tiptoed into my dormitory where I helped her out of her wet nightgown, guiding her twiggy limbs through the big, flapping sleeves of a dry one I'd found from the wardrobe. Her pale form was gossamer in the moonlight, bones protruding through paper-thin skin. When she dropped her arms, she looked like a bug-eyed moth about to take flight in her oversized nightdress.

I shooed her back to her room, but she stared at me with huge, dark eyes. Ignoring her, I went back to my bed, but her soft flapping feet followed. I widened my eyes and jerked my head toward the door. Instead of heeding me, she climbed into my bed and pulled the covers to her chin, her eyes plastered to my face.

There was nothing to do but shove the girl's wet nightgown under my mattress and climb in next to her. I'll admit it was comforting having her small, warm body beside me. She rolled over and tucked her knees against my thigh, blinking slowly until her lids dropped shut.

I waited until I was sure she was asleep before lifting her out of my bed, my skinny arms quivering under her weight. In the children's dormitory, I found her empty bed and laid her down, then tiptoed back to mine, remembering to collect my abandoned chamber pot on the way.

The next morning, I lingered behind until I was the last left in the dormitory, at which point I quickly pulled the girl's nightdress from under my mattress, stuffed it under my chemise and tied it around my waist, pulling and smoothing it out as best as I could before hurrying to chapel. It was nerve-racking, but also slightly thrilling having this nightdress secretly tied around my middle. I could only hope no one noticed the extra bulk or the sour smell of urine.

At breakfast, I spotted the girl three tables over, her head bent over her oatmeal. I tried to catch her eye, but she never looked up.

It was only after I made it to the laundry that I realized I couldn't possibly get the thing washed and dried without someone noticing. I became even more anxious when I saw Mable approaching with a cryptic look and told me I was to find her in the chapel room tomorrow night. If she knew I was hiding something, she didn't say.

I wore that smelly, damp nightdress all day and by bedtime all heroics were gone and I felt ridiculous slipping it off and shoving it back under my mattress. The little girl would just have to wear the too-big nightgown and hope no one noticed it was missing from the wardrobe. If discovered, it was not something that would go unpunished.

It was chilly and I pulled the covers over my head and breathed into my hands to warm them. Sneaking the nightdress reminded me of the time Luella and I snuck into Mama's room and tried on all her dresses, silk and lace hems dragging over the rug as we pranced around. We squeezed the little ball on her glass perfume bottle, dousing ourselves, the air, and dipped our fingers into pots of rouge and creams and powders. Naturally, we were caught. The perfume alone would have given us away. Remembering Mama's face when she discovered us made me smile. She'd tried to look fiercely angry, but had burst out laughing, delighted that we were playing at being her.

A poke to my shoulder startled me out of my reverie and I pulled the covers back. The little girl from last night stood over me, her eyes like misplaced buttons in her shrunken face, her arms wrapped around her skinny, shivering chest.

"Did you wet your bed again?"

She shook her head and climbed in next to me as if this were routine. I glanced at Mable, who slept with a pillow over her head, and then at Edna whose back was turned to us. The girl pressed her cold hands against mine.

"What's your name?" she whispered, her breath moist in my ear.

"Effie. What's yours?"

"Dorothea." She squirmed next to me. "It's cold. I don't like the cold. Will you tell me a bedtime story? My mommy knew lots of stories but she can't tell them anymore."

"Why not?"

"Because she got flattened into the earth."
She had a lisp and pronounced it *earf.*
"Sometimes she comes into my dreams. Not
pretty like she used to be, but twisted and
lumpy with her face smashed and her hair
burnt up. I won't see her if you tell me a
story."

Sickened by this image, I didn't know how
to respond. How could I erase a burnt face?
Children weren't supposed to know this
kind of violence, at least not in my old
world. In this new one, girls died in base-
ments and mothers were flattened into the
earth. I felt suddenly uncertain any of us
would survive. Then, in the dark, over the
creaking bedsprings and the wind sighing
around the gabled dormers, Marcella's
words came back to me; *you must keep your
imagination alive. That way you will have
somewhere else to look if things turn unbearable.* This was unbearable.

In a hushed voice, I whispered the story
of a gypsy boy named Tray and his selfish
sister Patience and their kind mother,
Marcella, how they played their music and
bewitched two sisters listening at the edge
of the woods. "The sisters disappeared and
they were never found again."

The girl scooted closer and pressed her face in front of mine. "Where did they go? Did the gypsies carry them off?"

"One girl was carried off and the other tried to find her, but that girl had a bad heart and the searching wore it out."

"Did she die?"

"No, but all the blood emptied from the hole in her heart and she became as hollow as a ghost, wandering forever in search of her sister."

"I don't like it," Dorothea said, with child-like frankness. "I want a happy ending."

"I'm not good at happy endings."

"Try."

I smiled. "Okay. The sisters find each other and Marcella creates a magic spell that heals the young sister's heart so she lives forever."

This made Dorothea smile. "Marcella's a good witch. My mommy told me of good witches. Did she have a wand?"

"Of course."

"And was she beautiful?"

"Very."

"If she could heal a heart, then she could heal my mommy's face, couldn't she? My mommy's waiting to heal so that God can take her to Heaven. I've seen the pictures of angels in Heaven and none of them have smashed faces." Dorothea squeezed her eyes shut, screwing up her delicate features in concentration, her whole body tensing. It seemed a long time before she opened them. "I saw her," she whispered, her wide eyes reverent as if she'd really seen her mother. "Marcella made Mommy pretty again. God will be happy now and help her to Heaven. And if I'm good and don't wet my bed, I will make God happy too and He will send Daddy to come for me."

The open trust in her face made me wish I was little again, and that I could still believe in magic. I wondered if I should warn her that no one was coming for us, that stories couldn't be trusted and happy endings were unlikely.

I wanted to tell her about my heart, how when you're dying from the beginning you view the world differently. I'd never been able to explain this to anyone. Since coming to the House of Mercy, I felt abandoned by my own deformity, betrayed by a thing I believed made me strong when it had been a weakness all along. What I really wanted was my sister. I needed to tell her that I was getting worse. My legs were swollen and I woke most nights pinned to my back as if the beams had come down on me. I needed to tell her that I was running out of time.

I should have at least told Dorothea, warned her that there was no magic Marcella to heal the hole in my heart, only a gypsy woman who hadn't told me the truth about anything. *Don't believe my stories,* I should have said. *I believed them, and that belief turned me into the fictional Effie Rothman. When I die, it will be Effie Rothman's death the sisters mark in their book for all of eternity. Effie Tildon will cease to exist.*

I didn't tell her this. I just stared at the cracks in the ceiling, crisscrossing like a complex railway system leading to dead ends. Dorothea's head grew heavy with sleep on my shoulder, and the ghost appeared in the rafters. Only it wasn't the strange dead girl I'd imagined, it was my sister, dangling her pointe shoes from their laces and calling for me to follow her. *Come with me.*

*I can't. I'm stuck, Luella. There's a boulder on my chest.*

*I'll lift it.*

*You won't be able to.*

*I can do anything.*

*It's too late.*

*It isn't. I never believed you were dying.*

*Is that why you didn't take me with you?*

Her shoes rotated in a slow circle above my head. *No. It was just a test, Effie. To prove you were strong enough to follow me.*

*But I failed, just like Mama.*

*You didn't. You simply followed me to the wrong place.*

*Then where are you?*

*I've gone again.*

*Gone where?* There was no answer. *Gone where, Luella? Gone where?*

But my sister was no longer there. In her place stood the apocalyptic lion from Tray's card who stretched out on the beam and laid his head in his paws, the numerous eyes filling his body winking out.

# CHAPTER SEVENTEEN: MABLE

When my mother and I arrived in New York City at Pennsylvania Station, it was like being hit by a tornado — men chugging past like they were their own small locomotives, shiny and fast in black suits and derby hats, train wheels screeching while voices rose and fell in one big shouting match. I stood stunned as air from the train blew up my skirt and I breathed the strong scent of grease and tar and sweat.

Mama hooked her arm in mine, told me to close my mouth and hurry up. She'd grown up in this and had no problem yanking me out into the bright street and up onto a trolley where I held on for dear life, the ground whipping past. Heat blew into my face and I closed my eyes and tried not to throw up, or fall off.

By the time we got off on Mulberry Street, the city grit was crusted on my skin. I read every sign we passed, twisting my head so as not to miss anything: *Frank Lava Gun-smith, Ravioli & Noodle Factory, Bicycles, Café Bella Napoli.* I'd never seen so much stuff in one place: cartloads of vegetables and fruit, baskets of bread and dangling sausages, people and carriages moving every which way and never colliding, as if everyone understood the same unspoken rule about space that I couldn't comprehend. My elbows bumped into every person I passed as Mama apologized for me.

Coming to a halt, she shielded her eyes with one hand and squinted up at a drab, dark brick building. "This is it." She pulled me down a narrow passage squeezed between the buildings, like a chute for pigs, that dropped us out into a large courtyard. The tenements in New York City were unlike anything I'd known. Clapboard siding rose up on all sides filled with windows and balconies, lines of strung laundry dangling between them. A group of grimy, barefoot boys screamed and kicked a ball that went smashing into the wall and bounced back at them. A busty woman with a scarf on her head leaned over a balcony shouting to a woman who stuck her torso out a window and shouted right back. A weary-eyed man sat on a barrel smoking a cigarette, looking as if he'd rather be anywhere else. Another leaned against a brick wall fanning himself with his hat.

The woman on the balcony paused her shouting as Mama called up to her, "Pardon me, I'm looking for Marie Casciloi?"

The woman pointed to an open door near a stairway that rose up on the outside of the building. Why anyone would build a stairway on the outside, I couldn't figure.

"Third floor," the woman said, and went back to screaming at the other woman who ducked her head in the window and slammed it shut.

In time, I came to love that courtyard. As well as my aunt Marie, a short, robust woman with a soft face who wept into my hair and kissed my cheeks whenever the mood took her. I'd never known anyone to weep from happiness. She had five children, three sons and two daughters, who she raised on her own after her husband, Pietro, died in a boating accident. At all times of the day, she'd whisper *Pietro,* with so much longing that it set off a fresh set of tears. Unlike Mama's tears, Aunt Marie's didn't weaken her. Instead, they propelled her into action and she'd bang around the kitchen, or strip the beds with gusto, crying and moaning and laughing all at the same time.

The two-roomed tenement turned out to

be smaller than our cabin. I didn't know so many people could squeeze in so tight together. The walls in the front room were papered in fading tulips and leaves that peeled at the corners and exposed gray strips of plaster. There was a big stove, a sink with cold running water and open shelving covered in cut-out paper and filled with floral china. A narrow table with a red gingham cloth took up the center of the room. An abundance of food, if not space, was at the heart of the Casciloi family. We shared one bathroom, down the hall, with three other families. And it always stank.

At night, the boys moved the table against the wall and shook their bedrolls out over a threadbare rug. Mama and I slept in the back room with Marie and her twin daughters, Alberta and Grazia. The twins were sixteen years old and full of sass, with olive skin and jet-black hair. Mama and I had been given one of the two iron poster beds, which meant the girls now had to sleep with their mother.

"As if it weren't crowded enough already." Alberta glared at me that first day I arrived, turning to the cracked mirror on the bureau and twisting her hair up.

Mama had left me to put away our few belongings while she drank coffee with Marie in the front room. So far, all I'd done was watch my shapely, older cousins tuck in their thin blouses, yank their skirts into place and pinch their cheeks red — the womanliness of it was enthralling.

"Yeah," Grazia said. "The last thing we need is a stinking cousin around. There are already too many of us."

The girls linked arms. "You've made our lives miserable, so we'll make yours miserable," Alberta taunted.

It was my twin cousins who taught me to be cruel. I learned how ruthless women could be long before I learned the wicked ways of men. First thing they did after I unpacked my bag was order me to light the gas lamp hanging from the ceiling.

"You have to turn the knob all the way or else it won't catch," Grazia said.

When I struck the match there was a flash and boom of gas that singed my eyebrows clean off. Mama and Marie ran into the bedroom while I held my face in pain.

"You trying to burn the building down?" Marie cried.

"No, ma'am," I said.

"You girls take care to teach her right, you hear?" she said to her daughters, who nodded and smiled.

They kept right on harassing me. If either

one of them chipped a cup, or stained a sheet, they blamed me. They'd claim they were missing a comb or hairpin, and say I'd stolen it. My drawers would be searched and sure enough, there would be the missing item tucked in with my underclothes. I'd declare my innocence, and one of the twins would start crying at what a wicked liar I was. It amazed me they could produce tears on cue. Aunt Marie would crack my knuckles or swat my behind with a wooden spoon. Afterward, she'd pull me into her plump bosom and kiss my head, crying and saying how sorry she was.

The boys were kinder, especially Ernesto. He'd quietly help me haul the coal bucket and empty the ashes from the stove. In the winter, he showed me how to trick the gas meter by sliding an ice chip in instead of a quarter and we'd have free gas for days.

Ernesto was fourteen and sold newspapers with his younger brother, Little Pietro. Little Pietro was only seven years old and seemed to think the joy of life came from stealing apples. No matter how many times the applecart owner, Mr. Finch, caught him and dragged him home, and stayed to watch and make certain Aunt Marie beat him proper for it, there were always more apples in Pietro's pockets.

Then there was Marie's eldest son, Armando. He was handsome and intimidatingly quiet. He worked as a clerk in a fur factory and wasn't around much. Aunt Marie said it was because of a woman, which made her wail that he was going to leave her. Mama told her it wasn't natural for a grown man to stay at home with his mother. It was natural to find a wife. "I'm here to help you now," she'd said, putting her arm around her sister and kissing her wet cheeks.

Mama was more affectionate with Aunt Marie than she had ever been with me. And yet, when we were out of earshot of others, which was rare, she'd tell me this was temporary and things would get better, even though I'd never once complained. Despite the twins' meanness, I liked the bustle of the place. It was Mama who seemed unhappy, lying awake nights, tense like a dry twig ready to snap.

By winter, our circumstances really began to wear her down. I could see it in her eyes, in her nervous hands and shrinking waist. She'd gotten a job at the shirtwaist factory where the twins worked, and the long days were hard on her. Nine straight hours on weekdays, and seven on Saturdays was grueling. Sunday was her one day off, and Marie insisted the family go to church. We'd never gone to church in Katonah. Mama and Daddy said it was too far, but I figured — even though they prayed — that they'd rather not face the Lord who'd taken all those babies from them.

I imagined it was for her sister that Mama put on a show of pretending to love church, when what she needed was to lie in bed and regain her strength. I told her I'd go to work for her, but Marie didn't believe in girls working outside the home before they were fifteen, and Mama told me I couldn't get my working papers until I was fourteen anyway, which still put me a year out.

Secretly, I was grateful not to work. It was a comfort being with Aunt Marie all day. She'd drag me along Mulberry Street to haggle with the food cart owners. "What is this?" she'd cry, finding the single, sprouted eye on a potato, or a tiny bruise on an apple. "How can you charge for this? It should be free! You expect money for worthless food? I will have to throw away half. Therefore, I will pay only half." She always got her way, the sellers shaking their heads when they saw her coming.

Aunt Marie knew all her mother's Sicilian recipes. We'd scrub the floor clean, then roll out long strips of pasta along the boards, hanging them to dry from the backs of the chairs, Marie talking the whole while. She told so many stories I couldn't keep them straight. But I loved the steady flow of her voice. She taught me to stew tomatoes and bake loaves of bread made from flour as white as snow, the centers soft and squishy, nothing like the dense bread Mama and I had made from ground wheat berries in the cabin.

At night, the family sat around the table — even Armando, who somehow managed to make it home for his mama's cooking — eating and talking, competing to be heard, the apartment warm and smelling of garlic and fresh bread. Marie told stories about Mama and her sisters and all the trouble they used to get into, their behinds welted with their daddy's belt buckle on a regular basis. They'd sing Italian songs I didn't know. The music made me think of Papa, and I'd picture him sitting alone in our cabin with his violin on his knee wondering where we'd gone.

After dinner, even though Ernesto and Little Pietro had been up at the crack of dawn to sell newspapers, they'd head out to Columbus Circle to sell more. Armando would slip away without explanation and Marie would shake her head and settle in at the table with Mama and a fresh pot of coffee. I'd be given a look that I was to give them privacy and I'd spend the evening in my bed with a boring old newspaper while the twins lay on their bed with a confiscated fashion magazine, giggling and angling it so I couldn't see their feminine secrets. I pretended I didn't care, but I was dying to get a look at those glossy pages.

Even with my worry over Mama and the daily tortures from the twins, I was happy. The rowdy life of a crowded tenement filled up the quiet, dead space inside me. The woods of Katonah, the cabin and Papa became distant and dreamlike.

Then I met Renzo.

It was early spring and most of the dirty snow had melted from the courtyard. Armando had moved out for good, and for weeks Marie shuffled about the apartment weeping and wringing her hands, falling to her knees in prayer and kissing the cross around her neck.

One day, she pulled me to my knees next to her and hugged me to her chest, smelling of onions and pine soap. "Thank the good Lord you and your mama came to me. You are my salvation." She pinched my face in her hands, kissing my cheeks with wet lips. "My daughters are hard workers, but selfish, wicked girls. Threatening to quit their jobs if I don't let them go to those dance halls in costumes that cost a week's wages! They can't be trusted. You, you are good. I see it in your eyes. You and Ernesto are all I have. And then there's Little Pietro." She threw her head back. "Always running off, always in trouble. He will be the death of me if the girls don't kill me first." She clasped her hands to her chest and dropped her chin, a prayer of salvation for her children flying from her lips. Then she rose abruptly, went into the bedroom and shut the door. I stayed where I was watching a mouse scurry along the wall and disappear down a crack in the floorboards as Marie emerged in her black church dress. She pulled on her satin gloves and took her straw hat from the hook on the wall. "I'm going out. I expect dinner on the table when I return."

I scrambled to my feet as she shut the front door. Marie had never left me alone in the tenement, and I took in the emptiness, sliding my eyes over the objects in the room feeling deliciously free. I could find the twins' magazines, use their hairbrush, try on their stockings and their Sunday dresses.

Since I didn't know how long Marie would be gone, I decided it wasn't worth the risk and busied myself by slicing onions and potatoes, then putting the meat to stew and setting the bread to rise. During the winter, the sounds from the outside had been reduced to banging feet in the stairwell and distant voices from the tenement above. With the arrival of April, windows were flung open and the courtyard noises echoed up, comforting and distracting, jump rope chants and shouting ball games.

When I finished preparing dinner, I went out to sit in the courtyard and wait for Marie. The ball game had moved into the street and I watched two little girls roll up their jump rope and run away down the alley.

The weather was mild and warm. A patch of sun lay over the bricks where a boy sat on an overturned crate rolling a cigarette. He wore a faded derby hat, with brown, crudely chopped hair sticking out from under it. He gave me an easy smile that filled me with nerves and I quickly looked away, wishing I'd worn my hair twisted up like the twins instead of braided down my back. Ever since I'd grown out of the dress Mama got me when we left Katonah, I'd become acutely aware of my looks. I'd been given a blue, cotton hand-me-down of Grazia's that accentuated my eyes and I had taken to inspecting my shape in the cracked mirror on the bureau.

The boy stood, offering his crate with a tip of his hat. "I'm Renzo."

"Signe," I answered, smoothing my skirt over my knees as I sat on the wobbly crate.

Renzo whistled. "That's no Italian name." He propped a foot on the crate next to me, leaned his elbow on his knee and pushed his hat farther back on his head. "I seen you go in and out of the Cascilois', but you don't belong to them, do you?"

"I do so," I said.

He raised a suspicious eyebrow and lit his cigarette, blowing smoke into the sky and pointing to a window above my head. "I been living in that tenement since I was born and the first time I saw you was a few months back, trailing Mrs. Casciloi up the stairs. So, either I'm blind or you're new, and I ain't blind."

He leaned close, his warm eyes on mine, and a flurry of activity started up inside my chest. I dropped my gaze. "It's my business where I come from."

"Fair enough." Renzo finished his cigarette, crushed it under his foot and sat on the ground next to me with his back against the wall. "If the Cascilois are anything like my family, there are far too many stories anyway. I'd rather sit in silence." Leaning his head against the bricks, he closed his eyes which allowed me a free look at him. He seemed about the age of Ernesto, fifteen, maybe, his features thin and boyish, only without the shadow of hair on his face Ernesto did his best to shave clean in the basin in the front room. Renzo's cheeks were as smooth as mine.

I stood up, resisting the urge to reach out and stroke my fingers over them. "I should get back."

Renzo nodded, keeping his eyes shut. As I went up the stairs to our tenement, a strange feeling moved through me and I felt hot from the inside out.

Every day after that, Marie left the house in her fine black dress and gloves and told me she expected dinner on the table when she returned. She'd come home just before the others, never saying a word about her absence. I suspected she was spending her afternoons in church, since her stories became threaded with biblical references and moral endings. She caressed the cross around her neck like a nervous tic, quoted scripture and prayed on her knees for hours.

I was lonely and bored and took to sinning like crazy while my good aunt was out praying for our souls.

As soon as Marie left the house, I prepared

food for dinner, then hurried into the bedroom to steal a dab of toothpaste from the pot the twins kept hidden under their bed. I'd rub it on my teeth, pinch my cheeks and bite my lips red before making my way to the courtyard. I'd started rolling my hair at night like I'd seen the twins do, and wearing it high on my head with wavy poofs around my face.

Renzo was always waiting. It became a ritual, him smoking with his foot propped next to me on the crate, the side of his worn shoe pressed against my thigh, the leather softening into me, my head dizzy with his presence and the warmth coming off the bricks.

By the time I turned fourteen, spring gave way to a broiling hot summer. Renzo and I no longer sat in the courtyard, but at the table in our tenement, drinking strong coffee like grown-ups. I never asked why he wasn't out working with the others. I didn't care. When his eyes moved from the top of his mug to my face and his mouth formed around a word, all I could think about was the way he kissed me that first time hidden under the stairwell in the courtyard, and all the times he'd kissed me since.

We made plans. We were going to get married and have a two-bedroom apartment all to ourselves, with a full kitchen and hot water that came pouring out of the tap. Renzo swore he'd be nothing like his father. "He's a fisherman and a fool," he said. "Does whatever's asked of him. Says it's better than where he came from and he knows not to complain. I'd complain. He's clean broke no matter how hard he works and comes home smelling of rot." Renzo banged his hand on the table, his hat jumping where it lay next to him. "It's because his English is no good. People don't take him seriously. I was born here, and I'm going to find me a job as a chauffeur driving one of those shiny cars. I heard —" he leaned forward, coffee splashing over the rim of his cup "— if you go to upper Manhattan where the houses are real big, they hire private chauffeurs and give them rooms of their own."

"What about our apartment?" I said, dotting at the spilled coffee with my napkin, worried about explaining the stain to Marie later.

Renzo smiled like he always did when I mentioned my place in his life, and I no longer cared a wink about the stain. "You can be a housemaid and have a room all your own too. We'll sneak into each other's rooms like we do now."

"Sneak?" I raised an eyebrow and he reached out and took my hand, stroking the back of it with one finger. A burning sensation ran through me.

I had only myself to blame for standing up and leading Renzo into the bedroom. At first, he held his hands politely on my hips while we kissed, but it didn't take long before they roamed elsewhere. I understood now how Papa's hands on Mama's waist made her melt into him, why she gave in all those times in spite of not wanting any more dead babies. When Renzo and I finally lay on the sheet with nothing but sticky skin separating us, I knew I had become the worst kind of sinner. One who enjoys it, and knows that no amount of damnation in the afterlife would stop me doing it.

I've paid the Devil back so many times since you'd think God would stop punishing me. Maybe it's because I still don't regret it. Those few months with Renzo — being wrapped up in the summer heat and the sounds of the city being washed away on our breath — took away a sadness I had always thought was the larger part of being alive.

It didn't last. In August of that summer the twins got their final revenge. Grazia discovered one of Renzo's socks on the floor near the bed and scooped it up, dangling it like a prize. "What's this?"

My heart stopped at the sight of it. I shrugged, playing it off. "What does it look like?"

Alberta sat cross-legged on the bed, smiling delightedly. "Mmmm, let's see. Why, I'd say it's a sock!"

Grazia grinned, swinging the thing back and forth. "The strange thing is, it appears to be a man's sock. What man could it possibly belong to?"

They both stared at me, waiting.

"How should I know?" I said, but my face was pink with guilt.

"Oh well," Grazia said, and tossed it onto my bed, the sock crusty with dirt. "Ernesto must have changed in our room. Why don't you give it back to him?"

"He's not home," I said.

"Leave it for him on his bedroll. Tell Mama he misplaced it, and find the other while you're at it."

I glared at her and slunk into the living room. Mama and Marie looked up from the table, but didn't question me as I shoved the sock at the end of Ernesto's bed and hurried back to the bedroom.

The next morning, Ernesto didn't say a word about it and neither did the twins.

When Marie left that day, I searched for the filthy thing, but it was nowhere to be found. I told Renzo about it, but he wasn't worried. A sock was a sock, he said, and who could trace it to him anyway? To be safe we stopped seeing each other for a week. It was torture. I ached with missing him, and was bored out of my skin.

When nothing came of that sock, we figured it was forgotten and Renzo and I took to our old ways, blinded by our need for each other.

Then, on a warm, wet day, we heard thumping up the stairs. The tenement door opened so fast that all we had time to do was grab our clothes from the floor. It didn't matter that I'd never met Renzo's mother. I knew her the moment her wide hips blocked the bedroom doorway and I froze with my dress held to my chest, a light spray from the open window dusting my bare hip. It was the same woman I'd seen that first day shouting out the tenement window. She waved that blasted sock in her hand like a war flag.

Renzo yanked up his trousers and pulled his shirt on with a look of horror. I expected him to say, "Mama, this is Signe and I plan to make right what we're doing and marry her so you needn't worry." He didn't say a

299

word. Not even when his mama slammed her fist into his arm and smacked the side of his head, screaming in an Italian I didn't understand. Renzo cowered and let her beat him like a child, his shoulders heaving. She wasn't a big woman. He could have stopped her if he wanted, and yet he stood letting her smack red welts into his cheeks. I wanted to lunge at her. Fight Renzo's fight for him.

Maybe I should have. Maybe if he'd seen that I was as strong as his mama things would have turned out differently. As it was, I stood mute while she shoved him out the door, glaring over her shoulder and spitting a string of Italian words at me.

To this day I know that woman put a curse on me.

Getting dinner on the table that night was like preparing the last supper. I was so shaky and nervous I thought I might throw up. When Marie came home I couldn't look at her. By the time Ernesto and Little Pietro arrived, followed within minutes by Mama and the twins, I wanted to blurt out everything I'd done and get it over with. That sock was the twins' doing and I knew it. They were sure to tell if I didn't.

Talk went the usual way over dinner. Ernesto was anxious to share how he'd pinned down a man who tried to steal a newspaper, and wrestled it out of his hands. After that, Grazia and Alberta jumped in with a story about a factory girl who was forced to urinate on the workroom floor because she wasn't allowed a bathroom break. It didn't seem like they knew anything about Renzo and me and I wondered if they weren't the cause after all.

"It's disgusting," Grazia grumbled. "They lock us in so they can check our purses and make sure we're not stealing thread."

"Last week a girl was docked a day's wages for a broken needle." Alberta sawed her meat with her knife. "We need Clara Lemlich to lead another strike."

"Don't cause trouble," Marie said. "We can't afford another strike."

"There's only been one!" Grazia cried.

"That lasted fourteen weeks," Marie said. "We can't afford fourteen weeks of no wages."

"It's worth fighting, Mama." Alberta put her fork down as if she was staging a dinner strike. "We didn't get union representation, but we got better wages and that's something."

"So, they dock you double for your mistakes and make up for it," Marie said. "You can't win."

Grazia stabbed her potato and Marie told her to sit up straight and be grateful she had a job.

I looked over at Mama eating as silently as I was. Unlike the twins, she never complained about the cuts on her hands or docked wages for thread and needle use, which sometimes resulted in her *owing* money for a week's work. She wore the same hardened resolve I remembered from the days after she lost a child, the skin under her eyes dark and sunken. I wondered what it would do to her if Renzo's mother came bursting through the door. I could see her forgiving me, no matter how painful, but Aunt Marie, rubbing her cross with one hand as she ate, was likely to kill me.

I excused myself with a headache and went to bed early, looking out my window for Renzo's light across the way. His window was dark. I wrapped myself in the sheet, remembering the touch of his skin and the feel of his wet mouth over mine. I wondered if he was sorry he hadn't stood up for me, or if confronting his mother was worse than abandoning me. Watching him cower under her made me think that he had no intention of marrying me, while the idea of going on without him made me feel desperate.

I closed my eyes and tried to empty myself

of feeling like I did when Papa left, but the face of that nameless baby we buried together rose up in front of me out of nowhere, and at that very moment a real baby began crying in the tenement above like God was sending me a message, its wail rising into a squall. I rolled onto my side and shoved the pillow over my head. I could still smell Renzo in the bed. I wondered why Mama had never asked about that smell, and it occurred to me that I hadn't done a very good job of taking care of her. Papa would be disappointed. Tomorrow, I'd tell her she wasn't to go to the factory anymore. I was fourteen now and I could get my work papers, whether Aunt Marie liked it or not. Getting locked out of a factory bathroom and urinating on the floor seemed a better prospect than being alone in the tenement without Renzo.

It was still raining when I woke the next morning. Dull light filtered through the murky windows, the air warm and heavy as a damp towel. I didn't want to move, but Mama wasn't in bed next to me. Sitting up I saw that the twins' and Aunt Marie's bed was empty too and I pulled myself up.

Still fumbling with a button at the back of my dress, I opened the bedroom door. In the same instant, Ernesto's ink-stained hand caught me across the face and sent me reeling into the wall. I cried out, my eyes landing on Little Pietro who sat cross-legged on the floor with a grin of amusement on his face. Usually, he was the one who got smacked. Marie paced back and forth in front of the stove, her eyes red, the cross around her neck pressed to her lips, sobs issuing between mumbled prayers. The twins sat at the table staring at me with satisfaction. Next to them sat Renzo's mother, the very sight of her knocking the breath out of me.

Then I saw Mama leaning against the front door with our leather bag at her feet.

"No!" I leapt forward. I hadn't thought about being sent away. "I'm sorry. It was a mistake. I'll go to work at the factory. I'll never see him again."

Marie wailed and sank to her knees, burying her face in her skirt while Ernesto slumped into a chair. I could tell that hitting me wasn't his idea and I was sorry he had to do it.

Stepping forward, Mama latched onto my forearm, her eyes steely. "You have disgraced this family. My sister will not have you under her roof, and if I had a choice, I would not have you under mine. You have brought me nothing but shame."

I no longer felt the sting of Ernesto's blow as she pulled me out the door and down the narrow stairs through the alley. Mulberry Street became a haze of shapes and sounds and odors with no meaning. Mama's words, and now her icy silence, sliced open a fresh wound in me. Stumbling behind her straight and unforgiving back, I realized how damning what I had done was. We were on our own now in the city with no one to help us.

# CHAPTER EIGHTEEN:
## EFFIE

Mable leaned against the wall in the room above the chapel with her arms crossed, watching Edna fetch embroidery rings from the basket. When I approached her, she said, "Don't talk to me. Go to the window. I'll meet you there when I'm good and ready."

I did as I was told, watching Dorothea on the rug next to another little girl, their legs sticking straight out as they warmed their feet by the fire. I was worried she might come over, but she only gave a low wave and tucked her hand behind her back.

Keeping her back to Sister Mary, Mable dragged two chairs over and Edna handed her an embroidery ring with a swatch of fabric, not bothering to include needle or thread.

Both girls sat smoothing linen over the wooden rings and cinching these into place. "Lean against the window and make like you're gazing at the stars," Mable said in a soft voice, her face animated, her blond hair pulled into a thick braid over one shoulder. I was glad to sink into the wall and gaze out at nothing. From behind me I heard Mable's low voice. "Tomorrow night is the annual Ladies Associates dinner. It's the best time to make a run for it. The sisters will be distracted and tired, plus they always go to bed early after an event."

I glanced over my shoulder. The glint in her eye was the same as my sister's when she was scheming a daring act of rebellion. "But the room will be locked," I ventured.

Edna pitched forward, with her elbows on her knees, and kept her voice low. "I can get a key. I discovered that Sister Gertrude's not the only one who carries them. I saw Sister Agnes lock the room the other night, and she doesn't wear her key, which means it's most likely in her room, and dear, trusting Sister Agnes doesn't bother to lock hers. I'll slip out during evening prayer, sneak into her room and hide the key under these beauties." She grinned and shimmied her chest at me.

"What if she notices they're missing?" I asked.

"We'll be long gone by then." Mable leaned forward in the same manner as Edna, their heads close together. "Once we're out the window onto the chapel roof, it's a straight drop to the ground. From there we'll have to run to the wall and find a tree to climb. You can climb, can't you?" She cocked an eyebrow at me.

I'd never climbed a tree in my life, but I nodded *yes.* "Good," she said. "Once we're on the other side, we make a run for it. Hopefully it's a dark night. The sisters will waste no time getting our descriptions to the police. There's a woman who houses escapees. 961 5th Avenue. Every girl in here's memorized that address. We just have to get to her before we're caught. Rich as the devil, I've heard, and kind as an angel."

"She's the only one worth praying to, as far as I'm concerned," said Edna. "I heard her speak at a rally once and I'll be if she ain't the most beautiful thing. I heard she employs the girls she can, and helps the others find work. She'll help you no matter what your story, but most of 'em's pitiful anyway, especially yours." Edna slapped Mable's thigh. "At least I was caught stealing a waffle from a vending cart, drunk off my rocker." She spat and cocked an eye at me. "Mable here wasn't even living in New York City when they locked her up. She came for a weekend to visit her aunt and uncle. Isn't that right, Mable?"

Mable kicked the leg of Edna's chair. "Shush up and don't remind me."

"Reminding ourselves is the only way to make sure we don't forget to hate the opposite sex." She pumped her fist in the air. "We've got to march against them so bastards like Mable's uncle don't get away with it. He took the liberty to shove his hands right up under Mable's skirt. The aunt caught him and he swore Mable lifted her skirt up for him. The aunt screamed at her for being a whore and the lying snake of an uncle dragged Mable off and locked her away to get back into the good graces of his devil wife. Never even got permission from Mable's father."

"I'm sure my father wouldn't mind a lick," Mable whistled through her teeth. "They're all the same. Wouldn't go home if I could. This rich lady is my only hope, or the streets, which I'd take any day over the sisters of this place. Why're you in here?" she said suddenly.

"Yeah," Edna said. "What'd you do?"

I thought of telling them the truth. It seemed fitting, as I was about to jump to my possible death with them. But something in me didn't *want* to give them my story. "I was caught with a boy," I said, sticking to the lie I'd told Sister Gertrude.

"You weren't selling yourself on the street were you? You look too scrawny for that," Edna said.

My face went hot and I shook my head. *Selling yourself* was a term I'd only recently understood.

"Ah," Mable crooned. "You've embarrassed her. Lots of girls in here are whores, or drunks. I could tell right away you weren't neither." She stood up and dropped her embroidery ring in my lap. "Put this back for me, would you?"

Edna, always following suit, stood up and dropped her embroidery ring in my lap as well. Linking arms, they sauntered off to join a group of girls gathered around a piano that no one played.

Lying in bed that night, thinking about escaping out a window into the dark terrified me. It didn't seem nearly as easy as the first time I'd imagined it. What if I did break an ankle? The consequences of being caught were far too real now. But what choice did I have? I'd given up hope my parents would find me. The oysterman was the only one who knew I was here. Even if my parents had put a notice in the paper, he most likely wouldn't see it. He didn't seem the type to waste a good penny on a newspaper. The sisters cared little for news from the outside world. I'd only seen Sister Jane — a small anxious woman who looked as if she questioned her faith on a daily basis — read the paper during our Saturday leisure hour.

The good sister reads the headline from *The New York Times,* Missing Girl. The name is familiar, but she doesn't recognize the surname, or the slightly blurred face of the young girl who looks like every other girl around her. She doesn't read on, turning instead to an article about the suffragette, Mrs. Pankhurst, being held at Ellis Island and threatening a hunger strike if barred from this country. Wondering if the suffragettes might be a more suitable calling for her, Sister Jane twists the paper and tosses it into the fireplace, warming her hands on the flames as they leap up.

This is what I told myself, that my parents had tried to find me and failed. Otherwise nothing made sense.

I rolled over, summoning the possibility of escape, picturing my parents' faces as I walked through the door, the shock and weeping. Luella would be there, and we'd fall into each other's arms crying apologies.

Dorothea appeared beside my bed, a slip of a figure in her white nightdress. I scooted over and let her slide under my covers, holding her frail hand while I whispered the best story I could think up, full of goblins and secret spells and fairy magic with a glorious, happy ending.

When I was done I said, "Tomorrow night, I want you to stay in your bed. No matter what happens, you're not to come in here. Okay?"

"Why?"

"Just do as I say."

Her eyes filled with doubt, but she nodded obediently and tucked her arm under the blanket, curling up beside me and closing her eyes. I brushed the hair from her sunken cheek, her lids marbled with blue veins, her face tranquil. I thought of all the nights I'd lain listening to Luella's complaints over her restricted life. What the girls in here wouldn't give for a life like ours, where sneaking off to a gypsy camp was the height of our danger. True danger was seeing your mother's face smashed in. True danger was being fondled by an uncle and unjustly locked away. True danger was being gagged and thrown in the basement by Sister Gertrude. True danger was leaping from a second-story window and making a run for it in the dark.

■ ■ ■ ■

Sunday was the only day we didn't have laundry duty, and the only day the Chaplain, Reverend Henry Wilson — a paunchy, abject man with roaming eyes and a high-pitched voice — graced us with his presence. His sermons were laborious and dutifully boring. He'd fidget at the pulpit, shifting from foot to foot until the sermon was over, at which point he'd slide his eyes around the room in silence, shaking his head at the hopeless task of redeeming even one of us.

The remainder of Sundays we spent reading and reciting scripture. There was a break for lunch, more scripture, dinner and finally evening prayer.

I was shaky with anticipation by the time I slipped into my seat in the chapel. As I repeated the litany of psalms on my transgressions and sins, I was itching to look around for Edna, but kept my eyes down. When we were finally released, I found her mounting the stairs beside me, flashing a triumphant grin. I had the urge to clasp her hand, but imagined she'd fling me into the wall if I dared, so kept my excitement to a quick smile.

The dormitory was frigid now that it was December. Girls no longer lingered in their underclothes, but jumped directly into bed and changed under their covers with a ruckus of chatter and creaking mattress springs. By the time Sister Mary stood in the doorway flashing the lights on and off to silence us, Edna and I were already in bed with our nightgowns pulled strategically over our dresses. Mable lingered, standing at the foot of her bed, looking around with uncharacteristic apprehension on her face.

"Stop it," Edna whispered from her pillow. "You'll draw attention."

"Sister Mary's blind as a bat. She won't see me from the doorway." Mable sat on the foot of her bed, her wool dress sticking out from under her nightgown. "You got the key?"

"Yes."

"Good." She lay down on her bed, keeping the covers tossed off. "I hate Sunday. All that kneeling and praying wears me out more than laundry duty. I'm bound to fall asleep, and Edna, you sleep like a log." She glanced over at me. "Can you be trusted to stay awake?"

I nodded, so jittery and nervous I couldn't imagine sleeping.

"All right then, I'll just close my eyes for a minute." She flopped onto her side and pulled a pillow over her head.

Edna stared at the ceiling. "I'm not falling asleep. Not worth the risk. I'll be the one caught with the key in the morning if no one wakes up."

After a while, despite her effort, Edna's breath deepened, her mouth went slack and her closed lids fluttered in her dreams. I stayed wide-awake, watching a three-quarter moon peek through a corner of the window. It was a brighter moon than Mable wanted, but I wasn't worried. Once I dropped on the other side of the wall, I knew exactly which direction to head home through the woods.

Once the moon reached the center of the window, I slipped out of bed and shook Edna awake. Her eyes flew open and she sat up, wiping a string of drool from the corner of her mouth. Staggering to her feet she snatched Mable's pillow from her head and Mable leapt up, bewildered for only a moment before her small, crooked teeth flashed a white grin. Without a word, the three of us shed our nightdresses and stuffed them under our covers, plumping them up to look as shapely as possible.

Stealing from the room, with Mable hauling a pile of sheets she'd taken from the wardrobe, we edged our way out the door . . . halting . . . listening. The only sound was the hiss of steam through vents, and the occasional creak of a wooden floorboard, and then, "Effie?"

We turned. Dorothea stood in the doorway of the children's dorm room, her hair tangled on one side. She looked dazed. "Where are you going?" she asked, dejected, as if I was running away from her.

"Go back," I said, angrily. She was going to ruin this for all of us. "I told you to stay in your room."

"Christ," Edna swore. "Get rid of her, and make sure she stays quiet." She headed down the stairs, moving quickly. Mable followed, the sheets billowing and trailing from her arms like disorderly ghosts.

"Go on," I said to Dorothea, but she didn't move. I went over and crouched down as her wide eyes filled with tears. "I'm sorry," I said. "If you're a good girl and go back to your bed, I'll try and find your daddy for you, okay?"

She brightened. "You know my daddy?"

"What's his name?"

"Charles Humphrey."

"I'll find him. Now go back to bed."

"Promise?"

I knew it was unlikely, but I said, "Promise," and Dorothea kissed my cheek, quick and soft, and then slipped into the dark room, the edge of her white nightgown fading like a ripple on a pond's surface.

I hurried down the stairs, worried that I was too late and they'd left me behind. But Edna and Mable were still fiddling with the lock on the door to the room above the chapel. The keys clanked and I froze as the metallic sound ricocheted off the walls. It was an eternity before Edna found the right key and the lock finally gave way with a small *click.*

The room was eerie and unfamiliar in the dark as we slipped over to the window where Mable dropped the sheets to the floor. "Tie them tightly. If a knot lets go, we're pancakes."

We shook them out, double knotted the ends and yanked the fabric as tight as we could, the sheets piling up like cording. Slowly, Edna eased the window up as far as it would go. The frigid air curled around us and it occurred to me that we had no coats. The sisters never permitted us out of doors in the winter, so there was no need for them; unless, of course, one was trying to escape into a bone-chilling night. Making a run for it would keep Edna and Mable warm enough, but I wouldn't have that luxury. Once I'd dropped to the ground, I'd have to go at a steady walk or else risk a blue fit.

Edna's full rump rounded in front of me as she leaned out, pushing the loose bars from the siding while Mable held onto one end of the sheet and dropped the rest onto the sharp, rising peak of the chapel roof below.

"You go first." Edna directed this to Mable. To me she said, "I'll go next while you hold the bars. You can slip out after. You're thin enough."

A leg of Mable's was already out the window, her dress hiked to her thigh, her bloomers exposed like a circus performer's pantaloons as she climbed with startling agility over the sill and dropped from view.

Edna nudged me and I leaned out and took hold of the frosty, wrought iron bars, resting my elbow on the windowsill, the wood cracked and splintering with age. The cold snaked up my sleeve and sent a chill down my side. Directly below, Mable sat on the ridgeline lowering the sheets into a crevice between two peaked roofs sloping away at frightening angles.

Edna was not as graceful as her partner. She lumbered one leg up, hauled over the other and then pushed herself out, her chest scraping the siding as she clutched the window casing and lowered herself down. There was more bulk to her than comfortably fit between the bars and she had to shove her shoulder against the side of the building to get out from under them. Mable, with one hand held tightly to the end of the sheets, tried to guide Edna's foot to the ridge, but Edna quickly lost her balance and dropped with a thud onto the ridge. There was a moan, followed by a stifled giggle as the two of them eased their way over the slates.

Neither looked up to see if I was following. I climbed onto the sill, dangling both legs out as I watched Mable slither down until she reached the crack where the two roofs met and propped herself with the bundle of sheets in her arms. Goose bumps rode up my legs and the bottom of my feet tingled. I clutched the bars with both hands and closed my eyes, paralyzed with fear. I thought of the Death card, that skeleton in armor. Tray had said it didn't mean Death. It was the unexpected, loss, misdeeds, lies. I was all those things. If I survived, maybe my outcome, The World, would be waiting for me.

It seemed, then, that I heard the far-off

tune of a fiddle and I opened my eyes and looked up. Cold, bright stars punctured the black sky. The hard light of the moon cast shadows over the field, and the wide swath of the Hudson yawned beyond the trees like a dark blanket tossed carelessly into the night. I was not mistaken. It was music I heard coming faintly over the hillside. The gypsies were here, and they were playing for me.

Easing onto my stomach, I looked toward the door, imagining Sister Gertrude storming through as I slipped over the edge. I lowered myself down, holding on for dear life as a shard of splintered wood jabbed into the center of my palm, a pain I wouldn't feel until later. The bars moved easily away from the crumbling holes in the siding as I pushed my back into them, my arms stretched like taffy, pulling from their sockets as my feet dangled precariously above the ridgeline. Craning my neck, I saw Edna scooting toward Mable on the lower roof. She hadn't waited to help me, and my fingers suddenly slipped. There was a terrifying whoosh of air as I crashed onto my stomach and slid down the shingles. Edna shot out an arm and caught me before I bumped into Mable and sent her flying off the roof with me.

"Blast it, you'll get us all killed!" she spat. "Smaller and clumsier than the both of us. Now hold still and go down slowly."

My heart beat wildly against my bruised ribs. Bracing my feet against the slick shingles, I eased next to Mable who had her dress hiked up and her feet propped against the gutter. Reaching between her knees, she double knotted the end of the sheet to the gutter. "That should hold, as long as the gutter doesn't give way. Edna, you go first. You're the heaviest. If it holds you, it will hold the two of us."

"And if it doesn't?" Our heart-pounding escape was not diminishing the scorn in Edna's voice.

"It's a clean drop to the bottom. You'll be fine. We'll be the ones stuck up here with the sheet come loose. Now hurry up!" Mable brushed a piece of hair from her eyes as she hurled the bed linen off the roof.

Edna gripped the sheet. "Here goes," she said, and pitched over the edge. The gutter groaned under her weight, but held. Mable and I leaned out, watching her swing into the air, then slam into the side of the house and slide down the sheets at a frightening speed until she let go and sprawled on the grass with her arms outstretched. A peal of laughter echoed up to us.

"Shhh," Mable hissed down, but Edna either didn't hear, or care, her laughter crackling into the night. "Hurry down and shut her up." Mable held the sheet out to me. "If you fall and hurt yourself, you're left behind, got it? I'm not stopping for anyone."

I took the sheet in both hands and wriggled over the edge of the roof on my stomach, my shoulder hitting the side of the building as I dropped over. I thought I'd ease down, clasping hand under hand like a dexterous rope climber, but the weight of my body was more than I'd anticipated and I found the cotton bedding skinning my palms as I slid to the bottom and hit the ground so hard I knocked the wind out of myself. I lay in a heap next to Edna whose laughter had subsided into hiccups. Despite my jarred body, a buoyant feeling bubbled up in my chest as I looked into the expansive sky, the grass cool and damp beneath my chafed hands. The stars looked like flickering Christmas lights. I remembered walking home from school with Luella in the early darkening days of December and seeing our tree glinting through the window. Maybe my sister was out here, right now, dancing with the gypsies in the moonlight. I'd forgive her leaving me. I'd forgive her anything to be near her again. We had so much to tell each other.

Catching my breath, I rolled to my knees and stood up, watching Mable leap to the ground and land on her feet as if she had spent her whole life scaling the sides of buildings. She pulled Edna to her feet and without a look in my direction they sprang forward as if a starting pistol had gone off. Their arms flapped from their sides and their skirts ballooned as they tore off into the field. For a split second, I was right behind them, my strength deceiving me until my heart surged and forced me into a fast walk.

It was then I heard the dogs. Not a distant, far-off braying, but a chorus of sharp, biting barks that started up out of nowhere and sounded frighteningly close. Not once had I thought of them until now and the sound sent terror up my spine. The ferocious barking grew nearer and fiercer and I sprinted forward, my heart throbbing, the air chiseling away at my breath. I slammed my fist into my chest, enraged at my heart, at my worthless body, at my gullibility.

I was smaller, weaker, slower. I was their bait.

As the dogs closed in, I watched Edna and Mable's silhouettes disappear into the trees at the bottom of the hill. There was a snapping at my heels and the sound of ripping fabric as a dog tore into the back of my skirt. I collapsed prostrate on the ground, gasping. There was a growl near my ear, and then a man's voice shouting, calling them off with a bark all his own. Here was my chance, I thought, to tell this man my real name, to reclaim my story.

But my words were lost, my intention betrayed by the simple effort of pulling air into my lungs. As I looked up, the edge of the sky dropped down like the lid of an eye closing over me.

The last thing I remember was the tip of a dog's tail slapping my cheek and the sound of a heavy voice praising him.

# CHAPTER NINETEEN: JEANNE

It was the turn of weather that finally broke me, the bitter winter laying claim over the cool of autumn. For the last month my daily telephone calls to the police department, walks through Penn Station and hospital visits were tearless. My quick, staccato steps down platforms and white-walled hallways, the endless, tight-lipped questions I asked nurses and porters, all measured.

I kept myself tightly stitched together until one morning in December, when I woke to see that the wind had ripped every last leaf from the tree in our yard. The bare branches of the oak spanned the white sky like stretch marks, and the frailty of those leafless branches, the permanence of the dead leaves on the frosty ground, filled me with immutable despair. Everything had fallen. Winter was coming, and my girls were lost in the cold. My love for them, my inability to hold them and keep them safe, surged hrough me, blew me wide open like they'd done once as small, helpless infants. I collapsed on my knees with my head to the floor, screaming. I didn't hear Emory leap from the bed, or feel his hands shaking me. All I felt were the cries lacerating my lungs, the air, the walls, until my voice went hoarse and I rolled onto my side in a heap of inconsolable sobs.

When I finally caught my breath, I saw the startled faces of Margot and Emory hovering over me. My husband tried to lift me, but I pushed him away. "I'm fine." My throat was sore, that was all. I held on to the windowsill and pulled myself up, looking at Margot who stood with her shoulders thrust forward, ready to leap at me. Evenly, I said, "It's surprisingly cold this morning. I think I'll wear my wool Tricotine today. If you'd be so kind as to fetch it from my wardrobe."

Margot hesitated, her eyes tracking me as she moved to the wardrobe to retrieve my black dress, severe and somber, a dress of mourning. Emory stood shivering in his thin nightshirt, speechless, staring at me as if I'd lost my mind. I wondered if losing one's children, and losing one's mind, looked the same in a mother.

"Madam . . . are you sure you're all

right?" Margot approached me gingerly, as if I'd crack.

"Yes, thank you, I'm fine. You can go. I'll dress myself." I slid the dress from Margot's arms. "You know, Margot, I can't remember the last time I ate anything substantial. Tell Velma I'd like two eggs, fried, with a piece of toast and cup of strong, black coffee."

Margot nodded, retreating out the door with a fleeting look at Emory who kept his eyes fixed on me.

I dressed in front of the full-length mirror under the confused gaze of my husband. With each fastened button and settled hairpin, I pinched shut the sensation of being torn open. Securing the last hook on my collar, I turned to Emory. I was done with pretense. I was sure of the truth, however hard it was to face. "Effie is dead," I said.

Emory came and put his hands on my shoulders, his touch tender and vulnerable. "We'll find her, Jeanne. She's a smart girl, and she's strong. Wherever she is, she'll get through it like she always has and we'll bring her home."

I shook my head, tears coming again. "We asked too much of her. We didn't see how much the loss of her sister was weakening her. She had a terrible blue fit after Luella left. She was in the yard, doubled over. She convinced me otherwise, but I'm sure of it now. Remember, as a baby when she'd cry and we'd be in hysterics? It was the most frightening thing to watch her tiny fingers and toes turn that ghastly blue. I remember wishing she would die just so I wouldn't have to go through it over and over again. Isn't that wretched?"

"No." Emory looked as lost as I'd ever seen him. "It doesn't matter what you wished, you were always there for her. Yours was the hand she held. I never watched her cry as an infant. I couldn't. I let you worry for both of us. I'm sorry for that." Emory dropped his hands from my shoulders and moved to the wardrobe.

I'd never seen him this defenseless, and I tried to will myself to feel some kind of forgiveness, but I couldn't. I watched him toss off his nightshirt, the hairs on his chest curled into little loops, and thought how absurd it was that we still went about our days performing menial tasks, like dressing and discussing our children in even-tempered tones, as if they were in the next room.

Since Effie's disappearance, we'd spoken of little else. We moved forward, did what was expected, but we were treading water, tiring out. I smoked constantly and ate little. I'd thinned to a wire, from which my shapeless dresses hung. Emory's good looks had slipped into drawn cheeks and puffy eyes. I watched him stuff his feet in his shoes, bending over to lace them into submission, and wondered which of us would drop first.

Emory righted himself, yanking his waistcoat straight, regaining control. "She's not dead, Jeanne. If she collapsed and was taken to a hospital someone would have identified her body from the story in the papers."

I tapped a finger against my ribs. "I can feel it right here. God is punishing me, carving a hole in my heart to match hers."

"Punishing you for what, Jeanne?"

"For not helping her. For not seeing the truth."

Coming over, softening to me in a way he hadn't in years, Emory reached out and slowly drew the gloves from my hands, his fingers on my bare skin startling. "It's not your fault," he whispered.

It was the touch I craved, but it was too late. His desperate attempt in this moment to try and regain what we'd lost long ago disgusted me. I looked down, imagining him holding the smooth, perfect hands of another woman. "God is punishing both of us for your sins."

Emory jerked back, dropping my hands. He looked betrayed, as if the removal of my gloves was a secret weapon that had failed him. "Are you blaming me? Do you think this is my fault?"

"I blame both of us. Effie should have been our priority. We got distracted, and we didn't do right by her. I won't stop looking, I'll just look in the right places this time. I'll seek the medical records from every hospital in New York City and Boston. I won't let our daughter die unidentified, without a proper burial."

"She's not dead," he said, his voice bone hard as he dropped my gloves he still held on the nightstand and headed for the door.

I did not try and stop him.

Sitting on the bed, I shoved my gloves back on feeling unapologetic at the lost moment between us. I didn't care where he was going, or who he gave his attention to. I just wanted my girls back.

Pressing my hands into my thighs, my spine straight, my feet flat on the floor, I wondered who I had in this world to protect me if not Emory. My brother, maybe. I had still not written to him. The guilt over failing my children bled right into the guilt I had for failing to protect Georges when I had the chance, leaving him that drizzly day at the Port in Calais. I'd had to pry his eleven-year-old fingers from the sleeve of my coat while he'd cried, "Jeanne, Jeanne, don't go. You'll never come back and I won't be able to find you."

"Don't be foolish," I'd said. "I'll write."

On the top deck of the ship, the salt air lifting my dress, Emory's arm secured around my waist, I'd watched my mother on the platform below reach out and smack Georges on the side of his head before sinking to her knees, weeping — not for the blow she'd inflicted, but because she was losing me. I was her favored one, cherished and applauded for reasons equally as elusive as her hatred for Georges. By the time the ship pulled away, Georges had stopped crying, and I watched him wipe his nose and give a courageous wave.

In my room, the morning light came through the window and settled over my lap like burnished powder. I thought I had a solid hold, as a parent, on what it was to love and be loved. I'd tried not to love my girls too much, not to smother them as my mother had smothered me, but maybe I hadn't loved them enough.

As I lay down in the heavy sunlight, I heard a small voice, my brother's, as clear as day, calling to me. It was coming from down the hall. I rose, drawn to follow it, to fold Georges in my arms and tell him how sorry I was. Then it was Luella's voice in the lisping high pitch of a child. "Mama, the baby's sick," and then the gasping sobs of baby Effie. A wave washed over me and I held on to the bedpost as if it were the mast of a ship and shook the voices from my ears. I was not insane. There were no children in the hallway. My brother was a twenty-eight-year-old man living in Paris, Luella, a young woman old enough to run away, and Effie . . . maybe the voices were Effie's? Maybe her spirit was trying to reach me?

I stepped into the hall. The feeling of death I'd woken with hung in the oppressive air. I knew a woman, Mrs. Fitch, who held séances to communicate with spirits. I thought it a lot of tomfoolery, but if you needed to speak with the dead what other way was there? I traced my finger along the wall, listening. I needed a medium, someone who had known Effie, and would know how to call her in.

A sudden thought crossed my mind and I hurried downstairs, snatched up my coat and left the house, baring my teeth against the cold as I plunged into the field, heedless of the frost ruining my leather boots. The sun had climbed into the clear, bright sky, but it offered no warmth and my breath fogged in front of me as I crossed the hill toward the gypsy camp. Black tendrils of smoke snaked from the chimney pipes sticking out of the wagon roofs. Children raced around shouting in a game of tag, a band of dogs barking madly at them. A girl in a dull brown coat with red buttons spotted me with a whoop and the game came to an abrupt halt as the children dashed behind wagons, their tousled heads peeking out to watch my approach. The yapping dogs, thank goodness, were tied up. As I neared a wagon, a skinny, wild-eyed boy shot from behind the wheel and flew up the steps, alerting a woman who appeared in the wagon doorway in a brown apron and headscarf, a plump baby on her hip. Her face looked windblown, rough and red, and a small, purplish bruise colored her jawbone on one side.

"Can I help you?" Her eyes were wary.

This wasn't the right woman. The one I was looking for was older, more experienced. "I'm looking for the mother of a boy named Sydney."

The boy poked his head around the woman's skirt and jabbed his finger at a wagon across the way. The woman slapped his hand and he disappeared behind her.

"What do you want with her?" The woman squinted, jiggling the baby up and down.

"Only a word." I turned, picking my way across a muddy patch of grass to the wagon the boy had pointed at. A large woman, with olive skin and eyes as black as coal, stood on the top step as if she was waiting for me.

I started to speak, but she interrupted, "I know who you are," and moved aside expecting me to enter that filthy place.

I hesitated. I'd seen a picture once of a woman getting her fortune told at a round table out in the grass. That would have been preferable, but the woman crossed her arms in a subtle challenge and I pressed my tongue to my teeth and mounted the wobbly steps, stooping under the low door frame into a dark hole of a room. The room — if it could be called that — was warm and smelled of wood smoke. There was a soft hissing sound that made me nervous.

"I'm Marcella Tuttle," the woman said, and shut the door.

"Jeanne Tildon."

"Sit." It was an order, not an invitation.

I sat on a bench along the wall behind a small table. It took a moment for my eyes to adjust and I saw that the hissing was coming from the kettle on a miniature, potbelly stove. The room was surprisingly tidy. Silently, the woman maneuvered her wide hips around the narrow space, spooning tea leaves into a pot and pouring hot water over them, a rich smell rising, something spicy and unfamiliar. A colorful curtain hung toward the back, which I imagined hid a bed. It was hard to understand how anyone lived like this, much less my own daughter.

Marcella set the teapot on the table with a matching mug, beige porcelain with tiny red flowers. She didn't pour the tea, as a hostess should, but sat on a footstool with her hands spread over her knees. I'd never seen hands that big on a woman.

"Don't expect me to read your fortune in those leaves. You wouldn't like what I would have to say," she grinned, toying with me.

I didn't reach for the pot. Tea was not what I wanted. I pressed my back against the wall, the curve of my spine into wood. "Can you summon the dead?"

Marcella laughed. It did sound ridiculous, now that I'd said it out loud.

"Is that why you've come? Magic and gypsy spells?" She leaned forward, her eyes hawklike and piercing. "I couldn't summon the dead any more than you, and I wouldn't want to. I'm a mother same as you are. Nothing else."

I looked away, exhausted with disappointment. Around the curtained window, light escaped in skinny stripes. A warm cup of tea sounded good to me now, practical. I wondered if it was rude to pour myself a cup, or if she expected it. I had no idea what social codes these people lived by.

Marcella reached out and put her hand over mine. A sturdy hand meant to steady me, I think, but the force only threw me further off balance. What was I doing here? "Why did my daughter leave?" I blurted out, thinking this stranger might actually have an answer.

"Why did my daughter? They're young and insolent. They thought they could do what they liked without consequence. They're paying for it now."

"Paying for it?"

"Guilt. Your little one's gone missing and they're to blame."

"You know about Effie?"

"Course I do. Your daughter's here, you know."

"What?" I leapt to my feet. "How? Where? Where is she?"

Marcella stood up, patting the air with her hands. "Luella, your older daughter Luella's here."

I steadied myself on the table. The room

was hot and cramped and I stumbled to the door, opening it just as my eldest daughter set her foot on the bottom rung.

The color drained from her face. "Mama?" she said, as if I was a questionable object instead of her mother.

I stood dumbfounded, utterly unprepared.

She moved back as I stepped forward and off the wagon. Her appearance was no different, other than her bright gypsy clothes and sun-lightened hair, and yet there was something I didn't recognize in her face. I expected her to purse her lips and meet me with defiance, but she just stared at me with the look of someone who had been betrayed, as if the world was against her, and not the other way around. Then she dropped her head and sobbed.

Chimney smoke swirled around me as the wind cut through my coat and the wet grass soaked the leather toes of my shoes. All the conversations I'd held with Luella in my mind, all the things I'd planned to say, vanished. My desire to reach her, to hold her, was gone. The fury I felt that she was right here in her own backyard and had not come home was too much. There was no excuse she could offer that would make this bearable.

From behind, I heard Marcella say, "She's

only here because she didn't know how to go home without her sister."

It was all I could do not to grab Luella. "How do you know about Effie?" I heard the demanding tone I used when she was little.

She looked at me, both of us recognizing that I could no longer demand anything of her. "Freddy read about it in the paper and came after us. He said we were to blame, and that there was no excuse for it. They're searching for her, Momma," Luella said, her tearful, urgent words meaning to heal something. "Freddy and Sydney and Job. They haven't moved on because of Effie. They said they'll stay all winter until we find her."

*As if that will make a difference,* I wanted to scream. *They* are the cause of this. *You* are the cause of this. I hated these people. Hated, even, my own daughter. Disgraceful. Selfish. Hate.

Luella's sniveling slowed to a hiccup and she wiped her cheek with the back of her hand. "I never meant for Effie to come after me. I never imagined she would. I told her I'd write to her as soon as I could. I don't know why she didn't wait."

And just like that, my hate slithered away. It was my fault. I had lied to Effie. I let her think her sister had abandoned her without a word.

A flock of geese flew overhead, calling out. I looked into the field that stretched in a wash of brown grass, dry and lifeless. "She didn't wait because I never showed her your letter."

Luella stood very still, staring at me. "What . . . *why* not?"

"I'm not sure anymore." I was not sure of anything. I felt weak, light-headed. I longed to reach out to my daughter, but the young woman standing in front of me felt like a stranger. The girl who left was now a woman, beautiful, estranged, alien. Waves of panic washed over me. "Come home."

Luella reached for my hand, her buff, weathered fingers curling over my sleek, bloodless glove. "I can't. I can't face Daddy. I can't face Effie's empty room. What would I do?" she implored, a gasp in her throat. "There's nothing I can do."

She was right. There was nothing she could do to bring Effie home, dead or alive. There was nothing any of us could do.

I looked at the rickety wagons with their wheels wedged into frozen ruts, at the hard field and the cold sky. "I don't understand any of this."

"I know." I saw acceptance in my daughter's empathetic face. There was so much about her I didn't understand.

I turned away, helpless and exhausted. I needed to go home. I needed to lie down.

"Mama?" I heard the young girl in her pleading, but I kept walking. She knew where to find me. And it helped to know she was right here, even if I didn't approve of this lifestyle. At least she was safe. The wagons were warm. There was food and hot tea. Maybe that's all she ever wanted.

Twigs snapped underfoot and a bird kept up a shrill call overhead like a single note on a piano. Behind me the gypsy camp was hushed, my visit having stunned children and dogs into silence. Luella did not come running after me as I'd dared to imagine, and I picked my way through the trees, down the steep hill and back across the field to the empty, silent hallway of my home.

# CHAPTER TWENTY: MABLE

Mama and I moved into a room on Worth Street. It was in a five-story building, the floors connected by a winding staircase that twisted up the middle like a screw. Ours was a single room on the fifth floor with a shared bathroom where we had the luxury of a bathtub and running hot water. The room was unfurnished, with whitewashed walls and a window at the end that looked out onto the street. Mama and I slept on bedrolls with our petticoats balled up for pillows. It was temporary, Mama said, just until we could afford something better.

It was so hot that August I spent most of my time leaning out the window trying to get a breath of air as I watched the tops of hats and carriages and cars in constant, glittering motion. Everyone seemed to have somewhere urgent to go, and I wondered how long Mama expected me stay up here watching traffic. Her anger had subsided, but I knew keeping me cooped up and bored was her quiet way of punishing me.

Those first few weeks I spent watching the street for Renzo, daring to hope he'd come for me. I'd know him by his easy saunter, his unhurried way. I'd call down to him and he'd look up and grin, confident I'd be waiting for him. He'd come and take me in his arms, apologizing and saying we'd find a way to be together, no matter the odds.

He didn't come. I tried to be angry, but all I felt was a longing as deep and gnawing as missing my papa had once been. I wished I'd kept something to remind me of Renzo, something with his smell, even that damned dirty sock. It was better than nothing. And nothing was precisely what Mama and I had been left with, by everyone.

I thought Aunt Marie would miss us enough to forgive me, but she didn't come either. It was cruel, her punishing Mama for something I'd done, and I vowed to make it up to Mama.

One night, I sat on the floor eating sausages and watching Mama shake out her dress and hang it on the back of the door. She'd come from the bath and her long, wet hair spilled to the crook of her back, the lines of her compact figure visible through the thin cloth of her nightgown. I thought of her standing in her mud-splattered nightgown the day she lost her last baby. She was so much thinner now.

"I'm going to work for you," I said. "I'm old enough for my working papers now, and you could use a rest."

"Over my dead body will you work in that godforsaken place." She put her hands on her hips, looking at me with determination, like she used to look at Papa. "I have a mind to find something better. In the meantime, I'll keep up at the factory and you'll busy yourself learning. It was boredom that got you into trouble in the first place. I didn't know Marie was leaving you alone. As long as I make enough to pay for this room and to keep us fed, you're to go to school."

I gaped at her, my sausage halfway to my mouth. None of the Casciloi children went to school. "We can't afford it."

Mama squeezed the water out of the ends of her hair, sprinkling the drops onto the floor as if watering the seeds of my future. "It doesn't cost any money. I've already looked into it. The school is five blocks from here and the first day is September third." She sat heavily on her bedroll, pulling her nightgown down over her legs. "I'm dead tired. Hurry up with that food and put the light out."

I protested. It would be *humiliating.* I was too old for school. I didn't know any facts. Mama rolled onto her side with her back to me and said facts were what I would learn and it wasn't up for discussion.

Three weeks later I found myself walking into a large brick schoolhouse on Chambers Street, the classroom packed with girls in neat skirts and white blouses, black bows flapping at the backs of their heads like the wings of shiny, dead birds. I felt ridiculous in Grazia's blue dress. Even the poorest girls with cracked shoes and grimy nails wore skirts and blouses. Some of their skirts, and sleeves, were too short and their arms stuck out past their cuffs, but at least they weren't in a foolish, old-fashioned dress.

I glared at the first girl who dared look at me, a plump, pink-cheeked thing bursting from her clothes. I had no interest in friends. The twins had taught me girls were mean and spiteful and you had to look out for yourself.

Our teacher, Miss Preston, a young, eager woman who seemed delighted to be crammed into the airless room instructing us, decided on the first day not to have anything to do with me. I could read well enough, but everyone else knew math symbols and places on maps and how to write in swirling letters that linked together. Miss Preston, with her wire-rimmed glasses and zealous smile, had no interest in a girl who didn't know these things. After testing me, she told me I was to sit in the back of the class and do the best I could to keep up. I spent the next two months gazing out the window making muddled designs on the pages where I was supposed to be solving problems.

It was no matter. School wasn't an option for long.

One night in mid-November, I stepped out of my dress and felt Mama's hand grip my shoulder. Her face was aghast, as if I'd grown a double head, or horns. Not even dragging me from Marie's had twisted her face like that. Her lips trembled and her hands shook from her sides as if she meant to wrap them around my throat. Even then, I didn't know what was happening, which was stupid of me, but I never claimed to be bright. My body had changed so much over the last few years I thought it was normal to keep growing round in places.

Tense and quiet, Mama said, "You are not to return to school tomorrow," and left the room saying she'd be back in an hour.

She was not back in an hour. I lay on my

lumpy pillow listening to the wind rattle the panes and whistle through the cracks, lapping its cold tongue at my face. Our sweltering room in the summer had turned freezing with the approach of winter. It reminded me of the cold seeping in through the walls of my loft bed. At least in the cabin there was the crackling warmth of the hearth. Here, the paltry heat came up through pipes, steaming and hissing and growling like it was being dragged out of someone's throat.

I must have fallen asleep because the next thing I knew Mama was leaning over me. My covers were tossed off and she was digging her fingers into my stomach, a fire on her breath.

"You're hurting me," I said, pushing her hand away.

Mama stumbled backward, dropping onto her bed with a thump. I hadn't put the light out and it flickered and trembled from the wall sconce. "I'm no midwife, but I know what a body looks like when a life's taken hold inside it." Her cheeks were bright red, her words slightly slurred, which shocked me as much as what she'd just made clear.

I hugged my knees to my chest, a numbness crawling over me. My mother was drunk and I was pregnant.

Mama pitched sideways and fell onto her pillow. "Maybe we'll get lucky and this one won't last either," she mumbled, her eyes dropping shut.

I watched her sleep, her chest rising and falling with each, slow breath. It never crossed my mind what Renzo and I were doing might have this outcome. I thought only grown women had babies. Now I saw how stupid I was. I hoped Mama was right and I would lose this baby.

Sliding over, I sat on the end of Mama's bed and unlaced her boots, pulling the thin, worn soles from her feet. There was a hole in her stocking and I found something childlike and disturbing about her big toe sticking out of it. I peeled her stockings off, tugging them around her heels and holding her small, bare feet in my hands. She didn't stir, her face slack, her mouth partially open. I was sorrier than ever for what I'd done. I never meant to cause her so much grief.

After a while, I drew her blanket over her and crawled back to my bed.

Before Mama left for work the next day, she put five cents into my pocket and told me I wasn't to leave the room for any reason other than to fetch dinner.

I didn't mind being alone. It was far better than a schoolhouse full of snickering girls and a teacher who couldn't be bothered to teach the dumb ones. The apartment building was quiet during the day. I roamed the halls undisturbed and stayed in the bathtub as long as I wanted with no one banging on the door for me to hurry up.

After a few weeks, however, I grew fidgety and bored and began lingering in the warm kitchen on the first floor. Our house was run by a thin woman with scaly skin that flaked at her temples and shook out of her hair like dust. Her name was Mrs. Hatch and she occupied the entire first floor where there was a parlor crammed with overstuffed furniture, a dining room that gleamed mahogany, and a full kitchen where she served food for her tenants at a price Mama and I couldn't afford.

She didn't ask any questions, which Mama said was a good thing, and she didn't seem to mind me sitting at the kitchen table watching her cook.

She made me think of Aunt Marie. I missed the simplicity of rolling dough out onto the floor or chopping vegetables. It was mind occupying, and I needed that. When I asked to help, Mrs. Hatch raised her eyebrows, her spoon pausing in mid-air. "You

348

know how to cook?" she asked, suspicious, glancing at my stomach — an embarrassment I could no longer hide.

"Yes, ma'am, I do."

Mrs. Hatch pinched her lips together, glancing at a pile of carrots, not bright orange like the ones I used to yank up from the crumbling earth with Papa, but dull, with winter fuzz over their skin. "Well, I suppose I could use the help," she sighed heavily. "But you're to keep out of the dining room, you hear?" She shook her spoon at me, broth spitting from the end of it. "It's mostly men who eat down here and they won't want to look at the likes of you. Reminds them of their own bad nature." She plucked an onion from a bowl and dropped it in my hand. "Chop it nice and small."

The skin crinkled and peeled away in my palm. I went to the counter, slicing it down the middle and exposing its crisp, white innards. A sudden sadness came over me as I remembered standing in the cabin kitchen, Papa's fiddle playing in the background and Mama humming beside me. I was grateful for the onion stinging my eyes.

I felt Mrs. Hatch watching me as she stirred her soup. "Nice and thin now, like I told you."

"Yes, ma'am."

I glanced at her and she shook her head. "It's a man puts a woman in your situation, and yet women are the only ones left paying for the sin. Not a fair world, but it shakes out as it does."

After that, Mrs. Hatch always had something set aside for me to chop or roll or pound. She never mentioned pay, or rent reduction, which I'd hoped for to help Mama out, but at least I had something to do. Mrs. Hatch was nothing like Aunt Marie. She spoke sparingly, and when she did it was to bemoan the entire human race, me being no exception. I didn't mind. Standing over the hot stove was a comfort, the smells brought memories of other kitchens, Aunt Marie's, and Mama's in a time already so long ago.

I took to walking to meet Mama when she got off work at the Asch Building. When my cooking duties were done, I'd hang up my apron, pull on my coat and step into the chilled air, letting the two-mile walk ease the restlessness in my swollen, tingling legs. I felt nothing for the growing thing inside me, except the inconvenience of its weight, and I didn't mind the cold. Moving kept me warm enough. Mama worked on the ninth floor and was always one of the last people out of the building. I'd stand on the sidewalk stomping my feet, watching the workers pour out, and string off every which way, until Mama's small shape emerged, her hair towering over her worn face.

Once, I spotted the twins huddled with a group of girls waiting for the trolley. It was snowing lightly and puffs of moisture twirled from their laughing mouths. When Alberta looked up, I ducked behind a large man smoking a cigar and talking loudly to the woman on his arm. I dreaded any thought of the twins reporting my sprouting belly back to Aunt Marie. I'd humiliated Mama in front of her sister enough.

Every so often on our way home, Mama would stop at a popcorn wagon and buy a steaming bag for us to share. We'd sit on a bench eating and watching people go by. Mama would let herself relax then. Her tired shoulders would sag and her body would sink into mine. It was the only time I saw her loosen her grip on life, and this ease opened up a pocket of happiness inside me. With the popcorn bag warm in my hands and the salty kernels melting on my tongue, I allowed myself to think things might not turn out so bad for us after all.

"What should we do with our Sunday afternoons when the weather warms?"

Mama asked one day, her voice light. It was still too cold to do anything but sit in our apartment reading the bible. There had been no churchgoing since we'd left Marie's, which I didn't rightly mind.

"We could go to Coney Island," I suggested. "The girls in school said there was a water carnival with high divers and log-rollers."

"I've heard it's best in June. Before it gets too hot."

"We'll walk on the beach and eat ice cream."

She smiled. "I'd like that."

We popped corn kernels into our mouths and talked about seeing the Barnum & Bailey Greatest Show on Earth, picnicking in Central Park, walking up Fifth Avenue and admiring the window displays. Maybe, if there was enough money, we'd dine in a real restaurant, Mama said.

We sat there planning our summer until the bag was empty and all I could do was dot my fingers into the salt at the bottom.

None of our plans involved a baby. Not once, since that first night, had Mama or I mentioned it. We made no preparations. It wasn't like Mama to make plans that would never happen, and I walked home thinking of our summer with that pocket of happiness expanding inside me.

By March, I was enormous. Mrs. Hatch continued to let me in the kitchen, but her frown deepened and I wasn't much help. I grew dizzy and began nicking my fingers with the knife and sucking off the blood so she wouldn't notice.

Most days now, I was too tired to meet Mama after work. But on March 25th, 1911, I had a hankering for popcorn, and to sit next to Mama and forget about what was coming. Thinking back, maybe it was Renzo's mama's curse, or the devil grinning at me, or God simply making me pay for my sins that had me walking up Green Street on a day when I could have easily stayed home. My feet ached and my stomach was heavier than a sack of flour, and yet I decided I wanted a bag of popcorn more than I wanted to lie down.

It was dreary out. Dark clouds suffocated the tops of the buildings. Every now and then I'd see a roof peeking out as if it was trying to catch its breath. I passed a waffle cart, the smell of sweet dough making my mouth water. I was thinking I'd try and convince Mama to buy me a waffle instead of popcorn when the loudest bell I ever heard rang so close I jumped, halting in my tracks, as a horse-drawn fire engine charged past me. The horses were brown, sleek as machines, their hooves launching them forward like well-oiled springs. They pulled a wagon where men in shiny hats clung around a silver dome, a storm of smoke billowing from the top of it. It was then I noticed a stream of dirty water collecting in the gutter even though it wasn't raining. I heard shouting, and there was a sudden hubbub of commotion. Men broke into a run, women started screaming.

A crowd formed, drawing me forward — curiosity and horror a powerful current. I found myself outside a gathering of police, their backs a wall of tense muscle. Swift, agile men leapt from the fire truck that had roared past me. They unwound a hose that hissed and spat a tube of water into the air, joining two other fire engines, the cylinders of water merging like a solid, white wing of salvation.

At first, my thick skull didn't register that it was the Asch Building engulfed in flames. I watched in fascination until I realized exactly what I was looking at and my gut twisted into a knot. *Mama's in that building,* I thought, and then, *surely not. They would have gotten the workers out.* Frantic, I looked around for her, but there were too many large bodies in front of me. I backed away under a striped awning, hoping from farther away I might be able to spot Mama in the crowd. A man stood next to me in a white apron, a hand clasped to his mouth. Everything was gray and dark and wet but for those flames. A spray of mist from the fire hose settled on my cheeks. I felt light-headed and nauseous, the heat from the flames licking the air like hot tongues. I could see the flames, feeding on the wind like a fat insatiable beast, and from an upper window a figure of a girl suddenly appeared. There was no pause, not even the briefest breath before she took flight. Her skirt and hair flew out, but her wings failed her, and she plummeted to the ground at a shocking speed. The sound of her body hitting the pavement vibrated through me. I doubled over. A woman screamed and I heard a collective gasp from the crowd.

After that, the scene became lurid, distorted, as if I was looking through glass, or a sheet of ice cut at an odd angle as woman after woman hit the ground. They leapt without hesitation, those wingless birds falling from the sky. One woman paused long enough that the flames trailed her to the ground, her burning hair a streak in the air.

I vomited all over my shoes. My throat burned as if the flames had found a way

355

inside me. The man in the apron put a hand to my back. "Don't watch," he said, but I shrugged him off, wiping my mouth on the edge of my skirt, my eyes fixed on the fire. Any one of those birds could be my mother.

People screamed and wept and women dove until the windows were blackened, charred holes and the disturbing thuds finally stopped. Steam hissed in the air like a serpent, the street continued to waver under me as I stumbled through the line of scattered policeman attempting to create some sort of order. As I approached the bodies, I looked into their faces, into their open, paralyzed eyes. These were nothing like the translucent, peaceful faces of my stillborn siblings. These were bodies startled into death, their rust-colored blood draining into the street.

A gentle hand pulled me from my knees where I'd fallen, staring into the face of a woman I'd never known. "Sorry, ma'am, but you can't be here. We're clearing the whole area."

I sank into his grasp, the policeman steadying me on my feet. "I'm trying to find my mother," I said, toneless, limp, emptied of feeling.

"We're taking the bodies to Charities Pier. Doors will open as soon as we get them laid out. Now get yourself home to your husband. This is no place for a woman in your condition."

"What if she's alive?" I asked.

"Then she'll make her own way home, I reckon."

There was a hush in the streets as the sky slipped from gray to black, the city lights blinking on cautiously, hoping to hide their eyes. The stairwell in my building was empty and I was grateful not to meet anyone as I climbed to our room and shut the door. I looked at the scant space with the sense that I had no idea how I'd gotten so far from the cabin and Papa and where I belonged. The only objects in the room, besides our beds and clothes, were a bible and a photograph Mama kept in a frame by her bed. We'd taken it the summer we came to New York. I'd never had my picture taken before. The photographer told us to stand perfectly still in front of a calico backdrop while he disappeared under a black cloth with one hand raised in the air. There was a pop and a flash and the man reappeared, flushed and smiling. I'd never liked the photograph, mostly because Mama and I looked dreadful serious, but Mama spent a whole week's salary on it so I lied and told her I thought it was grand.

I lay on Mama's bed and pressed the picture to my chest, staring at her Sunday dress hanging on the back of the door knowing that at any moment she was going to walk through it. There was a sour taste in my mouth, the sickness of the day a flavor on my tongue. I wanted a glass of water to wash it away but I didn't dare get up. I wasn't sure my legs would hold me.

The sound of those bodies hitting the ground rang in my ears as I fell into an exhausted sleep. I dreamt of Mama. She was young, kneeling on the floor of our cabin with an open-mouthed smile, her eyebrows arched in her smooth, high forehead, her arms outstretched, her dark eyes shining. *Come,* she said. *The baby chicks have hatched. I'll carry you out. The ground is frozen and we can't have you slipping on the ice.* I felt the softness of her chest as she lifted me in her arms. We stepped out into a pale dawn and I heard the sound of peeping chicks.

I woke with a start, shivering, my chest damp with sweat. I sat up. It was still dark and the bedroll next to me was empty. The photograph had slipped to the floor and I left it there, hauling myself out of bed and outside, making my way up East 26th Street. I'd never been out this late and was surprised at the pulse of the city. Windows blazed with light and people moved in and out of buildings and along the sidewalk as if it were the middle of the day. There was no need to ask where the morgue was. When I approached the dock on the East River, I found a line of people strung out along the sidewalk as if waiting for tickets to a theater. I slipped in behind a man in a tall hat and a thick coat. He beat his gloves against his palm, leaning over to the man in front of him to ask, "How much longer?"

The man lifted a pocket watch. "Five minutes," he said.

The doors opened the instant a distant church bell chimed midnight. I was impressed the police could be so prompt, given how devastating the fire had been. The man in front of me moved through the doors and I kept pace, trying to empty my mind of all thought as we walked slowly up one row of coffins, and down another. The muted shuffling of feet mingled with the lapping of water on the pier. Lights swung from the rafters, giving off a sulfuric glow that barely lit the dead faces. Policeman moved along with the mourners, lifting lanterns when requested, while cries rang out as one victim after another was identified. I was struck by how different these guttural, accepting cries

359

were compared to the panicked screams earlier that day.

I didn't expect to find Mama. None of it seemed real, the eeriness of the hour, all these strangers weeping. At the end of each row I came to, I felt more and more sure I had it all wrong and Mama was at home, frightened silly I was out so late.

And then I saw her. I didn't need the police lantern to recognize her. She lay in a coffin with her eyes closed and her head propped up as if she slept on a high pillow. Someone had taken the time to place her hands, one over the other on her chest. Her right cheek was dented and her eye sunken, but her hands were unscathed and her thick hair had stayed coiled on her head. The coffins were placed so close together I couldn't reach her hands and this made me panic. I sank to my knees at her feet, blocking the line behind me. No one told me to get up. The line stilled and people bowed their head in respect as I reached for Mama's feet, frantically unlacing her boots, sorry everyone could see the hole in her sock. I peeled them off, holding her cold, bare feet in my hands. I closed my eyes and lifted my face to the heavens. The lone cry of a gull came from outside. I wanted rain on my face and my papa's hand on my shoulder. This was his part. He was supposed to come and cover the body for me.

There was no hand. No rain, just the crushing smell of death. I scrambled to my feet. A roomful of dimly lit strangers surrounded me. None of them were Papa. The stench in my nostrils, the flickering lights and the yellow skin of the dead made the sweat jump out on my forehead. I shoved my way to the door, fleeing the rank-smelling building, leaving Mama's shoes to be trampled to dust by all those mourners. I didn't stay to identify my mother by name for a proper burial. I hadn't even said a prayer over her body.

By the time I arrived back in my room, I was shaking violently. I fell on my knees with my head to the floor, my belly hard as a watermelon beneath me. I was the one who should be lying on that pier, not Mama. If only she'd let me work for her like I'd wanted, I thought, considering how best to throw myself out the window. I wanted it to end. And not just today, every bit of my life leading up to today.

I rolled onto my side. The window above my head was black and spotted with rain. I thought of looking up into the dark night sky from the woods behind our cabin, and how the endless space and stars hadn't filled me with any kind of wonder or beauty, but a terrible fear. There was too much of it. Too much unexplainable emptiness. It was the loneliest thing I'd ever seen and I'd rushed inside, petrified I'd been abandoned with nothing but that black sky. Mama and Papa had laughed at me, but I was right all along.

The dark, inexplicable emptiness filled my body. I couldn't have jumped out that window if I'd wanted. The blackness had a weight to it that pinned me to the floor.

# CHAPTER TWENTY-ONE: EFFIE

It was cold when I woke up, and I ached all over. I lay with my cheek pressed to the floor, the cement cool against my spent rage. I'd screamed. I'd bitten and scratched. Now I was paying for it, but I didn't care. I'd do it again.

I sat up and gingerly touched my nearly shaved head. My palm throbbed where a splinter of wood had pierced it, my glorious wound of rebellion. The space around me was dark and dank and smelled like mold. Fear pricked the soles of my feet, but I refused to face the ghost of the dead girl and I shoved her away.

I had no sense of how much time had passed since I'd fallen with the dogs. I remembered being dragged, having my head tipped over a sink, the porcelain edge pressed against my windpipe like a cold hand around my neck. I remembered the sound of snipping scissors, wrenching my head around and biting the hand that held them with all the fury of both being betrayed, and failing to escape. The sisters meant to break me, but an anger I'd never felt before coiled in the pit of my stomach.

I peed in the corner, dried myself with the edge of my skirt, ignored the tray of water, stale bread and molasses. The smell of mildew and urine was nauseating. As time went by hunger became a familiar ache. I'd close my eyes and summon a taste from memory: lemon tarts from Velma, a stick of peppermint at Christmas, duck in all its salty, tender glory on the day Luella disappeared and Mama took me to Café Martin's. Hunger carved out an odd reality where my family became more elusive and surreal than the memory of a salty piece of meat.

I tried to conjure the touch of my father's fingers on my wrist, the pits in my mother's scarred hands, and the sound of Luella's dancing feet, but all I felt was the cold, damp floor and the only sound to be heard was a distant, steady drip of water.

Over and over I saw the shapes of Mable and Edna disappearing down the hill, hating how naive I'd been. I believed they'd chosen me, over all the other girls, because they liked me. Because I had "spunk," like

Mable said. To be liked. It was such a shortsighted, commonplace desire. Luella would have seen right through them, not caring if they liked her or not. "Watch out, Effie, they're up to no good," she would have said, tossing her head with a hand on her hip.

*Luella, where are you?*

After a while, time became blurred and boundless, with no seconds or minutes or hours to define it. The boredom was torture. I counted steps from one wall to the next, squaring up my room. I recited scripture, but became furious with God and switched to Shakespeare. I thought of the gypsy children performing *Romeo and Juliet* in the rain, of Tray and Marcella and the foretelling of my future. I thought of all the mistakes I'd made. I wanted to blame my father for them, for betraying our family and sparking our rebellion, but down here, trapped in the bowels of the House of Mercy, I'd forgive him anything, if only he would come for me.

Eventually, my breath became ragged and short and I was aware that there was something wrong with my legs. When I pushed my fingers into them, they felt tight and squishy like the frog's bellies Luella and I used to poke down by the stream. Sleep came in spurts, and I'd wake gasping for air, the pressure in my chest propelling me to my feet until I was too weak to get off the floor.

Death crept forward in small, seductive waves, drawing me in and out, pulling me from my body and dropping me back in. I wanted Luella, but there was only the lion in the corner of the room, watching patiently from his numerous eyes with his head in his paws.

I stopped being afraid of the dark, of the ghosts of my imagination, and became afraid only of the fluid filling my lungs, and the terrifying sensation that I was drowning.

When the angels of the Lord finally came for me, a soft light appeared and their faint, hushed voices soothed me. There were no dissolving edges, no falling away, just a sting to my arm and a tender sleep arrived as the pressure in my chest finally let go, the relief as sweet as flying.

In the end, Heaven did not greet me when I woke up, or God, unless God was a man with a tight mustache and a pointy chin leaning over me with a stethoscope in his ears.

"You're awake." He smiled, and his lids

pulled at the corners of his eyes. "Thought we'd lost you." The stethoscope dropped to his neck and he straightened his white jacket and jiggled the tube sticking out of my arm. My eyes flew open with the pain as the doctor patted my head and said, "Not to worry."

The doctor might as well have been God himself. *I'm out,* I thought. *My fabulous failing heart has landed me in a hospital.* I tried to speak, but couldn't find the use of my tongue. The weight in my chest and the swelling pressure in my legs were gone, and yet I was too weak to open my mouth.

Just then Sister Mary appeared beside the doctor, her coif fused so tightly to the perimeter of her narrow face it looked like she was shedding a layer of white skin. *What was she doing here?*

"Will she be all right?"

"For the time being. The mercury treatments will keep the swelling down." The doctor plunged his hands into a basin of water, shook them off and rigorously dried them on a towel.

"What do you suppose weakened her?" Frail lines creased the corners of Sister Mary's mouth.

"Stress to the body, malnutrition. Has she been eating all right?"

"She has," she said, her voice a faint peep,

like a mouse caught in a trap.

*Liar,* I thought, rolling my head to the side, my blurred eyes taking in the room. This was no hospital. The charitable sisters had simply dragged me from the basement to the infirmary. I wanted to scream at the doctor, to plead for help, but I couldn't lift a finger even to grab on to him. I was barely keeping my lips open.

"Well," the doctor said, as he peeled off his white coat and flung it on the back of a chair, "keep her off laundry duty. Let her rest and try to get her weight up."

The next time the doctor came, I was strong enough to whisper my name, my real name, but he only shook his head and stabbed a needle into my vein. "Don't bother confessing anything to me, missy. I hear all sorts of things in here. I learned to turn a blind eye a long time ago. They'll go easy on you," he said. "I've told them as much." He jiggled the tube and I winced. "Sorry." He patted my arm. "I'll be back in a jiffy."

Sleep came and went. I preferred sleep to staring at the ceiling. There was a fuzzy, unstable order to my thoughts. It was an effort to make sense of reality, and I forced myself to keep track of the little things. I was in the infirmary, in the House of Mercy.

The bed was soft, the lights harsh, the doctor civil but not kind, the broth flavorless, yet healing. Daily, a needle was jabbed into my arm and I was ordered to swallow a metallic-tasting tablet that made my teeth grind. Through the barred windows, the sky was white and a cover of snow lay over the world. It was winter. Time was passing.

One day, I propped up on an elbow to keep the water in my glass from dribbling down my chin and found that I was strong enough to sit all the way up. It was then I saw that I wasn't alone. A girl lay in the bed across from me, her eyes closed. Her head was shaven to a shiny scalp marbled with blue veins. It reminded me of a baby's head I'd once touched, perfectly smooth and vulnerable. A purple bruise bloomed on the girl's cheek. One eye was swollen shut and her lips oozed yellow pus.

It was unmistakably Mable, looking like a beautiful, battered statue beneath her wounds.

I slid down into my bed, unable to feel sorry for her. She didn't deserve the bruises, but a wicked part of me was glad she hadn't escaped.

When the doctor came the next day, I asked what was wrong with her.

"Her many sins," he said placidly, driving

the needle into my vein.

I tried to keep my eyes open, to ask more, but my tongue went slack and the ceiling rippled and blurred and disappeared.

At some point, an angry voice dragged me from a woozy sleep and I peeled my eyes open. Three men stood around Mable's bed in neat uniforms with brick hard faces. Mable was sitting up with her head propped against the iron bedrails. A heavyset policeman with a thick Irish accent shook a piece of paper in the air in front of her, looking as if it took all his restraint not to shake her. "This here, is not your name! Mable Winter is a Sunday school teacher at Church of the Most Precious Blood. We gave her parents a right shock telling them she'd leapt from a forty-foot wall!" He dropped his fists to the bed, sweetening his voice to something sarcastic and arrogant. "You be a good lass, now, and tell me your real name, you hear?"

Mable pressed her lips into a hard line as she stared straight into the policeman's eyes. This infuriated him — clearly a sore loser — and he backed up, waving the paper and shouting, "I'm not falling for this act. You're no simp. You're just another damn floozy. I see it in them keen eyes of yours." He pressed his face close to hers, rattling a chain that I now saw bound her wrists to the bed. "I *demand* you tell me your name or you'll end up in the pokey with girls far worse than the ones in here!"

The room was silent. One policeman coughed into his sleeve, the other looked at his feet.

The Irish policeman pulled himself away and spat on the floor. "Suit yourself," he said, superior and smug, as if he had won after all. "It's your sentence." He flicked his hand at the other policemen and the three of them exited the room.

Mable didn't move. She looked inwardly consumed, her eyes fixed as stone. Not once did she glance in my direction, and I lowered myself down onto my pillow burning with curiosity about her real name.

I wasn't about to forgive her, but I couldn't help admiring her strength of character. It was distinctly Luella-like. Even with the newfound anger coiled in my gut, I would never have been able to defiantly look that policeman in the eye. And to hold on to a lie even after you were found out took a single-minded tenacity every girl in this place would applaud, no matter how much they hated Mable. Or whatever her name was.

I thought of the rich baroness who'd gone missing. If she'd left on a boat with a circus man she would have changed her name too. Maybe Mable was a baroness in disguise? Either that or she'd murdered someone. I wouldn't put either past her.

I fell asleep working up the determination to confront her, but the next time I woke, Mable was gone. Her bed stripped bare. Only a thin, stained mattress left behind.

# CHAPTER TWENTY-TWO: JEANNE

When you become a person you no longer recognize, it is startling to find a piece of yourself intact.

Two weeks before Christmas, Georges arrived on our doorstep. I didn't believe it was my brother until he stepped into the parlor and I was met with the same sturdy boy's face I'd left on the pier, only thinner and stronger, with a few worn creases at the brow. He smiled playfully from the doorway, delighted to see my surprise.

I gaped, and became strangely self-conscious of my appearance. I no longer bothered with curling irons or face powders, and I was sure I looked hideously old to him. "What are you doing here?"

"Is that any way to greet your brother?" He came at me, folding me in a startling hug. I hadn't been touched since Emory had lifted me off the floor weeks ago, never mind a hearty embrace. My brother smelled strangely familiar, like a spice I'd forgotten about, and I could feel the scratch of his slightly grown out facial hair on my forehead.

I gently pushed him away, patting the sleeve of his heavy wool topcoat, his generous show of affection overwhelming me. "You've grown into a proper looking Frenchman," I said.

"That's a shame. I've been trying very hard to become a proper Englishman."

"Why on earth would you want to do that?"

"I'd planned to move to London right before receiving your husband's letter."

"Emory wrote to you?"

"He did indeed."

"What about?"

"All that's happened." Georges took my hands, squeezing them tightly. "I'm so very, very sorry, Jeanne. Why didn't you write? I would have come sooner."

A flurry of emotions rose up, his sudden presence melting a part of me I'd iced over. "I don't . . . I . . ." It amazed me how easily my brother offered his devotion when I had done nothing to deserve it. I'd thought of writing him many times, but could only stare stupidly at blank paper, my pen hovering.

"It's all right, Jeanne. There's no need. I'm sorry to upset you."

"No. I'm the one who should be apologizing to you."

"Goodness." Georges put his hands on my cheeks, lifting my face. His eyes were the softest green. "Don't be silly. It's understandable that it would be too hard to put it all down in writing."

"No, that's not what I mean. I'm sorry about Maman. About leaving you."

Georges laughed, and it startled a smile out of me. "You're sorry about that? You were a grown woman, Jeanne. You were meant to leave. As for Maman, I took my fair share of abuses, but she's harmless now." He let go of my cheeks with an impish look that flooded me with memories. "She actually begged me not to move to London, if you can believe it."

His comfortable manner, his ease and familiarity, sent a light feeling through my limbs. A sensation dangerously close to happiness. "I do believe it. You've been tremendously loyal to her, which is more than I can say for myself. And I'm sorry I didn't write to you. I wanted to. I tried."

"It's no matter. It was very thoughtful of Emory, considering he's never written a word to me before. He apologized for that, but said he was at quite a loss and couldn't think who else to turn to."

"He asked you here?"

"He did."

"That's surprising. My husband is rarely at a loss, and when he is . . . he turns to his mother."

Georges hesitated. "He's at a loss over you," he said gently.

This seemed unlikely. It was an outrageous gesture on Emory's part to send for my brother, and not at all like him. Whatever he'd told Georges, I was certain it wasn't out of any kindness for me.

If Effie's birth had been a crack, her death was a cleaving. There was nothing left of us. I couldn't believe he thought bringing my brother into it would do any good at all.

At that moment Emory entered the parlor, throwing his arm around my brother as if he was his dearest friend in the world. "Georges!" He gave him a hearty slap on the back. "You've grown."

Georges smiled. "I should hope so. I was eleven when I last saw you."

"Then I guess it's a good thing you've grown. I thought you were arriving this morning."

"You knew he was coming today?" I said.

"I arranged for his passage."

"Without telling me?"

"He's here now, isn't he? Brandy, my boy?"

Emory poured two glasses, handed one to Georges. Not only did he fail to offer me one, he didn't even look at me.

I suddenly understood why my husband brought Georges here. Emory was not at a loss over his love for me or how to heal our marriage, he was simply at a loss over what to do with me, and he no longer wanted the bother. Best to leave the task of handling my grief to another man, with my brother being the only option.

The flicker of compassion I'd felt when Georges first told me of Emory's letter slipped quickly back into bitterness as I listened to them converse about the weather, and how rough the seas were this time of year. Georges said the journey took nine days, and only once did he see the sunshine. I thought about my own passage: Emory and I not yet married, sleeping in separate cabins, tapping the wall between our beds at night. Two taps for goodnight, three for I love you. There had been something torturous and thrilling about being so near and not seeing him, about anticipating all that was to come once we married.

I broke into their conversation. "If you'll

377

both excuse me. I'll go tell Velma to set another place for dinner."

"Thank you," said Georges, squeezing my shoulder as I passed.

Emory said nothing.

Whatever my husband's intentions were, I was grateful to have my brother in the house. I began to feel human again. Georges was a quiet man with a softness that made revealing the state of my heart effortless. Even Emory found it impossible not to warm to his selfless, gentle soul. Especially when it came to Luella.

Emory had refused to see her after I told him about finding her at the gypsy camp. He never asked why I was there, and I never explained. I didn't dare go back, but a part of me waited every day for Luella to walk through the front door, uncertain whether I'd be furious enough to refuse her entry, or sorry enough to beg her to stay.

On Christmas Eve, Georges took it upon himself to visit Luella on my behalf, returning hours later declaring that the gypsies were a respectful people, and Luella a kind and thoughtful girl. "She's just confused with the desires of her heart," he said. A light snowfall had begun and he stood in the hallway dusting it from his shoulders.

"*Thoughtful* is the last word I'd use to

describe Luella." Emory stepped forward, took Georges's coat and hung it on the rack. "Have the gypsies changed her that much?"

Georges shrugged. "I couldn't say, as I didn't know her before. She had me to tea in a cramped wagon with all the grace of a woman in a great hall. I told her about the imperfections of my own mother and the mysteries of our family. She said little, but listened with quiet interest. It sets the young at ease to know their family history is made up of mistakes. Makes them feel less flawed."

"My flaws have not put her at ease," Emory said. "Quite the opposite."

Georges rested a hand on his arm. "Someday, it will be part of her past and she won't mind so much." I was grateful for the compassion he showed my husband — a compassion I didn't feel capable of.

I considered getting a Christmas tree this year, in honor of Effie who loved decorating it, but I couldn't bring myself to. Velma, at least, had insisted on making Christmas Eve dinner and we moved into the dining room where she'd laid roast pork, potatoes, carrots and jellied cranberry sauce. I wasn't hungry. Instead of eating I watched the snow fall past my reflection in the window glass, and thought about leaving my husband.

Since my brother's arrival, Emory had become more taxing than ever. I wondered how I'd borne it all these years, his thoughtless self-absorption. I stabbed a potato with my fork. The worst of it was, he was still seeing that woman, after everything that had happened. I knew her by the smell on his coat. A rosewater perfume he didn't bother to wipe off.

Over the next month, Georges visited Luella weekly, relaying the details to Emory and me afterward. I thought it a good sign she was receiving him. At least a part of her wanted to be near us.

"She's quite thin," Georges said one evening in the parlor, his hands clasped behind his back as he positioned himself between Emory and me. "It takes a resilient spirit to withstand that lifestyle. It's been a long, cold winter and you can be certain the glamour of gypsy life has worn off. Her sister's disappearance doesn't help matters. I'm afraid it's eating away at her. Effie is all she talks about. I don't think there's a detail of their childhood I haven't been privy to." He tried for a smile and failed. "I'm worried about her. I don't want to be alarming, but I'm concerned she might not make it until spring. They've already had one child die of fever. I've tried to convince her to come home, but she refuses. I hope it's all right, but I took the liberty of presenting her with the idea of going abroad. Before I came here, I'd already secured a house in London. Luella could stay there with me until she gets her bearings, with your permission, of course." Georges looked at Emory who rested an arm on the mantel in a careful pose.

I sat silent on the sofa, baffled to think that my daughter, exposed to fever and cold, still refused to travel the half a mile home.

"England might be a very good change for her," Georges pressed.

I could see that it hurt Emory to hear Georges speak of our daughter as if he knew what was best for her, and yet we both knew Luella had taken to Georges because he was unlike her father in every way: direct and honest and humble, without a bit of sheen to his personality.

"She's agreed to go?" Emory sounded unconvinced.

"She has."

"Well, then we're indebted to you. It's a very generous offer. We'll send her, of course, if she's willing." He left the room without a backward glance, his permission being all that was needed.

I thought it ridiculous, at this point, to pretend we had any say when it came to Luella, but Emory refused to admit his lack of control in any aspect of our life. He still insisted Effie was alive, posting weekly notices in the paper, calling the police for updates. None of which arrived.

Georges sat next to me on the sofa, concerned. "What are you thinking, Jeanne?"

Ever since Georges started visiting Luella, I'd let my thoughts stray to forgiveness and reconciliation, but her continual refusal to come home demoralized me. "You would go with her then?" I also couldn't bear the idea of losing my brother, which meant going back to being alone in the house with Emory.

"I would. She'll need someone. You're welcome too, of course, if you want to come."

I shook my head. "I can't."

Georges nodded in understanding. Every week, I still went to the hospitals and morgues. He knew I wouldn't rest until I'd properly buried my youngest. I stood up with a compelling urge to go lie in Effie's bed, something I did from time to time. It still held her smell, and the feeling of her small face on the pillow. Leaning over, I kissed Georges's cheek. "You're the dearest. I can't express my gratitude for all you've done. Luella would never have listened to us. I believe England is the best option for her, and she couldn't be in better hands. I will be sorry to lose you. You must, at least, let me see the two of you off. Tell her this, will you?"

"Of course."

Three weeks later, I sat at a table in Café Martin's with my eldest daughter. It had been six months since she'd left us, but her unfamiliar composure held a maturity that made it seem a decade. At least she'd abandoned her gypsy clothes and wore the traveling suit I'd gotten her. It was much too big, as she'd shrunk to half her normal size. But when I looked at her, I could almost believe she belonged to me again; and yet, I hardly knew what to say. I had only conversed with her as a child, and now we sat as two grown women.

We did not touch or hug in greeting, but sat formally across from each other as if we'd never dined in the same room together. I ordered liver, she ordered chicken. Neither of us ate much, and we spoke little. I asked her if she was looking forward to London.

She said, *not particularly.*

By the time the waiter cleared our plates and set down dessert menus, I felt the urgency of our last moments together. Her boat left in three hours. I had begged Georges to convince Luella to spend her final week at home, her last night at least, but she told him she couldn't. Not without Effie. This lunch was all I would have of her for a long time, and we were wasting it.

"This won't do," I said abruptly. Luella looked up over the top of her menu. "We must find a way to move forward with each other. For Effie's sake, if not our own. Do you remember when the two of you used to fight and she'd make you go out of the room and come back in and start over?"

Luella smiled. "I forgot that. It used to frustrate the dickens out of me that she never let me stay mad."

"I don't think she would want us mad at each other now."

"I'm not mad." Luella set down her menu. There was pride in her thin straight shoulders. "I was mad when I left. Mostly at Daddy, a little bit at you."

"What had I done?"

"You put up with him." She said this with such certitude, as if everything had become clear in her time away. Grief had matured

384

her, but not in all things.

"I loved him, Luella. You put up with people you love."

Luella looked startled. I clasped my hands on the table and leaned forward. "What? Did you think your father and I were always at odds? He loved me too, you know. He just grew out of it more quickly than I."

"Did you know what he was doing, and with whom?" she said hotly, a spark of the cheeky Luella returning. She had not changed entirely.

"Yes, my dear, long before you did."

"How could you stand it?"

*How indeed,* I thought, glancing at the neighboring tables, woman and men dining easily together. Her youthful idealism was touching. It was easy from her perspective. It was 1914, the world was an entirely different place than it had been in 1897 when I first met Emory. Luella's generation couldn't possibly understand. They were running off to college, dropping their waistlines and raising their hemlines, demanding the vote, independence. I could see now that my daughter's determination, her willingness to shake off what she didn't agree with, even if it was her own family, was admirable. I'd left my mother out of fear, not confidence, leaping from one suffocating rela-

385

tionship into the next. Luella was leaping on her own.

Without thinking, I suddenly pulled off my glove and reached across the table, opening my palm. I don't know why I offered her my scarred hand. Maybe because they used to comfort Effie, something I hadn't understood until Georges spoke about exposing our flaws, how it makes the younger generation less vulnerable to their own.

Luella stared at my hand without taking it. There were tears in her eyes, and her shoulders had fallen. "You used to let Effie hold your bare hand. I always wondered why." She looked up. "Why didn't you ever let me? There was one time I tried to take off your glove and you yanked your hand away. Why did you do that?"

"I don't know, Luella. I don't remember that. I am giving it to you now."

"It's not the same," she mumbled, but slipped her hand into mine anyway.

I folded my fingers over hers. "You must not blame yourself for Effie," I said, realizing this was at the core of the suffering that brewed beneath her cool eyes. It would resurface when she least expected, and I wasn't going to let her go without her understanding I wasn't condemning her.

She shook her head, the tears dripping down her cheeks. "It's entirely my fault. If I hadn't left, she would never have gone looking for me. Even if you had shown her that letter. I never told her where I was going, and I didn't write again soon enough. I've gone over and over what I could have done differently. I could have prevented what happened." She pulled her hand out of mine, sobbing into her palms.

I let her cry for a few minutes before saying, softly, "Effie was always dying, Luella. We never talked about it. None of us wanted to believe it, especially not your father, but every doctor told us the same thing. That Effie lived as long as she did was a miracle."

Luella yanked her head up. "She's not dead! I know she's not dead. I just don't understand where she's gone to. She got on the wrong train and ended up in a strange city, maybe she went all the way to California? You never searched outside of New York and Boston, but she could be anywhere."

"She would have made a telephone call."

"Maybe she ran out of money?"

"She's a smart girl. She would have found a way to reach us."

"What if she got picked up by police who thought she was homeless or something and got put in one of those homes for girls?"

"What homes?"

"Like the House of Mercy, or the Inwood House."

"Those are for girls on the street. They're like prison. They're court ordered."

"Daddy threatened to put me in there once."

"He wasn't serious."

"Well, a girl from school got put in there."

"She did?"

"Yes, by her father."

"For what infraction?"

"For getting a telegram from a boy."

"That seems extreme."

"Job and Sydney already checked the homes near us. The sisters told them there was no one named Effie Tildon. But you could check in other cities."

"Oh, Luella. Don't you think your father and I have? I've telephoned every hospital and institution I could think of. Not in California, mind you, but there's no way she'd get that far."

Luella sank into her chair. "Tray says she's not dead."

"Who is Tray?"

"A boy at the gypsy camp. He knew Effie. They understood each other."

"She never mentioned him."

"I think there's a lot she never told us."

The waiter approached and I quickly put my glove back on, managing a polite smile. "No dessert, thank you. We'll just take the bill." I took my watch from my jacket pocket. "We should be going. Georges will be waiting for us and you don't want to miss your boat."

On the dock, my daughter let me hug her as I openly wept, the icy wind off the water freezing the tears on my cheeks. Georges stood quietly beside us with his leather bag clutched in one hand. Behind him, the boat ramp filled with travelers.

"Go on," I said, but Luella wouldn't let go. She held my arms so hard they hurt.

"I don't think I should go," she said with sudden panic. "Tray says I should wait. He's certain Effie will come home. I'm only leaving because I don't believe him anymore."

"There's nothing more you can do, my dear. I'll send word the moment there's news of her. I promise. I'll recheck the homes you mentioned. I already check the hospitals daily." I gave a small laugh. "The operators know my voice before I even give my name. You should hear how they sigh, and they're always reluctant to put me through. It's no matter. I'm not giving up on her."

Luella's voice was shaky, her eyes red and

swollen from crying. "The truth is I feel guilty going. I don't deserve it."

"Nonsense. You must move on with your life."

"It's not fair."

"It's not. Nothing is. Come . . . you two will miss your boat."

Georges kissed my cheek. "You're to come for a visit as soon as you see fit."

"By then I hope you've fattened up my daughter on English scones and clotted cream."

"We'll do our best."

Luella wrapped her arms around me once more. "I'm sorry."

"Stop that now. What's done is done." I pushed her away and turned her toward the boat.

As the ship pulled away, I watched Luella leaning over the rail on the top deck waving furiously, her large hat tilting in the wind, her coat flapping open. She was a beautiful woman. I imagined her marrying an Englishman, and one day standing on some European coast watching her daughter depart, the women in our family stuck in a loop of attempted escape. Over time Luella would discover, as I had, as her daughter would, that we can't outrun ourselves.

I thought of my mother sinking to her

knees on the pier at my departure for America so many years ago, and how annoyed I'd been with her dramatic display. Now, it was all I could do to stay on my feet, weeping and waving even when I could no longer see my daughter or Georges leaning over the rail as the boat puffed and steamed out to sea.

# CHAPTER TWENTY-THREE: MABLE

I didn't get up for a week after Mama's death. Mrs. Hatch brought me food, standing in the doorway with the awkwardness of one who isn't used to helping people out of tragic situations. She said she was sorry about my mother, and that I could stay until the baby was born, but then I'd have to find new lodging. "I've heard there's homes for girls like you." She smiled at her own resourcefulness. "I'll find out the name of one if you like."

"Thank you," I said, not caring one way or another. I was already hollow and dead inside. It didn't matter where the shell of me landed.

One day Mrs. Hatch knocked on the door and said a Marie Casciloi was downstairs asking for me. "Claims she's your aunt. Thought you said you had no family?" Her words were clipped, suspicious.

I traced my eyes around a water stain on

the wall. "She's lying. I don't know her."

"If this is some kind of game, I don't like it." I could hear Mrs. Hatch scratching her scalp and I imagined it flaking all over my floor. "If you've got family there's no reason for me to be bringing you food. She the mother of the boy who fathered this baby?"

"No. I don't know her. I swear it."

"Well," she sighed, deliberating. "If I was you, I'd take this aunt whether she's real or not. Seems like she's here to help."

I didn't answer. Mrs. Hatch waited a minute, sighed with frustration and shut the door. I heard her light footsteps descending the stairs.

The idea of my weeping aunt in Mrs. Hatch's kitchen, her smell of onion and yeast and her soft bosom, made me feel a faraway longing, like a dream that is utterly ungraspable. Under no circumstance would I go to my aunt. It would have humiliated Mama if her sister so much as knew I was pregnant, and I was certain the last thing she would have wanted was for me to burden her family with a bastard child.

I had not done right by Mama in life, and I would be damned if I wasn't going to do everything I could by her in death.

That night, there was a note on my food tray, next to a plate of turnip, squash and ham. "I didn't read it," Mrs. Hatch said, setting the tray on the floor and turning on the light. "You best eat all of that," she said before leaving.

I rolled onto my side, poking a turnip with my dirty fingernail. I hadn't taken a bath in two weeks. All I wanted was sleep, which I had no problem falling into and the darnedest time getting out of. Opening my eyes felt like dragging myself up out of mud.

I ate the turnip, slick with butter, my fingers leaving greasy fingerprints along the edge of the note. The writing was small and hard to read. It took me three tries to make out that Aunt Marie had lost the twins and was sorry for what happened between us.

*When they didn't come home I went to find them,* she wrote. *By the time I arrived at the factory, the police were laying the victims out on the sidewalk, tagging them and putting them in wagons. I recognized Grazia by my grandmother's ring she wore. Her hair was matted around what was left of her face. All I could think of was how upset she'd be at the state of her hair. How ridiculous is that? You'd be amazed that I didn't cry. The shock froze everything inside me. When the policeman lifted her into a coffin, I grabbed at the poor man's arm and I told him he had to find my daughter's twin sister and keep them together, no matter what. "They've never been apart," I begged. That kind man took my hand and led me down the row of bodies until we found her. There was nothing left of Alberta's face either, her poor legs broken in a way that laying her straight didn't hide. I only knew her by the stockings I'd knitted for her at Christmas.*

*I stayed to make sure Alberta's coffin was put in beside her sister's. I couldn't stomach looking for your Mama just then, but first thing the next morning I went to Charities Pier. Someone had removed your mother's shoes and they were nowhere to be found. I went home and fetched a pair of my own for her.*

*The burial is tomorrow. I think the good Lord would want us to go together. After this, the sin of the flesh doesn't seem to matter so much. Please, Signe dear, call on us tomorrow. We're leaving for the funeral procession at 10 am. God keep you safe.*

*Marie Casciloi.*

The sin of the flesh mattered to Mama. It mattered so much she'd looked right past my growing stomach as if it didn't exist. I was sure it would matter again to Marie if she saw me in this condition. I tore the note into tiny pieces and let them drift through my fingers. I was sorry about the twins, but in the same numb, distant way I felt about everything. The reality of each day felt slightly out of my reach, like I was viewing it from far away.

The next morning, I got out of bed, dressed and fixed my hair. My legs were stiff and going down the stairs made them ache. Mrs. Hatch wasn't in the kitchen and the house was quiet. I pulled on my coat and stepped outside into the wet and cold. My coat no longer fit and a light rain settled over the top of my protruding middle. I'd forgotten a hat, and by the time I reached Washington Square my hair was limp and wet.

A solid mass of black coats and hats and umbrellas stretched as far as I could see. A horse-drawn hearse made its way down the street, the white horses grand as anything, with black netting draped over their powerful hides and tassels hanging from their ears. The hearse was covered in flowers, white and purple and pink. I didn't know if this funeral was for all the victims, or someone important, but I chose to believe it was Mama in that hearse.

Behind the hearse came a procession of mourners. I stepped in next to a woman with a wide, purple sash slung over one shoulder. She held a banner that said: *LA-DIES WAIST AND DRESSMAKERS UNION WE MOURN OUR LOSS.* The woman smiled at me, her face strong and handsome. I ducked my head and kept my eyes on the slick, wet pavement underfoot. Rain trickled down my neck and under the collar of my coat, reminding me of another funeral back at our cabin. I didn't know where we were walking and I didn't care. I only hoped Aunt Marie wouldn't see me.

I marched for hours, holding my weighted stomach up with one hand, my soaked shoes making a squishing noise, my wet skirt sticking between my legs. My hips hurt and my legs tingled as if they were going numb. I tried to pull strength from the woman next to me. She strode with her shoulders thrust back and her head high. There was a challenge in her eye, as if she'd been prepared and waiting for this day. I thought of the twins who had marched for women's rights, for unions. They'd been fighting a whole city of men, the same ones who locked them up and burnt them to death. Now, here was this woman, this stranger, taking up the fight for them. I moved closer to her, hoping her strength might infect me, that I, too, might feel passionate about something.

But by the time we reached the Brooklyn Bridge, all I felt was exhaustion. There was a sharp pain in my middle and the people penning me in on all sides made me anxious. I pushed my way through the crowd to Chambers Street where the sidewalk opened up and allowed me a path home. I barely made it to my room, collapsing on the bed with the weight of an elephant, the burning between my legs, and squeezing of my abdomen, a whole new kind of hell.

Mrs. Hatch heard me screaming and fetched a midwife, a sturdy, buxom woman who latched her hands over mine and squeezed so hard she practically pushed that baby out for me, talking the whole time, her voice velvety and soothing as candlelight.

Only, that baby decided to stick halfway and a doctor had to be called in. I was in such a state, I hardly noticed the man's head disappearing under the sheet over my knees. I can't be sure, but there was such an agonizing twisting and wrenching inside me I think that doctor stuck his hands right up and yanked the baby out himself. When it ended, I couldn't see straight.

There was a sharp cry and the doctor said, "Breech. Hardest kind to deliver, but you did it, young lady. Look at this pink beauty you've brought into the world." The midwife was holding the thing and I promptly turned my head to the wall. "Just a few minor stitches here and I'll be on my way," he said. Tears stung my eyes as a stab sunk into the fleshy part of my torn-open body. I clamped my teeth and clutched the sheet until he eased my legs down and adjusted the covers over them. "You've done good work. Get some rest, now, you hear? Mrs. Hatch is a kind woman. She'll look after you until you find your way."

The doctor left me with the midwife, who cooled my forehead with a wet cloth and smiled at me from her supple, fleshy face. I thought it was the kindest smile I'd ever known and I found myself wishing she were my mama and would stay the night with me. I didn't even mind so much when she placed that warm, slippery thing into my arms.

"A girl." She beamed, proud as if she was my mama. Looking at the empty bedroll on the floor she said, "You got someone to help you?" I nodded, but she looked skeptical. "It doesn't look like you've got any baby clothes, or even a blanket for the little one. You prepared for this?" She jutted her chin at my chest where the baby wriggled helplessly. "You bring her to your nipple. That's what she's looking for."

I turned my eyes to the ceiling and didn't move to help the baby. Reaching over, the midwife pinched my nipple and shoved it into the baby's mouth. The sucking stung like the dickens.

"Look what a good girl she is?" the midwife said. "That's all it takes, for now. I'm going to leave you two to sleep, but I'll be back to check on you first thing tomorrow morning. She'll stay warm if you keep her close."

I waited until the midwife was gone to pull the baby off, my nipple stretching out and making a popping sound when she let go. The midwife had given me a cotton blanket, torn at one edge like she'd ripped it from a bigger one, and told me I was to wrap the baby up in it until she brought something proper over. I did it like I'd seen Papa do with the others, tucking the blanket over the baby's feet and binding her arms to her sides. Her eyes were closed and she didn't move. She was either sedated from feeding, or dead. I poked her, wondering why I didn't feel any more for her than I had when she was a lump in my stomach. When she wriggled, all I could think was that I hadn't had the good fortune of birthing a dead baby like Mama. I placed her away from me on Mama's bunched petticoats and rolled over with my back to her, so tired the room waved around me.

I slept in fits, the baby's screams waking me, high-pitched and demanding. She wiggled periodically, stretched out a hand, gave a raspy howl, went silent. By midnight, I was itching out of my skin.

I blame what happened next on the fire and those burnt girls, on Papa leaving and Mama being gone, on all my siblings lumped under the ground. The dead occupied so much space inside me, you could say it was inevitable. Or, maybe it was just my lack of sleep.

In the middle of the night when the piercing cry of an infant started up again, I felt crazy. Not wild crazy. Dazed crazy, like someone who's been held under water too long and survives, but shouldn't have. All I wanted was for the screaming to stop. It never occurred to me to put the baby to my breast and set my nipple burning again. I got up and tugged my bloomers on, pulled my dress over my head and buttoned the back. My stomach was soft and bulky and would cramp in painful spasms. I put on my coat and lifted the wailing infant in my arms, holding her face to my chest to muffle the noise. Her mouth opened and she quieted, her head wobbling under my hand as I went down the dark stairs and out into the night, walking all the way to the pier on 26th Street with a throbbing pain between my legs.

I don't know why I went there, or what I was even doing out in the dark. All I remember was needing to get out of that godforsaken room, and since this was the last place I'd headed in the middle of the night, it seemed logical to go there again.

The building was quiet and dark, everyone gone to weep over gravestones instead of open coffins. The rain had stopped, but the sky was starless, the air cold and damp. At one point I looked down, forgetting all about the baby in my arms, and that's when I saw that she was dead. In the moonlight, she looked just like that pale baby I'd put in the ground. She didn't move or cry and I stared at her, not knowing what to do. There was no earth to dig. No hole to put her in. I rounded the back of the building where the dock yawned out over the East River, water slapping against the side of a steamboat. It smelled fishy, which made me hesitate as I dropped the bundle in my arms over the edge of the dock. She made the softest splash, and a drop of water hit the back of my hand. In that moment I thought I heard a sound, some small noise, but when I looked over the edge of the pier, the water was still and black, like nothing had been there at all. I told myself I hadn't heard anything. But I did. I hear it still.

I should have thrown myself into the river with her and why I didn't, I'll never understand. All the girls who'd been laid out in the building behind me had survived infancy and childhood, only to end up jumping away from a burning death and into the cement arms of another. Life wasn't worth it. Drowning in that dark water would have been a blessing, but I was without emotion. I turned from the dock and thought stupidly that I might go to Marie's now that I didn't have the baby. There was no evidence of her other than my sagging belly.

The street was quiet and dark. I could hear the slapping of water on the pier. Smell tar and fish rot. Not a single person was out. I hurried, thinking I looked suspicious out here all alone. I didn't know the hour, but whatever the time, I couldn't go to Aunt Marie's tonight. She'd know something was wrong.

Not knowing where else to go, I went back to my room and lay down in a silence that buzzed. I hated this room. I longed for my loft bed in the cabin, or the tiny room in the tenement with Marie's soft snoring. It dawned on me that the midwife was coming in the morning and I'd have to explain the missing child. The inexplicable nature of what I'd done roused me out of bed and

I locked the door, resting my forehead on the soft fabric of Mama's dress before lying down, but I couldn't sleep. I was wired, jumpy.

Morning crept in, a weak light that erased the shadows from the walls, Mama's ghost at the back of the door materializing as fabric and thread. A knock came, and her dress shifted slightly.

"Signe, I have your breakfast." Mrs. Hatch's voice was soft, hoping not to wake the baby, most likely.

"Thank you. You can leave it. I'm indisposed," I called.

"I see. Well, the midwife rang to say she's got another birth and can't come today. But she'll be here first thing tomorrow morning. For now, you're both to stay fed and warm." There was a pause. "Are you warm enough? Is the baby nursing all right?"

My breasts had crystalized and turned to rock in the night. "Yes, we're perfectly fine, thank you."

"Very well then, eat up and I'll be back for the tray in a bit."

I stood up, dizzy. The air vibrated around me, hummed and whispered. When was the last time I'd slept, or eaten? The night before Mama's funeral, I figured.

Quick and stealthy, I pulled in the tray

and relocked the door. I forced down the food, the slimy eggs harder to manage than the dry toast that crumbled all over the bed. The milk was pleasant, cold and refreshing, and I thought of our old cow, Mandy, and her sad, soulful eyes. I wondered if she was still alive. How long did cows live for?

When I finished, I left the empty plate in the hall so Mrs. Hatch wouldn't question my lack of appetite. The food made me drowsy, but I fought it. I liked the glisten of exhaustion, the tingle and brightness.

By late afternoon the air began to erode. Light popped at the corners of my eyes and it hurt to keep them open. I lay down, then, and despite my efforts, tumbled headlong into the deepest sleep I've ever known. I slept right through into the next day when a rapping woke me. It took me a moment to remember where I was. I felt heavy and disarranged, like I'd been shaken and left to settle with all my parts upside down.

"Signe?"

I sat up. "Yes?" My voice came out heavy.

"It's Mrs. Hatch. Are you all right?"

"I'm fine. Trying to get a little sleep is all."

"It's ten in the morning and you haven't touched the tray I left outside your door. Is the baby okay?"

"Yes. She's sleeping. Leave the tray. I'll

get to it when I see fit."

There was a long pause before she said, "The midwife was here earlier but said not to wake you. She'll be back this afternoon."

"That's fine." I crawled out of bed, struggling to lace my shoes. Sleep, and the stark, bright morning, made everything sharp and real. Lord almighty, what had I done? I was sure even dropping an already dead baby into the river was criminal.

I listened for the retreat of Mrs. Hatch, and then stuck my head into the hallway, making sure no one was about before snatching a hunk of bread from the tray and hurrying outside. Rain lingered on the sidewalks. Puddles glinted. Massive, white clouds floated above the buildings like a double world resting on top of this one. If only I could disappear into that soft world, I thought, as the one I was in felt brittle as bone.

I walked with no clear direction, the stitches between my legs stinging as my thighs rubbed together. I wished I had money for a proper meal. I'd finished the bread and my stomach still pinched with hunger. I thought of going to Mulberry Street. Maybe Renzo was sitting on his crate smoking in the courtyard. I could confess what I'd done. Burden him. Make him sorry he hadn't stuck by me. Or I could pretend I'd never had a baby and walk right past him to Aunt Marie's. She wanted me back. She said so, and now there was nothing left to humiliate Mama.

The sick reality of my situation kept me walking all day, despite the pain between my legs. I went up and down streets I'd never seen, watching cars and carriages rumble past, people swirling every which way like a directionless tide, the sun shifting the shadows of the buildings from one side of the street to the other. My stomach muscles felt torn and strung out, but the hunger pains were gone and I was only slightly light-headed from lack of food and water. The worst thing was the milk leaking from my breasts and wetting the front of my dress. I was grateful my coat fit over them. I buttoned it all the way up, shoved my hands into my pockets and kept my eyes on the ground.

It was dark by the time I made my way to Columbus Circle. Not until I stood in front of Ernesto did I realize I'd come intentionally, deluding myself that I could find solace in my cousin's kind, familiar face. His big eyes widened in surprise, and we looked dumbly at each other, neither one of us knowing what to say. A well-dressed man peeled a newspaper from the stack by Ernesto's feet and dropped a coin in my cousin's ink-stained hand, rolling the newspaper into a tube as he walked away.

Ernesto tossed the coin in the air, finding the nerve to say, "I'm sorry about your mama."

"I'm sorry about your sisters."

"Seems silly saying *sorry.*" The coin somersaulted through the air, smacking his palm. "It's so much bigger than sorry, but I don't have the words."

"Neither do I." There was an uncomfortable silence before I noticed Ernesto was without his brother. "Where's Little Pietro?"

"Mama keeps him home now."

"How does she afford it?"

"Armando's come home."

"That's good, I suppose. It didn't work out with the woman?"

"I guess not. He didn't say."

Another man stopped to buy a paper, dropping his money in Ernesto's hand without looking at him.

My eyes wandered to the stack and I heard Ernesto ask, "You doing all right?" at the very moment I read the headline: *FISHERMAN PULLS INFANT FROM THE EAST RIVER.* My breath froze. I reached for the paper. *A baby girl was found drowned in the*

*East River at 3am yesterday morning, April 6, 1911. Police are attempting to trace the fabric the baby was wrapped in and imploring any- one with information regarding this heinous crime to come forward.* There was no picture of the baby, just the torn cotton blanket displayed in a small square next to the words.

I dropped the paper and ran, Ernesto's voice fading away as he called after me. I darted around people. A woman gasped as I cut in front of her and turned blindly down a street, running until I doubled over with a sharp cramp in my side. A warm trickle ran down my leg and I wondered if my stitches had ripped open. *Drowned.* How did they know that? Was there water in her lungs? Her lungs would have filled with water even if she had died before, wouldn't they? It didn't matter. I'd hang, I thought, propel- ling myself forward and barreling down the sidewalk, no longer dazed, but frighteningly lucid. I had planned to tell Mrs. Hatch and the midwife I'd given the baby to an orphan- age. They'd never believe me now. The midwife had torn that cotton blanket her- self. She'd know exactly whose it was.

I thought of the photograph I'd left be- hind, Mama and me staring out with stern, colorless faces. My picture would be all over the newspapers. Marie would find out, Renzo and his mother. I wasn't a Casciloi, but they'd never live down the scandal. I had failed Mama again. *Signe Hagen convicted of murder.* In the end it was Papa's good name I'd ruin.

I thought of all those little lives we laid in the ground together. All those babies he'd hoped and prayed would live and here I'd gone and snuffed the life out of a perfectly good one for no reason.

I ended up on Green Street, walking past the burnt Asch Building and the restaurant where I'd vomited on the sidewalk. A couple came out of the door laughing as if nothing bad had ever happened here. The blood was washed away, and people traipsed without a care over the squares where the bodies had fallen. The only reminder of the fire was the blown-off top of the Asch Building, and a collapsed fire escape hanging like a mangled arm from its side. I looked at the charred, crumbled wreckage debating whether it'd be best to jump into the river from the dock, or over the side of the Brooklyn Bridge. I was clearheaded enough to do it now. I turned away from the building, deciding it didn't matter where I jumped. Either way, I couldn't swim and the water would take me quickly.

Heading east with my head down, deep in thought and moving quickly, I rounded the corner of 12th Avenue and walked smack into a man in a long black coat, his bowler hat falling to the ground.

"Good gracious!" he cried, catching hold of me as I lost my balance and stumbled into him. The impact was dizzying and I tried to steady myself and pull away, but the man kept a firm hold on my wrist. "Are you all right?"

"I'm fine," I said, but when he released me I slid to the ground as if my legs were made of jelly. I let out an embarrassed laugh. "How stupid of me."

The man crouched beside me. He was pleasant to look at, with a slight build and delicate, perfectly placed features. He picked up his hat, dangling it from the end of his fingers. "The sidewalk is not the best place to sit this time of day. Come." He offered his arm, hoisting me to my feet. "A bit of food might do the trick, yes?" he said, guiding me down the street.

I was too shaken to protest, or think past putting one foot in front of the other. At the end of the block the man opened a door and we entered a smoke-filled room, chaotic with noise and the sour smell of sweat and cigars. I looked around wondering how I could be so easily waylaid from my intention to jump into the river.

"This place isn't for everyone," the man said loudly in my ear. "But you don't look like a girl who's used to the finer things in life."

This insult smacked me in the gut. How the hell did he know what I was used to? I shifted my weight off his arm as he guided me to a slick, wooden bar where men and women mingled on high stools, swigging drinks and twirling cigarettes. A row of round tables, each with a lamp that gave off a dim, red glow, lined the wall up to a back room where loud music played over the ruckus of laughter and conversation.

Instead of ordering food, the man ordered me a drink that I coughed and sputtered out over the front of my coat. "Put some color back into those cheeks." He laughed, reaching an arrogant hand to the top button of my coat and carefully undoing it. I hoped he didn't notice the milk crusted over the front of my dress as he drew the coat from my shoulders and draped it over his arm. He was petite nosed and refined. Not at all the sort of man I imagined frequented a place like this.

"Never mind the drink. It's all about the music." He took my hand and drew me past the tables to the back room where a colored man sat at a piano, his fingers flying over the keys. The floor vibrated under my feet as people danced in ways I'd never seen.

The man cupped his hand over my ear and shouted, "Scott Joplin. The king of ragtime." His breath smelled of whisky. Something I remembered Papa drinking once in a while.

Without missing a beat, he took off his coat and hat, plucked my drink from my hand, dropped it all into the arms of a passing waiter and drew me onto the dance floor.

The only music I knew was Papa's violin, and the Cascilois' singing around the dinner table. I certainly didn't know how to dance, but the man grabbed hold of my hips and moved them in quick, jerky motions that somehow made sense. Everything fell away as the music vibrated up my legs and the floor rolled under my feet. The alcohol still burned in my throat and made me feel like I was floating. I was no longer hungry or tired and the pain between my legs had faded to a dull ache. I didn't even mind the man's hands roaming where they shouldn't. It reminded me of how good it felt to be with Renzo. I forgot all about my plan to jump into the river. And it was the first full hour since I'd woken that morning that I hadn't thought about what I'd done and the bad things that were coming.

After three numbers, we collapsed at the table, catching our breath. The man waved his hand at the waiter and ordered two more drinks.

This one was sweet and tasted of mint and lemons. I drank it quickly. "What is it?" I asked.

"Gin Fizz." The man propped his elbows on the table. "And what, my dear girl, are you?"

I watched a drop of water roll down the outside of my glass. It was clear what he meant, and there was no way he was getting any kind of answer out of me.

"A shy one?" He smiled. "At least give me a name to go along with that lovely face?"

The newspaper headline swam back at me. By tomorrow my name would be in every paper. The room swelled with music and the man said, "I'll get your name out of you one way or another," and lifted me to the dance floor. The piano was quick and lively and I moved next to him, loose and sloppy. Looking around at the dancers' arms and legs jiggling to the tempo, I couldn't help but think of the distorted limbs of the fallen girls on the pavement.

"Your name?" The man put his hand on the small of my back, his lips to my ear.

"Mable Winter," I said, remembering the name of the Sunday school teacher at Marie's church. I'd always thought it such a lovely name.

"Mable Winter." The man whistled, moving me slowly off the dance floor and pressing me against the wall in just the way Renzo had in the doorway of the tenement. My head swirled and my ears rang with the sound of piano keys, voices, clinking glasses and tapping shoes. The man's lips were salty and he tasted like the drink in my glass. This man was no good, and yet I let him press himself on me. I liked the smothering heat and whirlwind sensation. He either didn't notice the milk leaking down the front of my dress, or didn't care. He kissed fast and hard and I was hoping he'd suck the life out of me when the pressure suddenly let up. I opened my eyes to see the man being dragged off me by the back of his shirt.

"All right, that's enough." A wide, baby-faced policeman stood over us, his badge glinting in the lamplight.

The music had stopped and there was a commotion of angry voices. The room rocked and I felt dizzy and hot. Sweat trickled down my side. The midwife's al-

415

ready gone to the police, I thought, panic launching me forward. The policeman snatched my arm. "Oh no you don't. We've been through this before."

*We have?* I wondered as he pushed me out the door. Outside, the air was cool and damp. I heard shouting and swearing and the lights of the buildings tipped and swirled against the night sky, disappearing with a bang as I was shoved into the back of a police wagon.

Turns out that no-good man saved me. Isn't that the oddity of life? I don't doubt for a second I'd have jumped into the river, or wandered the streets until I was recognized and convicted as a baby killer, if I hadn't bumped into him. Instead, I woke up in a jail cell as a prostitute.

The booze made my memory of the night before fuzzy as that gin drink. Not until I opened my eyes to the light coming from a small, square window did I remember being arrested. I stood up, my body aching all over, and walked to that square of light. I leaned against the concrete wall and tapped the pain in my temples with my fingertips. There were six other girls in there with me, two slumped asleep against the wall, the others sitting on a bench with their elbows on their knees. They looked weary and angry, their eyes saying, *don't mess with me. I'm in no mood.* The pain between my legs was excruciating and it felt like a swab of cloth was stuck to my tongue. Not until midmorning did a policeman come down the hall, banging his stick against the metal bars so we had to hold our ears. He laughed, unlocked the door and led us, single file, down the hall and out a side door where another officer herded us into a police wagon.

We were taken to a glittering courtroom and sat shoulder to shoulder on sleek benches under bright lights. The judge called us up one by one, peering down from his perch. When my turn came, and he asked my name, I said *Mable Winter* without pause.

That idiot judge convicted Mable Winter to three years in a reform home for prostitution, as secure a place as any to hide out.

After that, Signe Hagen was as good as dead.

■ ■ ■ ■

# BOOK THREE

■ ■ ■ ■

# CHAPTER TWENTY-FOUR: EFFIE

I was released from the sanitarium on the day of my fourteenth birthday. It was New Year's and the girls had prepared a musical performance. In the room above the chapel, winter sunlight struggled through the dirty windows where Sister Agnes and Sister Mary ushered girls to chairs, fluttering their hands and clucking like anxious hens.

They glanced my way, whispering and nudging each other as I took my seat. I sat in a chair at the back looking around for Mable. When I didn't see her, I scanned the backs of the younger girls up front for Dorothea, but didn't see her either. A girl I didn't recognize took a seat at the piano, running her fingers along the top of the dusty fallboard with an exaggerated look of disgust that sent a round of laughter through the room. There was a sharp rebuke from Sister Gertrude, and the girl pinched her lips together in smug submission and lifted the fallboard.

As her fingers moved across the keys, I was stricken with homesickness. She was playing Liszt's *Années de Pelerinage,* a song I used to play for Luella while she practiced her arabesques. The grace of my sister's arms and the soft thud of her feet came back to me as the music played, the memory so abrupt it brought tears to my eyes. I tightened my jaw, shaking off the tears as I forced myself to remember the hard floor and the pain in my chest. I was not going to cry. My memories were trinkets of pain compared to the abuse my body endured.

The song came to an end with a burst of applause as the girl gave a dramatic curtsy. Other acts followed. Duets and solos were sung, more tunes banged out on the piano to cheers and boos, the girls getting restless. When it was over, there was yellow cake with white frosting — a gift from the Ladies Aid Society — which I ate reluctantly, my stomach shrunken and filling quickly. A few bites in I felt a hand squeeze my shoulder and looked up as Sister Gertrude's ageless, white face broke into a smile.

"I am glad to see you back with us," she said, her eyes fragments of a deceptively calm sky. *"Almighty God, the supreme Governor of all things, whose power no creature is able to resist, to whom it belongeth justly to punish sinners, and to be merciful to those who truly repent."* She released her grip. "The good Lord has given you a second chance. I trust you will use it wisely. Finish up." She gave a motherly nod at my plate, waiting until I lifted my fork.

Anger uncoiled in my gut, pure and huge and satisfying. I sliced my fork into my cake, glancing at Sister Gertrude's hands for signs of my teeth marks. Sadly, they were as smooth and unmarked as her face, and I wondered whose hand I'd bitten. "Where's Dorothea?" I asked, not daring to ask about Mable.

"Her father came for her." It pleased Sister Gertrude to say this, to emphasize the fact that no one had come for me. "You're to go directly to the dormitory when you've finished," she said, moving away, the hem of her black habit flicking like a cat's tail across the floor.

I bit back a smile, pieces of the sweet, spongy cake sticking to the roof of my mouth. Dorothea's father had come for her. She had her happy ending.

A man waits on the porch twisting his hat in his hands and stamping his cold feet, looking at the snowdusted hillside. He is

423

nervous, and wonders if he's made a mistake. This place is far nicer than anything he can give his daughter. The door opens abruptly, startling him, his daughter running at him so fast her thin frame hits his legs with an impact greater than either of them expects. She buries her face in his stomach and latches her arms around his waist. He hadn't anticipated crying. When he looks up, the sister standing in the doorway grimaces, as if reunions, or the weakness of a man in tears, disgusts her. He doesn't care. Lifting his daughter into his arms, he knows, without a doubt, that he has not made a mistake.

I held this image all the way through cake and up into my bed, letting the absence of Dorothea in the next room delight me, regardless of the fact that I missed her.

The sisters determined I was well enough for sorting, and the following day I returned to my old station in the laundry room. I expected the usual silence and stony glances, but as soon as Sister Agnes closed the door behind her, the girls flocked to the sorting table pressing me with questions. *Which window did you leap from? How far did you get? Did you see Edna fall? Was it very gory? Did the dogs get you? We heard you got a foot bit off? Can we see?*

Unused to popularity of any kind, I recoiled and dropped my eyes to the table in silence. *Come on,* they said. *You can't fool us with your timid act.* There was more urging and questioning until someone shouted, "Leave her alone!"

I looked up at Mable standing behind a steaming vat of water. She was thin, her features stark and chiseled, her face damp and sweaty, the muscles in her neck tensing. Her hair had grown into a yellow fuzz that crowned her brow and stuck out around her ears. Even from across the room, the spectral blue of her eyes was discomfiting. She kept them on me as she dropped her hand into the vat and resumed scrubbing, my popularity vanishing as the girls glowered and grumbled back to their laundry stations.

If she was looking for forgiveness, I wasn't going to give it. In the pit, I discovered anger was better than despair.

Over the next few months, I kept my resentment burning, growing a little hotter each day. I kept the image of Mable and Edna running away from me fresh in my mind, along with the memory of my father tripping up the stairs with Inez, and my fight with Luella the morning she went to the gypsies without me. I reached for memories that hurt, like Mama insisting I wear gloves to cover my clubbed fingernails and Luella saying she envied my blue fits, giving credit to something that kept me weak and her strong.

I learned of Edna's death in rumored fragments. One girl told me she heard Edna leapt blindly from the wall and landed on the craggy rocks bordering the Hudson.

"Broke nineteen bones!" she cried. "The police didn't find her until early morning and rushed her to Washington Heights Hospital, but she was dead before nightfall."

A girl named Tilly, who now slept in the bed next to me, said she heard Edna was alive for three days on the rocks before anyone found her.

Some of the girls claimed she'd escaped into the night and Sister Gertrude had made up the story to scare us. *Because how else did Mable survive?* they wondered. Easily, I thought, remembering how nimbly she'd leapt from the rope compared to Edna's ungraceful plummet to the ground.

No one dared ask Mable anything, but they didn't mind approaching me. I told them the truth. I never made it to the wall. I fainted on the lawn. I saw nothing.

"Then why were you in the infirmary for so long?" Suzie Trainer demanded one evening, as she and six other girls surrounded me in the hall as we made our way to chapel.

"Have you ever been in the pit?" I said with a satisfying edge I'd been honing. "It would make you sick too."

None of them looked like they believed me, but I wasn't going to show them my hand. I liked that the girls didn't know about my heart condition; not even Suzie Trainer, who had paid no attention to me in our Chapin School days. For the first time in my life, I was seen as courageous and daring. What did the truth matter anyway?

My truth had been that Luella was in here, and she wasn't. My truth had been escaping into the night, and I hadn't. The truth of my whole life had been that my heart was failing, and now it had stabilized, which meant this asylum doctor had done what my parents' doctors couldn't. Maybe I'd saved myself by locking myself away. Maybe that was the truth. And if Edna had died falling from the wall, then the truth was she and Mable hadn't left me as bait. They'd saved my life.

By March, the weekly mercury treatments

succeeded in keeping the swelling down and my blue fits under control, but a film lay over my mind that blurred my thoughts. I stopped imagining stories. The scene of Dorothea and her father was the last story I told myself, and it became a gold nugget I'd take out and polish to keep shiny, as if remembering it over and over would somehow bring clarity back to my senses. I had little appetite and often vomited in the bathroom. My collarbone protruded and my ribs became bumpy as a washboard. I tried to hide my tremors, but I could hardly hold a fork without it clattering against the plate.

"You've got to eat more," Tilly said one day as we walked into the dining room. "Keep up your energy. If you're well, you'll get to go to Valhalla in May."

Valhalla was a farm where a select number of girls were taken in the summer. A program designed to show the trustees what good work the sisters were doing providing work for the girls and extra funding for the grounds. "Truthfully," Tilly smirked, "Sister Gertrude pockets the money for her sherry and steak. Soil's so bad at the farm we can't grow a thing, but that's no matter. I'd grow weeds for a breath of fresh air."

"Who gets to go?"

"Only the most reformed."

Despite my exhaustion and loss of co-ordination, I was determined to set myself on a path of righteousness, arriving bright-eyed for the 7:00 a.m. Holy Eucharist, raising my voice in prayer, working at the laundry with my eyes down, my hate pulsing under my ribs.

Mable, I noticed, was doing the same. She made no waves; no longer slapped or tormented the new girls. She kept her mouth shut and her head high, meeting the gaze of any girl who dared look at her as if she'd eat them alive. We all steered clear of her, which was easy now that she was no longer head laundress. An Irish girl named Darvela had taken over. Bigger than Mable, she'd plant herself at the ironing table flicking her green eyes around the room, ready to smack the back of a lazy girl's head, or dash water in the face of anyone she disliked.

I kept an eye on Mable, wondering if she'd try and speak with me. I couldn't get the image of that policeman shouting at her in the infirmary out of my head, and how she'd held her ground. I wondered about her false name, and the oddity that we were both here under assumed identities. I wanted to know what she'd done as much as that policeman, and through the haze of my mind, a plan began to form. I didn't have the details worked out, but it involved getting Mable to trust me, which wasn't going to be easy. Her eyes still held the glassed-over remove I'd seen when the policeman stood by her bed, but at times, she did look at me from across the laundry room, as if contemplating our positions in a game neither one of us understood the rules to.

I began sitting with her at dinner and chapel. I didn't say anything, as I didn't want to be too obvious, but I needed her to believe I'd forgiven her.

It was the end of May, during lunch, when Sister Gertrude announced the girls who would be going to the farm. A wagon, she said, beaming, would be coming the following week to take twenty-five girls to Valhalla. I held my breath, my hard-boiled egg and spinach cooling on my plate. Since the weather had warmed, we were allowed a daily outing in the walled courtyard behind the chapel, a square of dirt peppered with rocks and weeds, the sky barely visible above the high barred windows and sloping rooftops. Just to stretch my eyes to a horizon, and wiggle my toes in the grass, would be a benediction. Escape, a miracle. But Mable had to go too, otherwise my plan would never work.

The names were announced with intentional slowness, Sister Gertrude's superior smile fueling the heat of anger in my belly. She enjoyed this torture. Mable's name was called and I sighed with relief, until she said, "That's all. Clear your dishes and head to chapel," and left the room. She had not called my name. Heat flared to my ears and set the tips on fire. Mable was not reformed any more than I was. Sister Gertrude had done it on purpose, to set us against each other. I cleared my dish, biting the inside of my cheek, determined to use her own tactic against her.

I lingered as the girls filed past, waiting to approach Sister Agnes who stayed behind to make sure we all kept moving. She hadn't forgotten the stolen key, and when I approached her she flapped her arms and lifted her plump chest like a penned-in bird ready to peck at me.

"Go on," she shooed, "get going with the rest of them."

I planted myself in front of her, noticing that I'd grown taller since I'd first arrived. "I want to speak with Sister Gertrude."

Sister Agnes ruffled the front of her habit. "You don't get to make that request, missy."

"I have important information about Mable's real identity."

It was delightful to see the stupefaction on Sister Agnes's face. She opened her mouth, snapped it shut, and then whirled me around by my shoulders. "You get back to work now and don't go making trouble."

I did as I was told, but within the hour, Sister Mary came for me in the laundry. Sister Gertrude wanted to see me straight-away, she said. I glanced at Mable, her eyes tracking me to the door as I followed Sister Mary out.

We went through the small waiting area into the room at the center of the house where, so many months ago, Herbert Roth-man had posed as my father. The lamp on the desk still leaked a pool of light over the shiny wood. Sister Gertrude shoved her arms into the glow and leaned forward, her face taut and bloodless, her white skin and black habit blending into the colorless room as if she sat in her own photograph, her magnificent blue eyes the only feature distinguishing her amongst the living.

Behind me I heard Sister Mary's shuffling retreat, then the click of the door. I fixed my eyes on the sculpture of Jesus on the side table, his outstretched palms and peaceful eyes as deceiving as Sister Ger-trude's. He hadn't cast any demons from the fallen girls in this place. The devil had bred them, as far as I could tell.

"I hear you have information for me." Sister Gertrude's voice was an octave higher than normal.

I steadied my breath. "Not yet, but I will have, if you send me to the farm with Mable."

A laugh cut through the room. "What gives you the right to stand here making requests of me?"

It was a dangerous move. Sister Gertrude wasn't beyond throwing me back in the pit. I planted my feet slightly apart, a posture I'd seen Darvela use to assert herself. "I know the police want Mable's real name, I heard them say as much. If you give me time, I can get it out of her."

My plan, when I had Mable's real name, was to tell Sister Gertrude that I would only disclose the information to the police. Once in front of them, I'd tell them who I was and make them contact my father before giving up Mable's identity. This was my last chance. Betraying Mable meant nothing to me.

Sister Gertrude leaned back in her chair, measuring me to the task. "Most girls are in here because they're either heading toward drink and prostitution, or have already arrived at it. There's no reason for Mable to give a false name unless she's hiding a greater crime. Knowing that girl, I would not put a more heinous act past her." From her pauses, and deliberate enunciation, it was clear that Sister Gertrude was trying to plant a seed of fear in me. "I don't like a girl being in here for a crime I'm unaware of. It puts us all at risk. You would be doing your duty to find out her real name. We don't leave for the farm for another week. I'm sure you can get it out of her by then."

I had no idea how I was getting Mable's name out of her at all. But there was no way I'd do it in a week. "I won't agree to it unless you send me to the farm too," I said.

A twitch started at the corner of Sister Gertrude's mouth and my heart gave a little jump. I glanced at the marble Jesus, his stony eyes as cold as the ones bearing down on me.

"Sister Agnes!" Sister Gertrude shouted, standing up and taking a lamp from the shelf.

Sister Agnes swooped in like a trained bird, plucked the lantern from Sister Gertrude with one hand and me with the other, her fingers curled around my upper arm as she marched me from the room and down the hall. When we passed the door to the laundry without stopping, my legs weakened. "You can't send me to the pit again," I cried. "I'll get sick and the doctor will have to be called in. You'll have to explain yourselves to him. I'm too weak for the pit."

I was met with a grunt, my legs collapsing as Sister Agnes swung open the cellar door. She hoisted me up by one arm and hauled me down like a rag doll, my shoes bumping each step with hollow clunks. She dragged me to the end of the hall, pulled a ring of keys from her pocket and shook them in my face. "I carry these everywhere with me now, thanks to you three." She set the lantern on the floor and slid back the bolt. "Go on. At least it's not winter-cold anymore." She shoved me in and the bolt settled back into place with a clang.

Darkness swallowed me. Sister Agnes's footsteps receded down the hall and I heard the steady drip of water plunking against the stone floor somewhere in the dark. A familiar tightness squeezed my chest and I pitched my head between my knees. The doctor hadn't cured me. He'd just dulled my symptoms for a while.

Instead of slinking into a corner or curling up in a ball, I unbuttoned my dress, pulled it over my head, wriggled out of my bloomers and lay stretched out with my bare backside on the cold floor. It made me think of the shape of my mother's back the day she undressed in front of me. I wanted my mother. I bit the inside of my cheek and spat the blood into the palms of my hands. I would not conjure the touch of my father's fingers on my wrist, the pits in my mother's scarred hands or the sound of Luella's dancing feet. These memories were no longer my foundation.

Closing my eyes, I thought of the final card I'd drawn with Tray. That was my truth. I conjured the lion who came to me in my dreams, the calf, eagle and man, and placed them in the four corners of the room. I gave them wings and eyes and set them chanting, *holy, holy, holy, The Lord God almighty.* I was the center, the naked woman with her wands. It was my mouth dripping bloodred saliva.

After a while I grew cold and I sat up and put my clothes back on. At some point the door opened and a tray of bread and water slid across the floor. I ate it, keeping the creatures dancing in the corner. They eased the tightness in my chest and made it possible for me to eat and sleep under their watchful eyes.

It couldn't have been more than a day or two before Sister Agnes came for me. She stood in the doorway with the lantern, shadows dancing over her face, and I was herded up the basement stairs and out the front door into the glaring morning sunlight, unsure of what was happening. A police officer, with a pasty, thick neck that squeezed out the top of his uniform like an overstuffed sausage, took me by the arm and helped me into the back of a black truck. I slid along the bench next to Tess, a big-boned girl I knew only by name. Other girls squeezed in next to me, and the policeman slammed the doors shut. The engine choked to a start and we lurched forward.

"Watch it." Tess shoved me and I braced my legs against the bench and tried not to slide into her as the truck came to a sudden halt. Male voices drifted through the slats. There was a gruff laugh and the sound of a gate clanging open and the truck moved forward again.

We were driving out. Half a mile and we'd be driving past my house. I held back the urge to jump up and press my mouth to the crack in the door and scream for my parents. What if Mama was crouched in the yard this very minute clearing leaves from her bulbs, or Daddy was standing in the doorway gazing at the sky? What if Luella had come home and was stepping out on her way to dance class, or devising some bright, spring-morning mischief without me?

We rattled on. The truck swayed and vibrated, the air thick and stuffy. Gas fumes, along with the smell of hot tar, leaked inside. City sounds bounced around like tennis balls inside the metal walls of the truck — horns, engines, clomping hooves and clanging trollies eventually giving way to the lone rumble of the truck, and the crunching of wheels over gravel.

Time dragged on in silence until the truck jolted to a stop and the doors swung open. "Come on out," the officer said, chipper, as if we'd arrived at a seaside vacation.

I squinted, my eyes adjusting to take in a dirt road and a wide, grassy field, the air sweet with honeysuckle. A second truck rattled to a stop behind us, kicking up a storm of dust. A disorderly group of girls tumbled out, Mable at the back. A police-man stepped out behind her, the dust settling over the shoulders of his dark blue suit. He and the other officer ushered us to the front door of a many-windowed farmhouse of whitewashed stone. I smiled. Sister Gertrude had sent me to the farm after all. What was a few days in the pit? I'd won.

Behind the farmhouse was a meadow sprinkled with purple wildflowers. A quiet thrill filled me as I realized that the only thing trapping us was a fence of skinny, hewn trees, bark flaking from the trunks like dry skin.

A sturdy woman with a deeply lined face met us at the door and exchanged a nod with the officers. She led us down a low-ceilinged hallway into a small, empty room with faded pink wallpaper and wide wooden floorboards. We stood penned in like cattle, the woman walling the doorway, her brown skirt ballooning out like a mound of dirt from which her torso had sprung.

"You see this room?" she asked, her eyes skimming over us. "Do you see a lick of furniture in it?" No one answered and she pressed a hand behind her ear with a piqued, "I can't hear you?" A few *no's* were mumbled. The woman smiled. "Very good. You're not nearly as stupid as the sisters make you out to be."

Around me, girls shuffled their feet and crossed their arms, the woman's hint of a smile enough to boil the coolest of blood.

"There is no furniture," she continued, "because there is no sitting other than at the table for meals. This is not a holiday, and I trust Valhalla will *not* meet your enthusiastic expectations. This is a working farm. You will rise before the sun and go to bed with it. You will be given rotating tasks, and if the work is too much, you'll work harder. Baths are on Saturday evening. Sunday is spent on your knees in prayer. I will answer to Miss Juska. If you think you've had a hard life, mine was harder. I do not take complaints and will punish the first girl who so much as hints at disquiet. These are not wrinkles of kindness on my face and I don't give a hoot about your salvation. You're all going to hell as far as I'm concerned. If those woods tempt you to sneak off, think again. Only one girl has ever tried, and she was eaten by coyotes. Forests are full of them. Bears. Wild cats. They'll tear your flesh from your bones before you get half a mile and there isn't another dwelling for twenty. No need for a wall when you've got the wild, is what I tell the sisters. If you choose to venture into it, you're only walking into your damnation faster."

Her speech ended with a grunt, her intention to frighten us succeeding as I glanced at the faces of girls who knew as little of the natural world as I did. We may have come from different sections of the city, but it was still a city. A forest with coyotes and bears was another peril altogether.

"Follow me." Miss Juska clapped her hands and we filed out of the room and up a narrow set of stairs, silent and ordered as ants, the wood creaking under our weight. At the top, Miss Juska's harsh voice ticked off the girls by groups of six, luck landing Mable and me together. Miss Juska drew a gold watch from her soiled apron pocket, clicked it open and instructed us to change and meet her at the bottom of the stairs in five minutes.

The rooms were small. Six beds each, three to a wall, crammed so close there was hardly space to walk between them. A single bureau abutted the far wall. Margaret, a girl with dark skin and bushy eyebrows, began pulling open the drawers and tossing rough linen dresses at us.

I changed quickly, looking out the small, paned window with its dirty, cracked glass. An ocean of thick, wavering trees stretched as far as I could see. It made the wall around the House of Mercy look like a bracelet you could fling off.

The only thing easing my mind, as I hurried down the stairs to Miss Juska counting the time, was the fact that I didn't have to escape. All I had to do was get Mable to tell me her name.

# CHAPTER TWENTY-FIVE: MABLE

The night we attempted our escape from the House of Mercy, all I could think about was my mother. If I was scared looking over the drainpipe, imagine her terror at jumping from the ninth floor of that building. It took Edna, flopping to the ground like a fish dropped over the side of a boat, laughing at the stars above her, to shake me out of my own fear. Edna could shake me out of anything.

During my first months in the House of Mercy, I went about my tasks with a listlessness that would have landed me in my grave if Edna hadn't hauled me out of my dark thoughts.

Our beds were right next to each other, and even though I didn't speak a word to her, she'd gab on and on until I'd fall asleep with her voice threading through my dreams.

"We're all hurt and broken," she said to

me one night, almost cheerful about it. "You're no different. You walk around with that sorry face, as if you're the only one's seen hardship. Have you tried looking at anyone else's face? Everyone in here's been put through the wringer."

She was beautiful, lying in moonlight, her dark hair spread out over the pillow. "Go on and tell me your story. No sense stewing in it. You say the words out loud, and you'll see it's not as bad as you think. Somehow, it's always worse in your head. No matter what you did, it's not your fault. None of this is. We're castoffs. That's why we got to fight for every bit of air we breathe. You go on and get it out. I'll shut my trap and listen."

I made up a story that Edna would believe, about an uncle who took advantage. *Men are the whole of our problems* I'd heard her say on more than one occasion. She was the protesting, fighting type. Talked as if she'd taken part in every march for women's rights there'd ever been. Edna reminded me of the woman I had walked beside during the funeral procession, and I found myself wanting to be near her all the time.

As resistant as I was to female friends, I began to find it empowering being sur-rounded by women who were ready to fight.

It was our strength in numbers that I grew to love. And Edna. I never loved anyone like I loved Edna.

Escaping was her idea. I tried to talk her out of it. "We've only got another year," I said. Truth was, I was scared of what waited for me out there.

"I'm done." Edna spat over the edge of the bed onto the dormitory floor. "If we can't fight our way out of here, how are we going to join the women out there fighting to get the vote?"

I'd crawled into bed next to her and we lay in the dark making plans for an impossible future: We would find the famed suffragette. She'd take us in and we'd march beside her, living off our victories, breathing in confidence and freedom. I liked this fantasy. I threw a sash over my shoulder and planted myself in the crowd with the same proud look on my face I'd seen the woman wear during the procession.

"If we're jailed —" Edna's voice rose and I pressed my hand to her mouth. She gently bit my finger and I stifled a laugh. "Like I was saying," she whispered. "It will be worth it. I'd take a real jail over this slave-labor-nunnery any day."

It was her idea to use the new girl, Effie.

Edna had a thing about weak girls. She thought they should all be sacrificed to make room for the ones strong enough to change the world.

The night we tore off into the dark, freedom alight in our limbs, I made the mistake of looking back. Edna never looked back. "Not my problem," she would have said. It was the pitiful look on Effie's face, and her thin helpless form in the dark, that sent guilt darting through me. My love for Edna was a double-edged sword, because it brought out a surprising set of emotions that I'd turned away from, feelings of shame and heartache. But when Edna reached for my hand, I thought no more of Effie as I dashed toward a future bright with deception.

At the bottom of the hill, the ground rose up unevenly and we stumbled, holding onto each other as we groped our way to the nearest tree. The sharp, insistent braying of the dogs reminded me of the yapping coyotes I'd listened to on full moon nights, with Papa sitting on the stone slab in the yard.

The dogs fell silent and I felt a flood of urgency. "Hurry up," I said, hoisting Edna onto the first branch and climbing after her, her dark shadow crawling overhead as she slid hazardously from the branch to the wall on her stomach.

"I can't move an inch or my fat bottom will roll right off," she said, laughing.

This was not a joke. The dark, the silence and the height of the wall unnerved me. "Hold still until I get to you," I commanded, easing off the branch onto my bottom, my feet dangling into a black abyss. All I could see were those girls leaping from the Asch Building. "Take my hand," I said, helping Edna to her knees. She sat up and pressed her body next to me.

"Praying never did me any good, but now might be the time for it, even if God's forgotten us," she said.

"The devil's the only one who's ever listened to me."

"We'll pray to the devil then. He's the only one who would want to keep the two of us fiends alive anyway."

I couldn't help smiling. "They'll be coming for us before we get a foot into freedom, at this rate."

"I'm ready." She squeezed my hand.

"On a count of three. One, two, three."

We dove into slippery darkness, our hands parting. It's amazing the pictures that can go through a person's head in a few seconds: my mother's battered face, Renzo's soft brown eyes, Aunt Marie praying on her knees and the twins twisting their hair in the mirror.

As I struck the ground, the images were knocked clean out of me. I landed so hard I couldn't breathe. I gasped and struggled to sit up, a slow pain rising up my right leg. "Edna?" Her quiet, dark shape next to me triggered the horror of the fire and the falling girls until her snorting, hiccupping laughter sailed out.

I dropped onto my back, tears springing to my eyes. "Stop laughing and help me up," I said. A trickle of warm blood ran down my calf, but I didn't care. We'd made it. We were over the wall. We were together. I could smell pine needles and hear tree trunks creaking in the high breeze.

"Lord have mercy on our souls, we did it!" Edna rolled over, the stars winking out as she kissed me, pressing her hands into my upper arms. The kiss was slow and tender, as if we had all the time in the world.

I could have stayed forever in that blessedly happy moment.

Naked branches snaked into view as Edna pulled away and stood up to help me to my feet. "Are you hurt?" she asked, supporting my waist with her arm.

"I think my leg hit a rock."

"Is it very painful?"

"No," I lied, wrapping my arm around her shoulder and dragging my useless leg along as we stumbled over roots and rocks, blood oozing into my shoe.

It was slow going and we'd hardly made a dent of progress before the dogs started up again. The sound sank me with dread, my leg throbbing with every howl like salt being rubbed into the wound. The memory of the coyotes came back, my father's clear, calm face in the moonlight as he raised his rifle and shot into the dark. It hadn't done any good. In the morning all that was left of our hens were scattered feathers. I remember thinking *you can't beat em, Papa.*

"You're going to have to go on without me." I slid my arm from Edna's shoulder, steading myself on one foot. "No sense us both getting caught."

"I won't leave you," she said, but in her voice, I heard she was prepared to.

"Weakness is a failure. Remember?"

"You're not weak, you're hurt."

"Same thing. Now, hurry up. Run as fast as you can. I'll tell them some nonsense to keep them confused for a while. You'll have time if you run hard."

It was too dark to see the expression on Edna's face as she grabbed me in a hug. I like to think it was a look pulled between sorrow and gratitude. "I'll never forget you, Mable Winter. You promise to find me when you make it out of this hell house, you hear?"

My false name soured in the air. "Without a doubt," I said as she pulled away.

Considering all I'd been through, it seems silly to say that Edna leaving me was one of the most painful. I knew I'd never find her in all that impossible space, and she'd never find me in my lies.

With a final squeeze of my hand, she turned and the forest swallowed her, the snapping of twigs and her quick breath consumed by the quickening yaps of the dogs. Bits of starlight flickered through the trees, and in seconds the growling mongrels surrounded me. A man approached, yanking at their collars and ordering them down. In whining protest, the dogs backed off, sitting on their lean, gray haunches. They looked as smug as the flushed faces of the two uniformed men who held up their lamps, trapping me in a pool of light. One was short and squat, the other taller, an air of authority in his massive shoulders. The short one took hold of my arm, disgust on his face. "Where's the other girl?" he asked, his foul breath forcing my head to the side. He yanked my arm and I wanted to spit at him. At least I was tall enough to look him in the eye.

"She fell," I said. "Jumped too close to the rocks near the river. She's hurt."

The other policeman said, "That's a forty-foot drop. We picked up a girl two years ago who jumped and broke nineteen bones. Never made it home from the hospital."

That was exactly the story I remembered reading in the paper, perched on a stool by the stove in the Cascilois' tenement. I wondered how these idiot policemen didn't see that I was recreating it. They probably didn't think I could read.

"You . . . come on and show us where." The one who held my arm pushed me forward and I sank to my knees with a gasp of pain. He held up his lantern while the other officer lifted my dress, sticky with blood, and exposed my shredded bloomers. An open wound tore down my calf. "Where exactly did you think you were going on that? Serves you right." He spit and it hit the ground with a soft hiss. "How far back's your little friend?" He pulled me to my feet.

"Back near the wall where the rocks start, I think."

From the shadows, a third voice broke in. "You two go. I'll stay with this one until you get back." When I looked up, all I saw was a man's silhouette stroking one of the dog's heads.

"Not up for a gory sight?" The shorter policeman laughed.

The man in the shadows remained silent. It was not a silence I trusted.

The taller policeman gave a sharp whistle and the dogs sprang forward, their barks piercing the air. The two policemen followed with a stomp of heavy boots. The light faded and darkness dropped over me.

I would have done anything for the use of my leg. I could sense that the man in the shadows was up to no good. Men who hide their faces never are. I moved. A twig snapped and he grabbed hold of my arms. My body went rigid with panic. I thought he meant to hold me still, but he pushed me to the ground, his boot on my chest. I prayed he'd keep his boot there. Better his boot, I thought. But he slid it off and kneeled over me, his black shape a vulture descending. This was not passion, or even a twisted desire. It was a cold power he knew he had over me.

I squirmed, but he flipped me over and held my head down, a knotty twig cutting into my cheek. His breath was wet on my neck and smelled of tobacco. There wasn't a sound other than his shallow, panting breath. A stone dug into my stomach as I focused on the throbbing in my lower leg instead of the hot pain shooting between them. Disgust and rage beat off the man with a fierceness that made me feel as if I was an enemy he'd been waiting to pummel for years.

It was over quickly, his body pulling away as suddenly as he had thrust himself on me. I clawed my way to the nearest tree, remembering how Mama clawed her way to her baby's grave. Steadying myself against the trunk, I pulled up my bloomers and shook my skirt over my legs, feeling sick and weak and dirty. I heard the man's belt buckle slip into place with a soft click. The stickiness he'd left behind dripped down my inner thigh and I wanted to rip off my bloomers and scrub my skin raw. Then the tears came. Another weakness. Edna was right to leave me behind. I pictured her arriving at a safe door and being ushered into a room glittering with promise. She'd be given food and a bath. Maybe a maid would sit on the edge of the bathtub sponging off her back. This maid would help her from the water, wrap Edna's untarnished body in a soft towel and lead her to a bed full of warmth and faultless dreams.

## CHAPTER TWENTY-SIX:
## JEANNE

It was Georges who arranged for my apartment since I had no control over my own money, and would have had no idea how to manage it if I had. Before Georges left with Luella for London, he paid a sum up front and opened a bank account in my name. I never told Emory.

Despite this careful planning, I couldn't bring myself to leave right away. Every object, every room, held memories of my children. Leaving Effie's bedroom behind was going to be the hardest, since Luella's absence now felt like a natural departure. She'd grown up and out of her room, but Effie still haunted hers.

I'd followed Luella's suggestion and gone to the homes for wayward girls, even though I didn't see how it was possible for Effie to be in one. The Inwood House wouldn't let me through the front door. A grim-looking sister had stuck her head out and told me, from where I stood on the massive porch, that they only admitted women over eighteen, and promptly shut the door in my face. The House of Mercy at least allowed me into the hallway where I was kept waiting for ages before a formidable sister came gliding toward me.

"Apologies." She smiled, her blue eyes reminding me of Emory's. "The girls are just settling into chapel for their morning prayers. What may I help you with?"

I gave a brief account of my missing daughter. "I don't know how it's possible she'd be here, but if a mistake was made somewhere . . ."

"No." The sister smiled sweetly. "There's no one by the name of Effie Tildon under our care, and besides," she placed her porcelain hand on my coat sleeve, speaking to me as if I were a child. "We don't make mistakes, my dear. No one is admitted on their own. A magistrate or a legal guardian must sign them in." Her voice dropped. "These girls are not innocents like your little one. They've all gone astray somewhere, and I assure you there aren't many who come from a family like yours. We'd notice if they did. I'm very sorry we couldn't be of more help to you."

From down the hall, I heard the drifting

chatter of girls' voices. "Thank you all the same," I said as she showed me to the door. Outside, I made my way carefully down the steps and along the icy road to the gate where a large, bearded man wrestled with the massive lock on the gate. The feeling of being stuck behind it was nerve-racking, and I was glad when he finally let me through.

One tepid day in April, snow melting in the city streets, I said a final goodbye to Effie's room and had Margot and Neala pack up my toiletries and clothing and send them to the address on 26th Street. For two months I'd carried the key secretly in my pocket. I considered making a scene, telling Emory I was leaving and confronting him about his mistress. Asking why he'd done this to us. In the end I couldn't. I was too tired, and confronting him was pointless. As far as I was concerned, my marriage was over and I wanted to start thinking of a life away from my husband.

When Emory came home from work that day in April, I was gone.

My apartment was small, but comfortable and well furnished. The first night, I removed my gloves and placed them in my handbag before eating dinner at a tea table by the window. The cool metal of the fork against my bare fingers was a startling sensation I would forever associate with independence.

Within a day, Emory discovered my whereabouts from Neala and came demanding I return. But his anger was defused the moment he stepped into my apartment. Neither one of us had strength left to fight. Even his confession about Inez was listless. He admitted he was in love with her, but since Effie's disappearance, he had little desire for anything.

It was strange having Emory in a space that was all mine. It made me feel oddly calm. At any moment I could order him out. This swapping of places clearly baffled Emory as well. He stood in the middle of the rug twisting his hat in his hands, looking pleadingly at me.

"How did everything go so badly?" he asked, as if genuinely expecting an answer.

I told him what I'd told Luella, that he shouldn't blame himself, which was generous of me. "We've exhausted ourselves trying to find the link in the chain of events leading up to Effie's disappearance. Any one of those links are to blame. It's useless to try and parse it out."

"What about the links leading up to us?"

456

The desperation in his voice surprised me. For a moment I almost weakened, but I knew this wasn't about me. It was about him losing all that he thought he was in control of.

"Too many to count," I said. "Would you like a cup of tea?"

"Do you have coffee?"

"I do."

I went to the kitchen at the back of the apartment, lit the stove and heated up a pot I'd made earlier. It was funny to think I'd never made my own coffee before, and here I was only a day on my own doing it easily. Margot had tried to do it for me but I'd insisted on doing it myself. "It's only the two of us for the time being," I'd said. "You can't be doing everything for me." I'd get a cook, eventually, just someone part-time, but for now, eating out and making my own coffee was sufficient.

When I returned with two steaming cups, Emory was seated at my tea table looking out the window.

"It's a nice view from here."

"It is." I set the cups down. "Two sugars, splash of cream."

"Thank you." Emory took a sip. "You know Mother is going to lose her mind over our separation."

I sat across from him, wrapping my hands around my cup to warm them. "She is."

"This is temporary, though? Isn't it? We'll tell her it's temporary. When Luella comes home, or Effie, you'll come home then too." It was not a question, but a statement. Emory glanced at my exposed hands. "I never asked you to wear those gloves, you know."

"You never asked me not to."

He looked into his cup as if contemplating this reality before swigging the rest of his coffee and standing up. He rounded the table, standing close enough for me to smell his cedarwood and pomade. Reaching out, he pulled me to my feet and leaned in to kiss me.

"Emory." I took a startled step backward. "It's much too late for that."

He held on to me, and it was the first time in years I'd felt his bare hands over mine. For a moment, I wanted whatever he had to offer. But it dawned on me, as I looked at him, that his hair was perfectly styled over his forehead, his cuff links buttoned, his coat crisply pressed. Clearly, he had not rushed out of the house in any panic over my whereabouts.

I pulled my hands out of his. "I think it's time for you to go."

He shoved his hands into his pockets. "We'll tell people you're taking time away. They'll understand, after all that's happened."

"You tell them whatever you want."

I walked him to the door, closing it behind him and leaning my forehead against the cool wood. A part of me wanted to follow him, a part of me always would. Just like a part of me would never give up looking for Effie. I no longer had either of them, but I'd never entirely let them go.

# CHAPTER TWENTY-SEVEN:
## EFFIE

At the farm, we rose at 4:00 a.m., dressed in the dark, ate breakfast by lamplight and were sent to work. Our jobs rotated weekly. The first week I hauled water from the pump to the kitchen, each step splashing water over the rim of the bucket and soaking my shoes. I raked coals from the stove, my arms black with soot; scrubbed floors, collected eggs, fed livestock, shoveled dung from stalls, filled those stalls with hay that stuck in my hair and on my dress. At night, I'd collapse onto my stuffed mattress, my aching limbs heedless of the prickly straw poking through my bloomers and itching like mad.

I was never alone with Mable. Even if I had been, I was too exhausted to convince her of anything, much less getting her name. At the farm, there were no mercury treatments. My legs were swelling again, and the increasing tightness in my chest was foreboding. The air was thick against my skin and I slept sporadically, the morning gong pulling me from dreams.

We ate our meals on benches pulled up to a long table made from barn planks set over sawhorses. It was imperative that you didn't drop your fork, or it would be lost between the wide gaps in the boards. There was no talking at mealtime; the slightest whisper raised Miss Juska's owl eyes from her plate. And she always found the culprit. Punishment was a skipped meal, and no one wanted to miss meals. Unlike at the House of Mercy, the farm food was hearty and filling: eggs, corn cakes, meat stews, fresh bread, milk, cheese and fruit pie. "Underfed girls underperform," Miss Juska said. "This way there's no excuse for weakness."

There were two other matrons at the farm, Miss Carlisle and Miss Mason, each silent and stern and built like small workhorses, permanent frown lines grooved each side of their mouths. Miss Mason ran the kitchen, instructing the girls she favored in cheese and bread making. The ones she didn't favor got to toss out endless, dirty dishwater. I wasn't a favorite.

This week I was on my knees between rows of potatoes pulling weeds that were nothing like the tender shoots I used to help

461

Mama pluck from her flowerbeds. These were gnarled and thick and held on to the earth like I was tearing out their souls. Blisters bloomed, and split open on my palms.

I had been at it for two days when I heard my name hissed under someone's breath. Straightening, I saw Mable one row over, pitched forward, her pale dress yellowed and streaked with dirt. It was early afternoon. There wasn't a cloud in the sky and the sun was blazing. Miss Carlisle had been stalking the rows before lunch. It appeared, now, as if we'd been left alone, but we knew better than to get comfortable. Someone always watched from the house. The moment one of us rested too long, or dared to stand up and stretch our backs, one of the matrons, or Joe, the farmhand who slept in the barn and wasn't right in the head, would come stomping out and order us back to work.

Inching closer to Mable, I dug up a weed, dirt scattering, the earthy smell reminding me of the stream and Luella. I wanted to take off my shoes and wiggle my toes in it.

"I'm gonna make a run for it," Mable whispered.

This wasn't how it was supposed to go. I had no intention of planning another runaway escape. My escape would be from getting her name, gaining her trust. "Right now?" Flecks of sunlight escaped through her hat and dotted her face like a double set of freckles.

"No, dimwit, and don't look at me."

She kept her eyes on the ground. I looked back at the spiny weed strangling a leafy potato top. Mable hadn't fallen into Miss Juska's calculated trap — plant fear in our hearts and fatigue in our bones so we thought of nothing more than meals and bedtime. I yanked the weed and a tiny purple potato came up with it. Quickly, I shoved the potato back in its hole and patted dirt over it, knowing it was only a matter of minutes before the green tops would wilt and give away my careless weeding.

"When?" I asked.

"Soon," she said. "You want in?"

"Why me?"

"Safer in numbers. Wouldn't do to be alone out there." Her eyes moved to the trees.

"Why not one of the other girls?"

She shrugged. "Can't trust um. Any one of these girls would rat me out. You're not a snitch. I know that much."

The strips of fabric I'd ripped from my petticoat last night to bind my bleeding hands had come loose, and I rested on my

463

knees and began rewrapping them, dried blood cracking on the linen. I was hot and thirsty and sweat trickled under the brim of my hat. "Why should I trust you after last time?"

Mable yanked a weed, tossed it into her pile and inched forward. "You don't really have a choice, now, do you?"

The anger that had loosened its grip from exhaustion came reeling back. "I can't trust someone who lies about their name," I said, the duplicity of this not lost on me.

Mable stopped weeding. She straightened her back, pressed her dirty hands into her thighs and scanned the horizon as if searching for a flaw in the landscape, hoping to find a green sky instead of blue, something to prove wrong. "Can't trust anyone anyway," she said. "You can come if you like, or not. Your choice." She reached into my row and plucked up the potato I'd reburied, rubbed it clean with her skirt and bit into it, the white flesh pearling with moisture. "Haven't you learned to get rid of your evidence *yet*?"

I watched her consume my potato with impressive stealth. Behind her, the dark, dense woods shadowed the edge of the field. I could not bear the idea of returning to the House of Mercy. My tremors were gone and my mind clearer, but my skin had cooled to a dull, pasty white and my legs were so swollen I imagined if I stuck a pin in them they'd burst like a balloon. My blue fits had returned and I woke at night feeling that the walls were coming down on top of me.

Finishing her potato, Mable moved down the row, pulling weeds as efficiently as she had worked an iron in the laundry. She'd led Edna to her damnation, and was most likely leading me to mine. But I couldn't see any other way out and my time was running out.

The next morning, we found a way to converse picking pole beans, the twisting vines providing partial coverage from the eyes of the house. It hadn't rained in days and the clumps of dirt exploded into dust under our feet. It was only 7:00 a.m., but I could already feel the heat of the sun creeping up behind the trees.

"Miss Juska wasn't lying about the bears," Mable whispered, her head bent so that all I could see was the brim of her hat. "We'll have to be careful. I wish I had a rifle. That'd be something. Although then I'd be tempted to shoot Miss Juska and let the whole lot of us free."

Cicadas buzzed and heat shimmered over the field. I felt light-headed. If anyone were going to get eaten by a bear it would be me. Was I going to be bait for her again?

"Don't look so petrified." Mable slapped at a mosquito on her arm. "Just steer clear of any cubs and you'll be all right. I know these woods."

"What do you mean you know these woods?"

"Never you mind, just trust me." She glanced up with a flash of her crooked teeth. "Or try."

A bean snapped off the vine in my fingers. I felt a twinge of revolt toward Mable. She was pulling me in her direction like she had with Edna, like Luella had with the gypsies. I didn't want to be led anymore. I didn't trust her, or whatever crime she'd committed.

Last night she'd whispered her plan to me while the other girls slept. Tonight, we would each steal a pair of boots from the matrons while they slept, sneak into the pantry for food, candles and a kitchen knife, tie it all up in a pillowcase and sneak out the back door. "Kind, trusting old dames." Mable had laughed in the dark. "Not locking any doors. Too bad for them they didn't count on me not being a city gal."

I looked toward the farmhouse. Miss Carlisle hadn't come out with us this morning and I wondered which dark window she watched from. "Let's go right now," I said.

Mable laughed, crouching down to search for lower beans. She wasn't even going to consider doing it my way.

The other girls were scattered down the bean rows, their hats tipped against the sun, their hands moving from the vines to their baskets with complacency. No one was watching. "The lunch bell won't ring for hours," I said.

"We'd never make it without food. It's too far. I don't know about you, miss never-did-laundry-before-in-her-life, but I'm not likely to kill an animal with my bare hands and eat it raw."

I wasn't afraid of death. I'd died when the walls fell away, when I'd tumbled from the bed with Mable's stupid rouge on my face, when I'd been left in the pit. What was one more death?

Mable stayed crouched where she was, plucking beans and dropping them in her basket, her skirt trailing in the dirt around her.

I didn't trust her, but for some reason she trusted me. I wasn't trustworthy. I was going to turn her in to save myself, the point being that I *could* save myself. I wasn't helpless. I didn't have to hover in between. I

467

could choose.

I stepped backward, the inviting shade of the forest stretching away to my left. Mable stood up, watching with disbelief, the look on her face taunting me to do it. She didn't think I had it in me, but what she didn't know was that my malformed body was the real prison, the forest nothing compared to waking up unable to breathe. I was dying. Running made no difference now.

Impulse leapt inside me. I dropped my basket, turned and ran, the edge of the forest catching me in cool shade, pine needles dulling the thud of my shoes. I sprinted, not caring if my heart kept up, my mind void of thought. Wind cooled my cheeks, and my hat blew from my head. Gradually, the ground rose and I was forced to slow down and hitch up my skirt in order to scramble over the large rocks jutting between the trees. When I grew dizzy, I sat on a boulder to catch my breath while my eyes readjusted. *I'll have to go slower,* I thought, *walk at a pace that won't turn the world upside down. I'll find a road, hail a passing wagon or car and find my way home.*

A crash through the brush brought me to my feet as Mable stumbled from a thicket of mountain laurel, her face aflame, her short hair damp with sweat and curled over the tops of her ears like the twisted ends of taffy.

"Come on, can't rest now," she said, scrambling over the rock in front of me. "You're the crazy one dashed off in broad daylight. I already heard the bell ringing. All we can hope is that they don't know which direction we've gone."

"I can't keep running."

She stopped and looked back. "Don't I know that? We'll walk, but fast. You got that in you?"

I nodded, hiked up my skirt and followed her over the rocks. After a while the hill evened out and descended to a flat forest floor. We kept up a good pace, the silence encouraging. No dogs or men were following, yet. I noticed Mable had taken the lead.

"Do you know where the road is?" I asked.

"No idea. Finding a road's a bad idea anyway. First person drives by will take us straight back to Valhalla. People love being heroes. It won't matter what we tell them. Girls always have a story and no one ever believes them." She looked up into the sky. "We're heading north."

I stopped walking. "No," I said. "I'm finding a road. Someone might not believe your story, but they'll believe mine."

Mable turned. "Your story's that good, is

it? The more outlandish the less likely they are to believe it." Her face softened. "If there's one thing I've shown you it's that people can't be trusted. Whoever's driving on that road will know exactly where you came from. Why do you think Miss Juska dresses us all alike? If it's a woman, she'll see it as her Christian duty to take our troubled souls right back, and if it's a man he'll take us for whores and do what he likes with us. These woods are the best coverage we have, and it wouldn't do to be out here alone. If something happens to one of us, the other's there to help. I need you as much as you need me."

Mable fell silent. Around us, the forest stirred with life, squirrels darted up tree trunks, leaves rustled and birds twittered. I suspected she was trying to even things up, but I still didn't entirely trust her.

"What's north?" I asked.

"Home."

The word was a longing in my chest. Thirst had set in and my legs were already tired, but I would have followed that word anywhere. "How far?"

Mable shrugged. "I have no idea."

# CHAPTER TWENTY-EIGHT: MABLE

When Mama and I were on the train heading to New York City all those years ago, I made a note of every town we passed. That way, I could go back and search each one for Papa when I grew up. Valhalla had only been a few stops away from where we started; twenty miles at the farthest, which meant Effie and I would reach Katonah in a day or two. Then again, I was never very good with directions.

By the third day, I began to lose hope.

The weather remained hot and dry. We'd drunk from a stream and slept under the stars, but we hadn't had a thing to eat and my limbs felt weak and wobbly. Why hadn't Papa taught me what to eat in the woods? I hadn't seen a single berry. Maybe bark was an option.

So far Effie had kept a steady pace, but she'd woken that morning looking like some vicious creature had sucked the blood out of her in the night. Not a word had crossed her lips since she'd shaken the pine needles from her hair, gazed at the sky and moved forward.

By early afternoon she was hardly moving. Each ragged breath sounded like a tiny saw hacking away at her lungs.

"I'm up by five points unless you hear a piping plover," I said. Neither one of us knew birdcalls, but we'd made up a game of shouting out whatever bird came to mind when one squawked or chirped above us. Five points a bird, and I was one up on Effie.

She stopped walking and looked at me, her eyes flecked with gold like tiny leaves had fallen into her irises. I waited for her to say something, but she only tilted her head to the side with a look of confusion and resumed her slow, deliberate steps.

I'd handed her that one. All she had to do was say *piping plover.* "This is your fault," I said, my shoes snapping a twig in half. "Running off without reason. I told you we needed to get supplies. If we'd stolen food from the pantry we wouldn't be in this situation." Luck landed me at Valhalla only to have me die of starvation in the woods, I thought. "We could pray," I said aloud. "It most likely won't help, but it can't hurt."

■ ■ ■ ■

Finding myself on the truck to Valhalla was a prayer answered, but I was suspicious of it. There was no way it was Sister Gertrude's merciful intention allowing me out. She had some greater gain. What, I couldn't be sure. I'd watched the dark edges of the House of Mercy fade away in the truck window like a picture fading from its frame, and knew I'd never set foot in that place again. Sister Gertrude had something on me and I didn't expect to leave the farm in anything less than chains.

Running was nothing, as I figured I was as good as hung already.

The sisters sending Effie to work on the farm made no sense either, being sick and all, but I figured it was my good luck. A chance to make amends. Not for my sins — they were too far-reaching — but because I owed Effie. Truth was, I liked her the moment she kicked me in the shins that first night. She wasn't weak like Edna thought. Lying in the infirmary, I overheard the doctor tell Sister Mary that people with Effie's heart condition rarely live past twelve years old, and that he'd never seen anyone live to the age of fourteen. Effie was tougher than any of us.

After the police beat me for leading them astray about Edna, and dragged me back to the sisters, I lay unwashed for three weeks with that man's filth on me, my face throbbing with pain. If my hands hadn't been chained to the bed I would have strangled the first person came near me. Not Effie. She came back from the pit and calmly let that doctor stab her with a needle every day. She didn't even put up a fight when the sisters sent her back to work in the laundry. Not an outward one, at least, but I could see she was fighting all the while inside.

Behind me, Effie's breathing suddenly changed to something shallow and dangerous. I halted. "I'm tired. I need a rest," I said, knowing she'd move forward until the last breath died out of her.

Dappled sun beat hot through the trees. Insects buzzed. Effie propped her hands on her knees and hung her head. Her knotted hair flopped over, revealing red, welted mosquito bites on the back of her neck. I itched my own, rubbing them with the flat of my finger so I wouldn't break the skin.

"Those cicadas are louder than New York City traffic," I said, hoping she'd laugh, or grunt. Anything. All that came out was her slow, sawing breath and I felt my own chest tighten. Then I heard something else, a steady, distant clop. I strained my ears, the sound growing distinctly louder. "Do you hear that? It's hooves! It's coming from that direction. Can you keep going?"

Effie righted herself, her face the blue of moon shadow. I put my arm around her, startled by her sharp rib bones. "You're going to be fine as soon as we get some food in you." She tried to reply but I shushed her. "Save your breath," I said, moving us as quickly as I could in the direction I'd heard the horse, panic rising when all I saw were more and more trees. Then the ground dipped abruptly and I held on to Effie as we stumbled down a bank and landed on a rutty, dirt road.

"Praise be to God!" I whooped, my muddled brain making me slightly hysterical as I eased Effie from my shoulder. Between the heat and lack of food, it was all I could do not to faint. I took a few breaths and looked up, the trees and road refocusing. "Whoa Nelly, I'm light-headed."

Effie sat in the road staring up at me. "You have to put me on a train. I need to get back to Luella." It was the longest sentence she'd strung together in days and the effort made her pitch forward. Through her dress, the spine of her curved back protruded like knotty wood.

I dropped down beside her, the ruts packed down hard and dusty around us. "I can't put you on a train without any money. Don't worry, I'll figure out a way to get you home. We just need to get some food and rest first. Then we can think straight."

By the time I heard the wagon wheels creaking, an orange sunset had set the tops of the trees on fire. Far down the road, a horse-drawn cart was making its slow way toward us. I jumped up, my head swimming and my heart racing. I licked my cracked lips hoping they weren't bleeding, my mouth so parched I could feel the grit of the road on my tongue. My shorn hair had grown out a little, and I tried to smooth it back but strands kept slipping into my face.

"Whoa." The driver pulled his horse to a halt, raising his bushy, white eyebrows in surprise. He wore a straw hat tipped back on his head, and the sleeves of his gingham shirt were rolled to his elbows revealing deeply tanned forearms. "You ladies need some help?" His voice crackled with age.

"Just a ride, if you'd be so kind," I said, my own voice dry and strained.

"Where to?" The man took off his hat and wiped his brow with the back of his arm. "Hot to be out and about. Your friend sick?"

He nodded at Effie, sitting in the dirt with her head between her knees.

"She'll be all right. She's just hot. We're looking to get to Katonah."

The man jutted his thumb over his shoulder. "Back that a way three miles."

"Is this Toll Road?" The man nodded and my chest swelled. We were so close. "You can drop us at the fork up ahead."

Lifting Effie to her feet, I helped her into the back of the wagon and climbed in after her, settling beside a pile of empty wooden crates. The man handed me a glass milk bottle, rinsed and filled with water. I let Effie take the first sip, water trickling down her chin, before helping myself. The water was warm, but clean and refreshing. I never thought I'd want for water so badly.

"I reckon you could use some food too." The man reached for a basket at his feet.

My stomach had long ago folded in on itself. "You reckon right," I said as he handed the basket to me over the back of his seat. "Thank you kindly."

The man clicked his tongue at the horse. "Walk on," he said, and the wagon lurched forward as the horse continued its slow gait down the road.

With shaky hands, I unfolded the checked cloth in the basket and ripped a slice of dark bread in two, handing half to Effie and stuffing the other half in my mouth, swallowing so fast my stomach squeezed in protest. I didn't care. There was sliced ham and yellow cheese and blueberry pie. Effie and I ate with our fingers, licking their blue tips without shame. The food put a spot of color back into Effie's cheeks and her eyes seemed to open up to the world again. When we finished, I slouched down and rested my head against the wagon, looking into the thick, green leaves passing overhead with a sense of deep gratitude. I'd been walled up for two years, four if you count my time in New York City. That was a different kind of walled in, but trapped just the same. Not until that moment did I realize freedom was a breath of clean air, a breeze in the trees and the silent tramp of a horse's hooves. Effie slouched over, with her head on her arms, staring into her palms. I wondered if she found her freedom there, in the small universe of her own hands. Her breathing seemed to have evened out and her chest rose and fell steadily.

"See," I said, "rest and food's all a person needs in this world."

"And family," she said, closing her eyes.

"I wouldn't know anything about that," I answered.

At the fork in the road, the man pulled his horse to a stop. The sky had dimmed from orange to a deep purple. "Which way are you headed?" he asked.

The path leading to my old cabin was only a short distance to the left. "We'll get out here," I said, climbing down and helping Effie out. She leaned against me, dust from the horse's hooves stirring around us.

"You got kin nearby?" The man looked concerned. "There's not a house for miles."

"We're fine, thank you."

He jutted his chin at Effie. "Don't seem right leaving you two out here. It'll be dark soon. You're welcome to come on home with me for the night. My wife's most likely cooked a peach pie. Peaches are falling from our tree like rain."

Peach pie sounded like a dream. I shook my head. "No, thank you, sir. Like I said, we'll be just fine." I was getting nervous at what a good look the man had gotten of us. Miss Juska would make sure our faces were in the paper. She wasn't the type to admit defeat.

Turning away from the wagon, I held on to Effie and led her slowly down the road in the opposite direction where I intended to go, the man calling after us, "Our farmhouse is only half a mile down. My wife would be happy to feed you. She wouldn't like to hear I let you wander off."

I waved my hand over my head, his voice trailing away as I kept on walking. I didn't turn us around until I was good and sure he was gone, making my way back to the fork and heading us in the same direction the wagon had gone. "We're close now," I said, a warmth of excitement filling my belly.

There was no path anymore, just brambles and hogweed up to my knees. It took me three tries to find the circle of pine bush where the path met the road. Papa used to say it was good luck to build your house near a perfect grove of pine bush.

How wrong he was, I thought, staring at that overgrown path for so long Effie finally said, "Is this where your house used to be?"

"Not exactly," I said, fear beginning to waylay my excitement. "Try and not disturb the brush. Even if that old farmer tries to turn us in, it's not likely anyone's going to find us out here."

The path seemed longer than I remembered, but it was slow going. New saplings sprouted up and the brush was thick and thorny. When we reached the crabapple tree and the stump where Papa and I sat waiting for coyotes, my heart turned over in my chest.

The cabin stood a few yards away, achingly familiar, the windows like curious eyes watching our approach. Moss covered the roof and weeds reached to the cracked panes. The barn roof had caved in and the chicken coop was a pile of sticks, but the five stones marking my siblings stood untouched, bumping up like bent knees out of the dry grass.

Effie hung back, silent. Reaching up, I plucked a crabapple from the tree and tossed it to her. "Come on," I said loudly, trying to break the bewitching feeling descending on me. I picked an apple off the ground and bit into it. It was hard and sour and filled with wormholes. I ate the whole mealy thing anyway, the taste on my tongue and the path under my feet taking me back to my childhood with a force I wasn't prepared for. A part of me wanted to run in the opposite direction. I imagined the cabin groaning and stretching out its arms as we entered, as if waking up from a long sleep. Only a scurry of mice welcomed us, darting across the floor and disappearing into the dark hearth.

It's amazing what emptiness can do to a place. The air was dead and silent, the floor scattered with leaves and dirt. Holes dotted the ceiling that was laced with cobwebs as if the spiders were doing their best to try and hold things together. Chairs had toppled over and the bedroom door sagged off its hinges.

"Doesn't make any sense . . . an unused door sagging off its hinges," I said, my voice unsettling the quiet. "What, did it just get tired of hanging there and think, *no one's using me anyway, might as well relax.*" I laughed, fighting the despair creeping over me. The dishes were still stacked on the shelves, canned peaches in their jars, the clock stopped on the mantel, the cast iron pan and the ash bucket exactly where Mama and I had left them. Everything was cobwebbed and dust covered, but untouched by anything other than wind and rain sweeping in through the broken window-panes.

Papa had not come back for us.

There was a creaking sound and I turned around to see Effie sitting in the rocking chair with a smile on her ashen face. "Feels wonderful to sit in a real chair. Do you play?" She nodded at the violin that had slid from the wall to the floor, the leather case partially hidden with curled, brown leaves.

"I used to, a little."

"Play me something?"

I righted a chair that had fallen on its side, too tired to do anything but sit, the wood groaning under me. "It's been too long," I said.

"Please?" She made her voice thin and faint and clasped her hands in prayer. "A last, dying request."

"You're not dying and don't joke about it."

"Oh, but I am. I've been dying since I was born." She smiled ruefully. "You can't refuse someone who's dying."

She had a point. "Fine." I got up and clipped open the violin case. Inside, the velvet was still smooth and bright. It reminded me of the tips of the red-winged blackbirds I used to watch prancing along the windowsill while Papa played. I had pretended they were jealous that his music was prettier than theirs, and they were listening to learn a thing or two.

The violin looked the same, the strings tight and unbroken. I plucked one and a pitiful note came out. I twisted and turned the tuning pegs, plucking the notes until they resembled something in tune. Effie watched, rapt.

"Now don't go expecting much," I said, tightening the horsehairs on the bow and standing with a curtsy. "Madame." I cleared my throat and lifted the violin to my shoulder. The notes screeched out like nails clawing the air and I dropped the instrument to my side. "Told you," I said.

Effie clapped her hands. "Don't you dare stop."

I grimaced and kept at it, pulling the bow along the strings until the sound smoothed out like wrinkles from a sheet. After that, the music flowed and the room brightened. I found myself thinking that if my last baby sister had lived, she'd be five years old now, sitting cross-legged on the hearth while I played for her. Mama would be at the stove with her hair wild and big on top of her head, humming while she cooked. Papa would be nodding in time with the music and stirring the fire, gently pointing out my mistakes when I was finished.

If that baby hadn't died, they'd all still be here.

Stringing one after the other, I remembered all of Daddy's songs. The music lifted the weariness out of me, and as I neared the final song, I let myself feel the truth of my situation. There was no Mama or Papa. No baby sister. There was no going back. I should find it in my heart to be grateful that God had seen fit to preserve my home of dust-ridden memories and give me a final chance at goodbye.

I played a final note, held on to it as long as I could, the sound moving through my bones. I knew then what I had to do. First thing tomorrow, I'd go into town and sell the violin. The money would be enough to put Effie on a train back to New York City and buy me a ticket west. Wild West, I'd heard it called, just the place for a girl like me to get a new start.

The room was hot and sweat dripped down my temples as I placed the violin back in its case. It's a funny thing knowing you're doing something for the last time. I felt tears in my eyes that I didn't want Effie to see. "I've got to pee," I said, heading outside and squatting in the grass, my eyes settling on dirt graves.

Batting my tears away, I returned and told Effie she looked like death was on her again and that she should lie down. The bed was stripped, the sheets folded and stacked on the bureau. I shook them out, dirt and mouse droppings flying off. There were holes all through them. "Those mice have been living pretty grand." I shook out the pillows and patted off the bed, making it up as best as I could, given all the dirt. Effie didn't mind. She sank onto the sheets as if they were made of silk. "Nothing ever felt so good." She smiled.

"I can think of a few things," I answered, kicking off my shoes and crawling in next to her, too tired to strip to my underclothes.

"Your playing was beautiful. It reminded me of my sister. She was a dancer."

"Was?"

"Still is, maybe." She gave a funny laugh. "I don't know anything about her anymore."

"At least you have one. All my sisters are buried out back."

Under the covers, Effie reached for my hand. It reminded me of Edna and I was tempted to pull away, but she kept her fingers tight around mine and I didn't have the heart to let go.

"I don't want to struggle to breathe anymore," she whispered.

It was strange to think that something so effortless for me could be so hard for someone else. "It's not something you can just give up on," I said.

"I don't have a choice."

We were quiet for a while listening to the scurry of mice and rustle of leaves across the floor. "Will you tell me a story?" Effie said. "Anything will do. I haven't been able to think up a good one since the mercury treatments. It's like a pillow's been stuffed in my brain."

"I don't know any good stories."

"Then tell me your story. I don't know the first thing about you. I'd tell you mine, but I'm too tired." Her words were shallow and breathy. "Go on." She squeezed my hand.

Maybe it was being back home after thinking I'd never see it again, or the faint, sweet smell of Mama's rosewater I imagined still lingered on the bed, or the music fading in my ears. Or, maybe it was because I knew Effie was dying and that made her a safe confidant. Whatever the reason, I told her my story, the words bounding out like caged animals.

The time of my childhood was vivid and bright, the time after Mama's death brittle and hazy, colorless as a photographic plate. None of it felt real. I thought Effie might fall asleep listening, but her eyes stayed alert. I left nothing out, telling her about bedding down with Renzo, Mama's death and how I dropped my baby in the river, how I hadn't wanted to escape the House of Mercy since only bad things waited for me, that I'd done it for Edna who left me wounded in the woods where a devil policeman had his way with me.

When I finished, Effie's hand was still in mine and there were tears in her eyes. "I'm sorry," she said.

I hadn't expected understanding. I shrugged it off. "No sense being sorry now. What's done is done."

"You haven't told me your real name," she said.

I rolled the name around in my mind like a dull object I was trying to shine into recognition. "Signe Hagen." It seemed fitting to put my name back on, in here, even if just for tonight.

She smiled. "I like it. It suits you."

"My papa named me. He used to tell me my name meant *victorious,* and that I should try and live up to it. When I was seven years old, I sewed a skirt up the middle like a pair of pants, smudged soot under my eyes, sharpened a stick and went running through the woods shouting like a warrior. I stayed out until long after dark just to test how brave I was. I thought I'd get a beating when I came home, but Papa only asked why I hadn't killed us anything for dinner and Mama set my plate of cold food on the table and told me to eat up. *A fighter needs a good meal to keep up her strength,* she said." I smiled to think of it.

"She sounds like a good mother." Effie shifted her eyes from my face to the ceiling.

"She was." I was tired now and didn't

want to think about the past anymore. "We should get some sleep."

Effie shook her head, her lips moving silently as if whispering something to the walls.

"Suit yourself." I rolled over to face the window. "I can't keep my eyes open another second," I said, though I lay for a long time looking past the blown-out windowpanes that bumped along the sill like tiny, translucent mountains. It wasn't quite dark yet, and outside I could see bright pink flowers blooming on the wild rosebush. I wondered if that was why I smelled Mama in the bed.

The sisters tell you that you'll feel lighter when you confess your sins. I guess there's some truth in that because now that I had, when I finally closed my eyes, I felt like I was made of air, floating. In my dreams, Mama picked a rose and reached through the window to put it in my hair.

# CHAPTER TWENTY-NINE:
## EFFIE

I felt the weight of my sister's body on the mattress beside me. When I reached out, I felt her warm, solid back beneath my fingertips. I tried to call her name, but the pressure in my chest pinned the words in my throat and I sat up, the moonlit room wavering across my vision like rippling water. This was not my room. I tried to ask Luella where we were, but all I could do was thump her back.

"What's wrong?" She jumped from the bed, banging her leg into the footboard and cursing, her voice groggy with sleep.

It was then I saw that this was not my sister, and the memories locked into place with sickening clarity.

Mable put a hand on my shoulders and shook me. "Can you breathe? What is it? You're a dreadful color. Why won't you say anything?" I dropped onto my back and she cursed again. "Damn it all! I didn't think to look for a light. I'm going for help. At least the moon's out. I'll see my way to the road. Don't die on me. You got it?" She eased a pillow under my head. "It's this house! This damned cursed house. I should never have brought you here. I'm going for that farmer. He's the closest. We'll get you a doctor, okay?" I shook my head and she leaned over me. "No? You're right. A doctor won't want you moved. He'll ask too many questions. We need to get you home. Do your parents even want you home or will they send you back to the House of Mercy? How have you not told me a single thing about yourself? What's your address? Where do I take you?" Her voice was shrill.

I squeezed her hand, managing to whisper, "Bolton Road."

This saddened her and she said, "The House of Mercy's not your home, Effie."

I shut my eyes, focusing on each shallow breath as the air receded from my lungs like the tide pulling away. I don't remember sleeping, but I was suddenly aware of the twitter of early rising birds. *Piping plover,* I thought, *five points for me.* When I opened my eyes the ceiling undulated. I thought I'd been left alone as the only sounds I heard were birds, and the occasional grasshopper pinging the side of the house. But when light came through the cracked window, I saw the creatures of the apocalypse crouching in each corner of the room. Silent. Waiting. Their wings tucked in like fledglings. The lion rested his head in its paws, and the eagle lifted his beak while the calf pawed the wood floor, their black eyes all looking at me. Only the man's eyes were the bright blue of my father's, and when I looked at him, he rose onto his knees and began unfurling his wings, light eddying from them and spreading over me like a cool wash of water. It felt familiar and wrong and I squeezed my eyes shut and tightened my body against it. I was not going without my sister.

The next time I woke, I was cradled in the arms of a large man with a white beard and squinty, kind eyes. My head bounced against his shoulder. I heard footsteps and heavy breathing and the rustle of leaves. "You just hang on, little lady. We're almost there," the man said, and when I opened my eyes again there was softness beneath me, and a wash of platinum overhead.

"I'll ride in back with her." Mable's face came into view and I felt my head lifted and settled on the lump of her thigh. Her chipped tooth winked behind her smile. "You see, all I had to do was get you out of that cursed house. You're breathing fine now, aren't you? At least your face is not so ghastly. Still white as a sheet, but the color of death's no longer on you."

Her lips continued to move, but I couldn't hear her over the creak of the wagon. Tree branches swayed, and a light mist dotted my cheeks. There was the rumble of a man's voice, and I was lifted and placed onto something smooth and cool.

Again, I heard Mable. "This man here's name is Joseph Idleman. He's going to take you in this fine car to the city. I've paid him a cabin's worth of stuff for it, so don't go letting him get anything else out of you, you hear?"

Her words snapped things into focus. She meant to leave me and a guttural sound escaped from my throat. I needed her. Without her, I was wordless. Story-less.

"Don't go upsetting yourself." Her face was over me now, her eyes flickering with agitated concern. "You're going to be all right. The farmer's a good sport. He hasn't asked a single question. No one's turning us in, so you needn't worry." I found the strength to grab her arm and she cried, "Blast it! You don't need me. You're the one who ran off first, remember?" Her brow furrowed. "Hang on a minute." She disappeared, returning with a slap of her thigh. "You win. Mr. Idleman won't take you without me anyway. Seems he doesn't trust you're not going to die and leave him with a body to contend with. I'm going to ride up front if it's all the same to you. I've never been in a car and most likely won't ever be again, so I might as well do it right."

A door slammed, then another. There was a rumble and a groan and I felt the speed under me. I slept in spurts, waking when we stopped for fuel, the smell of gasoline and rubber reminding me of Daddy. When we started again, the sun was hot and a forceful wind stung my cheeks. I wondered if I was going home, and this filled me with unexpected fear that things would not be as I remembered as I pressed my face into the back of the leather seat and slept again.

# CHAPTER THIRTY:
# MABLE

Rolling into the city was devastating, and not made any easier by the fact that it was happening in a shiny red car. At every turn I imagined a policeman waiting for me, beating his stick in the palm of his hand. Most likely he'd be fat and pasty with a pug nose and thinning hair. They were all the same, as far as I was concerned, and every one of them was after me.

Mr. Idleman was an unreadable type. Not once did his eyes wander from the road and he didn't speak a word the whole way, which wasn't surprising given the roar we made going along. I kept glancing back at Effie, her face pressed into the seat, her frame tiny beneath her linen dress. I'd told the farmer and Mr. Idleman where the cabin was, and said they could split the lot of it. I was never going back. I didn't warn them it was cursed with death. They'd have to figure that out on their own. Nothing comes free.

It wasn't until the car lurched to a stop that I let myself think of Edna, looking up at the magnificent building we'd parked in front of — high windows and turrets, and all sorts of fancy I didn't belong to.

Mr. Idleman came around and opened my door for me, helping me to the curb. The speed and wind and sun had dazed me.

"You sure this is the right place?" he asked.

"We'll see," I said.

He folded his stubby arms across his chest. "Why don't you see before I go through the trouble of carrying this girl to the door?"

"It'll look more desperate if she's in your arms."

He hesitated, looking at Effie's ghostly form in his back seat. "If you're turned away, I'm leaving her on the doorstep. This is as far as I agreed."

Mr. Idleman groaned lifting Effie from the car, huffing the few feet to the front door. I was sorry I'd left half the cabin to him. The old farmer had carried Effie as if she were as light as a bird. Better it all went to him, I thought, but there was nothing to do about it now.

I rang the doorbell, licking my palm and

smoothing my windblown hair as best as I could. A trim girl in a white apron and cap opened the door, took one look at Effie and ushered us in, shutting the door so fast you would have thought a squall was coming up behind us.

The hallway was dark. It took a moment for my eyes to adjust and take in the maroon-papered walls and the dusty rose rug running the length of the floor.

"You're lucky the mistress is home. Wait here." The girl disappeared behind a closed door, returning promptly with a woman wearing a shapeless, high-waisted dress that hung above her ankles and exposed her small-heeled shoes. The woman had a small birthmark on her cheek, and magnificent red lips. She stepped up to Effie, twisting the string of long black beads around her neck. She took no notice of Mr. Idleman, but turned her clear brown eyes to me and asked, "How ill is she?"

"Very," I answered. "It's something to do with her heart."

A quizzical look flickered across the woman's face as she put a hand to Effie's forehead and peered intently into her face. "What is her name?"

"Effie Rothman."

The woman's head snapped up. "Rothman, it is not." She looked from me to Effie, and then to the girl who let us in, "Amelia, show this man upstairs to the yellow room and then ring immediately for the doctor. Are you responsible for the girl?" she said to the man, her voice calm and urgent.

"No." Mr. Idleman shifted Effie uncomfortably in his arms, his face sweating. "I only drove her here as a favor to that girl." He jutted his chin at me.

The woman moved quickly now, eyeing me suspiciously as she snatched her hat from the stand. "What's your name?"

"Mable Winter."

"Are you responsible for this girl?" She secured the hat on her head.

"Sort of."

"Very well then. You're to stay with her until I get back. If she wakes, she'll want someone familiar. Amelia will bring you anything you need." She addressed the man. "After you've put her on the bed, Amelia will show you to the kitchen for food and then you're to be on your way." Her voice trailed behind her as she hurried out the door.

I stared after her, my palms sweaty. It was a gamble coming here. I had no idea what this woman intended. What if she had recognized me and was dashing to the authorities? I could still make a run for it. The door was wide open, the man already halfway up the stairs with Amelia leading the way.

"You can come this way," Amelia said, looking down from the top step. "I'll bring you something to eat as soon as she's settled."

Mr. Idleman grimaced at me, none too pleased to be roped into more than he'd bargained for.

Through the open door, the air filled with the rumble of traffic and the sun looked dim and hazy through the exhaust. Truth was, I was too hot and tired to run. I hadn't slept or eaten proper in days, and the thought of food and an inviting place to sit was all I wanted. I knew what I was risking by staying, but I receded into the cool of the hall and mounted the stairs anyway, wondering if this one, effortless decision was all it would take to undo all I'd fought for.

# CHAPTER THIRTY-ONE:
## JEANNE

On August 21st, 1914, when Inez Milholland knocked on the door of my apartment on 26th Street, I was sitting in the drawing room fanning myself with the newspaper. I'd given Margot the afternoon off, and the girl who cooked and cleaned for me had gone to the butcher's even though I told her I'd be happy to eat cold meat from the icebox.

As the maids were out, I was the one who opened the door to a flushed Inez. She was breathless, her cheeks dewy and her hat askew as if she'd run up the three flights of stairs to my door. We had never met face-to-face, and yet I knew her instantly. I'd seen her photograph in the *Woman's Journal and Suffrage News,* and her rosewater perfume confirmed it. She was more ravishing in person, with big brown eyes and shocking red lips. Her beauty stung, but only for a moment, out of habit, I suppose. Her appearance, ultimately, didn't fluster me, or the way she clasped a hand to her chest and apologized — a little too profusely — for disturbing me, asking that I come with her immediately. I took my hat from the hook and followed her into the heat without question.

Inez walked at an uncomfortably fast clip, her hands moving in nervous little circles by her side, and people parted to let us pass. I assumed this errand of urgency had something to do with Emory, despite the fact that his mother, good old Etta, had told me he'd put a stop to his relations with Inez.

Two weeks earlier, Etta had sat in my humble living room telling me, with the arrogance of someone who is used to being obeyed, that Emory still loved me and I was to end this ridiculous charade and return to my duties as a wife. I had just smiled and poured her another cup of tea. I didn't have the energy to tell her that duty meant nothing to me anymore. The landscape of my life had been irreparably altered. It was clarity I sought, and her son wasn't very good at that.

In hindsight, Inez's presence at my door that day should have been dismaying, and yet the real reason I hurried alongside her through the hot, dry streets never crossed my mind. I was worrying about Luella. Just that morning I'd read that the Germans had bombed a city in Belgium and killed nine civilians. The war was all anyone talked about. Georges assured me that Luella was safe, and yet I continued to read about bombs dropped on English Channel ports. Then there was my mother in Paris, who also assured me she was fine, in spite of the violence spreading to her city.

I still visited the hospitals looking for my youngest daughter, but I'm ashamed to say that with the war and the passing of time, Effie's absence had slipped into a dark corner of my mind that no longer believed she'd be found.

When I entered Inez's home and was led up the stairs to a room where a girl lay with her back to me, her short, dark hair cresting in little waves over the pillow, I was confused. I glanced questioningly at Inez who stood against a backdrop of lemon-yellow wallpaper, wringing her hands. There was a sudden ring at the door and she cried, "That'll be the doctor," and flew from the room.

"She's rather scattered, that one."

Startled, I turned to see another girl sitting in a chair, watching me with watery blue eyes. I assumed she meant Inez, who, moments later, swooped in with a portly man in a black jacket. I watched the man set his leather satchel on the side table, click it open and pluck out a stethoscope.

The sight of that stethoscope made me catch my breath, all the times I'd stood beside Effie while that contraption was pressed to her chest. My eyes moved to the bed. That thin shoulder poking up could not possibly be my daughter's. *Inez doesn't know her. She's made a mistake,* I thought, as the doctor rolled the girl onto her back and began to unbutton her blouse.

There was a moment of stillness, a vapid emptying, a caving in and a draining of sounds. Then a cry escaped me and I stumbled to the bedside. Effie's eyes were closed, her face a harrowing white. I thought she wasn't breathing until I saw her chest rise and a raspy sound escape her throat. I took her hand, soft and warm and delicate as a bird's wing. I couldn't believe it was really her. After all the searching and waiting and believing she was dead and here she had appeared so instantaneously.

The doctor tilted his head in silence, his eye gazing upward as he listened to her heart. I held on to her, refusing to give him her hand as he obligingly examined her clubbed fingernails on the other. He yanked back the covers and flipped up her filthy skirt and I stifled a cry, dropping to my knees. Effie's stomach was distended, her legs puffed and swollen and colorless.

The doctor drew his brows together and pulled the stethoscope from his ears. "Are you her mother?" he said, sharp and accusing. I nodded, unable to speak, hardly able to breathe. "How long has she been like this?"

I stared, the room closing in on me.

"She's been bad for days, but got real bad last night," I heard, and turned to see the strange girl rise from her chair and move toward the window. Freckles dotted her nose and her cropped, blond hair hung at an odd angle over her ears.

The doctor drew Effie's skirt back down and adjusted the sheet over her. He looked at Inez hovering in the doorway. "I don't know what shenanigans are going on here, and I don't care to." He moved his eyes back to me. "The swelling is from the accumulation of uric acid. If she goes on like this she'll slip into a coma, her kidneys will shut down, and she'll be dead within a week."

Sick to my stomach, I pressed my daughter's hand to my forehead and closed my eyes. I could not find her only to lose her again so quickly. God couldn't be that cruel.

"She told me they were giving her mercury treatments. Maybe that'll work again," the girl said, and I looked up to see her standing directly in front of the open window, the curtains fluttering on either side of her.

"They, who's they?" The doctor glanced in her direction, dropped the stethoscope into his bag and snapped it shut. "Never mind. It's no matter. Mercury reduces the swelling, but there are nasty side effects and her kidneys will shut down eventually anyway. The mercury just gives her more time, and in the end I'm not sure it's worth it."

I touched my daughter's forehead. She didn't move. She looked so frail and small, her hand like a withered leaf in mine. I remembered her as an infant, her exquisite feet and tiny hands, her soft, tender head. At every age, I'd braced myself for her death. After her disappearance I'd been certain of it. A hundred times I'd imagined how this would go; only to discover, now, that it was not a moment I could have prepared for. I felt gutted, hollowed, turned inside out.

"There is digitalis," the doctor was saying. "Foxglove. I have some at the office. It's known to help reduce the swelling without the side effects of mercury. It's not a cure, but it will help. Would you like me to fetch it?"

It was hard to take my eyes off of Effie. Somehow, I found the strength to shift my focus to the doctor's words and try to collect myself into a parental form. I rose to my feet. "Whatever you think is best," I managed to say.

But the doctor was no longer listening. He was staring at the girl by the window, his detached expression shifting to astonishment. "I know you," he sputtered, his mouth gaping open and then snapping shut.

The girl stared back, boldly, her eyes narrowing. I saw her hand creep along the window frame. "Can you be sure?" She tossed her hair from her eyes and lifted her head, her face open and fearless.

The doctor looked as if she'd struck him a blow. "Can I be sure?" Spit flew from his mouth and his face shot up in color. "That breech delivery haunts me nightly. I was made to visit your room and identify your photo, and if that wasn't bad enough, the police took me to the morgue to identify that dead baby." He spun around to a startled Inez. "I turn a blind eye when you bring me here to treat destitute girls with sprained ankles or syphilis, but this one I'm not overlooking. I imagine you don't know half the evil you bring under your roof, and I don't have the stomach to break the horror of this one to you. I'll let the police do that." Snatching up his bag, he made for the door.

Inez stepped quickly in front of him, her curvaceous figure filling the doorway, her voice commanding. "At this precise moment, Doctor, what that girl has or has not done is not my concern. If there's anyone you should recognize, it's the girl in this bed. Remember the newspaper stories about her? I do believe there was a reward for her return. Isn't that right, Mrs. Tildon?" She gazed steadily at me, an imposing air about her.

"There was. There is," I stammered, feeling that things were happening quickly, and out of my control. The girl glanced out the window, leaning over the sill as if she meant to jump from it. Inez raised her hand as if to steady her from across the room, a hand she then dropped flat on the doctor's chest with a seductive smile.

"I'm sure Mrs. Tildon will see fit to give you credit for finding her daughter, *if* you're accommodating. Won't you, Mrs. Tildon?"

"Yes, of course," I said quickly.

The doctor was not to be swayed. "I don't

give one whit about a reward! That girl —"
he pointed a stubby finger at her "— is going to prison and will hang for what she's
done if there's justice in this world. Where's
your telephone?" he barked.

"I'm afraid it's broken," Inez said woe-
fully, withdrawing her hand and fingering
the beads around her neck. "My dear Dr.
Langer, I assure you I'm not above the law.
I have no intention of letting this girl's
crime go unaccounted for. I'm just concerned with saving the sick child's life first.
If you go for the medicine, I promise we'll
all stay put until your return and then we
can call up the authorities and sort this
whole disagreeable business out properly."

"She'll give you the slip the moment she
gets the chance, and I'm not having her get
away a second time. Her getting away the
first has been the ruin of my conscience."

Inez looked at the girl. "You're not going
to give me the slip, now, are you?"

"No, ma'am," the girl replied, an exaggerated smile spreading across her face as she
angled precariously out the window.

I watched her rip a piece of skin from her
cracked lips with her teeth, a string of blood
beading on her mouth. Suddenly, she looked
at me, and I saw her confidence falter. Her
eyes seemed to be searching for help. I

gripped Effie's hand tighter.

The doctor shook his fist at Inez. "Get out of my way!"

Inez stepped aside and the doctor barreled out the door as Inez leapt at the girl and drew her from the window. "Falling dead on my stoop is no way to thank me. You have a lot of explaining to do, but there's no time for it. Truth is, I don't want to know. Whatever the crime, we'll owe it to circumstance and disadvantage. You've risked your neck bringing Mrs. Tildon's girl here, and I don't intend to see it broken out that window."

The girl wrenched her arm free. "I've leapt from windows before and I'm not sticking around for the authorities. I'd break my neck before I let them put their slimy hands on me again."

"I'm not calling the authorities." Inez sank into a chair and pressed her hand to her forehead. "But they'll be here soon enough with that doctor on the hunt. Even if you run, they'll find you." She dropped her hand to the arm of the chair and looked at me with tears in her eyes. "I'm so sorry, Jeanne. I'm so terribly sorry. About Effie, about everything." Her voice went soft. "I came to you first. It seemed a mother should be the first to know, but someone should fetch

Emory."

Through the commotion, the ringing in my ears and the noise from the street, my daughter's raspy breathing became my point of focus. It was not a sound I'd ever heard before. This time, her heart was truly failing. I'd lost the last year of her life, and this strange girl had brought her back to me at the risk of her own. I didn't care what crime she'd committed. This girl and my daughter were somehow connected, and I had the sudden sense that if I saved one, I might save the other.

The room came sharply into focus. I turned to Inez, finding the anguish on her face irritating, her intentions exaggerated for my benefit. "If you'd be so good as to send a maid to fetch Emory and stay with Effie for me, I'd be grateful." The moment I said it I wasn't sure I could leave my daughter. Effie hadn't seen me yet. She didn't know I was by her side. The last person I wanted her waking up to was Inez.

Inez moved quickly to the bed with a reassuring hand on my arm. "Where are you going?"

I looked at the girl edging back to the window. "I have an idea of where to bring you, if you're willing?"

She held suspicion in her eyes. "Why

would you help me?"

"I'm indebted to you."

"For what?"

"For returning my daughter."

"Why didn't you come for her yourself?"

"I didn't know where she was."

It took a moment for this to register. "Don't seem likely," she said. "But, I won't ask for your story if you don't ask me for mine."

"Agreed." I looked back at Inez whose warm hand was still on my arm. "I have no idea how my daughter came to be here, but I don't care. I'm indebted to you too. I'll be as quick as I can, but you must promise not to leave her for a second."

"I promise."

"If she wakes up, tell her I'll be right back and she's not to worry."

"Of course." Inez, earnest and obliging, stepped forward and took Effie's hand. "I'll be right here with her when you get back."

I moved reluctantly away from the bed. "Come, we must hurry," I said to the girl.

She hesitated, ripping another piece of skin from her cracked lips. "When she wakes up, will you tell her I said goodbye?"

"Of course."

At the door she turned to Inez. "A girl named Edna Craig ever come here?"

Inez shook her head. "I don't think so. No, the name's not familiar."

"Okay." The girl glanced at Effie one last time before heading out.

I glanced back too. Leaving Effie was agonizing, but what I'd seen in the girl's eyes as she'd looked from the window compelled me forward. No matter how destitute this girl's situation was, there was still hope in her.

# CHAPTER THIRTY-TWO: MABLE

Turns out I got to ride in a second car that day. The cab wasn't nearly as sleek as Mr. Idleman's car, but I was grateful it had a roof and kept the sun and wind off my face. I still hadn't had any food, and I'd begun to feel as if I'd slipped under water, things coming at me in a haze.

I knew that doctor the moment he walked in the room. I could have run, hidden my face and ducked out the door, but felt lethargic, tired to my bones. Maybe it was tramping through the woods for days without food, or just the years of grief piling up on me, but the idea of jumping out a window as I'd planned to do once before and ending it all seemed easier than running.

Now I was stuck crawling along in traffic. At any moment a police car could pull up and order me out. I didn't trust this woman claiming to be Effie's mother. Effie's last name was Rothman, and I'd begun to wonder if this Mrs. Tildon intended to take me to the authorities after all. I was suspicious of her wealth and shine. Only . . . she wore no gloves and her hands were scarred and ugly. Only working folks had scarred hands.

I pressed up against the door, easing my fingers around the handle thinking maybe I'd roll out into traffic. I might have done it too if that woman hadn't suddenly removed her hat and placed it on my head, tilting it so my face was hidden from view.

"Does that help?" she asked, keeping her eyes straight ahead.

I slunk down and looked out the window, deciding I didn't have much choice but to trust this woman.

The cab made a slow left and the houses dropped away, the spacious trees holding their branches over the road like protective arms. Not until we were driving past the gates of the House of Mercy did I recognize where we were. Alarmed, I yanked myself forward, but the car kept going and the gates slipped from view.

Not far ahead, Mrs. Tildon rapped her hand on the seat in front of us. "You can drop us here."

The driver pulled to the side of the road

and got out, helping Mrs. Tildon from the car. "There's nothing here, ma'am," he said, passing his hand to me. I ignored it and climbed out on my own.

"We'll be fine, thank you." Mrs. Tildon fished in her sleek handbag and retrieved a folded bill that she handed to the driver. He tipped his hat, thanked her and climbed back into his car.

When the cab disappeared, Mrs. Tildon glanced into the forest, her lips pinched, her face pale and determined. "This way," she said, stepping off the road into a clean cover of pine needles.

I followed, curiosity replacing my fear as we crested the hill and a ring of colorful wagons and sleek horses came into view.

Mrs. Tildon stopped and took the hat from my head, settling it back on hers. "I'm giving you the one-thousand-dollar reward for the return of my daughter, which you're to turn over to these people."

"Why would I do that?" I cried. One thousand dollars was an astounding sum of money.

"Money won't do you any good if the police find you. I'm sure the doctor has already informed them by now. I doubt there's a train you could board safely, and a cab would only take you so far. You're vulnerable alone. If these people are willing, you could hide amongst them. Only, I suggest you not let on that you've committed a crime."

"Then why, exactly, am I supposed to be hiding amongst them?"

She pursed her lips, thinking this over. "I'll think of something. One foot in front of the other. Come on."

Heat rose from the curled brown grass as we picked our way across the field toward a hefty woman watching our approach with apprehension, her face hard as she stroked the side of a dappled horse.

Mrs. Tildon stopped directly in front of her. The woman was as sturdy and bulky as the beast she stood beside. Without any greeting Mrs. Tildon said, "We've found Effie. She's sick, but alive."

The woman sank in on herself a little. "Tray," she called.

A slender, alert-eyed boy emerged from the back of a wagon and jumped to the grass with a thud.

"They've found Effie," she said, and the boy burst into a smile.

"She's all right, isn't she? I told you she'd be all right, didn't I, Ma?" The boy was as scrawny as they come, with a spindly torso and stringy arms.

"She's sick," the woman said.

"I want to see her. Can I see her?" The boy looked at Mrs. Tildon as she nervously ran her fingers over the backs of her scarred hands.

Without answering him, she said to the woman, "I've come to see if you're leaving or staying another winter."

"Leaving as soon as the cold sets in. Why?"

"I need your help."

There was obvious respect between these women, but also a clear, mutual dislike.

"With what?"

Mrs. Tildon touched a hand to my sleeve. "This girl is responsible for Effie's return, which means she's entitled to the reward. A reward she'll bring to you, if you're willing to take her in."

The woman rested her dark, unreadable eyes on me. "How much?"

"Ma." The boy nudged her as if she'd made a rude remark. I'd have asked the same question. "Can you work?" He looked at me, arching his brows earnestly.

"Done nothing else but work for the past two years," I said.

"See?" He threw an arm around his mother's shoulders. "She'll be helpful. We could use another set of hands now that Patience has gone off again."

Marcella ignored him. "How much?" she repeated, lifting her chin.

"One thousand dollars," Mrs. Tildon said.

Tray whistled. "You're worth a bundle. What do you need us for?" He leaned into his mother, his arm still around her.

"She needs protection," Mrs. Tildon cut in. "We'll leave it at that. The sooner she's away from the city the better. If you agree, the money is yours and I'll allow your boy to come see Effie before you set off."

In a startling motion Tray reached out and hugged Mrs. Tildon, who went rigid. "There now," she said, pushing him away. The boy stepped back with a bright smile.

"I need to ask my husband." Marcella kept her eyes on me. "But I know he'll say that if you're honest and pull your weight, the money's yours to do with as you wish. For now, Tray can show you around."

"Indeed." Tray extended his hand with a slight bow and I was suddenly aware of how filthy mine were.

I stuffed them into my skirt pockets. "I'll keep them to myself, thank you."

*"Though she be but little, she is fierce."* Tray smiled.

"I'm not little," I said defensively.

"No, you're not in the least. Taller than my mother here, and not many intimidate her. Come on, there's horse dung that needs cleaning up."

I followed him, feeling ungrounded as I walked into another new life. There was a shovel in my hand and the smell of manure, and I was suddenly digging a hole as I had all those times ago for my mama's babies. Only the ground was hard and dry and when I looked up, there was nothing to bury in my hand, no rain, just an arch of clear blue sky and a boy looking back at me.

"You're shaking," he said. "When was the last time you had anything to eat?"

"I can't remember."

"We can remedy that," the boy said, easing the shovel from my tightly clenched fingers. There was strength in the fine features of his face, radiance in his eyes. This time, I took the hand he offered, not knowing, yet, that this boy would grow into a man filled with a light impossible to extinguish.

His happiness would become infectious, and in him, I would find my identity.

# CHAPTER THIRTY-THREE:
## EFFIE

The slope of my mother's cheeks, the sharpness of her nose and the line of her lips seemed real. But it was the halo around her head, a golden orb of light crowning her thick, dark hair that made me realize I was only dreaming. She was crying, and when I touched her cheek I marveled that a dream could bring the dampness of tears.

"How are you feeling?" she whispered. Then my father's face appeared above hers, his forehead creased, the blue of his eyes achingly familiar, and something shifted. This wasn't a dream.

I tried to answer my mother, but couldn't. I had lost all of my words. My legs were anchored to the bed, my body tingled and my chest felt caved in against my backbone. I scanned the room for the apocalyptic creatures who'd been crouched with me for so long that their absence, now, felt like abandonment. My parents' faces hovered in their place and I wondered, as the room slipped from view, and the halo behind my eyes became warm and welcoming, why Luella wasn't here.

I woke up with a sharp clarity, the room bright and the heat from the covers suffocating. I kicked them off as my mother leapt to my side. She took my hand, her face pinched with worry.

"You're not wearing your gloves?" I said, feeling the uneven bumps of her skin.

"I never wear them anymore." She spread her fingers out over mine.

"I can breathe."

She nodded. "We've found a good medicine."

"There's a light above your head."

"It's a side effect."

"It's beautiful." This made Mama smile. "Where's Luella?"

"She's coming."

"And Daddy?"

"I'm right here." I turned to see my father on the other side of the bed. He took my other hand and pressed his finger to the inside of my wrist, his eyes crinkling at the corners. "Still ticking."

There was so much to say, so much I needed to know. Where was my sister? And how had I gotten here, and where was

Mable? But Mama pressed her fingers to my lips. "Save your breath. You've barely come back to us. Please, please don't exert yourself. There's plenty of time to catch up."

Plenty was an exaggeration. By the time Luella came home from England, the digitalis had taken the swelling down and I no longer had my blue fits, but I could feel my body slowly letting go.

The day she arrived, I dressed myself in a dark blue skirt and blouse and met Mama and Daddy for breakfast even though they pleaded for me to stay in bed. It was the end of September and the sky was clear and bright, the air slightly warm.

"I want to meet her by the stream," I said.

Mama and Daddy exchanged a worried look. They'd said *yes* to everything I asked since coming home, which I found pleasing and worrisome.

"It's a short walk and I promise I'll go slowly. I'll take my notebook. My hands are steady for the first time in a long while, and it will be nice to write again. I'd like to be outside before it gets cold."

Mama wrapped her hand around her teacup, running her thumb up and down the handle. I still wasn't used to seeing her exposed hands, but I liked it.

"I'll walk you there," Daddy said, and

Mama pinched her lips, keeping her eyes on her cup.

"I'll be okay, Mama," I said.

She gave a tight smile, on the verge of tears. "Of course you will be."

That afternoon, Daddy walked me across the field, the grass burnt golden from a dry summer. We went up through the trees to the edge of the stream where a trickle of water still flowed. Daddy shook out a blanket and left me seated with my notebook in my lap. "If the steamer's late, I'm coming for you myself," he said.

I nodded and waved him on, surprised at the relief I felt at being left alone in the woods. There wasn't a cloud in the sky and I lay on my back and stared into the pale blue abyss, a halo of yellow like the crown of God hovering across my vision. I preferred to think of this as the glow of an angel following me, rather than a side effect.

I was anxious about seeing Luella, which I hadn't expected. I worried our reunion would be cautious and hesitant. That we wouldn't recognize the changed people we'd fallen into.

As the wind rustled through the leaves, I thought of Mable, of the bond between us, how I heard the fiddle for the first time, in this very spot, and then how Mable played for me in the cabin. A week ago, when Tray visited, he told me they were leaving for New Jersey and taking Mable with them.

"She's fiercer than we're used to," he said. "Not even your sister had that much fire. But Ma's good with the strong ones."

When he left, I felt something smooth and cool under my pillow. Pulling it out, I saw that he'd given me *The World,* the card as crisp and new as when I'd first held it, the creatures still dancing around the voluptuous woman with her wands. In the corner Tray had written, *all good things in the end.*

Lying next to the stream, I pulled the card from my pocket and held it up to the sky. I owed being here to Mable, a girl I hardly knew and yet missed. Rolling onto my stomach, I opened my notebook and began to write.

I wrote until I heard footsteps crunching over the leaves. Looking up, I saw Luella coming through the trees. She stopped a few feet from me, her hesitation making me feel as if everything had changed between us. My sister's eyes were more serious than I remembered, her face and figure slimmer, her dimples diminished. There was an interval of stillness as we looked at each other. The world held its breath for us. And when it exhaled, I was the one who went to her. I didn't want her guilt, or an apology. I just wanted her to know me.

We hugged for a long time, words too much for either of us.

When I grew tired, I said, "I need to sit down," and Luella pulled away with a pained expression.

"Of course. How thoughtless of me to keep you standing." She took me around the waist and led me to the blanket where we sat leaning against each other.

"You're still writing?" She flipped open my notebook on the blanket beside her.

"I've only just begun again. It's a long story."

"Is it a good one?"

"Fantastically good."

"I haven't heard a good story in ages. Is it gory?"

"A bit."

"A dazzling heroine?"

"Yes."

"Well then, I can't wait to read it." We sat silently for a while before she softly said, "I never stopped believing you'd come back."

I rested my head on her shoulder. "I stopped believing you'd come back. That's what got me into so much trouble. I think it's easier to be the one lost."

"I'm so sorry, Effie. I'd take it all back if I could. I've gone over and over that day I left, and all the days leading up to it."

I pulled away, looking at my sister's bright eyes and the thin wisps of hair blowing over her forehead. In the sunshine, in our old familiar spot, she didn't seem so changed after all. "It's strange how little it matters now that we're together again. Do you remember how scared I was that night we got lost in these hills? I could sit here all night and through morning and not fear a thing now."

"You were always braver than you thought."

"Maybe." I scooted down and lay my head in her lap. "I want to hear all about the gypsies, and London and Georges, who Mama says is delightful."

Luella loosened my hair and ran her fingers through it. "I want to take you to London so you can meet Georges for yourself. I want to plan a future with you."

I didn't say anything, and we sat for a long time listening to the trickle of the stream and the scurry of small animals. Overhead, geese flew in perfect formation, their honking growing quieter as they turned to dark specks in the sky.

"We lost time," Luella said quietly, and in her voice, I could hear that she was crying.

"I know."

"I never believed you were dying."

"I know." I sat up and scooted to the edge of the muddy creek, the wet ground soaking through to my drawers. "It's not spring, but we might as well."

Luella scooted next to me, muddying her fine traveling dress as we unlaced our boots. Peeling off our stockings, we held each other up as we waded over the slippery rocks, Luella smiling through her tears the way she used to when she was getting away with something deliciously ill-mannered.

Even though it had been a dry summer, the cold water still reached to my ankles and tingled and numbed my feet. Beside me, Luella pulled the pins from her hair and let it fall around her shoulders. I watched her tilt her face to the sun, the arch of light I carried in my vision making her glow.

I walked out of the stream with my sister that day feeling stronger than I had in a long while, but by midwinter the creatures returned, their wings unfurling to greet me, expanding overhead into a shimmering sky as another stream swirled around my feet

*— enjoying the joys of earth while guarded by the divine watchers.* All at once time stilled, then raced forward. When I looked down, I saw the translucent arch of my foot and the hard, white stones of my toes. With the rustle of wind in my hair, and my sister's hand over mine, I finally understood what my fortune meant.

I was bone and skin and earth and sky. Death was not literal, just as Tray had told me. Time was infinite, my existence eternal.

■ ■ ■ ■

# EPILOGUE

■ ■ ■ ■

# JEANNE

Effie died on January 23rd, 1915. She was fifteen years old. As much as I wanted to believe she held on for us, it was the story she was writing that kept her going. She died the day she finished it, dictating her last words to Luella.

That morning, I woke before the sun had risen to check on her, as I always did since her return. Luella was asleep in Effie's bed, holding her sister's hand. Effie was barely breathing, pausing at the top of each breath as if deciding whether to try for one more. I held her other hand and traced her clubbed fingernails, listening as her breath became labored and shallower until her heart gave a final leap and settled silently in her chest.

Death was not what I expected. It did not strip Effie, or leave her empty and ashen. It laid itself inside her with a warmth that turned her cheeks baby pink. I watched her until the sun came up through the windows.

Luella stirred, and I called to Emory who rushed down the hall in his bare feet and nightshirt. It was the only time in my life I saw him weep.

Luella wept the hardest, climbing in next to her sister, refusing to let go. In the end, it was her father who lifted her from the bed. He carried her to a chair and sat holding her like an infant as she buried her face in his chest. With his free arm, Emory reached out to me. I went to him, and he wrapped his arm around my legs, holding on. For one last moment we were a family, one daughter crying on her father's shoulder, the other daughter releasing us with the blessing of having lived.

I had moved back into the house after Effie returned. While she was alive, I slept in the guest room, creating a space of my own and coming and going as I pleased. I had planned to move out again after her passing, but with the war, Luella could no longer return to England. And as I didn't want to leave her behind, I stayed.

It would take five years for Luella and me to make our way abroad. Luella returned to England where she eventually married an English countryman who let her wear short dresses and throw wild parties, as the world changed in a way that suited her. I returned to Paris, where Georges visited often and my mother relaxed into old age with the satisfaction that her daughter had finally come home.

Emory never left Bolton Road. During the years Luella and I lived with him, his habits didn't change. There was a period of mourning for Effie, and then he began slipping off to gamble, women flocking to him in even greater numbers as his hair peppered with graceful aging. It hurt only a little to be near him. The death of my daughter and the guilt over losing the last year of her life caused most of my pain.

I never told anyone about the girl I took to the gypsies. Neither did Inez. She told the authorities that the man who dropped Effie at her door had refused to give his name, and that no other girl had been with him. "Poor Dr. Langer," she'd said, with her smile beguiling a young and susceptible policeman, "to have let that girl slip away before . . ." She clicked her tongue. "I imagine the guilt makes him see her in everyone." The maids confirmed her story, as did I, and the police dropped the matter. I cashed in the bank account Georges had opened for me, and gave the reward money to the girl myself. She told me her name was Mable.

It was only after Effie died, and I read the story she'd written, that I discovered it was Signe.

For years, I devoted myself to getting Signe's story published. No one was interested. It told the story of a girl's struggle in our great city of New York that no one wanted to hear. Signe's truth was the last thing the world could handle. It was war-torn and damaged and wanted stories that glittered with luxury and pretense. Not until 1939, twenty-three years later, would others be ready for it.

When I opened the package from the publisher and saw Effie's book, the cover a joyful blue with a single white bird soaring over the page, it gave me more than closure. It gave meaning to the year I lost my daughter. It made me feel that in saving one girl, I had, in fact, saved the other.

# MABLE

It was Tray who brought me the book, placing it gently on the kitchen counter where I stood splitting peas. He'd been all the way to Boston that day to see his sister. It was one of those perfect days with the air soft and cool, the sun dipping in and out of the high, white clouds, the trees so thick and green they breathed abundance.

Not much took me by surprise anymore, but when I saw the title of that book, I'll admit it was like Effie reminding me how it felt to have your heart freeze in your chest. I must have blanched white because Tray eased the pea shells from my hand and walked me to the sofa. We had four boys, and I thought I'd faced every heart-stopping moment there was getting the older ones grown and out of the house without too many wounds and scars.

Tray placed the book in my hands. "The

animals need feeding," he said, and left me alone.

The book crackled with newness as I opened it, the pages crisp and white as the inside of an apple, with a sweet smell unlike our old, musty books. It's startling having your own story told back at you. Not since that night in the cabin with Effie had I ever breathed the name Signe Hagen.

Not even to Tray, who returned an hour later, leaning his thin frame on the doorway and regarding me with the ease he always had about him.

"You read it?" I asked.

"It's a long train ride home." He smiled, his eyes dancing as if he was still a boy. "Strangest thing, Effie telling me your story after all these years."

I slapped the book shut. "What makes you think this is my story? There's no Mable in it."

"Well now, let me see." Tray sat beside me, stretching out his legs and latching his hands behind his head. "This girl, Effie, goes all the way to escaping the House of Mercy with a girl who saves her life before disappearing into a cabin in the woods." He looked around at our farmhouse. "Not too far off."

"This doesn't mean we're talking about it."

"I suppose that would be asking too much of my wife of nineteen years."

"Yes, it would."

"All right then."

"And the children are never to know."

"Yes, ma'am." Tray dropped his arm around my shoulders.

Twilight warmed the room as I laid my head on his chest, listening to the faint beat of his heart and gazing out the window.

Our love had been a simple thing. I certainly wasn't looking for it. Those first few years with the gypsies, I kept my head down and did what I was told. I was grateful to them, and determined not to mess it up. But whenever I did raise my head, there was Tray smiling at me. He'd help me with my work, tell my fortune, make me laugh. I never laughed so hard in my life. The love part just snuck up on us. Tray was eighteen and I was twenty-one when we married. For a while we continued our life on the road, but the world changed so quickly there was no place to put a wagon after a while without someone yelling at you to get off their property. We used the money Effie's mom gave me to build this cabin and start raising animals. I'd handed all of it over to

Marcella and Freddy, thinking it would barely pay my way with them, but they'd sewn it into the underside of their mattress and held on to it for us.

For some reason, sitting there with the past rising up from that book, and thinking about how kind Tray's family always was to me, I started crying, which made me angry. I struggled to get up, but Tray tightened his grip and held me still. "It was a long time ago," he said. "You were a child, Mable. No one holds you responsible anymore. Time for you to stop too."

This only made me cry harder, my whole body shaking with sobs. I was grateful my two youngest were at Marcella and Freddy's for the night. I never cried in front of my children.

Tray held me in silence until I was cried out, at which point I slapped my hands on my thighs and stood up, grateful for the practical task of popping peas from their shells. "Now look here, we hardly get a night alone and I'm starving. No more talk of that." I shooed my hand at the book I'd tossed onto the couch.

I never told my husband about Edna, or escaping into the night, or about that policeman. There's not a thing in this world Tray holds against anyone. He'd forgive a flea for biting him. Still, since I could never bring myself to tell him what I'd done, or what was done to me, I was glad he finally knew. Even though it wasn't a surprise he'd forgive me for my wrongs, it was a relief.

"Signe is a beautiful name. It suits you," he said.

"That's exactly what Effie said, but I'm never changing it back."

"I didn't expect you to. I just wanted you to know that your real name is beautiful to me."

Tears sprang up again and I swatted his hand away. "That's enough of that," I said, going into the kitchen and putting on a pan of water.

Later that night, I eased out of bed with Tray sound asleep. Tray had placed Effie's book carefully on our bookshelf. I pulled it down and I snuck out of the house with it tucked under my arm, making my way to the boulder in the backyard that the children used to leap from, scraping every inch of their knees off. I clambered up and dangled my legs over the edge of smooth stone. The air was warm and comfortable. I looked up at the full moon, that cold, hard stone in the sky somehow casting the world in milky light. I had shot at coyotes with Papa under that moon, leapt from a roof under that moon, lost Edna under that moon and escaped with Effie. It was the same moon under which I'd dropped my baby in a river, the same moon that rose only hours after Mama's death, that fat, solid, dependable orb. Maybe Papa was sitting under it right now. He'd be sixty-nine years old.

Slapping at the mosquitoes eating my legs, I opened the book and thumbed through it to the end. If Tray had come across Effie's book so effortlessly, Papa might find it too. I always felt guilty taking away the name he'd given me. It wasn't a story he'd be proud of, but at least my name was here, preserved forever along with Mama's memory.

I looked at the cover, *House of Mercy, by Effie Tildon*. I was glad I'd given her my story. Her name got to be remembered too. Risking my neck to return her to her family was the only truly selfless thing I'd done in my life. Even letting Edna go had been self-serving. I'd loved her, and doing something for someone you love is always a little bit self-serving.

Lifting my face to the moon, I let the cool of it wash over me, sending a little prayer to Effie before making my way back to the house.

That night, the strangest creatures came

to me in my dreams. They were winged and full of eyes, and when they spread their wings their feathers rippled under me like a vast, dark body of water. From the surface came Effie, looking just as I'd seen her that first time in the laundry at the House of Mercy. She smiled, and I touched her soft cheek as the creatures' wings enveloped her and she slipped away, leaving behind a sky filled with the shimmering, white light of the moon.

# AFTERWORD

In 1891, the House of Mercy, a notorious asylum for "destitute and fallen women," stood on the highest point of Manhattan's Inwood Hill Park, a massive, foreboding building stretching the length of the plateau. The women it imprisoned were not privy to the view from the barred windows of their dormitory, or from the steaming laundry room, and certainly not from the basement, where they were isolated for the smallest infraction. These women were lucky if they made it through a day without crushing a finger or scalding their hands from the vats of boiling water as they scrubbed, ironed and folded. Their endless, long days were spent with overworked, aching limbs and searing headaches from the gas fumes in the enclosed laundry room, praying they wouldn't fall ill from tuberculosis and be sent to die, wretched and alone, in the House of Rest for Consumptives, another grand building just up the road.

I have stood on that picturesque hillside imagining the mansion that once loomed there, the women's faces pressed up against the bars, anger and injustice simmering in their eyes. The determination.

When I first began research for *The Girls with No Names,* I knew nothing about the House of Mercy. I was caught up in the horrors of the highly publicized Irish Magdalene laundries, asylums the church sold for millions of dollars with unmarked cemeteries containing graves that couldn't be accounted for — good stuff for fiction.

But once I dug in, I discovered a number of Magdalene laundries existed right here in the United States. The first one opened in Kentucky in 1843. By the end of the century, twenty-four more followed. These were religious institutions claiming to help destitute women, to reform them, put in place to convict women of crimes of a sexual nature. In actuality, they imprisoned women and children of all ages for any behavior deemed "immoral." They were, in fact, *prisons.* It made no difference what they were called: *penitentiaries, houses* or *laundries.* These socially acceptable establishments imprisoned, abused and enslaved women and children while the church made millions from their laundry service and lace making.

I spent hours unearthing articles on the House of Mercy in an attempt to give life to these women. As my research continued, I realized that at least Ireland had exposed the corruption of the church in the name of salvation, while the laundries masquerading as religious institutions in the United States were never held accountable. The women's stories about what happened to them inside *homes* like New York's House of Mercy are rarely spoken about, much less remembered.

From the lives of these real and daring women, Effie, Mable and Luella were born. Through them, I wanted to create a tapestry of New York City at the turn of the century made up of immigrants and tenements, of the Romani who camped in Inwood, along with the wealthy Victorians clinging to their traditional values, even as the youth of the gilded age shed these same values.

I would like to briefly address the use of the word *gypsy* throughout the novel. The word can be read as offensive as it fails to distinguish the Romani people — an ethnic community driven from their homeland — from travelers enacting a lifestyle choice.

And yet, I chose to use the word *gypsy* to maintain historical accuracy, because of the historical setting and the characters who would not be aware of different language to use. I am aware that the word *gypsy* is seen by many as offensive, and again, the usage here is meant to be indicative of a time and place and is not in any way reflective of my own views of the Romani community.

I thoroughly researched the lives of the Romani people in 1910 America with the desire to create characters that would reflect reality and not perpetuate stereotypes or disparaging beliefs. It is my hope that I have portrayed these characters — Patience, Tray, Marcella, Sydney — with accuracy and respect, and that through the flawed humanness of all of my characters, the lines of poverty and privilege and culture differences are challenged in ways that show us, in the end, how similar we all are.

In *The Girls with No Names,* all of these worlds collide and intertwine in unexpected ways while exposing the dark reality of what it was like to be a woman in each of these social circles in 1913. Effie's, Mable's and Luella's voices echo the voices of women whose stories were never told, women who suffered and endured and survived.

# ACKNOWLEDGMENTS

I am grateful to the following:

Stephanie Delman, for your devotion to my writing career, and years of encouragement, tenacity and insight that has carved our path together and made all of this possible.

Laura Brown — editor extraordinaire — for diving in with enthusiasm, clarity and heart and polishing this book until it shone.

To everyone at Sanford J. Greenburger Associates, especially Stefanie Diaz, for championing my books abroad. To the team at Park Row Books who I am blessed to work with: Erika Imranyi, Margaret Marbury, Loriana Sacilotto, Justine Shaw, Heather Foy, Linette Kim, Randy Chan, Amy Jones, Rachel Haller, Kathleen Oudit, Punam Patel, Canaan Chu, Tamara Shifman, Scar de Courcier.

My early readers, Ariane Goodwin, Michelle King, Christina Kopp-Hills and

Heather Liske for your acuity and wisdom. Sarah Heinemann, for slogging through research material at the New York Public Library (I owe you one), and Melissa Dickey and Julianna Comacho for exposing me to writers who challenged and expanded my way of thinking.

I am indebted to Rebecca Lea McCarthy's *Origins of the Magdalene Laundries,* Lu Ann De Cunzo's *Reform, Respite, Ritual: An Archaeology of Institutions,* Sidonie Smith and Julia Watson's *Before They Could Vote: American Women's Autobiographical Writings, 1819–1919,* Carol Silverman's *Romani Routes,* and Michael Stewart's *The Time of the Gypsies.*

There aren't words enough to express my gratitude to my parents and extended family for your unwavering faith and confidence in me, and to Silas and Rowan for patiently making room in your lives for this book.

Lastly, and most importantly, to Stephen, for giving us a life that allows me the freedom to write and the room to dream.